Suckled Brats 24-Pack : Books 1 to 24

*****

About This Book

The Suckled Brats 24-pack collection features books 1-24 of the series where feisty older men feast on the bounteous chests of the women in their lives in good, old-fashioned, lactation fun! Read just how naughty they get!

Stories include : *'Farmer's Prize Milk,' 'Holy Cow,' 'Boss's Magical Latte,' 'Training My Chest,' '21 Or Bust,' 'The Milkiest Showgirl,' 'Clean-Up In The Dairy Aisle,' 'Ice-Cream Fundae,' 'Sin On Splash Canyon,' 'Sexorcism,' 'Lacto-Park,' 'His Secret Milking Rack,' 'His Secret Milking Rack 2,' 'Bound And Satisfied,' 'He Suckled Me Before The Show,' 'My Milk For Free,' 'Coffee Liqueur,' 'Milk Trading,' 'More Milk Minister,' 'My Boss's Raffle Ticket,' 'Drinking My Nectar,' 'Draining My Milk,' 'My Dripping Milk Gave Me Away,'* and *'Lacto-Tolerant.'*

GW00730504

1. http://eepurl.com/b0ma0X

Table of Contents

Read An Excerpt

"More milk," he insisted.

"But Mr. Giles, you—"

"More!"

I hurried him the bucket and he clamored for it ravenously. He placed it to his lips and guzzled down the offering.

As I watched him feed from me I started to awaken. There was something inexplicably hot about nurturing him like that and knowing that he was absolutely relishing each mouthful. It was as though I'd offered him a home-cooked meal and he was gratefully devouring it. I felt proud and wanted all at once.

"That's fucking good, Agnes," he said. It was most uncharacteristic.

"You like it?"

He nodded. "It's yours isn't it?"

"No! No, it's not mine!"

Mr. Giles nodded to the long, smooth, glossy, metal containers that housed the milk from the other cows. Everything was spick-and-span in the barn, and the huge vats shone like mirrors. I realized all too late that he could see my ruse in the reflection.

At first I was mortified. I stared at him, horrified by what I'd done. But soon-after I realized that Mr. Giles had seen the whole thing and had still opted to guzzle it all down. He knew he was drinking my breast-milk, and he just didn't care.

"It was amazing," he confessed. "Do you have any more under there for me?"

I felt bashful and proud all at once. My hand fondled my pronounced nipples that were now punching out through the silken fabric of my gown.

"Under here?" I asked.

He watched and I ran a finger in a circle around my nipples

1

"Yes," he hushed.

He took a step forward and I slipped a hand inside my bra. I knew I was doing something utterly sinful and wrong, but I just couldn't help it. Mr. Giles seemed to have been bitten by the same bug, because he was being equally foolish.

He moved the middle of my gown open and I dropped my hands to allow him inside. The pressure in my tits was close to bursting. The steady drip of milk from my nipples increased into another fine-stream and then an outright spurt. The milk blasted forwards and I leaned back to groan at its release. It was exciting me beyond measure and I could feel my pussy respond by becoming as damp as my gown.

I watched now as Mr. Giles opened his mouth wide and met the fine jet of milk. It scattered on his face and then hit the inside of his mouth. He rolled it around his tongue and hummed, then he moved forward towards the source.

"That's it, Mr. Giles," I groaned. "This can be your breakfast."

His mouth opened again and he latched on to the life-giving breast, helping to relieve the pressure by sucking fiercely on the teat.

Like a cow's udder it delivered. I held his head on me and scratched at his scalp, encouraging him to feed from both of my charms.

"Don't forget this one," I offered, and Mr. Giles obliged by moving over and giving it the same treatment.

He guzzled down the ambrosia, then stood up and stared at me with a film of white about his lips.

"I fear I'm about to do something much worse," he hinted.

"Do it," I dared. "I want it."

Farmer Prize Milk : Suckled Brats 1

Farmer Gregor had raised dairy-cows for years, and Amber was one of his best. Her milk was the talk of the farmer's market. It fetched a hefty price due to its richness and limited supply. People would use it in cakes to give it a velvety, decadent texture, or put it in coffees for the ultimate morning pick-me-up. Others would drink it by the glass and savor the sweetness that no other milk quite achieved. Mr. Giles was proud of Amber, and rightly so.

All good things must come to an end though, and this good thing came to an end in a way so strange that I daresay you won't quite believe me.

You'll have to forgive my accent, by the way, and I hope it doesn't come across too British. I'm afraid Mr. Giles and I are as English as they come, right the way down to our tea-drinking and his tweed caps and jackets. He fell short of smoking a pipe, although I think that's only because his wife won't let him.

Anyway, I digress. Our story begins late one stormy night. The barn-door was going crazy in the wind and must have come off the latch. The second I heard it I was sprinting from my bedroom where I stayed as part of my job. The last thing you want is the cows getting out on a night like this.

So I ran across the muddy courtyard to the barn and thankfully managed to barricade the door shut before our inquisitive bovines had planned their escape.

I double-checked for Amber as she was the one cow we couldn't afford to lose. She seemed fine, although a little shaken by the rumbling storm overhead. I don't think my flash-light pointed directly at her face was much help either.

I stayed with the cows a while as they mooed uneasily, shuffling on their feet and unable to sleep a wink. I wasn't surprised. Out here there wasn't much shielding you from the wrath of the elements.

Suddenly there came a deep grumble of thunder. It started in the distance and came closer, as though the storm was targeting Mr. Giles' farmstead in particular. I wondered perhaps if one of his milk rivals had hired a shaman to send over a thunderstorm. Honestly, you can't put it past these people. They take their milk very, very seriously.

The barn was cold but the cow's coats are quite thick. It's their breed, you see. A benefit of that is that you can snuggle up against them if you happen to find yourself outside in a storm.

For twenty minutes I stayed and all the while the rumble grew nearer until the cracks and flashes of thunder were visible outside.

They lit up the sky, sparking through the sheets of rain that poured down. It was like the damn apocalypse. Mr. Giles was a deep sleeper and wasn't rousing, despite the incessant mooing of the worried cattle.

Amber seemed more frightened than most. She was shaking and shivering, and her silence was a stark contrast to the animated noises of the cows around her.

She was shaken up alright. I stayed until the storm passed, leaving only the rain in its wake. When things had quietened down and the animals seemed settled I locked them in the barn and walked back to the house.

After toweling off and getting warm I managed to sleep, waking only a few hours later to the sound of Mr. Giles downstairs in the kitchen.

"Fetch me some milk, Agnes," he shouted up to me.

I know, I know, 'Agnes' is a terrible name! My father was nothing if not traditional, and unfortunately the men in his family often name their first-born daughters after their own mothers. It made Grandma Agnes happy, but I'd have preferred Amber's name in all honesty.

"Coming, Mr. Giles!" I cried from the bedroom above. I was on the clock almost twenty-four-seven, but Mr. Giles paid well and the views from my bedroom window were to die for.

I dressed quickly in my gown and Wellington boots. Not the most chic of outfits, of course, but it gets the job done.

I ran back into the courtyard and noticed that Mrs. Giles's car was gone already. On Fridays she'd sometimes leave early for work. She was a 'networker' as she called it. She'd travel around and try to broker deals with traders and stores. Mr. Giles said it was better that she went alone, as the guys she often dealt with could be easily persuaded into a business relationship. She had all the sass and sex-appeal but Farmer Giles trusted her. Turned out there were about to be bigger problems back at home!

So I went out in the barn to fetch the morning's milk. Mr. Giles was old-school. He'd get it warm, straight from the cow and use it for his breakfast tea and porridge. It really did make the difference, trust me.

I grabbed a sterilized pale and walked over to Amber. She was still looking a little worst-for-wear since last night, but frankly so was I. My hair was all straggly from the preceding storm. With my dressing-gown half-around me I must have looked like a disheveled mess. Thank God we worked alone out here.

I set about squeezing those cutesy little teats that hung off her udder. The second the first spurt panged off the bottom of the bucket I knew something was amiss. First of all the milk didn't seem as pure-white as usual. It looked much more yellow. Secondly there came the smell. I'd long-heard of thunderstorms affecting milk, but I thought that was an old wives' tale. Farming is full of them, so it wouldn't have surprised me.

There was no getting away from it though, the milk just smelled foul. I brought the bucket cautiously to my mouth and took a sip. It was sour alright. The bit that I didn't swallow I spat back out in the bucket.

At first I was aghast at the taste, but then I realized the real worry. Farmer Giles's prize milk was ruined.

I wanted to run back the house and tell him, but before I did that the strangest sensation started to come over me.

I thought the milk had turned me woozy. I felt suddenly light-headed. There followed a sensation of great fullness. I held my stomach, wondering if I was going to be sick. Instead of that though I felt this intense euphoria blossom over me. Despite the circumstances, I had the pervading thought that everything was going to be okay. It didn't linger long. Following that quickly afterwards was an intense pressure beginning in my breasts.

Now I was nothing if not busty—and that's the one thing I can say about myself with confidence. Don't ask me why or how, but I had been bestowed a pair of breasts that at times were a burden due to their size.

Suddenly they felt inexplicably bigger, if that was possible. It was as though I was experiencing a growth-spurt, localized directly on my tits. In fact, 'spurt' was the best word for it, because not long after the sensation arrived, I felt a spurt of liquid shoot from my nipples.

I pulled my bra forward off my tits and inspected beneath. They looked wet. I watched them curiously and my eyes spread wide as they seemed to inflate further still.

When I dropped my bra back against my tits I could feel it digging into my skin. It was pushing my tits back against my rib-cage and cutting in to the side of my body.

I raced my gown off and unclasped the bra, feeling a great relief as soon as I did so. My brow furrowed as I inspected the inside of the bra-cup and found it wet with a hint of white about it. I looked down at my tits just in time to a see a bead of white appear on the teat.

"My God!" I hushed.

Amber mooed and I looked across at her. The cow seemed to nod, as though it had imparted some strange power.

Again I felt the sensation. This time my other breast was producing a teardrop of milk that turned into a gentle flow. It ran down off the nipple and curled under the curve of my tits. When it hit my body it started to roll down over my equally milky flesh.

"What's happening to me?!"

The veins in my breasts were more pronounced and the milk was flowing so freely that I needed another bucket to catch it. I took a clean one and squirted the milk inside. The feeling of relief was unsurpassed. It was as though the pressure that I felt inside me was being slowly relieved.

More and more spurts hit the bucket until I had a pale to rival Amber's. It looked just as creamy too.

Naturally I brought a sample of it to my lips and I was blown away. It tasted almost identical to the offering that Amber would often produce.

I bit my lip nervously and looked about the barn, hoping that inspiration would strike and I'd find a way out of this sticky mess. First though, I had to attend to Mr. Giles.

I pulled my gown back around me and left the bra where it was for now. I took the pale back inside and Farmer Giles grabbed it from me quickly.

"Took you long enough," he said. "My tea's almost getting cold."

He put the edge of the pale to his cup and started to tilt it. I watched my breast-milk flow into the cup and mingle with his dark tea. It produced a fantastically rich, tanned brown color. Mr. Giles swooned.

"As good as always," he smiled, and then he poured the remainder into a saucepan of porridge.

I was mortified, but I couldn't help but be curious. It's not exactly an every-day occurrence that your boss drinks your tit milk without even realizing.

"That might be the finest drop yet," he said obliviously, licking his lips.

I blushed with embarrassment. Not only was he drinking my milk, he was absolutely loving it.

He took a deep breath and closed his eyes, running his tongue over his lips where my milk still danced. He looked a picture of unadulterated bliss and I knew exactly how he felt. The milk seemed to inject a certain essence into the drinker. Mr. Giles looked so handsome, stood there enjoying it.

"I want more," he said, looking to me.

"More?" I was flummoxed.

"More," he said. "I'll fetch some."

He was on his feet and in his boots in no time. I pulled my gown tight across me and followed him into the courtyard.

"I can fetch it, Mr. Giles," I said. "It's okay."

"Nonsense, I'm half-way there."

He walked briskly in his boots and navy-blue pajamas, with his dressing-gown flowing behind him.

"I don't mind!"

I pulled at the pale and he tugged back. He opened the barn door and walked inside. The whole time I followed him close, fearful that he might discover Amber's plight and blame me.

"I'll do it, Mr. Giles I insist," I grunted, wrestling the pale from him.

He took it away from me and stared.

I swallowed nervously and tried to be calm, but his curious gaze was making me uncomfortable.

"What is it?"

"Your tits, Agnes," he said simply.

I looked down to see that I'd spilled completely out of my gown. Not only that, but the beads of milk were still steadily flowing.

"Oh, golly!" I cried, pulling the gown across me quick.

Mr. Giles seemed mesmerized.

"I'll ... fetch you some more?" I asked.

He nodded, keeping his eyes locked on my gown. There was a growing dark patch on each breast as the milk bled into the fabric and spread outwards.

I knelt to Amber and stealthily slipped out a breast. I pinched towards the teat and fired the cream into the bucket, hoping that Mr. Giles didn't notice where the fluid was coming from.

"There," I announced chirpily.

I covered up my breast and turned back to him, but Farmer Giles was still transfixed.

"I feel funny," he said.

I placed the bucket down and hurried to him. "Are you okay?"

"I feel funny, Agnes. I can't explain it."

"Are you sick?" I asked, worried.

I placed a hand on his forehead.

"Not sick," he said.

"Then what?"

"I feel like I need your Mrs. Giles back."

"I'm here. I can help. Mrs. Giles won't be back for hours."

"I need something," he urged.

"What? What do you need?"

"I need to do something with this."

He pointed down and I leaned back to look. The front of his pajama-pants was bursting forward, pushed out from his waist. There could only be one thing doing that.

"Mr. Giles!" I cried, shocked and impressed.

"I need Mrs. Giles."

"I'm here," I said. "It's okay."

All the while my breasts dribbled their milk and Farmer Giles's eyes targeted them, transfixed by their nectar.

"More milk," he insisted.

"But Mr. Giles, you—"

"More!"

I hurried him the bucket and he clamored for it ravenously. He placed it to his lips and guzzled down the offering.

As I watched him feed from me I started to awaken. There was something inexplicably hot about nurturing him like that and knowing that he was absolutely relishing each mouthful. It was as though I'd offered him a home-cooked meal and he was gratefully devouring it. I felt proud and wanted all at once.

"That's fucking good, Agnes," he said. It was most uncharacteristic.

"You like it?"

He nodded. "It's yours isn't it?"

"No! No, it's not mine!"

Mr. Giles nodded to the long, smooth, glossy, metal containers that housed the milk from the other cows. Everything was spick-and-span in the barn, and the huge vats shone like mirrors. I realized all too late that he could see my ruse in the reflection.

At first I was mortified. I stared at him, horrified by what I'd done. But soon-after I realized that Mr. Giles had seen the whole thing and had still opted to guzzle it all down. He knew he was drinking my breast-milk, and he just didn't care.

"It was amazing," he confessed. "Do you have any more under there for me?"

I felt bashful and proud all at once. My hand fondled my pronounced nipples that were now punching out through the silken fabric of my gown.

"Under here?" I asked.

He watched and I ran a finger in a circle around my nipples

"Yes," he hushed.

He took a step forward and I slipped a hand inside my bra. I knew I was doing something utterly sinful and wrong, but I just couldn't help it. Mr. Giles seemed to have been bitten by the same bug, because he was being equally foolish.

He moved the middle of my gown open and I dropped my hands to allow him inside. The pressure in my tits was close to bursting. The steady drip of milk from my nipples increased into another fine-stream and then an outright spurt. The milk blasted forwards and I leaned back to groan at its release. It was exciting me beyond measure and I could feel my pussy respond by becoming as damp as my gown.

I watched now as Mr. Giles opened his mouth wide and met the fine jet of milk. It scattered on his face and then hit the inside of his mouth. He rolled it around his tongue and hummed, then he moved forward towards the source.

"That's it, Mr. Giles," I groaned. "This can be your breakfast."

His mouth opened again and he latched on to the life-giving breast, helping to relieve the pressure by sucking fiercely on the teat.

Like a cow's udder it delivered. I held his head on me and scratched at his scalp, encouraging him to feed from both of my charms.

"Don't forget this one," I offered, and Mr. Giles obliged by moving over and giving it the same treatment.

He guzzled down the ambrosia, then stood up and stared at me with a film of white about his lips.

"I fear I'm about to do something much worse," he hinted.

"Do it," I dared. "I want it."

Mr. Giles downed his pajama bottoms and his engorged cock sprang upwards. I gasped and swooned at its size. He was so big and manly that I almost felt at a disadvantage.

When I saw that gorgeous cock of his I was utterly smitten and transfixed. My eyes could move nowhere else, even as the milk continued to spurt fantastically from my chest.

"Mr. Giles, that looks so gorgeous," I told him.

His eyes were on my tits but mine were firmly on his cock. As he had already had the delights of my breasts I felt it only right that it should now be my turn to sample him.

"I want to suck it," I urged.

"Suck it, Agnes. Put it in your mouth."

I dropped to my knees and the milk spattered his pajamas. I turned a shoulder in and aimed the jet of cream at his dick, pinching to the end of my nipples to increase the strength of the stream.

He watched carefully and groaned delightfully when the warm nectar glazed his cock.

"That's better," I smirked.

He let out a laugh too, but when I opened my mouth over the crown of his hard dick the laughter stopped. A heady groan replaced it as he cast his head back.

I could feel the strength of his arousal in my mouth. It was like hard rock-candy. I could taste the sweetness of my milk on him too and decided I needed more.

I started to lean back and apply more milk to his length, with Mr. Giles's encouragement of course.

"Coat my cock in your love," he said, moving my hair aside and holding it back.

I fed the cream over him, dousing his stiffness and then plunging it back into my mouth. I pressed him right to the back of my throat and felt my pussy awaken as my eyes bulged.

"Oh, Agnes, you are something else!"

I pinched my lips tight around him and pulled back towards the tip. He bounced free and then lifted my chin.

"On your back, Agnes," he said. "I want to fuck your tits."

I beamed with excitement and wasted no time at all. I fell backwards onto the hard floor and watched as Farmer Giles hopped out of his pants. His huge cock flailed and smacked against the inside of his thigh and then it started to come towards me.

He took off his gown and showed me the manly, big, hairy chest beneath. God I wanted to touch it so bad. I wouldn't have to wait long.

I bit my lip and held my breath, watching his cock descend and Mr. Giles with it. He took it in his grasp and I spread my tits wide.

"Good girl," he groaned, pressing his cock into my cleavage.

I pushed my tits up around him and a surge of milk fired up against his torso. It dripped down onto me as he started to pump his hips and send his huge cock gliding through my wet cleavage.

"Oh, that's perfect," he groaned. "Just like your Mrs. Giles. Agnes, that's so fucking perfect."

It was odd to hear him swear like that and odd to hear him compare me to his wife. But, the compliment was undeniable. He thought the world of her, so to be compared to her was a rare privilege.

"Where do you want me to shoot?" he asked, continuing to work his hips.

"Gosh, I don't know," I confessed. "Where would you like to?"

"I can think of a lot of places ..."

His cock moved up and out of my cleavage. I pressed my chin to my chest and opened my mouth to meet him, claiming the crown as he thrust forwards and popping my lips off him when he withdrew.

"Do it where you like," I told him. "I don't care. I just want to please you."

"You are, honey. You are."

He pushed my gown wide open now and it fell back against the floor like a blanket. His big, wet cock moved from my cleavage and he knelt between my legs. He looked down on me adoringly.

"You look so perfect, Agnes."

I bit my lip and scrunched my shoulders. "You look pretty good yourself."

I stared right at his cock and then looked back to him. "What are you gonna do with that?" I asked.

"The naughtiest thing I can think of."

"You're going to put it in my arse?"

Mr. Giles laughed. "Clearly you can think naughtier than I can."

"Oh!"

"I'm going to put it in this fine, tight pussy."

"Oh! That will certainly do."

His big hand rubbed at my panties and then he looked to me in amazement.

"You're soaked!"

I raised my eyebrows and bared my teeth. "Sorry!"

"Nothing to be sorry about," he said, moving the crotch of my panties over.

I let out a deep breath and realized that this was it. This was the moment that Mr. Giles was about to—

"Oh, fuck!" I groaned.

His big cock had spread right through my tight muscle, gobbled up quickly by my drooling core. I felt full immediately, but Mr. Giles had much more to give. He pressed onwards and moved his cock deep. I gripped him tight and grunted, sending a jet of milk firing into the air like the fountains of the Bellagio.

The pair of us groaned and the cows around us groaned too. They mooed and watched on, wondering what the hell the two of were doing on the floor in the middle of their barn.

Farmer Giles's big hands came underneath me and he wrapped me in his tight embrace. When I was lifted slightly from the floor he increased his thrusts, slamming into me and using his arms to yank me back against his thrusts.

"Oh, Mr. Giles! Oh, Mr. Giles!" I wailed, shaking like a rag-doll beneath him.

My tits wobbled against him and their milk sprayed out, hitting his chest and catching in his hair. I could feel the warm wetness between us. The embrace felt like the most erotic thing I'd ever done or witnessed, and in no time at all I was close to climaxing.

"You're gonna make me come," I moaned, gasping for breaths and clawing at his back.

"Come for me, Agnes," he dared. "I wanna feel you tighten on my cock."

Hearing those words leave his mouth was like a catalyst. The orgasm blossomed quickly and tore through me. I wept out my moans beneath him, biting into his shoulder as he continued to pound his huge cock through me.

"Oh, Mr. Giles, you're making me come!"

"I'm close too, darling," he grunted. "I'm really close!"

"Shoot it inside me. Give me your cum!"

I'd never wanted something so badly. The milk from Amber had sent me wild, and my milk had had the same effect on Mr. Giles. The two of us were feeding on each other's naughtiness and there was nothing to keep us in check.

"Pump your fucking cum in me!" I whined, and I opened my eyes and stared into his to show him I meant it.

"Oh, Agnes!"

"Come inside me!"

"Oh, Agnes!"

Mr. Giles's eyes closed and his whole body trembled. I felt the swell and surge in his cock. Knowing how imminent it was excited me further and I wriggled down on him with a grunt, relishing the moment.

I looked into his face and saw the pleasure wash over him. At exactly the same moment I felt the bursting flash of heat arrive inside me, followed quickly by a long, heady groan.

"I'm coming!" he cried.

He didn't need to tell me. I could feel the fierce lashings blast within and then the heat from him started to spread through me.

"Oh, Mr. Giles" I cried, my own orgasm still rippling within. "Oh, Mr. Giles, that's so nice!"

He pumped slower now, sending his cum deep as my tits continued to weep their milk. His cock became glossed in his cum and started to slide through me easier. The texture of his slippery stiffness cruising through me was second only to the sensation of his lips on my nipples.

As if he could hear my thoughts Farmer Giles brought his mouth to my breasts again and took one last feast, grinding his big cock into me as he exorcised the milk from my teat.

"Perfect," I whispered, holding him to me.

"You are."

I closed my eyes and melted against him. I felt a sudden pang of guilt that I tried to quash. It mingled with the danger of a pussy full of his cum and I had to fight hard to stay in the moment.

His eyes opened and he smiled. Everything drifted away suddenly. He pulled back away from me and wiped his mouth, then he pulled himself out.

His cock was still stiff with a delicious coating of cum over his length. He jerked it slowly, pinching out one last bead of cum that fell down onto my stomach. I rubbed at it and Mr. Giles squeezed at my tits.

"That sure was something," he laughed, running a hand through his hair.

"You can say that again," I giggled.

Thankfully the pressure in my breasts had gone and they were no longer leaking everywhere. The intense burning lust had also lifted, and I wondered if the milk had some kind of lusty time-limit, or whether our combined climaxes had signaled the end of our forays.

"I'll leave you to milk Amber," he said, and I didn't yet have the heart to tell him the bad news.

"Will do."

Mr. Giles dressed calmly and I watched that magnificent figure of his be covered by his morning attire. It seemed so odd to watch him leave the barn in his dressing-gown and pajamas, knowing that only a moment before he'd been naked and stiff and pressed against me.

Gradually I got to my feet and looked to Amber who seemed to have a smile in her dark eyes, as though she knew.

"What do I do now?!" I asked aloud. A moo followed.

There was only one thing to do. Pass my own milk off as Amber's and hope for first-prize at the farmer's market regardless.

I had become Mr. Giles's new prize cow!

THE END

Holy Cow : Suckled Brats 2

Our prize cow Delilah was an absolute dream. She produced a bounteous amount of milk good enough to satisfy most of the village. In fact, Delilah was the talk of our little community, and I think they thought just as highly of her as we did.

Farmer Giles was very protective though. He did everything he could to guarantee that Delilah kept on producing. He was so invested that he enlisted the village priest to bless Delilah, hoping to continue her fruitful supply of delicious milk.

I just had to be there. It wasn't every day that a priest came by to bless a cow, and I wasn't the only one interested. I guess village life was pretty slow, because on the day of the ceremony around thirty people turned up.

I recognized almost all of them. The village butcher was in attendance with his wife; the village newsagent had turned out; the head-teacher of a nearby school was there along with a host of others. All of them had sampled Delilah's milk and couldn't live without it. I knew exactly how they felt. As soon as I'd tasted her rich, creamy bounty I knew Farmer Giles would struggle to ever replace her.

So there we stood in the middle of his field, surrounding Delilah who chomped obliviously on the rich, verdant grass at her feet.

"We are gathered today to bless Mr. Giles's pride and joy. Delilah has touched many of our lives in ways we'd never imagined. Her milk surpasses anything we have ever tasted, and I'm sure the crowd here can attest to that," the priest began.

There were mumbles of agreement. I was trying desperately not to laugh. I mean the whole thing was just absurd. I almost couldn't believe it was happening, but the seriousness with which everyone else conducted themselves stopped me from outright erupting in giggles. It wouldn't be fitting for a worker of the farm to show such unprofessionalism.

"This cow has served the community for many years and we ask you lord if you can bestow us many more years of her glorious ambrosia."

'Glorious ambrosia,' I though, twisting my mouth. I mean, it was amazing milk, but it was still just milk.

Mr. Giles stood stoically at Delilah's side, rubbing behind her ear and patting her head as the priest continued the service. I stood on her other flank, tickling under her neck. Delilah seemed far more interested in chewing on grass.

"Lord, I ask your blessing," the priest continued. He raised his hand and made a cross pattern across his body, then he dipped his fingers into some holy water that he'd brought with him.

I thought that he'd probably just got it from his faucet at home, but who was I to judge? It seemed that the priest and many others genuinely thought this blessing was going to actually have an effect.

He tossed the water off his fingers and I felt some of it splash against my bare arm as I scratched at Delilah's soft coat. The water continued to sprinkle me as he rounded out his sermon.

"In the name of the Father, the Son and the Holy Spirit."

The whole congregation gave an "amen." The priest stepped forward and touched the cow's head, then he took a grip of my wrist.

I looked to him and we seemed to share a private moment. He locked on my gaze and I stared into his swirling blue eyes. My skin prickled with goose-pimples and the priest let go. He turned to Farmer Giles. No one there seemed to have paid any mind to the priest's hand on me.

"Thank you, Father," Mr. Giles said, shaking his hand warmly.

Everyone exchanged platitudes and the whole affair ended in a round of applause for both the priest and Delilah. It just made it all seem even more absurd.

I played the model farm-girl and gave warm smiles to all the well-wishers. Mr. Giles had even put on a buffet for them, which they dived into ravenously. It was then that I realized some of the people were just there to kill a morning and perhaps weren't as invested in the *glorious ambrosia* as others.

As the ceremony was wrapping up I started to feel strange. At first I thought I was coming down with something, but as I focused on the new sensations I realized it wasn't entirely unpleasant.

It was tingle at first, as though my breasts had fallen to sleep. They seemed all fuzzy, like they were experiencing a bout of static.

I shuffled my shoulders and felt the chill. As I looked around the crowd I spotted a pair of eyes staring right at me. The priest was looking over the top of his glass as he took a drink. He licked off his creamy moustache and held my gaze. Delilah's milk was the drink of choice, of course.

I walked to Farmer Giles and gave his shirt a surreptitious tug. He turned away from the village butcher.

"Everything okay, Lydia?"

"I'm gonna head inside," I told him. "I'm not feeling too great." I had a room at the farm as part of the job.

"Oh, Lydia, I'm sorry," he said sweetly. He always had time for me, even amongst the 'elites' of our little community. "Do you feel sick?"

I scrunched my nose. "I don't know."

"Go get some rest," he said.

I turned back and noticed the eyes of the priest on me again. I quickened my pace, folding my arms across my big chest and making my way back to the house.

That tingling sensation struck again. It seemed to radiate out from my chest. I took a look down and my eyes bulged. The front of my gray tank-top had turned a dark-gray on each breast. I looked back to the congregation, fearful that someone had seen the accident.

All I could see was the watchful eyes of the priest. He gave me a smile and I felt a chill. I hurried faster.

When I was inside the house I reached down inside the cups of my bra. I could feel the wetness on my fingers and I withdrew them to gasp at the white milk that sat on their tips.

"My gosh," I hushed.

My body seemed to awaken somehow. There was an intense pressure in my chest and I could feel my pussy swelling too, as though I was suddenly ripe to be satisfied.

I rushed to my bedroom to lie down, rolling onto the mattress and letting out a dissatisfied huff.

"What is *wrong* with me?" I asked aloud.

It seemed as though the priest's blessing had somehow been bestowed on me too. I wondered if Delilah's teat was leaking just like mine. The fact she was a cow meant that she had a better chance of getting away with it than me.

I felt the ache in my breasts for the next half-hour. I writhed and wriggled on the bed as they steadily started to leak, drip-by-drip, into my bra. It felt like I could do nothing about it.

Finally I heard Farmer Giles come through the door below and call out: "Lydia? Are you okay?"

I could hardly answer. By now I was contorting in discomfort.

"Lydia?" he asked, mounting the stairs.

I let out a whimper and heard his booming footsteps quicken.

"Lydia?" he said more urgently.

He arrived in the doorway and looked over me. To the casual observer it was tough to discern the cause of my discomfort. I don't think he noticed the wet patches on my chest at first.

He hurried to the bed and knelt beside me. "Lydia, are you okay?"

"Mr. Giles," I whimpered, pursing my lips. I felt as though I couldn't say it.

"What? Should I get a doctor?"

"No!" I burst. I was far too embarrassed for that.

"Then what is it? How can I help you?"

I cast my eyes down and nodded to my breasts. He looked to them.

"What? What is it?"

"They hurt."

"Let me see."

"Mr. Giles?"

"Let me see," he urged. "There's no time to be shy, Lydia."

I guess he was right, but it felt odd to expose myself to him like that. At forty-three Mr. Giles was over half my age.

He helped me take off my tank-top. Although the cause of my undressing was surreal, the act of having Mr. Giles help me was oddly sensual.

He was careful as he lifted it above my head and even more careful as he unclasped my bra.

"There's certainly a swelling," Mr. Giles laughed, trying to ease the tension.

I laughed too but felt a sudden squirt from each nipple.

He took the bra off my chest and the milk that had pooled inside ran down over my body. Immediately there was a sense of release and I exhaled deeply.

"I wish I'd have done that earlier," I confessed.

"I wish you had too," he said, ogling my breasts.

I let out a nervous giggle. It was rare for him to show this side. So long Mr. Giles had been the big gruff, reliable farmer. To know he had a weak spot was endearing, but then I guess there's only so long you can resist a nineteen-year-old woman.

"They're leaking," he said, reaching out to touch. "Can I?"

I nodded and bit my lip. The idea of having his big hands on me felt almost necessary now.

He touched them carefully and I closed my eyes to focus. I took a deep breath as he applied a little pressure.

I felt the milk spiral through my nipple and I gasped. I looked down to see it rushing from my breast and I felt the pressure lessen even more.

Mr. Giles was unabashed. He let the milk spurt skywards and fall back against him.

"Just like Delilah," he said softly.

"That priest was weird, Mr. Giles."

"He was?"

"So weird. His look ... it was just ... odd. I think he put a spell on me."

He chuckled. "Don't be silly, Lydia."

"But he put a spell on Delilah, right?"

"I hope so," he said.

"So why not me? Why couldn't he have done the same to me?"

He mused, and while he did so he continued to fondle my breasts. The milk flowed outwards.

"I have to check," he said, and he stooped his head to my breast.

"Mr. Giles?!"

"I have to check, Lydia."

"You're going to ... drink my milk?"

"Only with your blessing. I want to see if it rivals our Delilah's."

"Do it," I said, a sparkle in my eye. "Feast on my tits."

Farmer Giles hadn't quite expected that level of enthusiasm. He looked almost proud.

I beamed at him and watched as he closed his eyes and moved towards my nipples. He clamped his lips around me and I felt him begin to suckle.

The sudden bond felt incredible. It was like a bridge built between us. The act was so sensual and erotic that I could feel my swollen pussy begin to flood too.

He slurped my milk into him and swallowed it down gladly, taking much more than a taste. The creamy goodness filled him and from the glow of his face it looked as though he was enjoying himself.

I didn't stop him from taking more than his fair share. Instead I held his head against me and enjoyed the moment. His jaw dropped and bounced as he worked the cream through my nipple and it felt rewarding to nourish him.

Finally he pulled away, opening his eyes slowly and wiping his mouth.

"That was glorious," he said.

I blushed and giggled.

"I want more."

"More milk or more of me?"

"More milk," he said. "Although the idea of more of you is pretty delightful too."

I laughed again and bunched my shoulders together. His eyes shot to my tits as they moved between my arms.

"You like that?" I asked him. All of the pressure had been eased and an afterglow remained. I felt more of a woman than I ever had before in my life. If any other man was in the room I'd have taken him instead, but with only Farmer Giles there to satisfy my needs I was ready to break all codes and customs. I wanted him badly, and I think he knew it.

He rushed again to my breasts and I held them up to his mouth. Again he suckled, but this time I accompanied the sensation. My fingers teased at the crotch of my denim shorts and they were quickly joined by Mr. Giles's.

Soon his hand had replaced mine and I reached back to grip the posts of my bed. He sucked ravenously and fingered my crotch. I could feel the warmth of my pussy turn wet as he teased the flow from me.

"I want you," I hushed. I don't even know where the words had come from. It was as though my eroticism was talking for me. All my pussy wanted was to be filled.

"We shouldn't," he groaned, but his continued feeding on my tits told me that he didn't mean it. It would only take a little more cajoling.

"Do you think you could get hard for me?"

He broke his clasp on my nipple again. "I know I can."

"How?"

He stood up and I looked up at him, then he took a grip at the front of his pants. I looked at what was beneath as he uncovered it for me. I could see his huge thickness stretched across the front of his jeans, starting at the fly and curving up towards his pocket.

"Damn," I hushed. "That looks good."

"But we can't," he said unconvincingly.

"Sure we can."

I reached out and touched his package. I could feel how hard he was in his pants. He didn't stop me. I looked up into his eyes.

"Let me take it out," I begged.

Mr. Giles took a deep breath and then gave a subtle nod.

I rushed excitedly, kicking my legs off the side of the bed and scrambling at his belt. His rough hands hung at his side as he watched me slip the belt through the loops of his pants and then pop the button above his zipper.

I slid it down and stared forward. My eyes widened further as I tugged his pants down. I could see that sinful thickness ahead of me, covered only by his underwear.

I stalled for a moment, taking several deep breaths and listening to the steady drip, drip, drip of my milk on my wooden floor. It eased out of me at a steady, constant rate, sometimes falling from the nipple completely and other times curling round under my huge breasts and dribbling towards my navel.

"Put it in your mouth," he said.

"How can I refuse?"

I downed his boxer-shorts and his huge cock sprang out. I barely took the time to ogle it, instead rushing it right through my lips and sucking heartily on him.

Mr. Giles groaned wildly above me, letting out a series of pleasured noises that I'd never before heard him make before. It was so hot to see that side of him.

I drove his cock to the top of my throat and started to pinch at my breasts. The milk fired forward against his downed jeans.

"Wait," Mr. Giles said, and he took off his pants completely.

He hopped out of his underwear too, leaving his heavy boots on the floor by my bed. He stood before me again, naked from the waist down.

"Cover me in it," he smiled.

I took him in my mouth again and pinched my tits, firing out jets of warm cream all over his legs. I gave him a handless blowjob, shooting the milk all over him and listening to his soft moans above.

Eventually I pulled my lips off him and targeting his cock with my bullets. The warm milk spattered over his length, dotting it with white. It had never looked more delicious.

"Oh, Mr. Giles," I burst, and I raced his cock into my mouth again.

I could taste my own milk and I realized how closely it resembled Delilah's. I wondered if I might replace her should her stock ever dwindle, or God forbid anything happen to her. If we had both been bestowed with the exact same blessing then Delilah had nothing to fear. Whoever the mysterious priest was, it was clear to see that his powers weren't just for show.

I sucked more lovingly on his cock than ever, slurping out the beads of milk. My tongue pulsed along the underside of his dick, tickling the little hole at the top before I withdrew.

I giggled up at him and bounced his cock with my tongue. Mr. Giles looked impressed.

"Oh, Lydia, I wanna fuck you so bad," he grunted.

I sprang up and jumped back onto my bed. "So fuck me."

My tits splayed across my chest as I flailed my legs in the air. It looked as though Farmer Giles didn't know what to do with himself.

He took up his own cock and jerked steadily as he watched, then he seemed to come to a decision. He unbuttoned his shirt and pulled it off to reveal his barrel chest, then he reached forwards and unfastened the buttons at the front of my shorts.

"Are you gonna fuck me?" I whined, squeezing my tits. "Are you gonna fuck me?"

He nodded and tugged at my jean-shorts, dragging them under my ass and taking my panties with them.

I wriggled as the milk blasted upwards and fell back against me. Soon I could feel the air on the wetness of my pussy. When he had pulled the garment form my ankles he tossed it aside and pushed my legs open at the knees.

"That looks perfect," he said.

"I want you in there," I told him.

I hooked my heel around his midriff and pulled him forwards. Mr. Giles took a step between my legs and his big cock swung above my pussy.

He framed it above me as though he was gauging how far it might reach inside me. The tip of his cock hovered over my navel and his weighty balls hung underneath.

"Fuck me, Mr. Giles," I dared.

He pulled back his hips and took a hold of his cock, pointing it towards my tight, wet snatch. I bit my lip and held my breath as he approached, then I felt the smooth head of his cock smothering my folds.

He dragged the tip up and down as I shrieked with joy, pinching my nipples and firing the milk upwards like a geyser.

Finally he started to push forwards and I felt the weight behind his cock. It eased into my groove and gradually I spread open over him.

My pussy spread wider than ever. My brow furrowed in angst as I felt it stretch. I wondered if I could take it. Gradually the bulbous crown popped through and I exhaled.

Farmer Giles let out a grunt of approval and then continued, pushing the ensuing inches into me until I'd engulfed all that he had to offer. To feel him inside me like that felt like a strange kind of privilege. It was no secret that the bachelorettes of the village lusted after him. So too did many of the married women. Mr. Giles was a catch alright, and it was criminal that he hadn't found anyone yet.

But then perhaps he didn't need anyone. If I could cater to his sexual desires then we were all set, and it seemed my dripping udders were certainly catering to one of one of his desires.

"I want you on top," he said eventually. "I want you covering me with your cream."

I smirked up at him and he withdrew. His thickness sprang out of me and he sat on the bed beside.

I took his place as he got comfortable on his back, then he held his huge cock upright, ready for me to impale myself on it.

"Let me ride that thing," I cooed.

I straddled his muscled frame, putting my knees either side of his hips. I reached beneath and took a hold of the behemoth, then steadily I dropped on him until I started to swallow him up.

"Yes," he hushed, and I looked to his face to see him ogling my hungry pussy.

He watched the sinful union and I took my time, gradually sliding down over each inch until I was sat on his fat, full balls.

"Ride my cock, Lydia."

I didn't need a second invitation. I squeezed my way upwards and started to bounce on him, using the sponginess of the mattress to launch myself away from him over and over.

When I hit my rhythm I took a hold of my bouncing tits. I looked down on Mr. Giles to make sure they had his full attention, then I started to pinch.

The milk blasted down onto him and was greeted with an immediate, welcoming groan. He rubbed the pure liquid into his skin and I watched as it caught on the hair that adorned his torso.

More and more shot from me as though Mr. Giles was being baptized by it beneath me. He smothered it about himself, sometimes sucking his fingers and humming contently as he tasted me.

"You like my milk, huh? You like this fucking milk? Shall we put it on the shelves and have everyone taste it?"

It was a risky comment but Mr. Giles put his professionalism aside to enjoy the notion. He groaned as though he was imagining it.

"Have this whole village drinking my tit milk. They'd never know."

Again he groaned and I felt his cock swell within me, as though my dirty words were the catalyst he needed to come.

I rode his cock like he was my stallion, bouncing down on it and feeling it delight a place deep inside me that I didn't even know existed.

My hands found his chest and I squeezed at his pecs, running my fingers through the damp fur. My udders hung beneath me and dripped their milk all over him. Mr. Giles reached up and started to squeeze them.

"That's it," I encouraged, "squirt my fucking tit milk all over your face."

And boy did he! He was insatiable. He fired my cream all over himself and it showed no sign of abating. His mouth opened wide and the milk filled it, then he gulped it down gladly and set about delivering another load through his lips.

It was messy, but I wouldn't have it any other way. The sheets were sodden and so too were the both of us. It looked as though we'd just hurried in from a biblical storm, only instead of rain there was milk cascading from the heavens.

"I want to feel you come," I told him. "I want you to pump your cum into me."

Mr. Giles squeezed harder and groaned louder. The milk tore through my nipple and gave me a tingle that spread down my spine. I started to convulse in wild excitement, feeling my pussy contract around his burly cock.

"I'm close," he groaned, his eyes closed tight and his brow furrowed.

"Me too," I managed to reply.

My body was tight and tense, but still I bounced on him, jerking his cock through my tightening core over and over.

Eventually the levy broke and the climax began inside me. It rippled through my body in undulating waves and I rode them out on his pole, stirring him inside until he couldn't stand it anymore.

"Lydia!" he cried.

His cock swelled and stiffened, then finally he let out a huge croak and I felt his heat begin to rush into me.

The crazy thing was that as I started to come my tits somehow found another gear. The milk fired from them with wild abandon, steering my tits with its power. It absolutely covered my bedroom but neither of us cared.

Instead our orgasms carried us through, blasting out of each of us under different guises. Mr. Giles's shot from him as male orgasms often did. His pearly, hot cum fired up into my body and I wriggled down on him to claim everything he had to give.

My climax showed itself in an entirely different way. The cream sprinkled from my tits like Farmer Giles was on fire and I was trying to put him out.

Cascades of my nectar fell down on him and he opened his mouth, hoping that some errant drops would find their way inside.

They did. Shit, they went everywhere. By the time my climax was coming to an end the entire room was dripping in my prized milk.

Finally I came out the other side of ecstasy, breathless and confused. I looked around at the state of the room and then down at Mr. Giles. His eyes were still closed and I was pinching the last of his cum from his cock as I steadily rocked my tight pussy over him.

"Now *that* was amazing," I said, giggling.

He opened his eyes and surveyed the scene. "My God."

"He might have had something to do with it!"

I eased myself off him and felt him dribble a little ways out of me. The bulk of his seed stayed deep within. I closed my legs to trap it there and sat beside him.

Mr. Giles sat up and looked around the room. "Where do we begin?"

I started to laugh and he joined me.

"I'll grab a mop," I told him.

"Never mind a mop, I'll fetch one of Delilah's pails. I'm gonna fill it up while I have the chance."

Mr. Giles was serious. It's not every day your assistant's tits start producing milk that tastes like it was delivered by the God's themselves.

He was on his feet and carrying out the task in no time. He scrambled into his clothes and started to move with urgency, as though my breasts might shut themselves off at any moment.

He needn't have worried. As I watched him jog across the field from my window I could heard the steady, rhythmic drip of milk as it patted the wooden floor.

Its metronomic taps lulled me and I thought again of the mysterious priest who had seemed so sinister and yet delivered such a fine gift.

Eventually I fell back in the bed with a dreamy sigh, feeling the warmth of Mr. Giles's seed in my belly and the warmth of my own milk across my tits.

Heaven.

THE END

Boss's Magical Latte : Suckled Brats 3

Mysterious was an understatement when it came to Mr. Thompson's character. Despite being his employee for two years there was still so much I didn't know about him. He didn't talk much so I was often left to fill the void and as such he knew my all of my earthly desires better than I did.

I didn't even know what he did for a living, but it sure as hell wasn't: run a coffee shop. He was hardly ever here. He'd drop in once or twice a week in his business attire, as though he had another job elsewhere, and he'd always have a latte. That was his favorite. As long as he got his latte, he was happy. So happy, in fact, that in only two years he'd promoted me to manager.

I took to it like a duck-to-water. There was just something about it that really suited me: the way people drifted in and out; the way no two days were the same; the regulars who became friends; the sense of pride. I mean, it was just perfect.

And at the end of every week Mr. Thompson would turn up for a latte. It was on the house, of course. We'd sit and talk—or rather I'd talk—about anything that came up and he'd sit there looking amazing.

It was a Sunday and we'd been absolutely slammed. I think there was some kind of concert in the town-centre and the footfall absolutely killed us. I hadn't planned for it at all.

I'd sent the staff home early when everything turned quiet a little after five. They'd worked their asses off and gestures like that can really make the difference.

Mr. Thompson came through the door as he always did a little before six. He turned the "Open" sign over and put a bolt on the door.

"What a day!" I cried across the shop. I was behind the counter soaking the dried milk off the steam-nozzles. I hadn't quite been feeling myself but I wasn't exactly unwell.

He didn't say anything. Instead he picked a table and sat at it. He wore his suit-pants and shirt as always. He always dressed like a business-man, but I'd never seen him do any actual business.

"The usual?" I asked.

He nodded from the table, clasping his hands in from of him. His handsome face wore a sort of half-smile. He surveyed the scene.

"Busy?" he asked.

"You don't know the half of it. We made a killing, but damn, that was a no way to end a week. I covered so much ground that I won't be able to walk tomorrow. How about you?"

He tilted his head quickly and let out a small hum. I took it to mean: so-so.

I set the shot of espresso going and reached down to the fridges beneath the counter. My hand went mechanically to the where the carton of milk should have been, but instead I gripped thin-air.

I bent to the floor and looked inside, but there was nothing. The next fridge was just as empty and so was the third.

"Shoot," I cried, standing up. With my hands on my hips I looked across to Mr. Thompson.

He turned his head and raised an eyebrow.

"We're out of milk," I told him.

His nostrils flared and his eyes widened.

"Sorry, Me. Thompson."

"The coffee shop has run out of milk?"

"It's been so busy. We get another delivery tomorrow." I pulled at my shirt as I felt a strange tingling in my chest.

"And now?"

I shrugged and made a face. "Sorry, I don't know what to tell you."

"I didn't make you manager so you could do a bad job of it, Angela."

I held my tongue. I had so much to say but I knew better than to talk back. I felt another strange sensation on my breast and shuffled uncomfortably.

"Everything okay?" he asked.

"It's ... it's nothing."

I felt a sudden rush of something inside me. Mr. Thompson held my gaze as the bizarre sensation consumed me. It felt like my chest was going to explode. I reached out a hand and put it on the counter to steady myself.

"I feel funny," I said.

He was up like a shot and rushing towards me. "Angela?"

Suddenly my chest turned warm. I looked down to see the dampness spreading across the front of my gray t-shirt.

I looked to him in horror.

"Are you bleeding?" he said, advancing.

"No, I ... no, I don't think so."

"What is it?"

I took a step back and looked down at myself. Mr. Thompson did too. The pair of us watched the patch of damp spread over my chest.

I bit my lip, confused. "I think it's ... *milk*. Can you give me a minute?" I asked him.

"I can give you all the time you need."

He didn't move.

"I just need a second."

"I want to make sure you're okay, Angela. I'm worried about you."

His concern seemed genuine. I never thought I'd be stripping off in front of my boss. Actually, that's a lie—I thought about it more often than I care to admit, but my fantasies never looked like this.

"Okay," I said. "Okay, let's see what's going on here."

I un-tucked my t-shirt and lifted it over my head to assess the damage. My boss's eyes spread wide as he saw the milk running out from under the cups of each bra. It was kinda hot to have his eyes on me like that, I just wish it was under different circumstances.

"Where's it coming from?" I wondered.

"I can take a pretty good guess," Mr. Thompson said.

I let out a laugh. Without a second's thought I unclasped my bra. I pulled it forward off my arms and stared down in wide-eyed wonder. The veins in my breasts were slightly more apparent than usual and each nipple was letting out a steady, constant stream of milk.

"My, oh, my," he said.

"I'm leaking!"

"You certainly are. I don't think that latte will be a problem now."

"What should I do?"

"Give it a squeeze?" he suggested.

"I'm not sure I'd do it right."

"There's no right or wrong way, Angela. I was just thinking if it hurts or something t might be better to relive the pressure.

"Can you do it?"

"I—I *can,* I guess."

"Please, Mr. Thompson. I just don't know what to do."

He resigned himself to touching me, although it didn't look as though he needed much persuading. As he brought his hand up I tried to hide my naughty smirk.

I watched as he put it to my breast, stemming the flow of milk briefly before squeezing my tits and letting out a rushing blast.

"Oooh!" I cooed, feeling the rush of release.

"Feel good?"

"Better than I imagined."

"It's milk alright," he declared. He looked at the counter-top where some of it had sprayed.

"I know that! How do we make it stop?"

"Hmm," he mused.

He held his chin with one hand but continued to squeeze my breasts with the other. I felt ripe with an arousal that I was barely able to contain.

"Hand me the cup of coffee," he said and he nodded to the shot of espresso that I'd already poured.

I went to the machine and grabbed it, bringing it back over to the counter. "What now?"

He took the cup and brought it to his nose. He closed his eyes and inhaled, then he brought the cup to my chest.

He took my breasts again and squeezed it. A jet of milk tore through my nipple, tickling and exciting me as it spiraled outwards. It hit the coffee and turned it a creamy brown.

"What's that supposed to do?" I asked.

He took a sip and hummed contently. "Nothing," he said. "I just wanted my latte."

"Mr. Thompson!" I gasped, mock-offended.

He was chuckling to himself. "I can have my fun, can't I?"

"As long as I can have mine."

My face flushed red. I hadn't meant to divulge exactly how amazing this all felt. I'd never been this aroused before in my life and something about having my boss there to witness it was making the whole thing even naughtier.

"I do know of one way to make it stop," he said.

"What is it?"

"It's too risky, Angela. We shouldn't."

"What is it, Mr. Thompson? I'll do anything."

"Good, because it's very ... *unconventional*."

"I like the sound of that," I said wryly.

"I read about this in an article," he said. "It said that satisfying a person's arousal could be the first way to make it stop."

"What? How does that work?"

"The article said that any sex-act could work. It might be worth a try."

"What could I do?"

"Use the restroom and ... take care of it?" Mr. Thompson guessed.

"Don't you want to help?"

Mr. Thompson narrowed his eyes and quashed a smile. "Would you like me to help?"

"I—I don't want to go through it alone," I lied.

"Angela, I'm not sure I should be doing this with an employee."

"It'd be our special secret. I think we're already pretty involved together, don't you?"

I looked down at my tits again and Mr. Thompson did too.

"This is certainly a rare occurrence for me," he confessed.

"Let's help each other," I told him.

"How can you help me?"

"Take it out," I urged. "I'm not selfish enough to let you do all the work."

"What are you gonna do?"

"Suck your cock," I shrugged. I'd wanted to do that the second he'd hired me.

"You know that isn't necessary," he said, "according to article."

I stared at him coolly. "I don't care."

He opened his belt buckle and downed his zipper. I moved out from behind the counter and rushed to him, falling at his feet.

"Give me it!" I begged.

I scramble at his pants and he stumbled back, reaching out to hold a table-top to steady himself.

"Angela, you're gonna get me in trouble."

"I think we're in enough already."

I yanked down his pants and froze. In front of me stood his hard, upright cock, throbbing as his aroused blood beat into it. He was just as turned-on as I was.

"Oh, gosh!" I gasped.

"Put me in your mouth," he urged now.

"I didn't bend all the way down here just to stare at it."

I took a hold of his cock and held it steady. I could feel how stiff he was in my grasp and I could feel too the beat of his pulse.

I licked my lips. "Here goes."

I threw my mouth over him, driving down the tip and thrusting his cock right to my throat. He let out a groan of satisfaction as my nipples continued to flow.

The milk spilled down from the nipple and hugged the underside curves of each breast. It flowed down my stomach and dripped off me, leaving a puddle of white on the hard, wooden floor.

"They're still dripping, huh?" he said.

I pulled him out and held him. "Maybe I can get your cock dripping too."

"I'd like to watch you try."

I put his delicious cock back into my mouth and sucked with all my might, running my lips over him and turning him into a slippery mess of saliva.

"That's it, Angela, you keep trying!"

I gnawed down the length of his thickness and latched onto the low hanging fruit at the base. I rolled his balls through my lips and sucked them, jerking his cock and looking upwards as I did so.

I could see the familiar face of my boss, but it was stoic no longer. The pleasure etched across it was hard to deny and I felt privileged to witness it. It was an emotion of his that few women had got to see.

"You're really leaking," he asked.

I looked down to my tits to see them pumping their milk more fiercely than ever. "It feels so good!"

"Do you even want it stop?"

"Not right now, but let's see if this article was telling the truth."

I looked up into his eyes as it dawned on him.

"Stand up," he said. "Bend over the table."

I did as he said with great urgency. I bent forward and felt him at my pants, rushing them down beneath my apron.

"I wouldn't normally do this," he said again, "but in the interest of science ..."

It was cute to hear him pretend.

"Agreed," I said, desperate for him.

He rubbed at my pussy, finding it wetter than my chest.

"You're so ready," he said.

His finger probed a little ways inside and then he crouched to the floor. He pushed his face under my apron and started to tongue me.

"That feels so good," I groaned. "But I was hoping for your cock."

"I just wanted a taste."

He gave my pussy a few broad licks, and then rose to his feet. I felt his cock replace his tongue between my legs.

"Let's see if this works," he said.

He pushed forwards from behind and I felt my tight pussy spread over his thickness. It engulfed him and washed him in its juices—juices that he used to venture deeper.

"Oh, you're so tight," he moaned.

His hands came under my arms and he squeezed at my tits. They shot out a violent burst of milk that spattered the table in front of us.

"That's so good!" I cried.

The milk dripped from my udders as my boss started to fuck me. I was a mess of arousal and having his hard cock inside me wasn't calming me down. I tried to take stock of what was happening, but it was as though my mind refused to consider how naughty the act was. I was fucking my boss in the coffee-shop I managed while my tits leaked milk. Shit, that was some scenario.

"Keep fucking me, Mr. Thompson! Fuck this milk right out of me."

I think by now the pair of us was comfortable with the arrangement. I wanted my breasts to stop their flow—of course I did—but in the meantime Mr. Thompson's delicious cock wasn't hurting anyone. Quite the opposite. The more he drove that big thing through me the closer I got to climax.

"Keep fucking me!" I groaned, hanging my head and letting it bob.

He fucked me harder, slamming his bare hips against mine. The claps of our flesh rang out in the shop, interspersed with moans and groans and the dripping of my warm milk.

He squeezed and pinched at my tits and my orgasm approached steadily. Each time his cock drove into me I felt the meter of climax rise until it was close to bursting right out of me.

"Mr. Thompson!" was all I could muster.

He found another gear, using my moans as a cue to up his pace. Soon I couldn't contain myself. My tits were dripping faster until a constant stream of white ran out of them. The table was awash with it, but I didn't care.

I pushed my hands through it and felt my insides burst with ecstasy. I gasped as the climax tore through me, wriggling back against Mr. Thompson's stiffness and stirring him in my pussy.

"Let it all out!" he said, squeezing my hips as he fucked me.

My pussy gripped his cock over and over. I convulsed before him, the contractions of climax tearing through me violently.

"Mr. Thompson!" I wailed, pressing my chest to the soaked table.

He pulled out of me and turned me around. I jumped up onto table and fell back, rubbing my pussy as I lay in my milk.

"That's it," he said, jerking his cock as he watched me.

My fingers teased my clit and the orgasm continued, but so did the milk. Mr. Thompson took off my pants and moved between my open legs. He set the point of his cock towards its target.

He drove into my pussy and I let out a wail of delight as I felt him in me again. He pushed deep and spurts of milk erupted upwards from my chest like a geyser. The article hadn't been entirely accurate.

He opened his mouth and caught the flow like he was drinking from a water-fountain. He hummed contently and swallowed down my cream messily. It dripped down off his chin and fell to me, mingling with the ambrosia that already coated me.

"I want you to come too," I told him. "I want your cum."

He leaned over me and pushed back the torrent of milk with his mouth. It clamped down over my breast and he started to guzzle the ambrosia down like he'd thirsted for it for years.

I hummed contently and lay there, feeling his hard cock rocking through me as he suckled from my tits. Our bond had never been stronger, but the problem was not yet solved. The milk was ceaseless, blasting from me mysteriously with no hope of slowing down.

"Do it," I said. "Come in my pussy and let's see if that helps."

"I can't promise anything, Angela."

"I don't care. Do it! Come inside me. I want to feel it, anyway."

He smile and kissed me. I hadn't realized just how badly I'd wanted him until now, which was just as well.

"You want to feel me come inside you?"

I nodded. "Uh-huh!"

"Then I guess I have to," he said.

He clapped up against my pussy and I could hear the wet smacks as the milk dispersed. It was covering me from neck to thigh and flowing down off the edges of the table too.

"Give me your fucking cum," I grunted.

Mr. Thompson gripped my hips and pulled me back against him. He thrust forwards and bounced me away, only to pull me back all over again and repeat the process.

His hard cock drove through me, delighting my insides in a way that my fingers never could.

"Angela I'm gonna come inside you," he moaned.

"I want it. I need it!"

"You do, honey. You really do!"

It was the most I'd ever gotten out of Mr. Thompson. It seemed as though the only way to get him to talk was to cover his cock with my pussy. It certainly made for an interesting conversation.

The milk continued to burst upwards like a pair of Old Faithfulls and Mr. Thompson continued to slurp it down where he could. His appetite was insatiable.

"You feel so good in my pussy," I told him.

"It feels so good around me."

"I know, Mr. Thompson. Now shut up and fuck me!"

He pushed back my legs and started going for it. His cock slipped up through my folds, using the flowing milk as a lube to ease his passing.

He was stabbing so deep that I could see my stomach bulging. I looked down over my milk-strewn body to see that glorious cock disappearing inside me over and over.

"Oh, Angela," he grunted. "Angela!"

"Give me your cum!"

His thrusts slapped against me and I watched his face contort in joyous pleasure. The ecstasy arrived in his expression and he held himself at the peak of it.

"Yes!" I groaned, sensing the impending release.

Finally he exhaled, looking down at the source of his pleasure. His cock throbbed and then tossed its first rope of hot cum inside me.

He started to rock his cock through my glossy core, shooting off more and more of his seed. My pussy pinched it out of him. I stared at each nipple in turn, but the flow didn't stop.

It fired out of me at the same rate as Mr. Thompson's cum. Whenever I felt him let off a fresh lashing my milk would careen skywards and come splashing down over me.

"Take my cum," he groaned, pushing it deep.

"Give me every drop!"

As the torrent of cum died off so too did the bursts of milk through my nipple. The flow waned and the arc of the milk lowered. My breasts let out several shorts spurts of cream before finally returning to normal.

"It worked!" I cried, staring at my veiny, spent charms.

"It sure did," he said breathlessly.

He stooped his face to my nipples one last time and sucked them.

"Just making sure," he grinned.

I held his head on me as his tongue circled my nipples. His stiff cock rocked gently. After a moment he pulled away and wiped his mouth, then he pulled himself out.

"Look at that," I swooned.

His cock was covered in a sheen of his cum, glistening in the light.

"Can I taste it?"

"How can I refuse?"

"I've just always wanted to suck on a cummy cock."

He put his hands at his side and stood in place. "Suck away."

I jumped from the table and dropped to my knees in a puddle of milk. My mouth was over him quickly and I tasted the creamy, salty mixture of our love.

"Mmm," I cooed.

"Is that good?"

I nodded.

"As good as your milk, I wonder."

"Better!"

Mr. Thompson laughed. "I find that hard to believe."

"I'll know what to do when it happens again."

"You do," he said, then he raised a finger. "But you can't just do it with any man, do you understand."

I smirked. "I understand perfectly."

"Good."

I looked around the room. Before his arrival the place was a mess, but now I had a gallon of my own milk to contend with too.

"I should leave you to it," he said, kissing me. He pulled up his pants and fastened them.

"I'll see you next Sunday?" I asked hopefully.

He bit his lip and smiled. "Definitely."

He affected that same mysterious air again, drifting across the wooden floor and departing. I hurried to the door after him and locked it quickly, putting my back against the wall beside it. I started to giggle.

"Angela, you've done it. You've done the craziest fucking thing I've ever heard of."

I shook my head in disbelief. It was hard to imagine that only moments ago my tits had been shooting out milk like a broken faucet, but the proof was all around me.

I put a hand to my pussy. I could feel the warmth of my boss's cum inside it, but it didn't frighten me. Instead it gave me a sense of pride and contentment that I'd never quite felt before.

I couldn't wait for next Sunday.

THE END

Training My Chest : Suckled Brats 4

The story I'm about to share isn't exactly normal, but it's part of my therapy to write about it. Dr. Cooper said it will help, so here goes.

It all started just a little after my nineteenth birthday. The day had been fun and I'd seen lots of friends and family, but in the weeks that followed I kept feeling the strangest of sensations in my chest. It's kind of tough to describe, but it was almost like static, localized almost entirely in my breasts.

For the first few days I ignored it, thinking it would go away. It's stupid, I know! But the more it continued the more it played on my mind.

I'd given myself a check-over just to be sure, and in doing so I'd discovered that my tits had become *way* sensitive all of a sudden. I mean, even the lightest of touches was getting my pulse racing, which made the mammogram interesting. Shit, I'd barely even made it through without climaxing. Thank God the doctor was female. Not only did she understand, but I was less likely to launch myself at her in a horny frenzy.

It was only minutes after the check-up that I was in my car misbehaving. I just had to satisfy myself afterwards. I really couldn't help it. I hadn't even left the multi-story car-lot; I just went into the back seat and got straight to it immediately. It was one of the most incredible orgasms of my life.

The test-results came back all-clear, which was both a relief and a source of confusion. Everyone seemed dumbfounded by the sensation, but no-one seemed to care as much about it as me.

"Enjoy it," a friend had suggested. "Some women find it really hard to get turned-on and now suddenly you can do it instantly!"

But I couldn't enjoy it. I just had to know what was behind it, so under the advice of another friend I visited a psychiatrist that she said specialized in this area. I didn't even know there *was* an area.

I'd booked in through the receptionist as soon as I'd been given the number. Like I say, I just couldn't wait to get to the bottom of it. It was playing on my mind constantly and I needed some kind of closure, even if the sensation was to never go away.

I sat in the waiting room looking around and something didn't sit right. I couldn't quite explain it, but something was off, and it wasn't just the fuzzy sensation in my tits.

I looked to the plate on the door nearby. 'Dr. Cooper,' it read. *Huh ... that was my old science-teacher's name.*

The door opened suddenly a pair of breasts exited, attached to a young, blonde woman with a flush expression. She wore a naughty smirk and brushed her hair behind her ear as she passed, giving me a quick glance. Her physique wasn't too dissimilar to mine. I guess this was the place to be for women like me.

I sat in the empty waiting-room for a while with a confused look on my face. I wondered what fate awaited me, and the sense of unease grew. Eventually the receptionist got my attention and told me that the doctor was ready for me.

I took a deep breath and stood up. Beyond that door were the answers I was searching for. I was sure of it.

"Here goes," I hushed, looking down at my cleavage.

I gave the door a quick knock and entered. I was immediately dumb-struck, but so too was Dr. Cooper. Dr. Cooper: my ex-teacher!

"Lizzie?" he said, standing up.

"Mr. Cooper?"

"*Doctor* Cooper," he corrected. "Close the door."

I did as he said, shutting out the receptionist and leaving the two of us alone together.

"Is everything okay?"

"I—I came for ... ummm..."

"Look, I know why you're here and I know this must seem strange."

"You can say that again!" I laughed.

"I check breasts for a living," he shrugged.

"But you're a psychiatrist?"

"Sometimes women's problems are deeper than just the physical, Lizzie," he said sagely.

I could attest to that. No medical doctor had yet discovered what ailed me. I guess it was time for a different kind of doctor.

"Take a seat," he offered, sitting opposite and trying to remain professional behind his big wooden desk.

"I'm not sure about this," I said, looking back to the door.

"Lizzie, I'm here to help. And you do need help, don't you?"

I sighed. I did.

I sat carefully in the chair opposite, perching on the edge. Dr. Cooper sat patiently opposite, waiting for me to speak first.

"It's ... my breasts," I began, finally looking across at him. His expression was unwavering. It was attentive and non-judgmental and ... handsome.

"Tell me about them," he pressed.

God, this was weird.

"They've started to tingle."

"Tingle?"

"Yes. Like they've fallen asleep, you know?"

"I know," he said, clasping his hands in front of him. "How long have you had this sensation?"

"Gosh, a couple of weeks?"

"Interesting. And do you feel it now?"

"I feel it all the time! Every waking hour."

"Is there anything else strange about them?"

This is the part where I turned quiet.

"You can tell me," he said.

"They've become very ... sensitive, even at the lightest of touches."

"Let me see them."

I paused. "Ummm..."

"I need to see them, Lizzie, or I can't treat you."

"I thought this wasn't a physical thing?"

"You're my patient, Lizzie. I do this for a living and it's better if I just see them. Don't worry, I've seen plenty of pairs before. Lift up your top."

I thought about the woman who'd exited his office and how pleased she'd seemed. I wondered if she'd been on display for him only moments before I arrived.

He moved from behind the desk. He wore a pair of suit-pants and light-blue shirt with the sleeves rolled up. I could see his thick chest-hair in the open buttons at the top.

Cautiously I lifted my top until it was above my breasts. They sat in the hammocks of my bra, giving off that same aura, as though they were throbbing in front of me.

"Okay," he said, and he seemed to concentrate. His hands moved forward and my eyes opened wide as he touched them.

The second he made contact I let out a stuttered breath. I almost doubled forward as the rush of arousal arrived immediately.

"Do you feel it now?" he asked.

"Yes."

"Aroused?"

"Yes!"

He continued to squeeze gently, moving around the breast. The nipples punched out through the bra in an instant.

"Take that off," he said. "I need to see."

"You need to, or you want to?"

"What did you think would happen when you came in here? That we'd talk and it'd all go away? I'm an expert in this, believe it or not, Lizzie. So I *need* to see them to do my job."

I reached behind my back and unclasped the bra. I lifted it up and decided to take my top with it. No sense being coy now.

I bared myself to him and felt vulnerable and turned-on all at once. He'd never before seen me like this, but he was right. If I wanted to get to the bottom of it I couldn't exactly balk at the idea of showing him my breasts.

"I see what you mean by arousal," he said. "How does it feel when I do this?"

He touched again at my breasts, squeezing one in each hand and pushing them towards each other.

"Amazing," I gushed. I didn't know where to look. You try looking in the doctor's eyes while he's squeezing your tits.

"Anything more than that?" he asked. "Really focus."

I closed my eyes as his hands wandered over my stiff nipples. He rubbed softly and then squeezed hard.

"Relief," I hushed. "A slight ... relief."

"Good," he said. "That's good. How about now?"

He started to pinch up towards the nipple, massaging the breast with his fingers and dragging all of them off the teat.

"Oh, Dr. Cooper," I whimpered, losing myself.

"Concentrate, Lizzie."

"That's good. That feels good."

"Any better? Anymore relief?"

Again I focused. "Yes."

"Good," he said steadily, and he continued to massage.

Finally I opened my eyes and looked down at what he was doing. I was astonished to see my tits leaking a steady stream of white liquid. Most of it was covering his hands and I hadn't been able to feel the rest. The strength of my arousal was clouding my other senses.

"Milk?" I gasped.

He nodded. "It's more common than you think."

"How much is there?"

"From feeling your tits I'd say there was a lot."

'Tits' didn't exactly feel like a medical term, but I guess Dr. Cooper was being a bit more candid now that he was getting to the root of the problem.

"You're *milking* me?"

"It's a tried and tested technique," he said. "It helps to relieve the symptoms of your condition."

"My condition?"

"Yes. You have a fairly rare condition called lacto-aphrodisiacs. Your breasts fill with milk and give you an overwhelming arousal until they're drained."

"Wait ... so this is going to be a regular thing?"

"I'm afraid so," he said. "But we can manage it."

"How?"

"By repeated visits."

"You're telling me I have to come here regularly and get milked?"

"You don't have to."

"And what about the arousal?"

"I think you know how to cure that," he smirked.

"You don't have anything for it?"

"I have one thing," he said wryly, and he looked down at his pants.

"Mr. Cooper!" I gasped, but then I felt another wave of arousal as a spurt of milk fired from my breasts.

Everything below my nipples was covered in my cream, but Dr. Cooper seemed unabashed. I guess the leather chairs were mandatory in a practice like this.

"We can finish the session today if you're up to it?" he said.

"I want to. I want to feel normal again."

"I can help with that, Lizzie. It's okay. I can help you."

I felt so safe under his guidance. Obviously it was all kind of weird, but knowing that he had trodden this path before with other women gave me a sense of calm. It also gave me a sense of intrigue.

"Just how many women are on your books?" I asked.

"I can't give a specific number."

"More than ten?"

He gave me a look that told me everything I needed to know.

"They all come here to get milked?!"

"They come here for treatment," he corrected.

"Treatment that involves you milking their tits!"

"They leave very satisfied, Lizzie, I can assure you. I'm not some kind of pervert. This is my job."

"And do you satisfy them in other ways?"

"Only if they ask."

"If they ask?! What do you do?"

"I don't think we should get into this."

"Tell me."

He sighed. "I satisfy the cause and the symptom."

"The symptom being arousal, right?"

He nodded.

"So how do you satisfy their arousal?"

He raised an eyebrow. "How do you think?"

"I don't know, that's why I'm asking."

"You don't need to know, Lizzie."

"I do if I'm thinking of getting the same treatment."

The both of us fell silent. I hadn't meant to have put it so bluntly, but certainly the idea of my ex-teacher satisfying the intense yearning inside me was a notion that I was willing to entertain.

"Think about this carefully," he warned.

"I have. I want you to satisfy me."

There was no plainer way of putting it.

"How do you want me satisfy you?" he asked.

"I want it in a way that you don't do it with the other women."

"Lizzie, that's very *unconventional.*"

"To hell with convention, Dr. Cooper. Please. I want you to help satisfy me. Satisfy these ... *urges.*"

"I can do that," he said. "If that's what you want?"

I wriggled in the chair, feeling my pussy awaken further. It was throbbing with ecstasy.

"Yes!" I whined. "Satisfy me! Oh, suck my tits, Dr. Cooper."

There was a brief trepidation in his eyes, but when a pair of delicious, milky tits are hanging in a guys face he can't stay stoic for long.

I wriggled in front of him with my eyes closed, luring him to me like a fish to the bait. My tits bounced and I started to bunch them up, holding them against my body and running my hands over the flowing milk.

"Please suck my tits," I whined, and I wondered how much the receptionist outside could hear.

I heard him move and I looked through my lashes at him. His face was drawn towards my breasts and soon I could feel his breath tickling the wet milk that adorned them.

Finally his lips clamped over me and I let out a wail of pleasure. I'm sure I wasn't the only person to be in jubilant ecstasy in Dr. Cooper's office that day.

I felt the surges of milk leave my breasts as he suckled me. He squeezed my tits in combination with the pressure applied from his mouth and soon the milk was cascading into him with gusto.

He started to swallow it down, feasting on me and getting as much of my breasts as he could into his mouth.

The rush of milk felt euphoric as it left me, and so too did that dull sensation that I'd been experiencing. My pussy started to salivate as the sensations of his tongue and teeth against my node drove me to heights of pleasure that I'd never seen.

"Dr. Cooper, that's so good," I gushed, looking down on him. "You suck my tits so good!"

I held him against me as he continued to get his fill, draining me and training my breasts to release their life-giving nectar.

He seemed to glow from the nourishment and I felt a deeper bond between us form—a bond that would be even more earth-shattering when it was finally broken in the naughtiest way possible.

"Take out your cock, Dr. Cooper. I want to please you too."

He pulled back and looked uncertain, then he looked down at his pants and the pair of us saw the fantastic, stiff bulge that had formed across the front of them.

"Oh, fuck, you're hard," I swooned, looking at him. "Go on. Take it out for me."

"You're gonna get me in a lot of trouble, Lizzie," he said, but even as the words were leaving his mouth he'd started to open his pants.

I helped him with his belt, frantically clawing at it in order to release him as quickly as possible. Together we rushed it open and he pushed his hips forwards as he released himself.

Suddenly I had a face full of his delicious, engorged cock. It lunged out from his trousers, stiff and upright with thick veins reaching towards its tip. I didn't take it in for long.

Instead I opened my mouth over him and pushed down, smoothing my lips over the glossy, bulbous head. Dr. Cooper let out a groan of delight and looked down on me, holding my head steady as I treated him.

I rocked my head over him and jerked him with my lips. My hands would cradle at his balls and every so often I'd come away from him completely and gasp a few breaths as I pumped my fist over him.

The saliva became a lubricant and my closed fist ran along him, pushing all the way to his balls at the base and then running right off the end.

"You're good at that," he said, and he moved my hair aside for a better view.

I started to squeeze on my tits as I feasted on his cock and they replied with further spurts of milk that I angled towards him.

They struck the bottom of his shirt and he quickly opened his buttons, pulling it wide and revealing his strong, hairy chest beneath.

I giggled and bit at my lip, carefully firing more of my nectar across his body. Dr. Cooper exhaled and shook his head in disbelief, watching as the milk caught on his hairs and trickled down towards his cock.

I licked along the length of him and teased the droplets off, tasting the sweet nectar and finding it delicious.

"I can see why you like it," I beamed, licking my lips.

I lifted my breast towards my mouth and sucked straight at the source. He jerked his cock as he watched, nodding and giving me words of encouragement.

"That's it, baby. Suck the milk from your tits for Dr. Cooper. That's an option if ever I'm not available."

"I much prefer it when you do it," I smiled, and I stood up and held my breast up for him.

He was on me again in an instant, and this time when he sucked me I could feel his hard cock touching against my leg.

"Will you fuck me?" I asked. "Will you help me?"

"How can I refuse?"

"It would be in the strictest confidence. I wouldn't tell a soul, but I can't promise it'll be the last time."

"Your tits need regular milking," he said.

"And my pussy will need to be regularly fucked."

"Now you're catching on, Lizzie. Take off your pants."

He removed his clothes as I stood up and unbuttoned my tight jeans. I slid them down over my ass and down my legs, stepping out of them and staring at him in only my tiny panties.

"I can help you with those," he said.

He took me to the desk and placed my hands on it. I leant against it and my tits hung beneath me, steadily dripping onto the wooden floor of his office. It looked as though everything in the room was designed to be easily wiped down.

He came behind me but he didn't touch my panties yet. Instead he pressed his cock against the cleavage of my ass and I felt his thick hair against my bare back.

"You want Dr. Coopers big cock, huh?" he asked, and his hands came under my arms to cup at my tits.

"Yes," I nodded. It felt like I'd waited forever for it.

He pinched again at my tits and they leaked their milk in response. Their flow seemed unceasing and every time that Dr. Cooper touched them they gave up their goods.

"So much milk," he hushed, kissing my neck.

"Milk it out of me, Dr. Cooper. I'm yours. I'm your hucow."

"*Hucow in training*," he corrected, kissing my shoulders.

His wet pecks moved all the way down my back and his face approached my panties. When he made it down there he hooked his fingers over the waist of them and dragged them down slowly.

I arched my back and pushed my ass out towards him as he took the last semblance of modesty from me.

My panties peeled over my ass and the kisses continued. His mouth moved closer and closer to my most intimate of places.

He let go of my underwear and they dropped down to my ankles. I stepped out of them and Dr. Cooper moved my leg aside.

He eased underneath and kissed at my pussy. It was *soaked*. I could feel him tonguing out the wetness. I started to let out whimpers of pleasure as I fought to contain myself, trying to hold off climaxing until I claimed him for real.

"So fucking wet," he hushed.

He stood up behind me and I felt his cock against me again, pressing between my bare ass-cheeks. He started to move his hips, sending his cock through the channel and teasing me just that little longer. I could feel his stiff flesh slide over my asshole.

"Fuck me," I whined, looking back at him. "Please fuck me."

Dr. Cooper gripped me rough and claimed me as his own. He took a hand to steady his cock and he guided it towards me. He wasn't coy here. Instead of teasing he thrust it straight through my wet pussy lips and I found him deep inside me in an instant.

"Dr. Cooper!" I cried, pushing back against him.

As his cock pushed deep the stream of milk from my tits quickened. It fired out at the floor, no longer dripping but pattering instead. A puddle started to form beneath us which he was keen to add to. He took a hold of my tits and squeezed them against me, kissing at my neck as he did so.

"This is what you need," he told me, and he was right.

He started to buck against me and I lost myself immediately. I whined against him and felt my pussy contract and tighten around his shaft.

The ripples of climax shivered through me and I let out an unmistakable wail. His office was flooded with the sound of intense pleasure, and I'm sure that much of it also filled the waiting-room beyond too.

Dr. Cooper was unabashed. Instead he leaned into my ear and ordered me to ride it out.

"Come on my big, stiff cock," he said through clenched teeth.

And come I did. Shit, at that point I didn't have a choice.

I trembled against him and leaned back from the desk into his embrace. His strong hands wrapped around me and he held me tight, squeezing at my tits and rubbing the resulting flow of milk all over my body. I was a fucking mess, but I wouldn't have had it any other way.

"Now you," I said, breathing heavy and still convulsing from the orgasm. "Now you come. Come inside me!"

He took a grip of my hair and pushed my head forward. He bent me over the desk forcefully and I felt a pang of frightened delight. He was ravishing me exactly like I'd wanted for weeks; I just never knew that he would be the guy to deliver it.

His hips clapped against my bare ass and the pair of us moaned in unison. My pussy was gripping tight around his cock and from the speed of his thrusts I knew it wouldn't be long before my treatment was finished.

The milk spread out over his desk with spurts being added to it every time he thrust forwards. It was as though he was milking my breasts in a whole new way, but I didn't care. I'd take it any way I could get it.

He put my arms behind my back and pushed my face into the wet milk. I licked out at it and tasted it as he started to power-fuck me. I was helpless, but I didn't want to be helped. I wanted to take everything he had to give me in that moment. I'd never felt more alive.

Dr. Cooper's cock swelled and stiffened and his breaths became erratic. His thrusts lost their rhythm and he stabbed forwards wildly towards climax.

"I'm gonna come," he announced, straining.

"Do it!" I begged. "Come in my pussy! Fill me with your fucking cum!"

He strained and croaked and then I felt my pussy flood with his warm fluid. It shot powerfully from his cock and laced my insides.

"Oh, Lizzie," he groaned.

"Oh, Dr. Cooper! Fill me with your cum!"

He groaned out his release. Each time a cry left his lungs a shot of fresh cum came with it, until there was nowhere left to host it.

It pulsed back out of my pussy, flowing outwards in strings that dripped to the floor to join my milk.

Eventually he let out a long sigh and pulled back. My pussy pinched him free and sent another volley of cum falling to the floor as I became unplugged. It was such a fucking sinful mess, but I don't think either of us would have had it any other way.

Finally I stood up, feeling his warm cum dribble down my leg. I looked down at my breasts to see that the flow of milk had stopped. All that was left was streams of it that still adorned my body.

"It seems to have worked," he smiled.

"Best medicine I ever took."

I looked down at myself and then over at him. His cock hung from his waist, glistening in his cum and my juices.

"I think we better make it a weekly appointment, don't you?" he asked.

"Just try and stop me."

"The receptionist will book you in," he smirked.

"Does she know about this?"

"What do you think?"

I let out a laugh. It was a hard thing to keep secret, especially given the noise we'd been making. I heard the sound of a door opening and closing outside.

"That'll be my one o'clock," he said, looking at his watch.

"Is there anything I can do to stem the sensations? In the meantime, I mean—before next week?"

"You can write about it."

"Will that help?"

"No, but I'd very much like to read it."

I bit my lip and smiled. His smile sparkled back.

And so here it is, Dr. Cooper. Here's the story of how the two of us hooked up.

I hope I told it well.

THE END

21 Or Bust : Suckled Brats 5

Just another day in Sin City, or at least that's how things were headed. I was two hours in to my night shift and no-one had hit the jackpot on my table yet.

Around me the casino revelers delighted in what The Pit had to offer, which was mainly a whole lot of naughty fun. It was easy for a guy to part with his hard-earned if you hung a pair of tits in his face, and that was exactly the business model that The Pit had been built around.

Money flowed like water in here, which was one of the main reason I'd wanted a job there so desperately. The reason I *got* the job was because I was the proud owner of big set of tits.

Haha, it's kinda base, I know, but you've gotta use your talents, right? Well not only was I blessed with an eye-catching bust, but I'd also discovered that my breasts had some talents of their own.

Lactocopia; that's what the doctors called it, but the punters here had called it everything from weird to fucking hot. I had people visit the casino just for me, hoping to get a taste of the jackpot.

I dealt at the blackjack table under the game name 'Lucky Udders.' People would come into the casino and head straight to Lucky Udders, throwing money at me until they got a glimpse of my bare breasts or, even better, the grand prize.

The winnings were tiered on my table, ranging from a feel or a glimpse, all the way up to a spray of milk, a taste or more. Today no-one had gotten the least bit lucky.

That was until Tony Ponza walked in. He was the beating heart of Sin City, and when he heard about the unique game The Pit was running he'd started coming regularly. The bosses had told me to keep him on the line. They didn't want him succeeding, but they also didn't want to scare him off.

If I'm honest though I'd have let Tony suck my tits for free. The guy was fucking hot. He was a perfect mix of confident Italian, with black hair that matched his black suits. He was suave, sophisticated, dangerous and—most importantly of all—fucking rich. His father's empire was worth billions when he inherited. God knows what it was worth now.

"I gotta feelin' today's my lucky day," he said, sitting at the blackjack table.

In an instant the four other players got up and left. None of them wanted to be blamed for taking a card of Tony's that might have seen him triumph. So it was just me and him.

"And how's my favorite dealer today?" he asked.

"Just fine and dandy! But my titties are in need of some fresh air. Do you think you can help, Mr. Ponza?"

He smacked the table with an open palm. "That's what I like to hear! I wanna help, Cherry. Let me try and help, huh?"

"That's more than fine by me, Mr. Ponza."

He set down his chip-stack. Tony was playing with the Casino's platinum chips. One-hundred-thousand dollars per chip; they'd been made especially for him.

"Let's do this," Tony said.

The first hand was a dud. The more we played the more the audience grew, despite the fact that all kinds of crazy things were happening on the other tables. One of the dealers here put glowing dildos in her pussy and dimmed the lights around the table, and I know for a fact that people won often over there. And yet twenty people stood around and watched as Tony lost his money.

"Jesus fucking Christ," he said after drawing another dud hand. "You're bleeding me dry, Cherry."

"I'm just turning the cards," I teased. "All for a chance for you to *milk* me dry."

"Fuckin' hell, has anyone ever won? Is this rigged?"

"No," I told him. "It's not rigged. One person has won before."

"It's impossible," he declared, but he carried on playing anyway.

He was almost right. The odds of winning were ridiculously slim, but I had an ace up my sleeve. The bosses had provided me with a rigged deck. All I had to do was feed it into the machine and the rest was automatic. It'd set up a winning game for a one-man-table.

To win you had to get an ace and king of the same suit, beating the dealer's hand, which had to be two kings of the same suit. The odds were slim but not impossible.

"I've just about had it with this fuckin' game," Tony said, and I could see a red mist descend as he looked around at the onlookers. "And what are you punks starin' at, huh?"

A few shuffled back sheepishly before retreating. As they did so I pulled the 'booby' deck out and unwrapped it, feeding it into the machine. Now was the time. We'd milked him as long as we could. It was time to give him some milk back.

"Relax, Tony," I told him. "I think this might just be your lucky hand."

He threw down another chip and motioned for me to deal. I tossed a card to him. It was the ace of clubs.

"Now we're talkin'," he said, but when I dealt myself the King of hearts he cursed again and shook his fist at the heavens.

I tossed him the second card. Tony didn't even notice its suit at first. Instead he punched the sky and cried: "Blackjack!"

"Look at that, Mr. Ponza," I said. "They're both the same suit."

He looked across at my King and rubbed his hands. "Come on King of Hearts."

My other card lay face-down beside my upturned one. I felt a pang of nerves as I prepared to flip it. If this wasn't what I thought it would be there'd be hell to pay. Tony wouldn't forget the twenty hands he'd lost before his first win.

"Come on, Cherry. Give me something good."

I took a grip of the corner and turned it over. I felt an instant relief as I saw what it was.

"Un-fuckin'-believable," Tony cried, clapping his hands. "Un-fuckin'-believable!"

I pressed the button under the table and the victory bell chimed. I'd only ever heard it once before.

"Give me a taste of those gorgeous tits," Tony said.

"My pleasure!"

One of the staff came to secure Tony's chips and the table was cleared of cards. I mounted it and crawled forward towards Tony, watching his eyes settle on my big cleavage as my tits hung down. I wore a white shirt tied just beneath them with my blood-red bra visible between the open buttons. When I was close enough I gripped his tie and pulled him towards me.

"Congratulations, Mr. Ponza," I said planting a deep kiss on his lips.

The crowd around whooped and Tony sank his tongue into me. I met it with mine, kissing him back with the same burning intensity.

"So, uh, what can we do here?" he asked.

"Anything you like," I told him.

"Anything?"

"Anything."

Tony Ponza fed The Pit millions of dollars a day. That kind of cash talked. It talked loud enough for the rest of us to stay quiet.

"Take 'em out," he said. "Let me see those beauties."

Tony had seen them in the past, which I think was one of the reasons he'd kept coming. I sat back on my knees and my short skirt rode up my thigh. A whole bunch of people were watching, but I only had eyes for Tony.

"Good girl," he said, and his words sent a shiver up my spine. I wanted to please him more than anyone.

I popped open the buttons slowly. Someone from the crowd shouted for me to hurry up and Tony spun on his heels and shot them a look. He motioned something to his guards and they carried the guy straight out. He'd be dead by morning.

With the inconvenience dealt with Tony turned his attention back to me. "Where were we?" he said.

"I believe I was just about to do this." I opened my shirt wide and pulled it back off my shoulders. My tits bounced in their hammocks as I took off my top and tossed it behind the table.

"Bring those here," Tony said with a beckoning finger.

I crawled to the edge of the table and he buried his face between them. He shook his head and I started to giggle as he left wet kisses in my cleavage.

"You'll get a girl turned-on," I hushed.

"That's what I'm hoping," Tony said. "I wanna suck those tits dry."

"Then I hope you're hungry."

I reached behind my back and unclasped my bra. The whole place fell silent around us. You could have heard a mouse cough.

"Thank you, Lord," Tony said, clapping his hands together in prayer.

I smirked as I pulled the bra forward off my tits. I dropped and I revealed myself to him. He drank in the round, cherubic breasts, bringing his hands towards them immediately and pushing them together.

"Fuckin' magnificent," Tony rejoiced. I loved having his approval.

"Go on," I told him. "Suck them."

He shook his head in disbelief and stared ahead at my tits. He put his hand under them and lifted them towards his lips as he moved his face forwards.

"Yes," I hushed.

Tony clamped his lips over me and I tossed my head back and groaned. In an instant my milk had started to surge through my nipple and into his mouth.

He wasn't kidding when he said he wanted to drain them. He took several mouthfuls instantly and guzzled it down. Eventually he pulled back and wiped the milk moustache from his face.

"Like a gift from the Gods," he said.

"You're done?"

"Done? I ain't even started."

I giggled and Tony launched on me again, sucking my nipple back into his mouth. He switched between one and the other, getting as much out of them as he could and gulping it happily. He was like a babe in arms.

I looked over him at the watching crowd. They were stiff to-a-man and just as mesmerized. Tables sat empty as they watched the luckiest, richest guy in Sin City suck on the most sought-after tits in town.

"Good boy," I told him, smoothing my hand over his black hair.

He pulled away from me again and looked up with a deep, burning intensity in his eyes.

"Can we fuck," he said. "Here?"

"We can fuck anywhere you want."

"I wanna do it right here. I want the whole city to know who you belong to."

My heart skipped a beat. I'd be Tony Ponza's property any day.

"Show me what I'm working with," I said.

Tony unfastened his pants quickly and jumped back onto the table. He reclined and stared up at me as I moved over him.

"Pull it out," he said. "I ain't scared who sees."

"It looks like you don't have anything to be scared about."

The bulge in the front of his pants was intimidating. My hands fumbled for it and I reached inside. It was like Christmas morning and Tony was my last wrapped gift.

"Pull it out, that's it," he urged.

I brought him out from his boxer-shorts and stopped dead. Fuck, it was beautiful.

"What are you waitin' on?"

"I—I've never seen a cock so good-looking."

He laughed. "Shut up and put it in your mouth."

"You're the boss."

I curled my blonde locks behind my ears and dropped my head to him. The patrons around us watching as I sank my full, red lips over the beautiful head of Tony's beautiful cock. To feel that thick arousal in my mouth felt like heaven, and to know it was all because of me was the cherry on the cake.

"That's my girl," he hushed.

He held my hair behind me as I started to rock over him. He wanted to watch as I slid down his pole, but he wanted everyone else to see too.

"Show them how much you love it," he said.

I moaned and let the spit fall from my mouth, then I mopped it up and sucked it along the barrel of his meaty cock.

The veins pumped up its side like lightning, reaching towards that plump beacon on top. I jerked my saliva over him and spat on his cock again.

"You nasty girl," he said. "You gonna be Tony's nasty girl?"

"I'll be whatever you want me to be."

"Squirt some of that fine milk on my cock. I wanna watch you taste it."

I did as he told me, bringing my teat right to the tip of him. I rubbed his cock across it and then pinched the nipple until a spray of fine milk shot across him. It dappled his cock with spots of white that pooled together and mingled with my spit.

"That's it. Taste it. Taste your fuckin' milk."

I drove my lips over him again, pushing past the sweet cream and going all the way down to the hilt. My throat opened over him and Tony let out a roar so wild and sexual that you'd have thought one of the tigers had gotten loose.

Tony stood up with haste, holding his cock at the base and keeping it stiff. He gripped my hair and pulled me up and I sat on my knees in front of him.

"Let me fuck that pretty mouth," Tony grunted.

He forced his cock into me and I opened wide in compliance. I felt him rush straight to the back of my throat and beyond and soon my eyes were welling with tears as I gagged on him.

It felt fucking incredible to have him in my neck like that and I could tell that he was relishing how tight I was around him.

I squeezed at my tits as he throat fucked me, forcing more and more milk out from them. They hit his thighs and trickled down towards his suit pants. He stepped out of them and I helped him.

Around us the revelers watched enraptured. The acts in The Pit were debauched, but none were as debauched as this. Even the risk of watching one of the most dangerous men in Sin City wasn't keeping people away.

By now the table was a mess of milk. It had pooled on the fabric and left it sodden and off-color elsewhere. They'd have to change the cloth, but that was a minor expense when you consider what Tony had brought to the place. He could wreck a thousand tables and the casino would still be comfortably on top.

When he'd had his fill of my mouth he pulled his cock out. The thick strings of spit hung from him and my maw was awash with saliva. Tony wiped it across my face.

"I wanna taste you now," he said, "but not your milk. Take your panties off and spread your legs for these lucky fellas."

I looked beyond at the spectators. Their eyes had lit up. Tony was throwing them the smallest of scraps, but I didn't mind.

I peeled my panties down, looking at Tony as I did so. He was jerking his cock as he stood on the table. He didn't care at all that he was center-stage, and with a cock as gorgeous as that I can see why. It deserved to be on show.

"Sit up on the table," he said, and he dismounted and got back to the floor.

I hopped up and felt the wet milk against my bare ass. Tony pushed my knees open and looked eagerly between my legs.

"That's a fucking snack," he said, looking in my eyes. "One pretty pussy."

"Treat it nicely."

"I might."

He pushed my legs even wider and then buried his face between my thighs. I closed my eyes and held my breath as his tongue raced over me. Eventually I looked down on him to see him sensually enjoying me. He looked almost serene and at peace as he feasted on my pussy, and I wasn't about to interrupt.

My breaths were crashing out of me and my moans were rising over the dings and bells of the lively casino-floor.

"Such an amazing pussy," Tony said, pulling his face away to admire it.

He lapped across it slowly and then pushed back my legs even further. His tongue was on my asshole in an instant and I let out a giggle, followed by a coo of delight.

"Eat my ass, Mr. Ponza."

Tony didn't mess around. I couldn't believe he was willing to do that in front of everyone else there. He made a point of his tongue and pressed it as far inside me as it would go. Eventually he introduced a finger and pushed it up into my ass.

The crowd took a step closer, keen to see my asshole gripping around the intruder. His tongue lapped around my knot and at my pussy, but his finger remained inside me. He waggled it in my ass and my body seemed to respond. The milk was spraying up out of my nipples all by itself now, as though the pressure inside me was too much to hold it back and his finger was somehow relieving it.

"Get on your knees," Tony told me.

I did as he asked and Tony once again climbed up on the table. He took off his suit-jacket and opened his shirt, revealing his sculpted muscles beneath.

"Fuck me, Tony," I mewled.

He pointed his cock down at me and squatted. I wondered what hole he was aiming for, but then I felt him push into my pussy. It opened over him and he sank into the wet embrace.

"That's tight," he hushed.

He pushed all the way deep and my nipples sprayed their cream beneath me. Any time he pleasured me my breasts seemed to respond by dispelling some of their milk, but the flow seemed unceasing.

Tony bobbed on his knees, dropping down into me and giving me every inch of his thickness. He was so big that I could feel his cock bulging against my stomach from the inside, as though he was about to break out of me.

My udders hung beneath, all wet and dripping. Tony hung on my ass like a limpet. He reached beneath and squeezed at my tits.

"That's my fucking girl," he growled.

"I'm all yours, Tony."

He pinched my nipples and washed the resulting milk back against my tits. They slipped through his hands, all wet and creamy and delicious.

"Fuck me however you want," I hushed.

It must have been the permission he was waiting for. He dragged himself out of my pussy slowly and then set the enormous head of his cock at my ass.

"Is this what you guys want?" he asked looking back at the crowd.

There were cheers of approval.

"Don't wanna let down our fans," he said wryly.

He pushed against me and I felt my tight knot start to open over him. I bit my arm so as not to cry out in pain as his cock stretched me.

"Tony!" I yelped.

His delicious dick drove deep, giving me a feeling of fullness that I'd never experienced. I'd never had something so big down there, and Tony wasn't exactly gentle.

In an instant his inches had rushed inside me. I don't think he even realized that he was the first guy in my asshole, but boy, I sure did.

My muscle relaxed gradually until the sensation was no longer one of dull pain. Instead the intruder started to feel welcome, and as Tony stirred in my asshole I realized exactly what people enjoyed about this whole *anal sex* thing.

He plowed into me, pushing his cock all the way deep. The ring of muscle gripped tight around him at all times, pinching around the barrel of his cock and jerking him. It must have felt incredible to have that tight, cylindrical vice around him.

"I'm yours, Tony," I moaned.

"Best prize in this whole joint."

Tony pulled out of my ass and pushed down on my cheeks, separating them and leaving me agape. He seemed to be showing me off to the audience, but I didn't care one bit. I loved having their eyes on me. It was my job after-all.

"Turn over," he said.

I lay back in the wetness of my milk and Tony moved between my legs. He went straight back to my asshole, putting my ass on his thighs so he could get himself in there.

He pushed deep and a spray of milk shot skywards. Tony found it with his mouth and lapped it down. It was so hot to see it fire over his face like that.

With his cock in my ass he started to fuck me all over again, but this time he thrust his fingers into my pussy too.

"I can feel my cock in your ass," he told me.

"It feels so good," I whimpered.

Tony kept his fingers in me and he upped his pace in my ass. His cock sprang through the slack muscle, pushing all the way deep and delighting my insides from an alien angle. I'd never had anyone excite my pussy like Tony, and he'd got it wetter than I'd ever known it.

The milk blasted from my tits. Its flow seemed dictated by my excitement and Tony was doing an incredible job of that.

"Cover me in it," he moaned, sucking a breath through his clenched teeth.

He plowed on, sending his cock in and out of me with wild abandon. It sprang through my tight hole again and again and all of the signs on Tony's face pointed to one thing. Climax.

"You're gonna make me come," he grunted.

"Come for me, Tony. I want it. I want to see it. I've earned it."

"You have. You really have."

I felt his cock stiffen and swell within me. It was harder than granite now and Tony was breathless.

"Cover my pussy in your cum," I whined.

Tony hit the peak of his thrusts, blasting into my ass with his cock. I could feel my own climax arrive too and suddenly the both of us were in the throes of orgasm.

It had crept up on me quick, but once it took hold there was no stopping it. I breathed deep and hard and the milk fired upwards in a misty, continuous spray.

Tony pulled his big cock from my ass and groaned. All eyes were on it as he pumped it close to my pussy, then suddenly he let out a roar and a fat rope of cum leapt from the tip.

It splashed across my pussy and I convulsed with glee. He felt so hot against me, but I had to feel it for real.

I moved my hands to my pussy and moaned with him. Another jet of spunk hit me and I spread it over my flesh with my fingers, rubbing it across my sensitive skin and feeling it turn all slippery and creamy.

"You're beautiful," Tony said over and over. "You're fuckin' beautiful."

He showered me in his cum and I continued to rub it across my sex. I pushed my fingers into my pussy and felt it spasm around them.

Tony rubbed his spent cock across my flesh, teasing my hard clit and spreading his cum around me. From there he moved the tip of his cock to my tits and gave it a spray of cream. Finally he brought the cocktail to my mouth and I opened wide.

"Good girl," he said slowly, moving my hair aside.

I tasted the creamy saltiness on my tongue and felt the bliss envelop me. I belonged to him now, just like I'd always wanted. Tony hadn't just won the jackpot, he'd won me.

"You don't need to work here anymore," he hushed. "What do you think about leaving this place with me?"

"I think I'd like that."

By now the patrons were applauding the show. They clapped wildly. The Pit had never seen anything like it.

"Come on," he said. "Toss some clothes on if you like."

Tony dressed calmly, giving a bow to the crowd.

"Now fuck off," he told them.

They didn't hang around. The men dispersed quickly, leaving the two of us to dress.

"Come on," he said, opening his arm.

I fell into it and leaned against him and Tony Ponza led me away from that life. Suddenly I belonged to the richest man in Sin City, and my problems didn't seem so big anymore. All I had to worry about now was where his next cumshot was going, and I didn't mind that at all.

THE END

The Milkiest Showgirl : Suckled Brats 6

Mr. Fantastic's circus was the talk of the towns we frequented. People flocked for miles around to come and witness the main-event: me. I'd been training my breasts for years now. They were my pride-and-joy. It was in Mr. Fantastic's best interest to keep them primed with milk too and between us we had it covered. He'd insisted on a rich vegetable and fruit diet that he said kept the milk creamy and flowing.

"We have to make it look real," he had always insisted.

I mean, it *was* real, but we ran a family show, so there was some dressing up to do around my breasts. We cut a hole in a conical bra and the stream fired out from there. The audience sometimes thought it was one big trick, but I can assure you it's completely real. I sometimes offered the adults to stay behind afterwards so I could show them the real thing, but Mr. Fantastic didn't like that. If I'm honest I'm not sure how I'd feel about a bunch of people watching it for real.

"People enjoy mystery," he said. "Besides, those tits belong to us."

He was right, I guess. We were a team, Mr. Fantastic and me.

"If people find out its real they might start trying to copy our act," he said. So the next show I kept them guessing.

We had lions, tigers, bears, trapeze acts, fire acts and everything in between, but none of them elicited the same reaction as the grand finale.

Mr. Fantastic and I had dressed it up like a burlesque act. The women seemed to love it just as much as the men.

It was a stage-act, playing to the audience as I danced around a chair to the music in the middle of our arena. A spotlight shone down on me and at the end of the performance I'd lean back in the chair and the milk would fire right from my nipples.

I think that's where people got confused. You see, I don't really need any prompting to shoot the white nectar from my breasts. Over the years I've honed it to a point where I merely need to *think* about it and it happens. It's as easy to me now as moving my arm.

Once again the crowd went wild. The milk blasted out in a shooting arc and the audience got to their feet to holler and applaud. My sequins twinkled beneath the spotlight's heat. I felt more alive than ever.

I looked off to the entrance to our circular arena and saw Mr. Fantastic with a beaming smile. He loved it when I brought the house down. He started to clap along with the crowd and then stepped into the arena himself. He held a cane and wore a huge top-hat. He presented me to the crowd.

"The Milkiest Showgirl, ladies and gentleman," he said, and the onlookers' cheers and whistles intensified.

"Take it off!" one guy shouted.

"Now, now," Mr. Fantastic said, holding up a finger. "This isn't that kind of show."

There were laughs and groans amongst the audience. Some of the guys often got the wrong impression, but for the most part everyone left satisfied.

After the show the arena felt like a different place. I liked to walk out there when it was quiet, dressed in my cream jodhpurs and high, black boots. It was just a different kind of feeling, you know? I liked to be there late, when all the other acts were in their trailers.

"Another great show," I heard a voice say.

I turned to the shadows at the edge of the arena and saw Mr. Fantastic's silhouette. It was unmistakable with his top-hat and long coat.

"They really seemed to like it," I said.

"Shit, who wouldn't?"

He flicked on the spotlight and I was illuminated in the middle of the arena.

"Stay there," he said. "I wanna look at you."

Now I couldn't see him at all. There was something intimate about having him as my only spectator.

"You're making me nervous."

"The Milkiest Showgirl, nervous?" he laughed. "She fires milk from her tits in front of hundreds of people, and now she gets nervous."

I heard a grunt from him as he vaulted the barriers, then he appeared in the light in front of me, emerging from the darkness.

"Feel less nervous now?"

I laughed bashfully. "A little less."

He took my hands and we swayed, pretending to dance to some music that wasn't playing.

"I've been thinking of ways to spice-up the act," he said.

"Spice up?"

"Give the audience more of what they want, you know?"

"I'm not going topless, Mr. Fantastic."

"And I'd never ask you to," he said. "I don't like the thought of guys looking at you as it is."

"So how do we spice it up?"

"We could do something with the milk. It always felt like such a waste having it shoot right out onto the dirt like that."

"Offer milkshakes to the crowd?" I laughed.

Mr. Fantastic didn't. He stared in thought.

"Seriously?!"

"It's an idea," he said.

"I'm not sure I want stranger's drinking my milk."

"What if they weren't strangers?"

"Who?"

"What if it was me?"

Now it was my turn to think in silence.

"I could show the crowd a big, milky moustache, you know. Make a real show of it."

"That ... could work."

"And we need to dress you a little skimpier. Make the *illusion* that some of the crowd think is happening feel even more impossible. *Where could the milk be coming from?* That kind of thing."

"It's coming from my tits!"

"I know that, but those guys don't."

"I worked hard for that. It's annoying that some people don't believe."

"Forget them, Charlotte. Whether they believe it or not, they leave here talking about you. That's all we need."

"But you want them to talk more?"

"Don't you think it'd be fun to have me catch it in my mouth?"

I bit my lip as I thought about it. "I guess that'd be pretty fun. Naughty too. Won't someone say something?"

"That's exactly what we want! We can put on more shows and fill this place."

I thought for a moment, but truthfully I'd already made up my mind.

"So what do you say?" he asked, presenting the floor.

"Now?"

"There's no better time."

"But I—I don't have my special bra on."

"You don't need it," he said. "I've seen it all before."

"You've seen *breasts* before; I've never shown you mine."

"You haven't?"

"No."

"Huh..." he put a hand to his chin, confused. "I could have sworn I'd seen them."

"You haven't!" I laughed.

"I guess that's the end of that idea then. Goodnight, Charlotte."

He turned to leave, walking away from the spotlight.

"Wait," I told him. "Wait."

He turned to me.

"I'd like to try," I said. "I think we should try."

"Are you sure?"

"Yes! I'm sick of doing the same old act. It's been over a year now."

"You know you'll have to ..." he trailed off and nodded at my breasts.

"I know."

"How far can you shoot it?"

"A couple of meters I think."

"The further the better. It'll be a real spectacle."

"You get on your knees and I'll find my range."

Mr. Fantastic knelt in the dry dirt and looked across the illuminated circle at me. I took a deep breath to calm my nerves and then unfastened my tight waist-coat. I opened my shirt beneath and bared my big tits to him.

He was quiet. I looked across at him and he swallowed nervously. His gaze was unwavering, as though he was desperately trying to keep eye-contact.

"You can look," I told him. "I don't mind you looking."

He exhaled and his body became more relaxed. He looked at the floor and took several breaths. "Jeez, you don't know how hard that was."

When he raised his head again he looked right at my tits.

"What do you think?" I asked him. I was genuinely curious.

"They're beautiful," he said. "You're beautiful."

"*Mr. Fantastic*, stop! You're spoiling me."

He laughed with me and then took a breath. "Okay," he said. "Fire away."

He settled in on his knees and I took up my tits. Ordinarily the bra would point the nipples out of the makeshift hole, but now I needed to aim it.

I lifted my breasts and then thought of exactly what I wanted to do. I wanted to shower him in milk and I didn't care who watched.

Just like that two jets of milk burst from my nipples. I overshot the mark. At first it cascaded over him but then the stream slowed and it poured over his face.

He let out a breath of desperate relief, as though he'd been waiting to be bathed in my milk for the longest time.

He opened his mouth and let it fall in and I watched it under the spot lights. This was way more erotic that I could have ever imagined, but I didn't want it to stop.

"You taste so good," he groaned, then he started to swallow down my nectar. If I'd have known better I'd have thought that this was his intention all along.

I started to pinch towards my nipples and they began to turn stiff. That wasn't part of the act. My nipples only ever got stiff when I was excited. As a result of their tightening the milk shot out of me in a finer spray. It washed all over Mr. Fantastic in a shower, covering his long, red jacket.

He brought his hands to his shirt and tugged hard. The buttons popped open and his glorious chest was revealed beneath the lights.

I steered the milk towards it fiendishly, and giggled as it cascaded down over his pecs. It sprinkled amidst his hair, dappling and hanging on it like pearls.

"Fuck, Mr. Fantastic, that's hot. That's too hot for the show!"

"Then let it be our show," he said. "This can be just for us."

He stood up and advanced towards the stream. I bit my lip and fired a faster jet at him, as though I was trying to blast him backwards.

He fought his way forwards, thrashing through the milk until he arrived before me. When he was only a foot or so away I stopped and stared.

The two of us were breathing heavy, staring across at one another with the devil in our eyes. I dropped my tits and they hung there like spent udders. Milk dripped steadily from them.

"May I try it from the source?" he asked.

I pushed my shoulders back. "Be my guest."

Mr. Fantastic took off his top hat and shook out his long, black hair. He was such a magnificent showman. He looked good from every angle—or at least every angle I'd seen so far. He still held some mystery and I hoped to uncover it.

"Suck my tits," I urged, breathing heavy so that they rose and fell to tempt him.

He pounced and his beautiful mouth raced over my nipples. He sucked hard and the milk flowed into him without me even having to think. He drank it thirstily and let it fall down off his chin. I held him against me and ran my hand through his lustrous hair.

Finally he emerged from his feast and looked me dead in the eye. The milk was lacing his lips. I looked down my nose at them.

"Taste it," he said.

I put my lips on his and started to kiss him. My tongue burst through his lips and I tasted my sweet nectar inside his mouth. His tongue fought with my own and my pussy came to life.

"You're getting me wet," I told him.

"You're getting me hard," he replied. "I can think of a way to satisfy both our ailments."

"That sounds naughty."

"It's the naughtiest thing I know, Charlotte."

Fuck, he was too handsome to turn down; stood there with my milk all over him. His muscles were glistening, for Christ's sake. *Glistening!* How can I be so tempted and not act on it?

"Well, if you think it'll help," I said, playing coy.

"Let's start by taking our boots off and then we'll see what happens."

Shit, I knew full-well what was gonna happen, and that's why I didn't waste a second. My boots were off before Mr. Fantastic had even started on his.

"Someone's eager," he grinned.

"How's this for eager?"

I dropped to my knees in front of him and stopped him part-way through. With one shoe on Mr. Fantastic stood upright, realizing quickly what I was about to do.

"Oh, Charlotte," was all he could say when I started to unbuckle his shiny, black belt.

I could already see his big hard cock stretching across his jodhpurs. The material was tight and thin, and usually that wasn't a problem. I don't imagine he got too many erections during his performance, but he had one now. A big one.

"Fuck, you're ready," I cooed, looking up at him with a smile.

"How could I not be?"

"I hope I'm ready ..."

I pulled down the front of his pants and his huge cock shot upwards. I stared in wonder at it, watching it bounce steadily. It was long and smooth, with veins just beneath the surface. It bobbed gently as I stared, moved by the force of the arousal that was pumping into it.

"It's so big," I swooned.

All he did was raise an eyebrow and nod. He knew.

"I don't even know where to start!"

"There's no wrong answer to that."

I pushed his cock back against his stomach to try and get a better measure of its size. It came up right to his belly-button.

"I think I'll start with your balls," I smiled.

"A fine choice," he said, nodding like a gentleman.

I looked ahead at the low-hanging fruit. It looked just as delicious as the main-event. Mr. Fantastic was shaven close and it seemed to make everything look bigger.

"Fuck," I hushed, and I pushed my face in towards him.

I sucked the orb into my mouth and he rejoiced above me. His groan filled the arena.

"Good girl," he told me, and hearing his encouragement was like a drug.

"I want to please you," I moaned, gnawing at the hilt of his big cock.

"You are."

"Tell me what to do."

"I want you to lick all the way to the head of my cock and then put it in your mouth," he said.

"I think I can do that."

I closed my eyes to perform. Mr. Fantastic moved my hair aside and watched. I pushed my tongue out and licked up his shaft slowly.

"That's my girl," he hushed.

My shoulders rocked as I shivered with excitement. I found my way right to the crown of his cock. I pulled it back off his stomach and bent my neck over him.

"I want to be in your mouth, Charlotte," he hushed.

I opened wide over the crown of his cock and felt it slide past my lips. To have such power in my mouth like that gave me the oddest sense of privilege. I knew from travelling with him that his conquests were few and far between, despite his handsome looks. He seemed to distance himself from women. Perhaps he'd been saving himself.

"Good girl," he groaned, nodding and looking down as I opened my eyes.

I stared up at him with a mouthful of cock and batted my lashes. Slowly I withdrew, letting him watch his wet cock emerge.

It felt like the whole crowd was watching. The seats were hard to see and for all we knew one of the lion-tamers had walked in and sat down to watch.

The craziest thing is that I wouldn't have cared if they did. This was a once-in-a-lifetime opportunity and I wasn't about to squander it. Let the whole world watch for all I care.

"You're good at that," he said.

I looked up and smirked. "You haven't seen anything yet."

Mr. Fantastic was curious. So was I. I hadn't yet determined exactly what I was going to do, but then the naughtiest of thoughts struck me.

I leaned back and put a hand under my breast, angling it towards his cock. I let out a strong stream and listened to him groan in delight as the milk blasted against his shaft.

It covered it in a white film that I very quickly relieved him of with my mouth. It seemed so sinful and debauched, but also tinged with a deep love, as though I was giving nourishment to him.

Again I fired my milk from my tits, but this time I sandwiched his wet cock between them and started to bounce them over him.

"Does that feel good?" I asked him.

"Oh, Charlotte. You don't even know!"

I looked down and watched his delicious, big cock burst out of my fat cleavage over and over. My tits continued to leak milk and it dripped down over my stomach until it started to wet my panties.

"I don't want you to come yet," I whined.

"Then you're gonna have to stop doing that!" he laughed.

I slowed the pace and French-kissed the top of his cock. My tongue wound round him slowly and I listened to the gasping breaths above me.

"I want it inside me," I told him.

"Stand up, baby."

I did as he said while he removed his other boot.

"Turn around."

I turned around.

He took me from behind, gripping my body close and grabbing my tits. I could feel his stiffness against my ass.

"You want me inside you?"

"Uh-huh," I nodded.

He rubbed the milk over my tits and then reached to the back of my pants. The jodhpurs slid down over my ass and he took my panties with them.

"That's what I want," he said. "You don't know how long I've stared at this hot ass and wished I could see it for real."

"Don't waste your opportunity," I giggled.

His hands were on it immediately before my pants were even off. He gripped and squeezed. He kissed my neck and shoulder and whispered dirty things close to my ear.

"I want to fuck your pussy," he said. "Fuck, I'm twice your age. Is that wrong?"

"I don't care, Mr. Fantastic. I want it too."

"You want this big, hard cock inside you?"

"Please, give it me!"

"Bend forwards."

I bent at the hip and looked back. My knees were together with my half-downed riding-pants and underwear around them.

He looked to my bare ass and grabbed his cock. He jerked himself and the put the tip to my soaked puss.

"That's it," I hushed, closing my eyes to focus on him.

His stiffness spread through me, parting my lips and pushing through the tight muscle of my O. I cried out in pained pleasure as I felt his size.

"Oh, Mr. Fantastic!"

He took a hold of my hips and I fell forward further, pushing back on his cock and claiming as many of his inches as I could fit inside me.

He thrust forwards and clapped against my ass. I let out a yelp and then he did it again, and again, and again until he was fucking me so hard that my tits were bouncing beneath me. As they rocked they let out their milk and it dribbled on the dirt in circular, arcing patterns.

Mr. Fantastic leant over me and gripped my tits, rubbing the milk over me and making even more of a mess.

His wet hands came back to my ass and he took a big squeeze of it, letting out a grunt as though he found great release from burying his fingers into my soft skin.

I leant back against him now and he hugged me from behind. My tits burst with their nectar and he spread it all over me, running his hands under my open shirt. I felt so safe in his grasp and so in love.

My ass wriggled on his thickness and he stirred inside me. He started to buck into me again and our milky fantasy continued, but from his fast breaths I knew it would be over soon.

"Come inside me," I hushed. "I want to feel it."

"We're putting on some performance, huh?"

I looked out again from under the spotlight. It felt as though I could see the silhouettes of people watching us and it gave me a deeper thrill. Maybe a saucy after-show wouldn't be a bad idea.

"Oh, Charlotte, honey, I'm close."

"Give it me," I yearned.

His cock seemed to stiffen, pushing through me with greater intensity. He felt primed for release and there was only one place it was going.

His back arched and he folded over against me, kissing my shoulder. I felt the first throb of his cock and then a delicious warmth flooded into me.

"Charlotte," he grunted, straining out his release.

"Fill me up, Mr. Fantastic!"

My tits burst with pleasure and the sound of milky puddles could be heard forming beneath me. I took everything he had to offer, and he had to offer a lot. So much, in fact, that there was no place to hold it all. It streamed from my pussy and ran down my leg.

He held me close and breathed deep after his climax, kissing at my neck before finally slipping out from behind me.

I turned to look at his cum-soaked cock and I dropped to my knees to taste it. It went right into my mouth and he hissed another moan.

His fingers were outstretched and his arms tense as I sucked him one last time, and then the moment took me completely.

I lay back in the dirt in euphoric delirium. I moaned and rubbed my tits, feeling his slickness between my folds.

I pushed my hips up off the ground and Mr. Fantastic watched as I fired a jet of milk up in an arc that finished right on my clit.

"Fuck, girl, that's something," he marveled. "Does that feel good?"

"So good," I whimpered.

My fingers started to rub the milk against my clit and Mr. Fantastic got to his knees for a closer look.

I guess the both of us were getting carried away, because he went on to do something that I'd never known or even heard of.

"I want to taste that," he said.

I tried not to act too surprised. "Do it," I told him. "I want to feel your lips on me."

The milk spattered on my pussy as he moved in for the kill, putting his face between my legs and taking no shame in tasting himself. His mouth enveloped my pussy and I moved my hand away to let him explore.

His tongue washed over me, eating milk and cum as one. I could hear him slurping away busily beneath me and in that heady moment I started to come.

"That's perfect," I whined. "Don't stop!"

He redoubled his efforts, tonguing my petals and sliding his tongue up to tease at my clit. He feasted on the cocktail of sin until my pussy started to contract with joy.

"You're making me come," I told him.

My stomach tensed as I dropped my ass and leaned forwards. My milk sprayed against his face but he took it in his stride. He opened his mouth to take some of it in, then he let it fall out against my cum-filled pussy as he tongued the rest of the climax from me.

My legs shivered wildly against the side of his face and finally he broke away from me, looking down on his masterpiece. My pussy flexed and I looked at him with adoration.

"That was incredible!" I burst, and I felt a great need to kiss him.

I came forward quickly on the dirt and put my mouth on his. I could taste the sweetness of my milk, mingled with the salty-caramel of his cum. It was a heady cocktail that I'll never forget.

"You think we can make an act of that?" he asked.

I giggled and fell against his shoulder.

"Or do you think we need to rehearse some more?"

I smirked. "I think we need more rehearsals. Much more."

THE END

Clean-Up In The Dairy Aisle : Suckled Brats 7

I'd work in Mr. Portland's store for a couple of years, but honestly I hated it. I hated the feeling that I was destined to stay there forever. I took night-classes to try and plan my way out of there, but it made the following day at work hell. It was so hard to concentrate on so little sleep.

He ran the store like a damn SS Officer too and was known for being strict. He was always way stricter with me though. He said he had to set an example to the staff and for some reason I was that example.

It was just another Tuesday when things turned crazy. I'd had the worse night's sleep ever and was bleary eyed and tired.

I was stocking the milk aisle and filling the shelves. It was mindless stuff and I was kind of minding my own business and day-dreaming. I'd totally forgotten Mr. Portland's rule of not fully filling the shelves. They weren't built to take the weight of all the milk, so he had us face-up the milk at the front of the shelves and leave a void behind it.

Because of that it needed extra attention throughout the day because it emptied faster. And milk isn't light, you know? After a while your arms really start to ache, but Mr. Portland would never hear it. He was a *big, strong man*, after all, right?!

Anyway, his stupid rule had slipped my mind. I didn't even notice the shelf begin to sag in the middle. I just kept tossing on these huge gallons of milk. It wasn't until a bolt popped and shot across the aisle that I realized what I'd done.

One of the customers backed away from the creaking metal and left the aisle in a hurry. I was frozen on the spot. Everything seemed to go in slow-motion.

The gallon jugs cascaded to the floor one-by-one at first. They hit with a splat and milk leapt out, covering the lower part of my pants.

I backed up into the shelves of cream opposite and they started to rain down behind me too. I didn't know where to look. It was like the fucking elevator scene in *The Shining*, only instead of blood there was a river of milk flooding the store.

The jugs and cartons fell to the hard floor and exploded open. I was absolutely covered and so was everything else in the aisle. It started to flow out into the store and I heard the murmurings of people elsewhere in the shop as their feet became wet with milk.

My friend Ellen came to the end of the aisle and looked down it in horror. I stared at her from my spot against the shelves. My foot slipped and I stumbled back even further. I wound up with my ass sat in the milk and heavy cream raining down around me.

Ellen put her hand over her mouth and her look of shock turned to a shrieking laugh. "Clean up in the dairy aisle," she giggled.

She looked to her right and her expression dropped quickly. She hurried out of view and she was replaced with Mr. Portland who strode into shot at the end of the aisle. He stood stern, his hands on his hips. He tapped his foot into the wet milk and looked down at it as it spread out beyond him.

"Are you okay?" he asked, but there was little concern in his voice.

"I'm okay," I told him.

He left me there for the moment. I heard his voice on the PA system overhead.

"Ladies and gentleman, the store is closed for the next few hours due to an incident in the dairy aisle. Apologies for the inconvenience. Please make your way to the check-out.

I got up steadily from the floor and shook out my hands. Shit, I didn't even know where to start with this. Ellen brought a mop and bucket to the end of the aisle, but she was still giggling in fits of laughter that flared up as more gallons of milk dropped from the shelves.

"Not helping, Ellen!" I told her.

"You're in trouble."

"No shit!"

"What happened?"

"The milk fell, Ellen, what the fuck does it look like?"

She laughed again and left me on my own in the aisle. I stepped carefully towards the mop and ran the head of it over the floor. I twisted it into the bucket and squeezed out some milk. It was immediately about a quarter full, but the store was still about a centimeter deep in dairy.

About ten minutes passed and Mr. Portland finally returned.

"I've sent everyone home," he said.

"Sorry, Mr. Portland, but the shelf it just—"

"Did you overfill it?"

I paused just long enough for him to know that what I was about to say was a lie. "No."

"Don't give me that shit, Clara. Look." He pointed to the countless busted jugs and cartons. "That's *way* more than we usually stock on the aisle."

"I—I didn't over-stock it!"

"You're lying," he boomed, and his voice filled the store without the need of a PA system. "What did I tell you about that?"

I stayed quiet.

"Huh?"

"Not to overfill the shelves."

"And what did you do?"

"I ... overfilled the shelves."

"What are we going to do now, huh?"

I loved him when he was angry. He looked adorable.

I shrugged. "Clean up, I guess."

"It's some clean-up operation, isn't it?"

"We're gonna need a bigger bucket," I teased.

"Not now, Clara. Have you any idea how much money is all over my floor right now?"

"A few hundred bucks?"

He was taken aback by how accurate my guess was. "That's ... about right."

"You gonna take it out of my wages?" I teased.

"I'm gonna take it out of you," he warned, pointing.

"Haha, what? As milk?"

"I just might."

"I'd love to see you get a hundred dollars of milk out of me," I told him.

"Be careful what you wish for, Clara."

"You can't do that."

"I bet I can," he said, and he seemed confident. "You've no idea what I'm capable of."

It sounded like a threat, but it was too hilarious to take seriously.

"You gonna milk these udders," I told him, and I shook my chest in his direction.

He wasn't impressed. "Don't start playing-up Clara. All of your friends had no issues abandoning you in your hour of need."

"I don't blame them. If you'd told me to go home I'd have left before you'd finished the sentence."

"You're welcome to leave whenever, Clara, but last I knew you need to pay rent. Has your situation changed?"

I sighed. "No."

"So should we clean this milk up or do you want to push your luck some more?"

I couldn't bear the thought of ceding to him. It was a real battle of wits.

"I wanna see you try and get it out of me," I smirked.

"I don't think you want that, Clara."

"I do," I cried proudly, setting the mop back in its bucket. "I wanna see you take the milk out of my big tits."

I shook them in his direction again.

"Then unbutton your top," he said calmly.

Everything turned serious all of a sudden. I'd have to put up or shut-up, and I didn't much feel like shutting up.

"Okay," I said defiantly, and I opened the buttons of my shirt.

He looked back over his shoulder and then down the long aisle that split the store.

"Scared someone might see you fail?" I asked.

"No. I don't want anyone to see me succeed but you."

"You're not gonna succeed."

"Not if you keep your top on."

"I'm supposed to just get my tits out right here?"

"If you want me to prove myself."

"I'm not getting them out because there's no way you'd be able to milk me. I'm not a cow."

He raised an eyebrow suggestively and I put a hand on my hip.

"You're gonna go there?" I asked.

"Open your top," he said. "I wanna see what I'm working with."

"You're not working with anything."

"You said you wanted to see it, Clara. So I was going to show you."

"Shit, then show me. I *bet* you can't do it."

"Okay; if I succeed I get to do whatever I want to you."

"Whatever you want? You're making it sound weird."

"It's not weird already?"

"Shit, if you even get a drop of milk from these I'll work here for free."

He clapped his hands. "That's quite the offer. Take your shirt off."

"No."

"You want me to take it off for you?"

I nodded.

Mr. Portland moved behind me and things turned eerily sensual. I wasn't used to him being so tender. He carefully took my shirt off both shoulders and untucked it from my pants. Slowly he removed the garment and finally I turned to him, showing him my bursting bra. I'd always had a big, full set of tits, but the idea that they'd been filled with milk the entire time was absurd.

Well I guess it's a day for absurdities, because what happened next was like something out of a Brothers Grimm fairytale—the adult version.

He made a move for my tits and I took a step back. My work-shoes squeaked on the milk beneath.

"I can't milk you if you don't let me touch you."

"It's just ... you're my boss."

"Not for the next twenty minutes."

I started across at him. His expression was like nothing I'd ever witnessed. He looked ... *nice*. He looked approachable and welcoming. He looked ... *handsome*.

"Okay," I said finally. I arched my back and pushed my tits forward. "Have at it."

He reached forwards and touched me gently at first. I felt a tingle in my breast the second his magic hands touched me. I let out a soft whimper.

"I haven't even started yet," he laughed.

"Then start," I grunted. "I wanna know what it feels like when you touch me for real."

He took a step towards me. The silence around us was filled with the steady dripping of milk from shelves.

He hooked his fingers down the front of my bra and pulled both cups down. My nipples sat stiff on my chest, pointing straight at him as though he'd been targeted.

"They look ready," he said.

I looked down to see what he meant. I could see the soft, bluish-green veins beneath the surface. I'd never noticed them before.

"They look ... *bigger*," I hushed.

"The look gorgeous," he hushed.

My nipples had never been stiffer. The whole thing felt naughty, which perhaps explained why my nipples were punching out so far from my breasts.

"One drop, wasn't it?" he asked.

"Huh?"

"One drop of milk. That's all I have to get, right."

"Well, I said that but—"

He put a hand on both of my breasts and pushed them together. He squeezed them each and I felt a euphoria wash over me like nothing else. His touch was like a drug. My eyes rolled back and I let out a whimper.

"There we go," he said.

His thumb sprang over my stiff nipples and left a wet trail in its wake. I startled and looked down. There was a line of white running across my milky skin.

"What's that?"

"Your milk," he said.

"That must be from the floor or—"

He squeezed again and this time I watched the bead of milk burst right out of my nipple and hang on it.

"No way!"

"And I haven't even started," he said. "One drop. So you'll work here for free, right?"

"I was just kidding!"

"Then there's no reason for me to stop?"

"Don't stop," I whispered.

"What did you say?"

I closed my eyes tight and tried to fight against the deep yearning I felt inside me. It was no good. "Don't stop!" I burst.

"I thought that's what you said."

He squeezed again more forcefully and this time a jet of milk burst from my tits. My eyes opened wide as I gasped and I stared down at the release.

"Oh, Mr. Portland!"

My voice was tinged with shock and arousal. I'd never known anything like this sensation before in my entire life. It was like a jolt of electric bliss, focused entirely on my tits. It spread out from them in waves of ecstasy that made my whole body weak.

"Look at that," he said steadily. He continued to squeeze and the milk burst out of me, firing in fine sprinkles and then long jets that pattered on the wet floor.

I stumbled backwards and then sat to the floor. My legs refused to keep me upright and Mr. Portland refused to let me go. He fell to the floor with me, straddling me. He knelt in the milk and I lay back in it, as though it was a baptism of creamy sin.

"That feels so good," I groaned.

I squirmed in the floor and felt the milk bleed through my pants and touch my legs. Mr. Portland didn't seem to mind it either.

He kneaded my tits like they were big balls of dough. Each time he massaged up towards the nipple my tits responded with another jet of milk. He was like a damned tit-whisperer.

"You're spoiling me," I told him. "I want to spoil you too."

"I'm just doing what you bet me I couldn't."

"You're not enjoying it?"

He took his hands off me and leaned back. He looked down at his pants. "I didn't say that."

I looked to his pants too and noticed the thick bulge. It was more than apparent, but I wasn't content with that view alone.

"Show me what I've done," I told him.

"You gonna be my naughty girl?"

"I'll be as naughty as you need me to be."

"Promises, promises," he smiled.

He unbuckled his belt and then opened his pants.

"You wanna do the rest?" he asked.

I scrambled at his pants desperately and made ripples in the milk beneath me like snow-angels.

Mr. Portland stared down in wait as I released him. I could see the arousal in his fat pupils, but it was punctuated by the thick cock that suddenly sprang from his pants.

I startled and then began to giggle, putting a hand over my mouth.

Mr. Portland laughed too. "I've never had that response before."

"No ... no it's ... *amazing*."

It was. It was beautiful. It lunged from the kempt fur like a beacon. He was pumped full of blood and his pink crown was taut and primed.

I leant up out of the milk and opened my mouth for him, but he was just out of reach.

"Oh, you want that, huh?" he asked.

I fell back in the milk and nodded.

"Stay where you are."

He sat over me and started to unfasten his light blue shirt. I watched his magnificent figure become revealed slowly. I'd never looked at him with this kind of eye before, but I felt nothing but lust for him. I knew it was wrong but I didn't care. Mr. Portland didn't seem to care either.

"I'm gonna put it in your mouth," he said. "But I don't want you to move. Can you do that?"

I nodded. I could feel the milk turning my hair wet. The back of my shirt and the back of my pants was already soaked. My crotch was starting to get soaked too, but it wasn't from the milk.

He tore his shirt back off his shoulders and then leant forwards. His chest moved above my face and he put his hands into the milk to support himself in a kind of press-up pose above me.

It felt so surreal to be doing this in the middle of a store. Somewhere so public and we were doing something so sinful that to even do it in private would be crazy.

His big cock swung over my face and then he eased himself down onto me. I opened my mouth over the tip of his length and he pressed himself all the way in deep.

His dick pushed through my lips and he filled my mouth. I let out a splutter and groaned around him. My tongue pushed back and forth along him. He didn't let up. He pushed right the way down into me and threatened to burst through into my neck.

I thought I was going to gag but instead my throat opened right over him. I managed to suppress the sensation and soon he was pushing right into my gullet. I lent my head back like I was a sword-swallower and I took him right to the hilt. His hair tickled my top lip and I listened as he let out a deep, heady cry. It filled the store.

He pulled himself out of me and I gasped off his cock, breathing heavy. I wiped at my face and then opened my mouth again quickly as he returned.

He went straight back into my throat and started to fuck me, bouncing his waist down and until he was making rough love to my mouth.

I took it all like a champion slut. I felt a strange kind of empowerment. I hadn't expected to be able to take him so easily.

The moment took me and I started to squeeze my tits as I sucked along him. They fired their milk up against his pants and it dripped back against my milky tits.

"That's perfect," he hushed.

I looked up to see him staring down on me. My mouth was agape and full, but still I tried to smile.

"You're one naughty slut, Carla," he said. I hadn't felt like one until five minutes ago. It was like he'd cast a spell on me without doing anything.

The next time he pulled out of me I gasped a request up at him. "I want you to fuck me," I blared, surprising myself with how loud I'd demanded it.

"You think you can take this big cock?"

I nodded. "I'm so wet."

He dragged his dick down my body. He gave me a kiss on the lips as our faces met. I melted against him, uncaring for the puddle of milk that I lay in.

But then he continued down me further. He settled at my tits for a moment and sucked my nipples hard. I felt my milk rush into his mouth and then I heard him happily swallow it all down.

"Drink me in, Mr. Portland," I told him. It felt so special to be nourishing him like that. It felt as though I'd turned provider.

"My naughty, milky slut," he declared.

"I'll be your slut."

"You don't have a choice."

He continued downwards until his face was over my crotch now. I wriggled beneath him, trying to tempt him onto me.

He kissed at my pants, moving his face down into my crotch. He bent my legs back and kissed the hot spot that covered my pussy. I whimpered and wriggled, yearning for his mouth for real.

"This is my pussy, you understand?" he said.

"Uh-huh."

"Say it."

"It's your pussy, Mr. Portland."

"That's right."

He popped the button at the top and then pulled hard, neglecting the zipper. It sprang down quickly and then the fabric tore.

I wriggled impatiently and looked down through my cleavage. My tits wobbled and dripped their milk steadily. It flowed in a little stream that ran down off the side and joined the dairy milk beneath me.

"Get it," I told him.

He reached beneath and grabbed my pants at my ass. I lifted my butt out of the wetness and he pulled down hard.

I hear some more fabric rip, but he wasn't stopping and I didn't want him too. He took my panties and pants as one, dragging them down under my ass.

I sat back in the puddle of milk and felt it against my bare skin. Mr. Portland dragged the pants down and thrashed off my work shoes. Soon I was wearing only my white socks. My bra was underneath my tits and Mr. Portland was waiting over me with his cock lunging out from his open fly.

"You want this?" he asked, shaking his thickness.

"You daren't," I told him, wriggling.

"Naughty girls deserve punishment," he said.

He took a grip of the hilt of his cock and steered it towards my soaked pussy. I pushed my ass up off the floor and he washed the tip of his cock through my soaked petals.

"I'm so wet," I told him.

"I can feel it."

"Fuck me, Mr. Portland, I deserve it. I deserve that big cock as punishment."

"Yes you do."

"Stop teasing me!"

He spread his cock through my lips a little longer. I reached down to try and take charge but he moved his cock away.

"Ah-ah-ah," he said, wagging a finger. "I'm the boss here, remember."

"Oh, Mr. Portland, be the boss of me," I whined. "I can't take it anymore."

"You want this big cock?"

"More than anything!"

He pointed it down towards my eager pussy. He started to push forwards and I felt the pressure of his girth on me. My pussy spread over him slowly and I felt myself stretch around him. I hadn't felt that sensation in so long.

"Oh, punish me, Mr. Portland! Punish me with your big cock!"

"You deserve everything you get," he said, and he pushed himself deeper.

I closed my eyes in a wince and then opened them to groan. I gasped up at him and saw the arousal in his eyes. I mirrored his lust.

"All the way," I nodded, whimpering. "Give me all of it."

I kept nodding as he pushed deep. My body was trembling with excitement. The milk made waves beneath me, then he gave one more thrust that shot a yelp from my lungs.

"Mr. Portland!" I burst, and he pushed all the way deep.

I felt him tap on the door of my cervix, but he wasn't asking permission to enter. He was coming in whether I was ready or not.

He put his arms under me and lifted my upper back out of the milk. He held my torso off the floor and bore down on me, keeping his cock deep.

"Fuck me," I whispered.

He gripped me in a tight hug that made me feel safe and apprehensive all at once. I was at his mercy, truly, and I wondered if I could keep up with him.

He started to pump into me slowly, dragging his cock almost all the way from me and then surging it deep. He struck me over and over, hitting my clit with his pubic bone.

Each time he slammed down I heard the wet slap of my ass against the floor. My ecstatic cries almost drowned it out completely.

My pussy was soaked for him and the way he fucked me was only making me wetter. His cock rocked through me, bathed in my cum. He sprang through the muscle over and over. The head of his cock started to get me off.

"Every fucking inch" I told him. "I want it all."

He took the challenge masterfully. He pounded me, crashing into me over and over and raising my excitement like a pro. He pulled me against him and my tits bled milk into the hair of his chest.

"You made me do this," he told me over and over. "You made me do this, you naughty slut."

"It's all my fault, Mr. Portland. I deserve everything I get."

He pulled himself out of me suddenly and scrambled back towards my mouth. He put his cock to me and I ran my lips over him, tasting the sweetness of my pussy on him.

This time I jerked him over me, then he put his balls right on my mouth. I wasn't going to say no to that. I sucked him right in and listened the to impassioned moans lurch from his lungs.

He moved back down and settled his cock between my big tits. I looked at the wet head peering out between them and watched as he dragged it back. My cleavage swallowed him up but then he pushed forwards.

He fucked my titties in the wet mess of the dairy aisle, surging his cock through me. The whole time they continued to leak their milk. I pushed them around him and another jet fired up against him, hanging in his hair like little pearls.

"That's it," he said. "That's my little slut."

It felt like I was being rewarded rather than punished, but I didn't want to tell him that. Instead I let him continued to fuck my tits and each time his cock sprang up out of my cleavage I'd open my mouth and pop it off the tip of his length.

"That's perfect," he growled. "You're fucking perfect, Carla."

He'd never been so nice to me.

Eventually he pulled his cock from my cleavage and jerked himself hard over me. I braced myself for his cumshot all over my face, but instead he moved back down and put himself in my pussy.

"You think I was going to waste it all over that naughty face of yours?" he asked.

"I was hoping so."

"It's going inside you," he said, "where it belongs."

"Pump it into me," I dared, pushing out my lower jaw.

He upped his pace inside me. "You want my cum, huh?"

"I want it!"

He pounded me, putting his weight on his hands that gripped my tits. He squeezed hard and the milk fired up and out, shooting into the air like the fountains at the Bellagio.

He opened his mouth and caught the stream. He stopped squeezing and then let the milk fall from his mouth.

I opened mine and the milk poured from him into me. It tasted creamy, thick and sweet. Some of it dappled my face and Mr. Portland rubbed it over me.

"You look like such a beautiful slut with that milk all over you."

"It could have been your cum," I told him.

"You need that inside you."

"Fucking breed me," I told him, and that seemed to really get him excited. He upped his pace and his expression turned stern. He'd set his sights on the target.

"Fucking breed me, Mr. Portland," I told him again.

"You want my fucking cum?"

"I need it!" I told him.

He gripped my tits and pinched to the nipple again. They blasted upwards and the milk hit his face. This time he didn't open his mouth. Instead he let it all fall back against me. He kept his pace, firing into me so fast that the milk on the floor pattered between my ass cheeks.

I stared right into his eyes and watched the climax arrive. "Shoot your cum in me!"

"Oh, Carla!"

He strained and let out a growl. His cock swelled and turned stiffer than I'd ever known. The milk fired from my tits all by itself, as though it was responding to Mr. Portland's imminent release.

"Pump me full of cum!"

Fuck, he did. His cock pulsed and then I felt his warmth strike inside me. It lashed against my cervix again and again and he marked each release with another deep groan.

He pushed himself all the way deep and sent his cum even deeper. I felt the warmth spread inside me and felt his weight against my body.

My tits continued to leak mysteriously, and Mr. Portland's climax continued inside me. He filled me with so much cum that it started to dribble out of me and mingle with the spillage on the floor.

He kept his cock in me, fucking me slow and passing it through the sticky deposit that he'd left within me. The texture of his cock felt different now, slipping through his velvet seed.

Finally he pulled it from me and set himself between my breasts. I rocked my tits over him as he breathed heavily above me.

"That feel good?" I asked him.

He ran his hand through his hair and looked down on me. He pulled his sticky cock from my cleavage and pushed it into my mouth one last time.

I opened over him lovingly and took his spent cock inside me. It slid right back into my throat and I tasted his bitter, caramel seed. He pulled himself out of me and then moved his leg from over me. I bathed in the milk on the floor and stared up at him, fuck-drunk and satisfied.

"Don't tell Ellen," he said. "I know how much you two talk."

I started to giggle. "I'm not sure I'll be telling anyone," I told him. "I don't want them to know."

He almost looked put out, but his smirk told me he knew that I was joking. If I could have let the world know I would have. Shit, it's not every day your tits leak milk and your boss fucks you—as much as I wished it was.

"You gonna tell me how you did that?" I asked, sitting up and looking down at my tits. Milk dripped slowly from the nipple.

"It's a family secret."

"Mr. Portland!"

"I'm afraid I can't divulge."

"Will that always happen now?" I asked.

"No," he said. "Only with me."

I didn't know whether to sigh or rejoice.

"So how are we gonna clean this up?" I asked, looking around.

Mr. Portland was getting himself dressed. "*We?*"

I slapped my hands down in the milk. "Mr. Portland!"

"I'll be back to check on you in an hour," he said. "I have to do the payroll." He gave the mop-bucket a tap with his shoe. "You might want to get some more of these."

I sat naked in the pool of milk in the dairy aisle, with Mr. Portland's cum slowly leaking from my pussy. My legs were outstretched and my tits sat exposed above my bra. My hair was wet with milk and my chest was flushed with a red hue of excitement. I must have looked quite the picture.

Mr. Portland gave me a little wave as he put his cock back in his pants, then he disappeared from view.

"This fucking job," I cursed, slapping down on the milk with a splash.

I got to my feet steadily and grabbed the mop. I started to soak up the spilt gallons, moving through it barefoot and naked. Every so often I'd pose for the CCTV camera that moved above me. I just knew he would be watching in his office and it gave the task a bit of added spice that it desperately needed.

I didn't want that to be the last time we were naughty together, but I didn't want to spend hours mopping up milk every time I wanted Mr. Portland to fuck me.

I'd have to get creative ...

THE END

Ice-Cream Fundae : Suckled Daughters
8

Mr. Luther had always called it his greatest acquisition. The beach-side ice-cream parlor was prime real-estate, and in the summer we did an eye-watering amount of trade.

You wouldn't think it, but selling ice-creams is big business, and with everywhere getting hotter Mr. Luther had gripped the opportunity with two hands when it came his way. Now the beach-side shack was worth hundreds of thousands.

It wasn't Mr. Luther's main job. He worked in the city—the kind of job where he's so high up that he doesn't even need to dress smart anymore. The ice-cream parlor was his plaything, and he mainly left it to me to run.

I loved it. I got to meet new people every single day and I pretty much got to do what I wanted. I was my own boss really, even though Mr. Luther was top-dog. He only rarely swung by to check on things and it was nice to have that kind of responsibility at nineteen. It really made me feel like I was part of something. All I needed to be was stocked up on ice-creams and I was set.

The cabin was fitted out with four chest-freezers—three regular and one display at the front—and two big drinks fridges. With no air-conditioning it could get pretty hot in there, even on a cold day. Even the sea-breeze wasn't enough to cool a gal down.

And that day was *hot*. The fact that it was so hot is pretty much the only reason this sinful story exists in the first place.

The queue started at a little after nine o'clock in the morning. It sounds crazy, I know, but people really do want to eat ice-creams that early!

People would pitch up on the beach for the day, grab a drink and an ice-cream and most likely come back later for a second helping.

Mr. Luther said that I was so cute that people were guaranteed to come back a second time. I did my best to connect with them in the brief moments me and the customers had together and I'd usually see them again later in the day.

That day the rush of customers was intense. There were only a few minutes where I didn't have a queue at all, and in those moments I was able to quickly eat a sandwich that one of the guys who ran the mini-golf had dropped off for me.

"Rather you than me," he'd laughed, spotting the queue when he called by with my food.

I gave him a smile. The queue was nothing, really. Everyone was pretty chill and when they finally made it to the front and saw me busting my ass off they went pretty easy on me.

"Can I get three scoops of rum and raisin," asked Craig. He was a regular that always came by. I think he worked on the trampolines further down the beach.

"Coming right up," I told him.

I leaned forward to the front of the display freezer and rolled the ice-cream into the scoop. Craig always paid particular attention when I got his ice-cream. My friend Charlie said she's pretty sure he picks the ice-creams nearest the front so he could look at my tits when I lean forward. I didn't care. They were big, but they were mine so I wasn't going to have any hang-ups over them. I sometimes found it pretty flattering to be honest, and I loved it when husbands came to the shack and did their best to avert their gaze in front of their wives.

"Is that enough, babe?" I asked, pushing the third scoop into the cone.

"More than enough," Craig smiled.

To be honest I loved the chill of the freezer on my skin, so the more time I got to spend reaching in there the better.

"That's six dollars."

"Always happy to pay it," Craig smiled.

The next customer came along and did a double-take at my chest. When I turned back to grab their drink from the refrigerator I looked down to see my nipples punching through my t-shirt. Even with a bra on it was obvious.

The guy paid and tried to take a few more surreptitious glances to my breasts, which were all too obvious. When I handed him the change I decided to go all out.

"Man, is it *hot*," I huffed, and I took my t-shirt up over my head, wearing only my bra and jean-shorts now.

The last customer still hadn't left.

"Can I help?" I asked, blowing a jet of air up my face.

"I'll take some—uhh"—he looked to the display of flavors—"mint choc-chip," he pointed.

"How many scoops?"

"Two," he said. "Big ones."

"You talking about me or the scoops?" I smirked.

He seemed shocked at first but then let out a laugh that seemed to ease the tension.

"The scoops," he confirmed.

I leaned forward and my bra fought to hold my tits back. They made a huge cleavage as I struggled to make balls of the stiff, cool ice-cream.

The chill felt even better this time around. It was like it was actually doing something, other than just giving me a brief respite. I could feel it catch the dapples of sweat on my chest and turn them cold.

"There you go," I told him. "Four-fifty."

My new choice of attire was already paying dividends. Not only was I much cooler, but the patrons tended to linger longer, buy more and even return later in the day.

I couldn't believe the amount of money that the till was holding. It was practically overflowing. It made me wonder if I should have a security staff on days like this, but who would ever think to rob an ice-cream shack?

As things started to wind-down I messaged Mr. Luther. I told him about how crazy the day had been and how I was pretty sure it was a record. He told me he'd come by later.

I shut the shack doors at around six. It was a long-ass day, but man it was worth it. I closed the doors and locked myself inside, counting the money in the still-sweltering heat. I took a drink from the refrigerator and put it to my forehead. I put it on my chest and felt the condensation run down into my cleavage. I took a long swig and then startled as a knock sounded on the shack door.

"Clara?" came Mr. Luther's voice.

"Here," I told him. "Let me unlock the door."

It opened and Mr. Luther stood there in his shorts and sandals. He wore a light shirt and looked fresh and immaculate as always.

"So how much did you make?" he beamed. He took a step inside and then stepped back out when he felt the heat. "Jesus!"

"I know," I told him. It was then that he looked to my big tits and bra.

"Was it *that* hot?"

"Mr. Luther, you wouldn't believe it. It was so hot that I think we broke the record. I've never seen so much money."

"You don't think your new choice of uniform helped?"

"I ... I'm pretty sure it did," I confessed.

"Because I'd be back double-quick time," he laughed. "I wouldn't be able to get enough."

I started to laugh. Mr. Luther had never been so open about my body before and I felt like I needed to return the compliment.

"Well if a guy like you was serving me some soft-scoop I'd be back for more too."

There was brief moment's silence in which I wondered if I'd gone too far.

"So how much?" he asked.

"Come in," I told him. "Lock the door."

"It's sweltering!"

"Security, Mr. Luther. It's bad enough you put me in here alone all day. Besides, I've just had a whole day of this heat. You can't stand twenty minutes?"

He sighed and stepped inside. He closed the door behind him and the shack instantly got hotter.

He grabbed a drink. "You want one?"

"Vanilla coke," I told him. He handed me a bottle and I twisted off the cap.

"So come on. Spill!" he urged.

"Well, so far I count four-thousand dollars."

"Damn."

"And there's still more to count. Could be about six-thousand."

"From this little stall?" he marveled. He pulled the front of his shirt out a few times to try and get a draft going. "I need to get you a treat as a reward."

"Crazy, isn't it. Look at the empties!" I pointed to the corner where the empty tubs of ice-cream were stacked high.

"You think you need a number two?" he asked.

"I think it wouldn't hurt; even if you just employed someone to blow on me all day."

"I think some of the guys out there would do that for free," he joked.

The whole time we talked Mr. Luther couldn't stop his eyes from wandering. He kept glancing at my tits but by now I just thought it was normal.

"Let's count the rest," he said, nodding to the pile of cash I'd set aside.

He took roughly half of it and moved it to the top of the big chest-freezer near the door. He started to count it out, wiping his brow frequently.

I was across from him, taking plenty of sips of drink. I was way more acclimatized to the heat than Mr. Luther was, and I was wearing fewer clothes too.

"Take off your shirt," I told him.

He looked back at me with surprise.

"If you're hot, I mean."

"You don't mind?"

"Why would I?"

"I thought watching an old man undress might be something you didn't want to see."

"It's hardly undressing, is it? And you're not *that* old."

"It kind of is undressing, but I'm not gonna argue. It's fucking *hot*."

He started to unfasten his buttons and I turned to him with a tongue in my cheek. "Take it off!" I whooped.

"Clara!"

"Take it all off!"

He shook his head but he didn't stop. He popped the buttons and even did this thing where he grabbed either side of his open shirt and ran it back and forth across his back.

Mr. Luther started to laugh, not realizing that his little act had had an effect on me. I swallowed hard and tried to imagine something else, and not a topless guy standing in front of me with a body to die for.

"I'm not getting you flustered am I?" he joked. I think if he genuinely realized he was then he wouldn't have made the comment.

"Uhh, no," I lied. "Just keep counting."

He turned back to his pile and started to count the coins. I watched him, running my eyes down his strong back and following a drop of sweat as it rolled slowly down his spine and into his shorts.

I bit my lip and felt my body start to respond to the sight. My pussy dampened and not just from the sweat. Something about the summer's heat always got me kind of horny, you know?

"I've got one-thousand, eight-hundred and fifty," he said, looking back. "You?"

I realized I was staring and shook myself from the daydream. "I haven't finished yet."

"Jeez, Clara," he teased. "You need a calculator?" He came over to me and leaned over my shoulder. "Where are you at?"

I could feel his warm body against my bare skin. I took a deep breath. "I've just gotta do the coins. The notes are done."

"Here," he said, and he reached around and quickly started to sort and count the pile.

I didn't move. Instead I let him count against me. Being in his embrace like that was driving me wild, but I don't think he even realized what he was doing to me.

"Twenty-two-fifty," he said. "How much are the notes?"

"Nine-hundred," I said quietly.

"Plus the four-thousand we already have ..." Mr. Luther did a bit of arithmetic. "That's six-thousand, seven-hundred and seventy-two dollars and fifty cents!"

"Fuck," was all I could say.

"Fuck, indeed. That sounds like a record to me."

"I've never known a day like it."

"So is this your new uniform from now on?" he asked, and he turned me by the hips and looked me up and down.

"It can be."

"Why not go the whole hog," he said, and he tugged at the waist of my jean-shorts.

I smiled and bit my lip. I felt suddenly shy and nervous. I never knew I held thoughts for him like this.

"I could take these shorts off it's that hot in here," he said, and he took a long swig of his drink.

I watched his throat gulp it down and followed it down past his pecs and to his stomach.

"I could just wear panties," I told him. "Or maybe a bikini is more acceptable?"

"Show me," he said nonchalantly, screwing the top back on the bottle. He leaned back against the chest freezer and watched me.

"Show you what?"

"What you were thinking for your new outfit."

"You mean ... take my shorts off?"

"Yeah. I wanna see."

He made it sound so innocent—like it was no big thing. I was almost convinced he was right.

I popped the button at their waist and wiggled out of them. I was wearing a tiny pair of black panties that matched my black bra.

"That looks good to me," he said, watching. "Do you want to see something?"

My eyes bulged. "What?"

"A trick," he said. "Or a skill. Whatever you like to call it."

"What is it?"

"I'll show you," he said, stepping forwards. "Something I learned years ago."

"Is this my treat?"

"It can be."

Mr. Luther came behind me again, but this time his intention wasn't to count coins. He put his whole body against me so that I could feel the bulge in his pants.

"Relax," he said, and he brought his hands up slowly.

I marveled as he moved them towards my tits. I wasn't about to stop him. His hands cupped them and I closed my eyes and sighed dreamily.

"I haven't started yet," he said.

"Then show me!" I giggled impatiently.

He started to squeeze and rub my tits, which was nothing unusual to begin with.

"Is that it?" I scoffed. "That's my treat?"

"Wait," Mr. Luther said patiently.

His hands continued to move and my nipples turned stiff. It felt good, but it didn't feel like anything particularly special. Until ... *oh gosh*.

"You feel it," he said, sensing it.

"It feels *wet*."

"Uh-huh," he said, not stopping.

He rubbed at the cups of my bra and I felt my breasts turn wet. Suddenly the fluid started to seep out under my bra and run down me. I giggled as the flow tickled my skin and then looked down.

"It's milk!" I cried.

I pulled away from him and looked down. Mr. Luther was laughing to himself.

"Did you put ice-cream down there?"

I pulled out my bra and looked in at the white cream inside it.

"No," he said. "It's yours."

"Mine?"

"Your milk."

"My milk?!"

He nodded. "That's my treat. Feels good, doesn't it?"

I was dumbstruck. I mean, it *had* felt good, but that was before I knew that it was mine.

"Where did it come from?"

"Do I really need to tell you that?"

"But how? How do my tits have milk?"

"Ahh," he said, wagging his finger. "That's the secret."

"Tell me!"

"I can't," he said. "I've been sworn to secrecy."

"Tell me!"

"I can only show you."

"So show me."

"You liked it, didn't you?"

"Yes, goddammit, now show me!"

I flashed the front of my bra down and showed him my big, milk-strewn tits. He drank them in, biting his lip. It looked like he was having some naughty thoughts himself.

"Show me," I told him again, bouncing them above the bra-cups.

He moved forwards and put out a hand. "May I?"

"Do it!"

He touched me again and I closed my eyes, focusing on the dreamy sensation. My breasts tingled and then gave up their milk all on their own. It flowed out of me in abundance and Mr. Luther rubbed it back over my tits until my skin was a milky white.

"There you go," he said steadily.

I looked down and watched him fondling them. "Taste it," I hushed.

Mr. Luther looked at me and smiled. He moved his face forwards and I closed my eyes again. I felt his mouth envelop my nipple and a heady cry leapt from my lungs.

"Yes!" I gasped.

It was so hot in there, but I could tell it was about to get a whole lot hotter.

Mr. Luther rubbed at my tits and pushed them together around his face. He sucked on each nipple in turn and they gave up their milk in an instant. I didn't even know that I could do something like that, but Mr. Luther had started the procedure with such conviction that it made me wonder if every woman had milk in their tits.

"Yes, boss," I hushed. "Keep going."

I leaned back against the freezer and felt its chill on my back. Mr. Luther reached behind and unclasped my bra. He took it off my shoulders and wiped the milk from his mouth before latching himself back on me.

It felt so special to be nourishing him like that. It gave me this odd kind of euphoria and arousal—the likes of which I'd never known. My pussy started to dampen more and then I felt his hand grip at the inside of my thigh.

"Oooh," I whimpered, looking down. I was hoping he wasn't about to stop there.

He teased his finger around the crotch of my panties, touching the sensitive skin and teasing ever-so-close to the real thing.

I felt impatient for him and wondered if he didn't want to smash the last taboo. With my tits in his mouth it felt like we'd started at the more extreme end anyway, so I grabbed his hand by the wrist and put him right on my pussy.

"That's what you want?" he asked.

"I want a whole lot more than that."

I lunged forwards and started to kiss him. Our lips entwined and Mr. Luther's tongue pushed through against mine. I could taste my sweet cream on him. Then I felt him start to rub at my groove.

"Yes," I hushed, breaking off him.

He put his forehead to mine and I closed my eyes tight, letting out a strained whimper as his fingers started to work me.

But again I wanted more. I took his wrist once more but this time I pulled out the front of my panties and thrust him inside there.

His fingers pushed through my short fur and went straight to my clit. He circled slowly and nudged the sensitive node. It sent chills through me.

"That's it," I moaned, leaning back.

I pushed out my chest and felt more like a woman than ever. Whatever Mr. Luther had done to my tits wasn't stopping. They still continued to leak their milk without any provocation. Every time I moaned they let out another fine spurt which spattered forwards against his chest. He seemed to love it.

"Cover me in your milk," he groaned. I never thought I'd hear that sentence.

I fired the nectar all over him and got off on his moans. My milk showered him and I rubbed it into his chest, pushing my fingers through his hair and feeling his stern pecs.

"This is so fucking *bad*," I giggled.

His fingers teased around my pussy, rattling my clit until I couldn't take it any longer. He curled his fingers inwards and pushed two of them inside me. My pussy engulfed him in its juices. He started to shake his entire arm and my whole body turned tense.

"Mr. Luther!" I squeaked, rising on my tip-toes.

My pussy started to gush and so too did my tits. He took the whole blast against him, unflinching. He let my pussy squirt all over his legs as the milk careened from my chest and struck his.

He slowed the shaking of his arm and then pushed his fingers through me slowly.

"I'm soaked!" he said, looking down at his drenched shorts.

"Take them off."

The two of us were sweating heavily but we weren't about to stop. There were so many fluids crashing around in that tiny shack and I was sure we were going to add one more to the mix before the day was out.

Mr. Luther popped the button of his shorts and let them fall down his legs. My hands went straight to his boxer-shorts and I rubbed over the thick, stiff cock that sat inside.

"Take it out," he said.

I dropped to my knees and rushed down his boxer-shorts. His huge cock sprang up and out, bouncing in front of me. Mr. Luther watched, waiting for my reaction.

"That's one sexy cock," I swooned. I looked up into his eyes and he nodded at it.

"Taste it," he said.

I wrapped my big lips over him in an instant, driving the stiffness right to the back of my throat. It was smooth and long and delicious.

My hands teased at his weighty balls and I hummed along with him as the first moan of pleasure soared from his lungs.

"That feels so good in your mouth," he groaned.

I pushed him deep and started to jerk him through my lips. Mr. Luther held my head and watched. I stared up at him and sank his cock all the way deep.

He shook his head in disbelief. "You are something else."

"Here," I told him, and I rose up on my knees and pushed my tits towards him.

A jet of milk fired over him and he jerked it across his cock. He stooped his knees and set himself in my cleavage, then I started to bounce my tits along him.

"Yes!" I cried, watching his delicious, milky cock burst through my cleavage.

"This is the best fucking thing that's ever happened to me," he laughed.

He sucked a breath through his teeth and pumped his cock along me. My smooth breasts enveloped him in a cushion. The tit-job was so slippery and milky that I thought he was about to burst right then and there.

He moved above me frantically. He went to the freezer and I stopped jerking him for a moment to watch. He pulled himself a scoop of ice-cream and then dropped it right onto my tits.

"Oooh," I winced, feeling the sudden chill.

"Use it," Mr. Luther said.

Well fuck, I didn't even know what that meant. I settled the scoop of cream in my cleavage and smothered his cock again. Mr. Luther pressed the icr-cream down and soon he was getting a chilled tit-fuck and loving every second of it.

My nipples pricked stiff and fired out their cream. Mr. Luther's thighs caught the brunt. His hips thrust slowly and his cock sprang through the milky, creamy mixture.

Eventually he took out his cock and gave it to me. It looked like a whole new type of ice-cream and I wasn't shy in trying it.

I opened my mouth over him and tasted the sweet, cool cream. I didn't stop until his cock was completely cleansed of it. The whole time I could feel the last of the scoop sliding down my body.

If my boss was going to use props from the stall then so was I. Without thinking I grabbed the strawberry syrup and laced it along his cock like I was putting ketchup on a hotdog.

"Good girl," he said. "You gonna taste that too?"

I nodded and then drove him into me slowly, pushing my lips down over his smooth crown and feeling it slide into my mouth. I'd found a new favorite way to eat ice-cream.

"Be a good girl and lick all of that off," he hushed, smoothing my hair aside to give himself the best view. "Then afterwards I'll give you your real dessert."

I tried not to race, but I couldn't help it. I licked him clean, tending to his messy cock like it was part of my job.

When I was finished he took my hand and lifted me to my feet. I stood across from him, breathing heavily.

"Where do you want me?"

"Bend over that freezer," he pointed.

I walked forward and did as he said, pressing my tits on the top of the plastic unit and looking back at him. Mr. Luther was surveying my curvy ass and looking at the slender strip of pussy-flesh that stared back.

"Fuck me," I told him.

He took a grip of his cock and took a step forward. "You don't have to tell me twice."

I grinned but my expression suddenly turned to moaning pain. Mr. Luther was big, and that was no more apparent than when his huge cock was pressing into me.

My pussy stretched over him and my body tingled. The act was so crazy that it felt like a dream. I couldn't believe what we were doing, but then there were so many crazy things that had already happened.

"Oh, Mr. Luther," I wailed. I wondered if any of the passers-by could guess what was going on in the closed ice-cream shack. The moans were tough to confuse with something innocent.

"Give me your pussy," he hushed.

I pushed back with a grunt and sent his thickness deeper inside me. It felt like he was going to blast right through my cervix. As he pushed deep my tits became even more charged, shooting their milk onto the chest-freezer until it pooled beneath them.

He bucked forwards and my breasts swayed in a pool of their own milk. It tickled the nipples and caused even more to flow.

He put his hands under my breasts and held them as he fucked me. He went off at a crazy pace that I hadn't saw coming. After the initial surprise I realized I was right on the edge of climax.

"You're gonna make me come!" I cried, and just as I was finishing the sentence I felt the first spasm.

A long, ecstasy-laden grunt left me. It sounded like something straight from the jungle. Mr. Luther pushed himself all the way deep and held his cock there as I started to spasm around him.

"Come on my cock," he demanded. I didn't have much of a choice.

He pulled both arms behind my back and pinned my tits and face in the milk. He continued to fuck me and I continued to come, wailing and at his mercy.

"Fuck me!" I dared, vying to regain a bit of control.

Mr. Luther didn't let up. His cock sprang through my tightening pussy over and over and I rode out the orgasm.

I wanted nothing more than to expel him. My pussy had turned so sensitive that the slightest of movements were making me spasm and writhe wildly on the freezer.

"I'm gonna come," he said through clenched teeth.

"I want it! I want it! Come on my tits!"

I was fucking ravenous for it. I could hear his breaths crashing out of his lungs behind me and I was matching their pace.

The heat of the room sucked into my lungs over and over as he rammed his cock into me in one final flurry.

I was off the blocks like a starter-pistol had sounded when I felt him pull out of me. I turned around and got to my knees instantly, rubbing my big tits and offering them up for him to cover.

He ran his hand over his cock and looked down expectantly. His mouth opened in a silent moan. His body was so tense and perfect.

"Come for me!" I begged.

He finally exhaled a long breath, following it with a grunt and wrap of his fist that saw the first hot lashing leap from him and crash against my milk-soaked tits.

"Yes!" I gasped. "Yes! Yes! Yes! Come all over me!"

I rubbed the cum into my tits, moving my hands in a circle as though I was massaging his spunk into me. More and more of it crashed against me, thrown from his cock in messy ropes.

My nipples sat proud and leaked slowly, mixing with his love. They glistened in the light overhead, as though they were shrink-wrapped. I'd never known them look so fucking good.

"Every drop," I begged, looking into his eyes. The look of euphoria in his face was heavenly.

"Good girl, Clara," he said, taking several deep breaths.

He pinched off the last of his cum and rubbed his cock over my taut nipple. He let go of his dick and leaned his head back to take a deep breath. With it hanging there right in front of me I couldn't help but put it in my mouth one last time.

He hissed a breath and stared down, running his hand over my hair. "Good girl," he said again.

I popped him free finally and got to my feet. Now that the act was over my tits seemed to be calming. They leaked slowly, with only a drip-or-so appearing every few minutes.

"That's some end to the day," I giggled.

"You're telling me. I think we broke a couple of records in here today."

"We broke a couple of laws, probably," I laughed.

Mr. Luther did too but then turned a little more serious. "You can't tell anyone about this, okay?"

"It's okay," I smirked. "I like a secret—especially a naughty one."

"Then perhaps we can share a few more dirty secrets in future."

"Is that a promise?"

"Keep up this good work and I'll give you anything you want," he said.

"Hmm," I mused, running through a list of fantasies in my mind. "That sounds good to me." I thought for a moment and one request came instantly to mind.

"I do have one idea," I said wryly.

Mr. Luther smiled keenly. "What is it?"

I looked around at the mess. "A cleaner?"

He let out a big belly-laugh. "Agreed!"

THE END

Sin On Splash-Canyon : Suckled Brats 9

Fuck, it was the naughtiest day of my life. To this day I still can't really believe that we did it, but you know when you get so caught-up on being horny that you lose all sense of danger? Well, that!

It was a Thursday and Clark had decided to treat me to an impromptu visit to the local theme-park. I'd known him for so long now and he was always the sweetest of guys. He was like my gay best-friend, only not gay, if that makes sense?

I was off work as I was getting to my due-date. The father of the baby had split before he even realized I was pregnant, but I was nineteen and broody. Or foolish. I still haven't decided which.

So anyway, I plowed on through the trimesters and now all I could think of was getting this thing out of me! I was over eight-months gone, but I hated the wait.

I loved the theme-park close to us. It was about an hour-and-a-half drive away. It was called Pleasure Land, which Clark and I always thought sounded like some sleazy strip-club, but whatever.

"It'll be nice, you know," Clark had said. "The two of us. Some time before you're up to your neck in baby stuff."

Anything to take my mind off it I figured.

So Clark and I headed out there. He drove and acted like the perfect gentleman. It really felt like a date and I think some people confused it for one. On more than one occasion during the day people mistook him for my sugar-daddy. I could kind of see it, I guess.

But he really spoiled me. He satisfied all of my many cravings, lavishing me with greasy junk-food and milkshakes. He even came on the big roller-coasters—something I'd never known him do. Listening to him scream was hilarious!

We'd just got off one of the faster rides and I was laughing so hard I thought I was going to piss myself.

Clark was an almost ghostly white. He was playing it up a little, but on the ride he'd been genuinely terrified. You don't fake those kinds of screams.

"You're a big wuss," I laughed.

"Those things are a *death trap*," he said, pointing back.

The people on after us streamed overhead on the track, screaming down on the crowd beneath them.

"I'll tell your families you love them!" Clark shouted after.

I shook my head and sniggered, but suddenly I felt the strangest sensation come over me. I winced and Clark's face transformed immediately.

"Clem?" he said, rushing forwards. "Clem, are you okay?"

"I just feel *funny*," I squirmed.

"What is it?"

"Like a *pressure* ..."

"Shit. Is this it?!"

He looked around, panicked.

"No, no. I just feel strange."

"What kind of pressure?" he asked. He was looking into my eyes so intently. Fuck, I loved him.

"Like, in my chest."

I placed a hand on my tits. They were big *before* pregnancy, so now they sat on my chest like balloons.

"Anything I can do?" he asked.

"I don't know. I think I just need to sit down."

"There's a bench here?"

"Or maybe we can try a more sedate ride," I said, looking around.

"Sure," Clark said. "Something easy. Shit, I'd kill for something easy. Let's look at the map."

He took the map from his back-pocket and unfolded it. I stepped close to him and we both perused the cartoony cartography.

"The Slow Train," he said, tapping the map.

"I'm not five," I drawled.

"Splash-Canyon!" he said, pointing hopefully.

"People already think we're a couple."

"So what? We might as well try it then, hadn't we?"

Splash-Canyon was well-known as the ride you took your crush on. It was a fifteen-minute water-ride that circled the entire park, yet somehow the whole route was secluded. It was obviously a teenager's dream amongst an otherwise raucous theme-park and it had got a reputation off the back of it.

"Come on," he pressed. "It's real close."

"Okay, okay," I said, and we walked off in its direction.

"I feel like a need a change of pace anyway," Clark said. He put an arm around me and looked at me. "Are you sure you're okay?"

"I'll be fine," I told him.

The pain in my chest was still there. It felt like a zit that was about to burst or something. Thankfully the queue was short. We got a few wry looks from the ride attendants as Clark and I got into our own private boat.

The boats were round, rigid-inflatables that seated six. Clark and I sat opposite at first and the current took us away from the public area and along the private route.

"Any better?" he asked.

I wriggled in the seat.

"We're fifteen minutes from safety," he said. "You better be okay!"

"Not helping!" I laughed.

Suddenly a spike in pain arrived and I sucked a breath. My back straightened. Clark rushed across from his seat, sitting beside me with his arm around me.

"Clem?"

"It's fine," I said, breathing deep. "It's fine."

I could feel my breasts pressing against the front of my button-up maternity shirt.

He rubbed my back. I guess he didn't know what else to do. Suddenly the boat got bumpy and Clark looked back at the advancing frothy water.

"I forgot this part," he said.

We bounced against each other and I tried to calm my discomfort. When my ass hit back against the plastic seat one of the buttons of my shirt popped clean away and my cleavage burst up out of the shirt like something from a cartoon.

"Whoa!" Clark cried.

I pursed my lips and tried to hide my modesty, but that wasn't exactly my priority. Mostly I just wanted this horrible sensation to go away.

"You're bursting out of your shirt," Clark said, ogling my jiggling charms.

"It does feel better though," I confessed.

The shirt felt constricting, like it was pressing down on me. When the button popped off I felt a kind of immediate relief.

"I'm gonna take it off," I told him. "Just while we're on the ride."

He scanned the surrounding flora for people. There was no-one in sight. "If you're sure, Clem."

I popped the remaining buttons and pulled the shirt back off my shoulders. I felt an immediate relief. There was something calming about feeling the cool, fresh air against my bare skin.

Clark didn't know where to look though, bless him. He was doing everything that he could to not have to look in my direction. The rough water was making my tits bounce all over the place.

"Better?" he asked.

"A little," I said, wriggling.

But it was no good. I could still feel *something* and I just wanted to do everything I could to stop feeling like that.

"I'm gonna take my bra off," I announced.

"Wh-what?"

"I'm just gonna take it off. Just while we're on the ride."

"But, Clem ..."

"What?"

"I ... I don't know if you should."

"It hurts, Clark."

"Okay, okay," he said. He clenched his fist and seemed anxious. "Okay."

"Can you unclasp it," I asked him, and I faced my bare back to him.

"Jeez, Clem. The stuff you get me doing."

He popped the clasp expertly with one hand. I felt a relief so immediate that I couldn't stop myself from moaning.

"Clem?" he said, worried again.

He turned my by the shoulder and the bra straps fell down my arms.

"That's so good," I groaned. I closed my eyes and sat back in the seat. I couldn't have given a shit if I was topless.

"Better?" he asked.

I opened my eyes gradually and looked through my lashes at him. He was staring right at my big tits with a terrified look on his face. I found it pretty funny.

"Getting a good look?" I asked.

"They're just—uhh—there."

"It feels so much better."

"How long have you been ... *producing*?"

"Huh?"

I sat up and noticed Clark nod again to my breasts. I looked down and saw a bead of milk on the nipple.

"Whoa!"

"It's milk, right?" he said.

I laughed. "I hope so!"

I lifted my breasts for a closer look. The second I did so I felt a rush that fired right out of me. It startled me. I flinched and watched in awe as a fine burst of milk fired right out from my breast and struck Clark.

His eyes bulged in shock and he looked down on the milk as it dripped down his shirt. He was open mouthed. I started to giggle.

"Sorry," I said, but then it did it again! Another spray of milk left me and when it did it felt *so fucking good*.

"Jeez, Clem!"

My eyes rolled back as the pain left me. A deep euphoria replaced it. Everything felt *amazing* suddenly.

"That's so good," I groaned.

"When it squirts out of you like that?"

"Yeah! It's such a release."

"I remember what those used to feel like," Clark joked, but he was so good-looking that I don't think he ever struggled.

"Can you squeeze them?"

"Clem?"

"Milk them," I said. "See if you can get more out. I think that's why it's been hurting."

"Because of the milk?"

"I guess. I mean, I can feel the pressure going away every time I let some out."

"So you want me to ..." Clark nodded at my tits.

"Yeah. Please? If you can?"

We swept down Splash-Canyon and Clark reached out slowly. I couldn't wait for him to touch me. I just wanted to feel that amazing rush all over again.

He put both hands on one of my big breasts and then squeezed towards the nipple. The fluid burst out and Clark moved out of its way. It sprayed into the center of the boat, audibly hitting the floor like a leaking drainpipe.

"Fuck, Clem," he hushed.

I think he was getting crazy too. Something about that sinful river ride was affecting the both of us.

"I'm gonna take my shirt off," he said. "Just in case it hits me, you know?"

I nodded and watched. Clark's body was well taken care of. His skin was tanned and hairy in all the right places. He set his t-shirt down on one of the empty seats and moved his hands back to my tits.

This time he took both and bunched them together. I let out a wail of pleasure as both breasts gave up their nectar at once.

I opened my mouth to look down at the stream of cream bursting from me. Clark was letting it fire right against his chest and he was breathing deep with excitement too. His pupils were fat and his face wore a look of pleasure that I'd never seen before.

"It's crazy, huh?" I hushed.

"You can say that again."

He looked down and noticed how the milk was running down his stomach and hitting the top of his shorts.

"Take those off too," I told him.

Clark seemed to pause and think, but he didn't think for long. He looked ahead at the water and then stood up.

He downed his shorts quickly and I could see immediately that he was packing something serious in his boxer-shorts. What's more, it didn't look flaccid. When he moved *it* moved.

He stepped out of his shorts just as we hit a bump in the stream. He fell forward over me and put his hands on the top of my seat.

His boxer-shorts were right in my face. I knew his cock was right under there. Clark didn't correct himself straight away. Instead he stayed exactly where he was. I needed to make a move.

"We don't want these getting milk on them, do we?" I asked, and I pinched at the fabric of his boxer-shorts.

"We don't," he agreed. "Want to take those down for me?"

I swallowed nervously. Fuck. I mean, it was Clark, you know? Clark! All I could think of was that there was a big, hard cock close to me. That same euphoria still coursed through me, like some weird kind of drug.

I moved a hand up to his waist and pulled his boxer-shorts down. Fuck, it was a rush. I watched the hair turn thicker as it ran down from his stomach. Suddenly I caught the unmistakable sight of hard, veined flesh. It sprang up out of his boxer-shorts and bobbed right in front of my face.

"Oh, Clark," I hushed.

"Look what you've done to me, Clem," he said, looking down.

I looked up and then back to his cock. It was so close that it was almost touching my face. It seemed as though the next step was obvious.

I eased my head forward and kissed his dick softly on the tip. His head was a different shade to his shaft, all smooth and clean-looking. It looked so at odds to see that, and see his familiar face above it.

"Yes, Clem," he hushed.

I opened my mouth and French-kissed the tip now, using my tongue to tickle along the little slit at the top.

Suddenly the boat bounced beneath us and several of his inches rushed quickly into my mouth.

"Shit!" he cried.

My mouth was too full to say anything. I was in shock to begin with. His cock was right at the top of my throat and filling my mouth.

"That feels good," he hushed.

I pulled my lips back off him slowly and then started to jerk him with my mouth. At first it was gradual and sensual, but soon I was rocking my lips over the tip of him and we were both losing control. Our moans were louder than the sound of the water beneath us.

"That's perfect," he said. "So fucking perfect." His high energy was rubbing off on me and soon I was thinking of upping the ante.

"Put yourself between my tits," I told him, leaning away and offering up my cleavage.

Clark put an arm back to hold the central ring of metal and used his other hand to steer his cock right between my breasts.

He sat between them and I enveloped him in my soft tits. His groan told me that it felt amazing immediately. To know that I was having that affect on him was a dream. All I wanted to do was please him, especially after the day he'd given me so far. I just wanted to give a little back, but I don't think Clark was anticipating some tit-milk as a reward.

I pressed my tits around him and a jet of milk surged forwards against his calves. I started to rock my breasts over him, relishing the sounds of pleasure that escaped him.

"Clem, that's so *fucking good*, you don't even know."

"I can take a good guess," I smirked.

His beautiful cock kept peeking out from between my tits each time I ran them down around him. My milk was the perfect lubricant to it all. He ran right through my tits as I showered my cream all over him. It was so fucking naughty and even crazier that we were out in public like that. I mean, we could even hear the screams from the park above us. I just hoped our moans weren't making their way out of the canyon and into earshot.

"Look at that," Clark said.

He moved his hips slowly and fucked my cleavage. Watching him spread through me like that was giving me crazy ideas. I wanted more.

"Give it me," I said now with a sparkling smile. "I want it for real."

He stepped away as I got to my feet. I pushed back my pants over my ass and turned around to show him my curves.

"Take down my panties and fuck me, Clark."

"Right here?" He looked up at the tree-lined walls.

"Right here."

To tempt him even more I pushed my panties back myself. I put my knees on the seat and angled my ass back at him.

"Fuck me on Splash-Canyon, Clark."

The most fucked-up thing was, we probably weren't the first to do something like that. I'd heard rumors of people getting frisky on here, but I'd never heard of a guy fucking a woman twenty-years his junior.

"Fuck, Clem," he said.

"Time's ticking," I said. "We're ten minutes in."

"We are?!"

"Uh-huh."

Honestly, I had no idea how far in we were. It probably wasn't ten minutes yet, but Clark looked like he needed that final push to convince him.

He took a hold of the hilt of his cock and jerked himself, stepping forwards. He put one hand over me and then steered himself up between my legs.

I didn't realize how wet I'd gotten until his hard cock touched me. It slid right through, spreading me open and satisfying me. Clark's hands held my big belly, rubbing the taut skin as he pushed himself deep.

"That's it!" I moaned, closing my eyes.

Clark made me feel fuller than ever. When he pushed his cock deep it felt like it belonged there. I swelled with love for him. I could feel the ecstasy surge around my body. My tits seemed to balloon even further and the milk began to drip freely from them.

"Open me up, Clark," I begged.

He pushed deep and gave me everything that he had to offer—which was a lot! I could only fit a little under half of his cock in my mouth so when he put it in my pussy I knew it'd be a struggle. He made me feel tighter than anyone ever had before. Older guys' cocks just feel bigger like that, I guess.

"That's it," I grunted. "All the way."

He held me steady, not resting until his cock was tickling at my cervix.

"Oh, Clark," I burst.

I moaned against the seat as we wound around the river-rapids. Clark started to fuck me slowly, getting his footing on the rocking boat. His delicious cock spread through me, collecting my cum all along it until he cruised through me with ease.

My tits hung like udders beneath me. The milk flowed from them, making patterns beneath me like a spirograph with the trail of white that it left behind.

"Fuck the milk out of me," I dared.

Clark upped his pace and put both hands on my hips. He fucked me hard and fast, then leant over me and cupped my tits in his hands.

He squeezed them and the milk flowed into his palms. He pushed it back against my skin and rubbed it over me, then he moved his hands up to my face. I kissed at his fingers and tasted my milk, then Clark pulled out of me completely.

I turned to him and he held my face with his hand. He looked into my mouth and then kissed me, moving his tongue around mine and tasting the sweet cream.

"You're so fucking perfect," he said. "I should have done this sooner."

He rubbed my pussy with his fingers and stooped to suck on my titties. His mouth enveloped the nipple and I felt the fluid rush through me again. It was like a different kind of heaven. The release was incredible.

Our bond strengthened like nothing else. It was like I was nourishing Clark—like he *needed* it, you know? The way he drank it down it certainly seemed that way.

He feasted on my tits, moving between each in the brief interlude of breast-feeding. I was happy to let him have his fill.

I fell back in the seat and held his head against me, moaning and swaying as the boat careened down the rapids, pushed along by the artificial currents.

He pulled his mouth off me and let the milk fall from his lips all over me. It was so fucking messy.

I opened my legs and rubbed at my soaked slit, looking to his cock hungrily.

"You think you can come in five minutes?" I asked.

"Are you kidding?"

"Come and prove it."

Clark walked forward wielding his cock like weapon. He bent his knees and angled it in towards me. I watched as it approached. The tip disappeared under the fur of my pussy and then I felt him stretch me wide again.

He was focusing on the sinful union of our flesh too. It must have looked so good to see his pregnant friend's swollen pussy gobble up his cock like that. I'd have killed for the view he had.

"Oh, fuck, Clem," he said, looking at me and shaking his head. "You feel so good around me."

"Give me your cum, Clark," I begged. "Give me your cum!"

His cock felt so fucking stiff—way stiffer than before. The look on his face seemed to match the euphoria that I'd been feeling this entire time.

His stiffness ran through me and I focused on it. My whole pussy became charged with excitement and over-sensitized. Even his smallest movements felt huge.

"You're making me come!" I told him.

I closed my eyes and whimpered softly, writhing and struggling to contain myself. My tits started to leak freely. The current of milk flowed down over my breasts and ran into the boat, mingling with the water on the floor that had splashed in over the sides.

"Clark!" I burst.

My pussy pinched him, but Clark was quietly focused. His muscles were taut and strained all over him. He fucked me hard and drove on, pushing past my contracting pussy.

"Clem!" he strained.

"Fill me with it!"

His cock throbbed and he let out a huge roar. The cum surged along his length—I mean I could really feel it. It burst right up though him and poured into me with force. It turned me hot in an instant.

"Yes!" I wailed. "Yes! Every fucking drop!"

He continued to fuck me, pushing his cum deep and squeezing my tits roughly. The milk fired out against him and he threw his head back. The boat rocked and bounced and Clark swayed, keeping himself inside me as best he could.

"Oh, Clem," he grunted.

I looked down as he came out of me, then he sent the final few ropes up over my pussy and across my swollen stomach.

I felt like such a slut. My body was covered in milk and cum, and I could feel his cum sliding out of my pussy like rich cream.

He put his knee up on the seat beside me and brought his cock up to me. It was lavished with seed. The whole length looked slippery and shiny and the tip held one last bead of his love.

"That looks so good," I confessed.

I raced my lips over him and tasted his richness. He was sweet, salty and bitter all at once, but it was so fucking moreish. I sucked everything I could off him and giggled up at him as I fingered more of his cum off my plump stomach and fed it to myself.

"Has that satisfied a craving?" he asked.

"More than one."

I smiled up at him and pursed my lips. I felt suddenly bashful and exposed. Now that the fog of eroticism had lifted it was easy to see how fucking crazy we'd gotten.

"Get dressed," Clark said, looking ahead. "We're almost back round."

"Shit!"

We rushed out clothes on as fast as we could.

"They're soaking wet," I cried.

"It's a water ride," Clark shrugged. "So we got wet."

He put on his damp t-shirt and pulled up his shorts. I was just about decent when we rolled back in to the ride's entrance.

"Fun journey?" one of the team asked, steadying our boat against the moving platform beside.

"Very," Clark said.

He jumped from the boat and helped me out of it. We were getting looks from every member of staff there.

"Come on," I said. "Let's get out of here."

I grabbed Clark's hand and led him quickly through the exit. It was then that my stomach dropped out of my body completely. There on the wall sat a bank of televisions, each with pictures of that day's entrants.

Cameras, I thought. *Of course there are fucking cameras.*

I looked to Clark and didn't even have to say anything. He was thinking the exact same thing I was. Our walk turned into a jog and then an outright run as we made for the park exit.

I started to laugh and so did Clark when he looked back to see my tits bouncing all over the place.

"Let's get the fuck out of here," I cried.

"And never come back," he laughed.

I mean, how could we show our faces there again after that. We'd be the talk of the park. They'd be sharing the footage around like a porno. *'Remember the time when that woman squirted her tit milk all over her boyfriend?'*

Clark and I didn't talk about it again. I guess it was just one of those moments, you know? It was special and unique and hard to replicate. I mean, how often does something like that happen spontaneously? It's not like I could just walk up to him and ask him if he wanted to feast on my leaking tits again—as much as I wished that I could.

So we kept it a secret to ourselves and kept away from the theme-park for a few years until our performance on Splash-Canyon had transformed into legend. Shit, you might have even heard about it? Well there's the truth anyway, for what it's worth. I hope you enjoyed it as much as I did.

THE END

Sexorcism : Suckled Brats 10

I didn't know what had gotten into me. It was tough to pin-point the exact moment that I started to lose my mind, but it felt like it definitely started *after* we moved house.

There was just something about our new home that gave off a strange vibe. Things wouldn't stay where you left them; rooms fluctuated wildly in temperature and breezes ran through the corridors with all the windows closed. It was just bizarre. It really gave off an unsettling vibe.

Nevertheless, we plowed on. Mom and Dad went straight back to work and would help me decorating whenever they could. I barely left the house in those opening few weeks and the place started to consume me.

It was my Dad who first noticed the change. He said I'd seemed distant and unfocused. Mom too said she thought my body had changed. She said my breasts had gotten bigger and it was hard to disagree.

By the second month there I was bed-bound. At the time we hadn't linked any of this to the house so holing up in one of its rooms didn't seem like a bad idea. I thought I just needed the rest.

But things didn't change. If anything they got worse. I was breaking out in cold sweats and the whole time the pressure in my tits increased. They felt as though they were about to burst.

Eventually my parents requested the help of Mr. Matthews, a priest. He'd never seen anything like it either and he quickly enlisted the help of Father McShane from Ireland who had seen many more things in his storied life. He immediately knew what was going on.

Even in my stupor I could spot a stud when I saw one and both Mr. Matthews and Father McShane had a certain something to them. Father Ian was well-built and had a command about him that I didn't get from nineteen-year-old guys my own age. He just seemed so *alpha*, you know? Him and Mr. Matthews were like no man I'd ever met before, and they were in very close contact with me all of a sudden.

"Has to be an exorcism," he insisted one day in his Irish twang.

I stared at the both of them from my bed as they surveyed me. "What do you suggest?" Mr. Matthews asked.

"I wonder... " Father McShane said.

He moved around the bed and I followed him with my eyes. I remember wanting to speak to him but I couldn't convince my mouth to form the words.

"She's more than cogent," he said. He snapped his fingers in front of my eyes and I blinked.

"My tits!" I burst suddenly.

The pair of them looked to each other and back at me.

"Oh, Mr. Matthews, my tits!"

Mr. Matthews walked quickly to the door and closed it. "She's been saying that quite often," he said.

"And have you checked them?"

"*Checked them?*"

"If she's talking about them so much, maybe there's something wrong with them?"

"There's nothing wrong with them," Mr. Matthews said, and he motioned to my breasts. "They just seem bigger that's all."

"*Bigger?*"

"Yeah. Sheila, her mother, says they've gotten bigger. I'm ashamed to admit I've noticed it too."

"No shame in that," Father McShane said. "She's a beautiful woman, Florence."

"I just wish we could get her back to her old self."

I felt locked in. I wanted to scream at the pair of them and answer their questions, but whenever I tried I found myself blaring something about my tits.

I wriggled in the bed and pulled the sheets down off myself a ways. I wore a thin, silken night-gown but I still felt as though I was burning up.

"My tits!" I whined again.

The pair of them looked to my chest.

"Are the nipples usually ...?"

"Stiff?" Mr. Matthews answered. "That's not normal, no."

"Interesting."

Father McShane moved closer and looked down on me. He stared into my eyes and I stared back. I felt such an unimaginable lust for him in that moment. When Mr. Matthews's face appeared above me the feeling was shared between the two of them. They looked so much alike and I wasn't thinking straight.

It was as though this terrible affliction was forcing the truth out of me, and that truth was that I had the hots for not only the Priest, but Father McShane too. That kind of thing can get a woman in trouble.

"My tits!" I whined again.

I felt a gradual easing of something through my nipple and I saw their eyes widen above me. The front of my grey gown turned a darker grey at each nipple.

"Is that blood?!" Mr. Matthews asked.

My eyes opened wide, belying my shock, but I couldn't make myself look in the direction I wanted. Instead I studied their faces, trying to determine the cause and severity of this new affliction.

"No," Father McShane said slowly. "No, not blood."

He became animated, rushing around suddenly and pulling out his phone.

"What is it?" Mr. Matthews asked, looking to him. "Is everything okay? Should I call an ambulance?"

"No," he said. "No, don't."

"Then what?"

He swiped quickly over his phone. "It's something—something I've seen. I think I've seen this case before. What's coming out of her chest there isn't blood, but milk."

"Milk?!"

"Yes. There was a case back in Ireland not all that long ago," he said, moving his thumb over his phone-screen. "The patient had—here!" He pointed his phone at Mr. Matthews. "Here it is."

Mr. Matthews peered into the screen, scrunching his eyebrows. As he read each line of the story his mouth opened wider.

"Local woman has spirit milked from her," he read.

"Quite the headline, huh?" Father McShane laughed.

"You can say that again."

"She'd been possessed by the spirit of an old wet-nurse, apparently."

"You think Florence could have too?"

"It's possible, isn't it?" said Father McShane.

"My tiiiiiits!" I wailed, right on cue.

"How did they cure her?" Mr. Matthews asked.

"They drained the spirit from her."

"*Drained*?"

The Father nodded slowly.

"Drained? Like ... *milked?*"

He nodded again. "It worked."

"But that's crazy!"

"But it worked," he shrugged. "I don't have many other ideas."

I could feel the pressure mounting in my chest again. The brief, short release had barely set me at ease at all. I needed much more than that exorcising from me.

"When can we do it?" Mr. Matthews asked.

Father McShane stared at me as I wriggled in clear discomfort. "No time like the present," he said.

"Gosh," Mr. Matthews hushed. "And how do we do it?"

The Father shrugged. "It can't be too hard, can it?"

Mr. Matthews shook his head. "This is so crazy."

"We have to do it. It's the only way."

"Okay," Mr. Matthews said, then he turned to address me, shouting out the instructions as though I was deaf. "We're going to take off your night-gown Florence, okay?"

"My tiiiiits!" I moaned back.

"That settles that," Father McShane said.

Mr. Matthews moved close cautiously. He looked to my expression for a sign that I might suddenly strike and lash-out. Slowly his hand moved down the shoulder-strap of my gown and then he moved across to the other side.

"Just try to relax," Father McShane said, his voice smooth and calm.

Mr. Matthews carefully took down the other shoulder strap. I pushed my chest up and out and he moved the gown lower.

"It's like she's helping me," he said, then he addressed me again. "Are you helping us, Florence? Is this what you want?"

I tried to cry out 'yes,' but it left my mouth as: "Mr. Matthews, my tits!" That was progress I suppose.

"She wants our help," he smiled, and now the both of them scrambled to take down my gown.

They pulled it down off of my tits as I lay there, then both of their eyes spread wide.

"They look so full," Father McShane said.

"They look incredible," Mr. Matthews said. The pair looked at each other curiously.

"We've got a job to do," said the Father, ever the professional.

Mr. Matthews cracked his knuckles. "Right."

He moved his hand steadily downwards and started to apply pressure around my nipple.

"Have you any idea how to do this?" Mr. Matthews asked.

"Can't say I have much experience. Not in my adult life at least."

He pressed at my breasts but nothing happened. If anything the pressure increased.

"Nothing," he cursed. "How the heck are we supposed to get it out?"

Father McShane illuminated suddenly. "Not in your adult life ..." he repeated slowly.

"Huh?"

"How did you used to get milk out of a breast," he said.

I could see where he was heading with this even in my state, but I guess Mr. Matthews was slow on the uptake, or perhaps he didn't want to face the reality of the situation.

"I sucked," he shrugged.

Mr. Matthews stared blankly and Father McShane nodded, urging him the come to the conclusion himself.

The penny dropped. "Oh, Ian. No way. Fuck."

"Only way, Ted," he said as they became more relaxed. "Florence doesn't seem to care."

I was pushing my tits out to the both of them, trying to offer myself up to each of them.

"Help her, Ted," Father McShane said.

Mr. Matthews stood conflicted but the longer he stared at my big tits the more his resolve waned. I could see the angst in his brow flatten out as he surrendered.

"Come on," Father McShane urged.

Mr. Matthews rubbed at his chin. "And you say it's the only way?"

"The only way."

He took a deep breath. "Then here goes."

I remember feeling impossibly excited when he moved his mouth onto me. The sensation of his lips wrapping over my nipple was like nothing I'd ever experienced, and when his tongue teased over the stud I started to lose it.

I writhed in the sheets and my nipples gave up their milk almost instantly. It burst through the tight aperture and Mr. Matthews recoiled. He swallowed and then looked to the Father.

"Do we swallow?" he said.

"The article said it was the only way to banish the spirit," Father McShane said, then his face turned curious. "What do you mean 'we?'"

"She's got two tits, doesn't she?" Mr. Matthews pointed. "It'll surely help quicken the process."

"I couldn't possibly," Father McShane said. I was delirious at the idea of both of them on me.

"Bullshit," Mr. Matthews said. "If I'm doing it then you are too. Jump on."

Mr. Matthews moved back to my breast and he motioned for his friend to settle on the other. Father McShane moved in slowly as Mr. Matthews started to drink down my nectar. I looked down on my breasts and watched as his mouth settled over the nipple too.

He started to suck and my breasts lifted towards his face. The milk fired through and into his mouth and he mimicked Mr. Matthews, swallowing down the ambrosia and filling his mouth with more of it.

I could feel the pressure lessen as the two feasted on me. The more they continued the more I felt able to communicate.

"That feels good," I was finally able to say.

The both of them pulled off my tits and looked up to me. "Florence?"

"Don't stop!" I groaned.

They raced back to my breasts and I held each of them to me. I could feel an unbreakable connection begin to form between us all. It was as though I was nourishing them although the reality was almost the opposite. The more they fed on me the stronger our bond became.

"That's good," I hushed, tickling at their ashen hair.

Mr. Matthews finally pulled off with a smile and beamed up at me. "Better?"

"Almost," I said.

Father McShane came off my tits too. "What else can we do?"

Jeez, I'd never get a moment like this again in my life. In the ecstasy of the occasion I decided to go for it.

"Maybe I can suck on you two in return."

"Florence?" Mr. Matthews said.

"She isn't thinking straight," said Father McShane. "We're men of the cloth."

"I am," I asserted. "And I want to return the favor."

"I'm not so—" Father McShane began.

"Let's not be too hasty," Mr. Matthews said. "We need to make sure she's regained all of her faculties, don't we?"

Father McShane smiled and nodded. "I guess we do."

"So show me," I nodded. "Pull out your cocks for me."

Both of them got on their knees and knelt up on the mattress.

"You're both so hard!" I pointed. They each wore a black cassock but it was obvious.

The pair looked down and then across at each other.

"It's tough to suck a beautiful pair of tits without getting hard," Father McShane confessed.

"I think the same about a nice, delicious cock," I said, licking my teeth.

Mr. Matthews didn't waste time. He pulled off his gown, unbuckled his belt and opened his fly. The Father saw how quick he was moving and started to rush himself, as though it was a race to my mouth.

"We've enough time for both of you," I said with a wry smile.

Mr. Matthews was the first to reveal himself. He pulled his thick cock up and over the top of his pants and it bobbed there, stiffened by the bluish purple veins that searched up towards his smooth crown.

"My gosh," I hushed.

I'd barely had time to drink it in before Father McShane pulled a similarly huge and engorged cock out from his pants too.

The two of them presented themselves proudly and they had every right to.

"Bring those here," I told them.

They hurried up the bed until their cocks hovered above my face. I sat up and leant back on the pillow, then I looked up at Mr. Matthews.

"You first," I told him.

It looked as though he was holding his breath. When I took him in my grip I heard him exhale.

"Good girl, Florence," Father McShane said. I felt so special and wanted in that moment. I transferred the energy into the blowjob and started to slide faster along Mr. Matthews's cock. My neck worked and my head bounced back and forth.

Eventually I sprang all the way off him and left his cock hanging there, wet and wanting more. I turned now to Father McShane and looked right up into his eyes.

"I've always wanted to do this," I told him.

I kept my eyes on him as I opened my mouth and took hold of his cock. I pointed it right at me and swallowed over the tip. Watching the ecstasy flourish on his expression was incredible. It was exactly how I'd pictured it

Mr. Matthews shook his cock close-by, keeping himself stiff. As I feasted back and forth between the both of them I felt the pressure begin to mount again in my breasts.

"My tits," I hushed.

I could sense the alarm in the both of them as they heard that phrase uttered all over again. It was like a call to action. In an instant the both of them were back on my breasts and sucking hard. The nectar flowed into them and I felt the spirit lift again from me.

I started to moan as their tongues pleasured me and eventually my hand found its way to my pussy. I played beneath my night gown, sliding my fingers down along my petals until they were soaked.

"Yes," I moaned softly. I looked to Mr. Matthews. "Put yourself between my legs."

He looked across at the Father for guidance.

"You heard the lady," he said.

"What will you do?" Mr. Matthews asked.

"He'll stay here," I answered. "If he's good I'll let him fuck my tits."

Father McShane swallowed and then looked to his friend. "She's a wild one."

"I'm finding out," Mr. Matthews said.

He took off his the t-shirt that hid under his cossak and Father McShane did the same. Their big barrel chests looked a perfect match.

Mr. Matthews stood up now and took off his pants completely.

"You too," I told Ian.

He moved off the bed and took down his pants. His hard cock shook on his waist as he did so. I looked between the both of them as I continued to play with my pussy.

"Fuck the demons out of me, Mr. Matthews," I told him.

He got onto the bed and put his knees underneath the top of my thighs. I pushed my pussy up to him as he settled there, holding my hips.

"Fuck me," I whined.

He took his cock and pressed it down against my pussy. He felt so hard against it. The underside of his cock rubbed at my clit and then he pulled back to ready himself for the real thing.

Father McShane watched, stroking his cock slowly.

"Watch close," I grinned.

The smirk didn't stay on my lips for long. Suddenly I felt my pussy spread over Mr. Matthews's big crown and my expression turned to a desperate frown of angst. Gosh, it felt so good.

He pushed into me and a wail left me in return. It bounced off the walls and came back to me. Father McShane stared at the union of our flesh, watching his friend slide slowly into me until he had nothing left to give.

"That's it, Mr. Matthews," I whined.

My breasts were letting out a spurt of cream as though they were powered by Mr. Matthews's cock. The deeper he delved the higher the arc of milk became. It spattered back against my chest. Father McShane paid closed attention.

"And you want me between those?" he said.

"Jump on," I told him.

He straddled me and sat over my stomach. His cock rocked on his hips. I held my tits open and waited for him.

"Right there," I said, and I ran a finger along my rib-cage in-between my two leaking tits.

"I think I can do that," Father McShane said.

Mr. Matthews pumped slowly into me, waiting for his friend to find his spot too.

Father McShane settled his cock into the milky liquid. I pushed my tits around him and blanketed him in my cool flesh.

"It's so soft," he hushed.

He started to push through me and a look of delight flourished on my face. "You're fucking my tits!" I burst.

"That I am," he said.

He moved slow and relished the sensation. Shit, so did I. Even against my tits I could feel how stiff he was. He was such a *man* too, you know? At nineteen I was used to guys with less hair that were less sure of themselves, but Mr. Matthews and Father McShane had none of those hang-ups. They exuded confidence. I felt looked-after and safe, which is the perfect combination for a woman who's set her sights on climaxing.

So Mr. Matthews continued to fuck me slowly and Father McShane did the same between my tits. The pair of them used my body just like I wanted and the sensations began to overwhelm me.

My tits leaked their milk into my cleavage and the Father fucked through it, using the nectar as lube.

My pussy was leaking fiercely and I had no lubrication issues down there. Shit, I could hear the smacking of Mr. Matthews's cock as it sloshed in my wetness.

"You're gonna make the both of us come, you know that don't you?" Father McShane said.

My eyes sparkled. "I think I may beat you to it."

Mr. Matthews pumped through me and my pussy let out a spasm. It pinched on his cock and I felt him even bigger inside me. The sudden realization was enough to start a chain of events.

I started to moan, gasping my breaths. As I did so my tits heaved too and Father McShane fucked harder. My nipples fired out their milk and it blasted against the Father's barrel chest. It hung in his hairs and dropped back to me.

"Come for us," he told me, looking down. It felt like an order straight from God.

I remember that look so vividly. There was a yearning in his expression as though he really wanted me to come. I wanted it too, but seeing Father McShane's excitement for it only helped to bring it to the fore.

"Mr. Matthews!" I whined and I let go of my tits and gripped two fistfuls of duvet instead.

Mr. Matthews rocked into me and rode out the pinching of my pussy as it fought to expel him. Finally he popped free, resting his cock against my petals and working it back and forth. I wriggled and writhed and he watched close.

Father McShane beat his cock over me quickly, watching the pleasure spread across my expression. I convulsed beneath them, pinned down on the mattress and with nowhere to go. It was like my own kind of heaven.

Father McShane moved his way off me and clamped over my tits again. I let out a yelp of pleasure as I felt his tongue on me all over again.

My milk burst into him and he gulped down a fresh load of it. Quickly Mr. Matthews found his way to the other one as my climax slowly started to fade from me.

"Keep sucking," I told the both of them. They didn't disappoint.

The milk flowed into them and they swallowed down the evil spirit like it was nothing. They seemed to thrive on it in almost the opposite way to me.

Finally the flow ceased and the both of them looked up at me for their next instruction.

"It's stopped," I hushed. I bit my lip and smiled. "But you don't have to."

The pair of them smiled and then raced around my nipples again. Finally I was ready to give them their last instruction.

"I want your cum," I told them with fresh confidence. I'd never been so sure in myself.

"Where do you want it," Mr. Matthews asked.

"I think it's only right that I watch you both cover my tits, don't you?"

"That sounds fair to me," Father McShane said.

"I can live with that," Mr. Mathews smiled.

They both got up and knelt either side of me. They started to jerk above me and I felt like I was being worshipped. Something about being masturbated over like that by two older guys was indescribable. It was as though they'd both put aside any of their differences in order to pay tribute to me; a tribute of cum.

"Give it me, boys," I urged, tickling at their hanging balls. "I think I've earned it."

"You have," Father McShane strained.

"You've earned this cum," Mr. Matthews agreed.

The two of them pumped fiercely and I watched the muscles in their bodies go tense. Their forearms worked busily and their hands rushed over their big cocks. They seemed to share a similar technique too, sliding their fists along the entirety of their lengths from hilt to tip.

"Cum for me," I hushed, looking between the both of them. They'd never looked so stiff.

The pair began to get animated, as though they were working in tandem to arrive at the exact same time.

"Give it me," I demanded, putting the same amount of vigor into the request that the two of them looked to display.

"Oh, Florence," the Father hushed.

"I'm gonna come," Mr. Matthews strained.

"Come on my tits! Come on my fucking tits!"

Mr. Matthews flurried too, racing his fist along himself so fast that it all became a blur.

My pulse raced and my stomach fluttered with excitement. They were beating themselves to frenzy over me and it was only a matter of seconds before their arrival.

"Come on my tits!" I cried again.

I gasped as the first jet leapt from Father McShane. He let out a groan and then Mr. Matthews joined him, firing the hot cum from his cock and lashing it right across me.

My hands spun on my tits and I worked the cum into them, circling out from the nipple until my entire chest wore their glaze.

Mr. Matthews and Father McShane added to it again and again with fresh ropes. Eventually I let them cascade over me, looking down on myself at their white seed.

The two strained out their release, pumping until the cum hung from the tip of their cocks and dripped out slowly.

I took them in each hand and beat slowly, watching their cocks move and push out the last of their offering. I pinched right to the tip and watched the final beads ease out and slide down onto me. I was a sticky mess of milk and cum, but I wouldn't have had it any other way in that moment.

"I think she's fully exorcised, Ted" Father McShane said, looking across to his friend.

"I know I am," Mr. Matthews laughed.

I started to giggle too. "Well, that was naughty, wasn't it?"

"It was necessary," Father McShane said, raising a finger. "We *had* to do that, okay."

I nodded and tried not to laugh. "Okay."

Mr. Matthews agreed too. "And you feel better, don't you?"

I nodded. "Much, much better."

"So there you have it," the Father declared.

The two of them leant over and kissed my forehead.

"I'll be back with something to clean you up," Mr. Matthews said. "But you make sure you get some rest, okay."

He left and Father McShane sat at the top of my bed beside me. I could feel his eyes wandering over me as I lay there breathing hard.

"You were incredible," he said finally.

"I've wanted that for so long," I confessed.

"Two men?"

"Is that wrong?"

"People would tell you that it is," he said diplomatically. "I don't agree though."

"I'm gonna ignore them."

"I think that's wise," Father McShane said.

He moved to my lips and kissed me for real. I pushed my tongue into his mouth and then felt his hands massaging my tits one last time. The cum slipped over them and felt incredible.

"Thank you, Father" I whispered. "I don't know what I'd have done without you two."

THE END

Lacto-Park : Suckled Brats 11

Mr. Masters knew I was a wild-child. I wasn't too shy about it either. I'd talk openly about my fantasies and conquests when he tutored to the point where it was now normal to him and his wife. I'd been going to his house for years to learn the piano.

He knew me better than anyone, so when my nineteenth birthday rolled around I just knew he'd be getting me the perfect gift.

It took me a while for it to register when I opened the thin envelope and pulled them out.

"Tickets?" I asked.

I looked to Mr. Masters who was beaming. His wife was curiously spying close-by.

"To what?" she asked.

I read them and my face lit up. "Lacto-Park!"

I bounced towards him instantly with open arms.

"Hank!" Mrs. Masters said.

"Thank you, thank you, thank you!" I cried, kissing him over and over.

He laughed, trying his hardest to ignore the intense, angry stare of his wife.

"*Lacto-Park?*"

"I've always wanted to go, Mrs. Masters," I told her, hoping to deflect her anger.

"And I assume you've only got two tickets?" she asked, raising her eyebrows at him. She knew he could be a bit of a lothario.

"It's bonding, Carol," he teased.

"Bonding with your student and her tit milk."

He gasped, mock offended. "Don't be so crass. There's plenty else to do there."

"It's a park centered around making its female attendees lactate, Hank, what else is there to do?"

"The rides!" he said, then he turned to me. "Excited?"

I nodded, bouncing on the spot so excitedly that my tits damn-near hit me in the face.

"Let her be happy, would ya?" Mr. Masters said, trying to turn things back on her. She kind of had a right to be offended, but it was my birthday and I really wanted to go.

As the days passed before our trip Mrs. Masters had relaxed a little. Eventually she was stood on the driveway, waving the both of us off and wishing us a good time.

"No funny-business," she said, pointing a finger at Hank and smirking. "I know you, Hank."

He stopped the car and held up both hands, laughing.

She continued to wave as Mr. Masters reversed off the driveway. Before we knew it we were on our way.

On the trip over we talked about all the things we wanted to do once we got there and all the rides and games that we wanted to try.

"Do you think the pill will work?" I asked him, suddenly fearful.

"It's only ever failed once, to my knowledge," he said.

The park required all of its female residents to take a pill that induced lactation before they entered. Once inside the fun began.

For the moment we steered clear of the inevitable decision that would be coming our way. Mr. Masters would at some point be faced with the prospect of drinking down my milky offering and I wasn't sure how he was going to react. I hoped he didn't heed his wife's words. I wanted all the funny-business I could handle!

We arrived and moved slowly through the queues of cars, following the attendant's instructions until we found a spot. Mr. Masters parked up and we got out of the car to stretch.

"Lovely day for it," I beamed, squinting to the sun.

Mr. Masters wasn't looking at the weather though. He was staring at my chest as I stretched, watching my breasts press against the front of my tank-top. I hadn't bothered to wear a bra. It all seemed kind of pointless.

"Shall we," he said eventually, offering his hand.

I took it and swung his arm as we walked towards the park entrance.

"Thank you so much for this, Mr. Masters," I beamed.

"That's okay, angel."

"I know those tickets aren't cheap."

"Then we have to make sure we enjoy it."

I stopped dead in my tracks when I saw the queue. "Holy shit."

"Never fear," he said valiantly. "I have queue jump!"

He led me forwards and I wore a smile the whole way as we walked down the narrow, empty corridor between the velvet ropes. I could feel the jealous looks of the people who queued alongside us. I tried my best to ignore them, staring forwards adoringly at the back of Mr. Master's head as he led me forwards.

"Hey," he chirped as he arrived at the booking booth. "Reservation for Mr. Masters."

"Certainly," the attendant said. "I see I've got you down here ... a Mr. Hank Masters and a Ms. Maya Croft."

"That's us," Mr. Masters said.

"Please read and sign this consent form," she said.

I did a quick cursory scan. It was basically to absolve themselves of any wrong-doing, should our tit-milking escapades lead to something unsavory. I signed it and Mr. Masters did the same.

"And this is for you, Maya," the lady said. She smirked and pushed forwards a gold plate. In the centre of it was a small, smooth, glossy pill."

"That's it?" I asked.

"That's it," she said. "Would you like some water?"

"I don't think I need it."

The thing was smaller than a pea. I popped it in my mouth and swallowed it down.

"It should start to work within the next few minutes," she said. "Some of our luckier guests find that they have absolute control of their newfound powers."

"Oooh, I hope that's me."

Mr. Masters was looking at me with a curious smile.

"Good luck, Maya," the lady said, "and enjoy the park."

"We will," Mr. Masters said, with just the slightest of suggestive hints.

The lady's gaze lingered on him as he turned to leave. He had a way of making an impact on people without really doing much. I think his movie-star good-looks played a big part, or maybe she was just looking at his ass move in his shorts like I was. Mr. Masters was cute for an older guy.

He led me into the park and then looked back at me as we got inside.

"Is it working?" he asked.

I tried to focus on my tits, searching out any kind of fresh sensation that I hadn't felt before.

"Nothing yet," I concluded.

"Never mind," he said, "let's take a look around."

Everything in the park included milk in some way. I had no idea where they shipped it all in from.

Just then a roller-coaster blasted overhead and the sounds of people cheering could be heard above. Shortly afterwards a scatter of liquid hit the ground.

"Haha," Mr. Masters laughed, and he bent to look at it. It was unmistakable. "They're shooting it from the rides!"

I looked back to the fast-moving carriage and noticed that the women on the front-row had their tits outside of their tops. They were bunched together and firing out their milk all over the park.

"Look at that!" he beamed, and he pointed off to a stall with people at it.

I couldn't believe what I was seeing. They were aiming their milk at empty vases and trying to fill them before a timer ran out. It had cuddly-toys to give away just like a normal park, but the rest was far from fucking normal.

"Can you believe this place?!" he cried.

"It's like an oasis of tit-milk."

We rushed to watch the games and on the way the nearby log-flume splashed down with a ceremony of gleeful wails. A burst of milk crashed over the side of the ride, hitting the floor beside us and being swept into the long drains that ran across the floor all over the park.

"It's everywhere, Mr. Masters!"

He shook his head in disbelief as we continued on our way to the stall. A woman in her forties was happily angling her chest as a fine arc of milk sprayed out everywhere.

She was laughing along with what looked like her husband. The stall's attendant was giving a joyous running-commentary as she went head-to-head with another lady who looked as though she was employed by the park. She wore this gloriously devilish burlesque outfit.

"Roll-up, roll-up," the guy said. "Can you beat The Great Lactini!"

The lady waved as she fired two huge jets of milk from her sumptuous tits. Fuck I was jealous. Just then I felt a tingle.

"I think I feel something," I hushed, looking to Mr. Masters.

His face lit up. "It's working?"

The sensation came at me stronger. I bit my nip and nodded excitedly.

"Think you can beat The Great Lactini?" he asked.

I shrugged.

"If anyone can do it, you can," he said proudly, then he turned to the guy manning the stall. "Here!" he said. "She'd like to try."

He volunteered me forwards.

"Another victim," the guy said, tongue-in-cheek. "What say you, Lactini?"

She took a look at my tits. "She won't fill the vase with that tank-top on, that's for sure."

The previous contestant stepped back, laughing with her husband.

"A valiant effort," the guy said. "Ma'am, would you like to try?"

He offered me the spot in the middle of the table. The Great Lactini stood along the other side of the stall. He set up two fresh vases.

"Go on," Mr. Masters urged.

"What if they don't work?"

"Can she just test them out quickly?" he asked.

"Be our guest," the man said.

It was no time to be bashful. I whipped up my tank-top and my big tits fell out underneath them.

"A fine pair," The Great Lactini said, smiling. She looked to be around thirty and was more than comfortable in her own skin. She wore a playful smirk that put me at ease.

Mr. Masters was staring at my ripe tits. "They look full," he said, mesmerized.

"They *feel* full," I told him.

I turned away and tried to focus on the sensation and set it free. I hoped I had the skills to control it all.

"You can beat her, honey, I know it," he said, massaging my shoulders.

When he touched me a fine jet of milk sprayed out.

"It's working!" I told him.

He was just as overjoyed as I was. When I turned back to the stall I could see my elation was shared amongst its staff.

"So you can control it," Lactini said. "Show me what you can do."

I put my game-face on. The stall's attendant reset the clock and made sure the vases were on their marks. They were a meter or so in front of both of us.

"On your marks," he said, and I shifted my weight. "Get set."

"You can do this," Mr. Masters said, squeezing my shoulder.

"Go!"

I focused on my tits and the spray began, but The Great Lactini had already started. Not only had she started, but her flow had immediately entered the vase and it was starting to fill up.

"No match for me," she cackled, playing-up her villainous role.

"You can do it, sweetie," Mr. Masters said.

I scrunched my face and took hold of my other breast. A stream left it too and I angled it towards the vase, filling it at twice the speed.

There was a look of genuine alarm in The Great Lactini's face as the level of milk rose to match hers.

"Cheap tricks!" she scoffed, and she too used her other breast to fill the container.

She was just too good. She raced ahead of me until the vase was overflowing. She locked her gaze on me and kept on filling her container without looking.

"Easy," she said.

"You did great," Mr. Masters said, massaging my neck. "I'm proud of you."

I stopped the flow and the milk dripped off my nipples like the end of a garden-hose.

"You win this round, Lactini," I said, joining in with the act. I held up a finger and turned away from her.

"Come back when you think you're ready," she challenged.

I took one look back, frowning and looking her up and down. Fuck, she was a sight. I hoped to have a job just like hers one day.

"You'll beat her one day," Mr. Masters said, and he patted my ass as we walked away.

There was a building all on its own now in front of us. At first sight it looked like a public toilet, with a men's sign on one-side and a women's sign on the other, but instead of the regular bland affair there was a neon sign atop it. *The Milk Hole*, it read, and below it smiling revelers left through the doors, wiping their mouths and smirking.

"What the hell is that?" I asked, pointing.

Mr. Masters spied it too. "I don't know."

We walked to the building and stood outside it between the two doors.

"Looks like we have to split up," Mr. Masters said, looking to me. "I'll wait here. You go ahead."

"You're not joining me?"

"My wife would kill me," he said. "I promised no funny-business and, uh, that looks pretty funny."

"I wanna see what's inside."

"Okay," Mr. Masters said. "I'll meet you out here after?"

"Sure."

I walked off towards the women's entrance.

"Enjoy," he waved.

I turned to walk inside and a giggling, big-breasted blonde stumbled out. "You're gonna love it," she laughed.

I was more than a little intrigued. As I stepped inside I noticed it wasn't unlike a women's restroom. There were stalls on one side running the length of the room and mirrors were on the wall opposite with basins in front of them. Unlike a women's bathroom, though, I could hear the sensual, unmistakably sexual moans from the people in the stalls. Women's heady sighs and men's groans filled the place. It sounded like a brothel.

Gosh, it was so naughty, but still I found myself intrigued. I moved down the row of stalls, checking the locks until I found a green one.

I opened the door and inside there were two holes ahead of me at chest-height. Another hole sat below, nearer waist-level. It looked like the whole wall was adjustable.

"My God," I whispered. It was like a glory-hole but for tits. I moved forwards and set my breasts in the holes, trying out the fit.

I adjusted the walls a little and then suddenly I felt a suck on my tits. I recoiled backwards in shock. For whatever reason I wasn't expecting that. I could see the sensual lips of a guy in the stall opposite.

"Sorry," I said nervously. "You caught me by surprise."

"That's alright," the voice replied, and it was quite obviously Mr. Masters. I didn't say anything. I thought that if I acknowledged that it was him the fun might stop there.

"Think I can carry on?" he asked, and he wore a naughty smirk.

"I don't see a problem with that."

I put my tits back to the hole, resting them on the cool wood. This time I felt a hand fondle them. Around me women groaned and moaned, doing God-knows-what in their own stalls.

"That's good," I whined, looking up at the ceiling.

I felt his stubble against me as he rubbed his face to my tits, then I felt his mouth again clamp over the nipple. I focused on my breasts again and fired a warm jet of cream into him. I could hear his appreciative hum come from the men's stall opposite, along with gulping as he swallowed down my nectar.

"It's so sweet," he said, and then his mouth raced back on to the flow.

I closed my eyes and pictured him on the other side of the stall. I could imagine his serene face as he sucked on me, his eyes closed and his mouth working hard to draw the nectar from me.

I pumped it into him lovingly, feeling a bond between us grow. Along with that I felt a unique kind of power, as though I was a giver-of-life.

I listened to his groans as I fed him. I could hear too the jangling of a belt-buckle, mingled with the heady cries from the adjacent stalls. Everyone in there was having fun, and I'd be damned if I wasn't going to join them.

I moved my hand down to my jeans, pushing against the crotch. I could feel the warmth from my pussy below as the blood rushed to it.

I felt something against my hand and pulled back to look down, doing an immediate double-take. I could scarcely believe it, but it was there as clear as day. Mr. Masters' hard cock was venturing from his stall into mine, and it looked delicious.

"Oh my," I cooed.

I looked to the hole where my tits had been and saw his chest in its place. His navy-blue t-shirt really gave the game away that it was him, if it wasn't already obvious.

"Is that for me?" I asked.

"If you want it," he said and his cock bounced as though he was shaking it.

My hands moved to it and I tickled him gently, listening to him moan.

"That's it," he said, and he pushed more of himself through into my stall.

I stroked softly, bouncing the tip on my fingers. Slowly I got to the floor. I could see his open shorts pressed against the wood. His huge cock hung there, waiting to be claimed.

"Let me taste you," I hushed, and I kissed the head.

Mr. Masters groaned. "Oh, Maya."

I opened over him and sent his thickness into my mouth. It was so hot to be feeling his stiffness like that. He felt hard against my tongue as I slid it back and forth along the underside of his dick.

"That's so good, Maya."

I kept my head in place and he started to fuck my mouth slowly. He eased back from the wall of the store and I felt him slide back out of my mouth. He pushed forwards and his dick slid slowly to the back of my throat, tickling me and testing my gag-reflex.

I kept myself there on my knees for the moment. In the stall beside me I could see the feet of a woman in a similar pose and I could hear a similar noise. It was the wet smacking of lips as she sucked ravenously on her man.

"That's such a beautiful cock," I whispered, kissing his smooth head over and over.

I could sense his heady arousal beyond. His cock was stiffer than any I'd known and the veins were so pronounced that I could feel them against my tongue as I licked him.

Finally I pulled back and beat my fist over him, studying his dick like it was a work-of-art as it moved in my hand.

"That's it, Maya," he said, and then he said something that made my whole body turn tight with adrenaline. "Put me inside you."

My mouth hung open in shock. A smile blossomed on my face and I let out a laugh of disbelief.

"Is that what you want?" I asked.

"Yes," he answered quickly. "I want you bad."

Mr. Master's cock was pulled back away from me. His hand came through to replace it and he searched ahead. I walked on to him and he gripped the inside of my thigh. His hand moved upwards and I watched it.

I looked to the holes for my tits and saw nothing but the back of the door of Mr. Masters' stall. He was crouched now and reaching through to touch me.

His hands moved up my legs and he went to my crotch, rubbing it and getting me excited. I closed my eyes and whimpered, feeling the wetness break out of me.

I popped the button of my jeans and he grabbed down the zipper. He was stroking impatiently as I downed my jeans. His hands quickly found my crotch again and this time he moved the fabric aside to get at me for real.

I gripped the rim of the hole ahead of me and let out a grunt. I'd had people touch me before, but knowing that it was Mr. Masters doing the touching made the whole event ten-times more sinful. I fed off the debauchery of it all. My body was shaking immediately and I could feel the excitement ramping up inside of me. I felt like I could come any second.

"That's what I want," he said.

He thrusts his fingers deep into me and I folded over in a joyous moan. He was inside me. His fingers pulled back against my spongy g-spot. As he excited me my tits started to leak their milk, this time without any effort. The nectar spilled all down me and ran onto his hand as it worked it through me quickly.

I moved forwards and let his fingers do their work. My mouth hung open in a silent moan and my tits fired out their bounty against the wall of the stall. It dripped down messily.

Finally my voice broke through and a joyous, unmistakable moan of ecstasy escaped me as I started to come.

I rose on my tip-toes and my whole body tightened and shook. Mr. Masters felt my pussy squeeze him but he kept himself inside me for now. His thumb rattled my clit and finally I broke away, unable to stand it any longer. I was just too sensitive.

"Yes!" he said, and I could sense a smile in his voice.

I started to giggle, drawing long breaths in between. "Holy shit, Mr. Masters."

"That was hot," a voice beyond said.

I put a hand to my mouth and stifled my laughter. Mr. Masters' hand came through the breast-holes and he offered me his fingers. They were soaked with my juices.

I took a hold of his wrist and looked at them, then I plunged them deep into my mouth and tasted my sweetness.

"Good girl," he said. "Good girl, Maya."

To hear his encouragement was like nothing else. Before now it had been reserved only for his classes. Now though his encouragement was for something much more sinful and it left me with a warm internal glow.

I cleansed his fingers of my sweet cum and then pushed them back through the hole. I pressed my tits to it and his mouth raced onto me again.

This time he sucked with much more passion and intensity and my tits gave up even more of their milk. It sprayed into him and Mr. Masters swallowed it down. He pulled back and squeezed them with his hands, milking me like I was his prize cow. Fuck knows where the milk was going in the stall beyond, but there was a lot of it.

"I want you to fuck me," I told him now.

"I want it too, Maya."

"Fuck me, Mr. Masters," I begged. "Fuck me!"

I pulled away and turned my back to the wall. I bent over and pushed my ass back to meet the hole.

Without warning his cock spread through me as he put it through the hole. I hadn't anticipated him to be so quick on the draw. I gasped and my back straightened as he filled me. He was big.

"Oh, Maya," he groaned. "You're so fucking wet."

He pushed into me and I felt him fill me completely. I pushed back to try and fit even more of him inside me but my cervix had other ideas. He teased at it, venturing deeper than anyone I'd ever known.

"Fucking give it me," I whined, and I pinched at my tits.

The milk flowed out of me as he pounded forwards. If it wasn't for the wall between us he'd have bounced me right against the door, such was the force of his thrust.

He fucked me like an animal, spreading his cock through me over and over and coating it in a thick film of my cum.

"Mr. Masters!" I strained, biting at my arm as I reached forwards and pressed against the door.

My tits dripped in a long flow. The milk pattered on the floor beneath me and I looked down. I saw a mop-head cleaning the stall beside me and I got a sudden reminder of just how fucking crazy Lacto-Park was.

"I want your cum," I told him. "I want your fucking cum."

"You better give it her," a female voice said in another stall.

"She's getting it all," Mr. Masters said in response.

"Give it to me," I whined. "Give it to me!"

I didn't think it was possible, but somehow Mr. Masters increased his tempo. My pussy jerked his thickness and squeezed tight around it, trying to milk him for all he was worth as he'd done to me.

"I'm gonna fucking come," he cried, uncaring of our fellow patrons.

"You better," the same woman said. "Give it to her, baby."

It gave the moment and added tinge of naughtiness, if it even needed one.

"Give her that fucking cum," the woman said.

He railed into me and his groans rose. They hit a peak and finally he let out a long wail that was unmistakable in origin. As he did so I felt the first warm blast of his love.

"There you go!" the woman said. "Take that cum."

And take it I did. As Mr. Masters throbbed and filled me my tits spurted too, matching the spasm of his cock. Each time he shot a lashing up into me my breasts fired their milk at the floor. I watched it flow into the drains, all milky, white and pure—unlike what the two of us were doing.

"Oh, Maya," he whimpered, and more of his seed poured into me.

It started to flow back out of my pussy with nowhere else to go. It stringed to the floor messily and I watched it mingle with the milk, creating a kind of marble effect.

"All your cum," I told him. "I want it all, Mr. Masters!"

"Every drop," the lady said. She seemed just as invested as him and I.

Mr. Masters did as the audience requested. He fed each and every last drop into me and then pulled out quickly. I heard him fall against a wall and let out a chuckle before sighing happily.

"And he's spent," the lady said, and the three of us laughed.

"Oh, gosh," I hushed to myself, standing up and feeling his cum slide down my legs towards my panties.

I put a hand over my mouth, trying not to think too hard about what we'd just done. We'd only been in the park for forty minutes, but already its energy had infected us.

"Good girl," he said, and I heard him buckle himself up.

I pulled up my panties and trapped his seed inside. It turned my crotch warm, but I didn't care. The sensation was a sinful reminder of what we'd done.

Mr. Masters left the stall and I left mine, fixing myself in the mirror briefly. The bathroom's janitor leant on her mop, smiling.

"Sounded like you enjoyed yourself?" she asked.

"You can tell?" I laughed.

I tried to look as presentable as possible and then I went for the exit. I could see why so many people left there smirking.

I walked out of the doors and saw Mr. Masters standing there waiting as though nothing had happened. He wore a naughty smile himself.

"Have fun in there?" he asked.

"I did," I told him. "I met an amazing guy ..."

"You'll have to tell me all about him," Mr. Masters said coyly.

He put his arm out and I fell into it, leaning against him. We walked away from the building and in the direction of one of the roller-coasters.

"What do you think?" he said, watching the carts fly around above us.

"I think it could be my second-favorite ride of the day," I smiled.

THE END

His Secret Milking Rack : Suckled Brats 12

Kelsey and Anthony had split about a year ago. I hadn't lived with them long when it happened but I'd stayed there with Anthony.

Kelsey and I didn't always see eye-to-eye, but when she asked me to search the attic for some of her old photographs I wasn't going to say no.

The attic had always been off-limits but I never really had a reason to go up there anyway. I figured it was just to do with how dangerous it was pulling down the ladder to get up there and everything, so I just never really thought about. Until now.

Anthony was out in the garden, which is where he spent most of the sunny daylight hours since Kelsey had left. It looked immaculate, but he couldn't stop tending to it. I guess there are worse ways to pass the time. Maybe it's just what forty-year-olds did, who knows?

I grabbed a chair out of my room and set it under the attic hatch, climbing on it and reaching for the handle above me. I gave it a pull and then what felt like a set of hydraulics opened the hatch the rest of the way.

A ladder sat on the underside of the hinged opening. It was folded over a couple of times. I gave it a quick look-over and then tugged on the bottom rung of the outer set of steps. It all flowed open wonderfully and looked so easy. I couldn't believe Anthony was worried about *this*. Even a child could have done it.

The ladder went all the way down to the hallway floor, clicking into place. I got off the chair and gave it a waggle to test it. It felt like it wasn't going anywhere.

I walked a little ways down the hallway to the staircase. I took a look out the window to see Anthony tending to the flowers in one of his raised beds. I took out my phone and read Kelsey's message again.

'The white box in the far corner of the room. DO NOT touch anything else.'

Jeez, that was an intriguing text. How are you gonna say something like that and expect someone to listen? Shit, perhaps she knew that there was no way I'd pay attention.

Anyway I climbed my way up the ladder and peered into the attic. It was fairly bright up there with some light coming in from one of the windows but I flicked the switch close to the hatch anyway and whole room illuminated just that bit more. A girl alone in the attic wants as much light as she can get!

The first thing that struck me when I rose up into the room was how clean it was. Anthony had kept it immaculate. Everything was all neat-and-tidy around the edges. I scanned the far corner and saw the box that Kelsey had spoken about.

I walked over to it and knelt on the wood-boarded floor. I opened the box to check and a photo of her and Anthony sat on the top of a pile of many others. From their hairstyles it looked like it was taken back in the nineties. You could see the love and laughter in their eyes. That had faded a long time ago.

I took a hold of the box and turned back for the attic-hatch. Something across the other side of the room caught my eye immediately. It looked kind of like a gurney, but neither Kelsey nor Anthony was in the medical profession. Straps hung off it all about the place and it also had these curious crank-handles positioned on its side.

I set the box down at the exit of the attic and walked over to the strange contraption. It was made of polished metal with leather straps set across it like a hammock to hold whoever lay in it. More straps hung down off the sides. I couldn't make head-nor-tail of it.

"Jessica?" I heard suddenly.

"I'm up here," I shouted.

"I told you not to go up there!" Anthony said, and then his head appeared, rising up through the hole in the middle of the room. He turned around and spotted me. His expression turned cold.

"What are you doing over there?" he asked.

"What's this?" I toyed with one of the straps and looked at him.

"Don't touch it. Don't touch that."

He hopped up the ladder quickly and took a few quick steps towards me. "Don't touch that," he said again.

I knew immediately that it was something important. Telling me not to touch it was as good as Kelsey telling me not to look around up here.

"What is it?" I asked again.

"It's not for you, that's what it is."

"Jeez, you're protective."

"What are you doing up here?"

"Kelsey asked me to fetch some photos," I said, pointing to the white box.

"Oh," was all Anthony said.

"What is this? Like a stretcher?"

"It's nothing."

"It's clearly *something*. Come on. What's the harm in telling me?"

He looked like he didn't want to play any games. I thought I might have pushed him too far, but to my surprise he actually answered me. It was *not* the answer I was expecting.

"It's a sex-rack," he said.

"A ... *what?*"

"A sex-rack," he repeated. "Kelsey and I used to use it."

I was dumbfounded. "Sorry, it sounded like you just said it was a *sex-rack?*"

He looked off distantly. "I'd strap her into that and milk the life out of her."

"Anthony!"

"What? You asked!"

"I didn't think *that* would be the answer. You used to *milk* her?"

He leant over and grabbed the leather. "These straps used to go over and around her. They'd tighten across her skin and bunch up her tits until they were nice and ripe."

I wanted to shout and stop him, but another part of me wanted to hear the rest. This was a fucking revelation. Nothing this exciting ever happened in our family.

"I can't believe she produced for so long," he said. He seemed to be thinking aloud. "It was like it was just *always* in her, you know?"

He stared off into the middle-distance.

"You used to *milk* Kelsey?"

"Once a week without fail," he said.

"Yuck!"

He started to laugh. "There was nothing yuck about it. It was the most exciting time of our marriage." His nostalgic smile faded. He looked back at the box of photographs. "Go on," he said. "I'll carry those down."

He left through the hatch and grabbed the box, taking it down the ladder. I lingered at the edge of the hole, looking back to the sex-rack. I tried to imagine Kelsey in it. I tried to imagine myself in it.

"Come on," Anthony said.

***

For the next few days it was all I could think of. I'd go to sleep and stare at the ceiling at where I knew the sex-rack was above me. I'd fantasize about exploring it, but I had no-one to explore it with.

It was like a whole swathe of revelations had been dropped on me at once. You never really think too much about older people having sex, but now it was all I *could* think about. Kelsey and Anthony didn't just have regular sex either; he strapped her into that device and really went to town. *I wonder how it felt to be strapped in and helpless like that.*

My fingers toyed at my panties and I felt my pussy turn sodden at the thought as I lay there in bed. It was late at night but I didn't care. The sex-rack was beckoning me towards it like some kind of magnet.

I left my bed and walked out into the quiet hall. Anthony's room was at the end of the house. The loft-hatch was just before its entrance.

I tip-toed carefully down the hall-way in my night t-shirt and panties. The wind blew outside. As I approached Anthony's door I heard the soft snoring coming from within. *Perfect*, I thought.

I hurried back to my room as quietly as I could, grabbing the chair. I set it beneath the hatch and stood up on it. I paused again and listened for his snoring. When it caught my ear I turned the latch and let the hydraulics do their thing again.

In no time at all I was back in the attic. I switched on the light and stared across at the sex-rack again. It sat there ominously with all of that sordid history emblazoned in its metal and leather. Fuck, if objects could talk I think that'd have some stories to tell.

I fingered at the straps. They were worn slightly around the little puncture holes where they fastened like a belt. My heart raced as fast as my mind. I closed my eyes and explored under my t-shirt, finding my crotch all warm.

"Anthony," I hushed.

My eyes gasped open. *What was I saying?*

A voice startled me. "Jessica?"

I turned back to the attic-hatch. Anthony stood up out of it and looked across at me. He was in his tight boxer-briefs.

"What are you doing up here again?" he asked.

I didn't say anything. Instead I stared at him—at his body. He was well put-together, even for a guy in his forties. I hadn't seen him like this in a long time and in my heady, aroused state I started to think things about him that a nineteen-year-old woman probably shouldn't.

"The sex-rack, Jessica? Again?"

"I want to know how you use it," I said.

He came over, grabbing some of the leather and giving a half-assed explanation.

"You strap the hands here, the legs here and then the other straps go across the chest. The crank moves the rack up and down." He walked back to the hatch. "Now come on. Out of here."

"I mean ... show me for real."

I stared at him to let him know I was serious. Suddenly he didn't look tired anymore. His eyes spread wide and he stared back.

"What do you mean 'for real?'"

"Strap me in it," I asked him. I pulled the contraption out from the wall.

"Will you go to sleep then?"

I nodded.

"Okay," he said.

He walked over the sex-rack and started spinning the crank. One end of the stretcher dropped to the floor and the other rose to the ceiling.

"Lie against that," he said. He used his foot to put a brake on the wheels. "It'll hold you."

I turned back and leant against it. Anthony looked at my t-shirt.

"Should I take this off?" I asked.

"Do you have anything on under there?"

I didn't. "I want to try it properly though," I told him.

He sighed. "Take it off."

I tried not to smile as I rushed the t-shirt up over my head. Anthony tried to look away but my big tits were very demanding of attention. I lay back against the cool leather. He bent to my feet and strapped my ankles in, then he came up and strapped my wrists to the side of the frame too.

"Mmm," I groaned, wriggling. "That feels good."

"We've not even started," he laughed.

I looked down at his boxer-shorts and noticed the unmistakable erection bulging against his underwear.

"This awakening something inside you, Anthony?"

He looked at me and then looked down. He let out a soft laugh. "I guess I'm conditioned to get turned-on by this thing."

"You're not the only one."

We shared another moment as he looked into my eyes. Before it became something weird Anthony started to turn the crank and suddenly I started falling back. The leather strappings caught me, holding my weight as my tits fell off to each side of my chest. I watched the room turn until I was staring right up at the angled ceiling.

He came to the side of the stretcher and looked down. "Feeling good?"

I nodded. "What's next?"

He smirked. "That's my girl."

He strapped more leather over my chest, fixing the belts tight. I could feel the mounting pressure in my tits as the bindings tightened around them.

"Just like Kelsey," he said, looking down on me proudly.

"And how did you used to treat her in this position?" I asked.

I lay there helpless. He could do anything he wanted to me. Fuck, I hoped he would.

"You really want to know?" He asked.

I nodded.

Suddenly he turned the crank again and I let out a little yelp. This time my feet rose to the ceiling and my head dropped to the floor. I could feel the blood rush to it.

Anthony stopped turning the crank. My head was about two feet from the floor. The whole room was upside-down now. I watched his hairy legs move around the stretcher until he was stood near my head.

Without a word he downed his boxer-shorts and suddenly I was looking at his hard upside-down cock. The underside pointed up to the ceiling and his delicious, smooth balls hung underneath. My heart pounded against my rib-cage. I couldn't believe what was happening, but I wasn't about to stop it.

"That's a sight," I groaned as Anthony stepped out of his underwear.

His cock wobbled on his hips. He took a grip of his length and then pointed it down towards me. His body approached and blocked out the light. Suddenly all I could see was cock. I felt it touch my lips and my mouth opened in compliance.

His stiffness burst inside me and I let out a groan. He was in full control when it came to how much of his cock he wanted to give me. He pushed it right to the top of my throat. I breathed hard out of my nose then he pushed just that bit further, easing the tip of his cock into my throat.

I felt it spread over him and he let out a terrific moan of pleasure. It felt like he was coiled spring of lust. It must have been a year since he'd been intimate with anyone after Kelsey left. I wasn't exactly experienced myself. The most I'd ever done was touch one of my friend's dicks on a dare and yet here I was with Anthony's mature cock teasing at the top of my throat.

He dragged himself out of my mouth and I let out a gasp. My spit hung off the tip of his cock. I thought he was done but then he came back. This time he placed his balls against my mouth. I opened my lips around them and sucked them like they were hard candy. Anthony's deep groan made my pussy salivate. I'd never heard him call out in pleasure like that and it was all because of me. What a fucking privilege. What a gift.

As I sucked on him I felt his hands come to my tits. He massaged them gently. They felt so fucking sensitive. He touched them softly, circling his fingers carefully around my nipples that sprang to attention quickly. I'd never been so *charged*. It was tough to describe. It was like I was holding back a flood.

He gave my breasts another squeeze. I felt a unique sensation. Anthony stepped back and I gasped off his balls. I could feel something wet on my chest, but I wasn't sure if it was just the burning of the tight bindings.

"Milk," he said.

"Huh?"

I tried to lift my head to look. He turned the crank again until the stretcher was parallel to the floor. He stood naked beside me and marveled at my tits. I looked down at them. A bead of pure white hung on my nipple.

"Is that ...?" I began.

"Milk!" he rejoiced.

I watched his mouth drop to my tits. He licked off the drop of nectar and then clasped his lips around my nipples. I felt the pressure as he sucked and then I felt the beautiful release as a bounty of milk that I didn't even know I had rushed through my nipples.

He hummed contently, swallowing down my offering gladly. I watched close. His shoulder rocked as he jerked himself. He was clearly enjoying the nourishment.

"That feels so good," I hushed, and my head fell back.

I closed my eyes and focused on his busy mouth. I could feel his stubble grazing at the soft skin of my breasts. His tongue wound around my nipple and then he changed breasts, sucking the nectar from the other side now with just as much effect.

"I didn't even know," I moaned.

"Me either, baby," he said, and his voice sounded so loving and euphoric.

"Do I taste good, Anthony?"

He didn't answer. Instead he took a big suck of my tits. He moved off and then brought his lips to my mouth.

I put my lips to him and opened my mouth, startling slightly as the cream rushed through between us. I swallowed it down and then felt his tongue writhing against my own. I kissed him back and tasted the sweet cream that was fresh and warm from my tits. It tasted *good*.

He broke away and smiled down, smoothing the hair out of my face. "You're beautiful," he told me.

Fuck, I felt *adored*. I'd always felt a kind of love from him but now I felt lust, both from and *for* him. He stood beside me with a cock so stiff that it felt like it could smash granite.

"Put it in my mouth again," I moaned.

"Here," he said. "Don't swallow."

He sucked the milk from my tits again and then moved it from his mouth to mine with another messy kiss.

He turned the crank and I held the warm nectar in my mouth as instructed. Anthony moved around and then pushed his cock into my mouth to bathe it in my ambrosia.

I moved my tongue around him and sloshed the milk around his smooth, swollen crown. Anthony's moans were so laden with eroticism that I started to tremble because of them. I could feel my pussy tingle with delight. The fact that I couldn't satisfy the urge to touch it was turning me on even more.

I swallowed down my cream and Anthony pulled his cock out from me again. He turned the crank some more and my head moved closer to the floor. The blood rushed down with gravity and my head felt light and tingly. I could see his feet but not much else.

I felt him push my panties upwards and bare my pussy. It must have been so soaked but it was about to get even wetter. He moved close and then I felt his mouth on me. It was unmistakable. His tongue worked over my folds and he scooped out my juices. I burst with a groan immediately. It rattled the whole house.

I started to tremble so violently that the whole sex-rack shook. Anthony kept his mouth on me, tonguing beautifully at my folds and my clit. I'd never had anything like that done to me before and it was an immediate improvement to my quiet, late-night fingerings.

His tongue washed my pussy of all of its juices and the whole thing swelled terrifically. My tits leaked their nectar as the orgasm grew within me. The nectar streamed down over my breasts and ran up my neck. I felt it on my face.

"Come for me," Anthony said, and I took heed of his words immediately.

My pussy spasmed and my older friend ate it messily, slurping on my flesh and really giving me all of his mouth. I throbbed on him, wriggling in the bindings but with no hope of moving anywhere. I'd never had a climax like it. My head was already light and this felt like it was damn-near floating off. I almost passed out from the sheer joy of it.

He pulled his mouth off me and my pussy continued to contract and relax slowly. I whimpered like a trapped creature—shit, I guess I was.

He turned the crank and leveled me out again. I breathed hard and deep, trying to drop back down to reality. If I woke up suddenly in my bed I wouldn't have been surprised. The whole thing felt like a fucking dream.

"Oh, Anthony," I moaned. "Please fuck me. I want you to fuck me for real."

"You don't know what you're saying," he said.

"I do, Anthony. I do. Please fuck me."

Again he spun the crank and this time I faced the right way up. I stared ahead at him when he came back in front of me. He jerked himself a few feet away, looking me up and down. I was a mess of milk and it continued to tease its way out of me.

He reached forwards and squeezed one of my breasts. They let out a burst of milk that rolled down my body.

"You're my naughty girl, aren't you?"

"I am."

"Say it."

"I'm your naughty fucking girl."

"Yes, you are, baby."

He stepped into me and put his mouth close to mine. I reached forwards to kiss him but he moved away with a laugh.

"Don't tease," I whined.

"How's this for teasing?" he said.

He put his cock between my legs and set it against my pussy. I stared down, bound and unable to move. I'd have snatched his cock and put it inside me if I could, but instead I had to watch as he stroked the head of his cock back and forth along my folds.

"That feel good?" he asked, and we both watched now.

I clenched my fists and let out a grunt. "Please fuck me, Anthony," I moaned.

He angled his cock up and then thrust forwards, pressing his whole body against me.

"Oh, Anthony!" I burst, feeling his stiffness rush up into me.

He snatched my virginity with ease. My sticky pussy sucked tight around him. His lips touched mine and we started to kiss again, but if I'm honest I couldn't focus on that.

Instead *he* kissed me. My mouth hung open and I trembled. I couldn't believe what we'd just done, but I didn't want it to end at that.

"Oh, Anthony," I groaned, kissing him back finally.

He pulled back and started to fuck me standing up. I hung there in the tight leather bindings, motionless apart from the jolt that would surge through me each time he thrust his hips against me.

He pressed his bare chest to my tits and I felt the milk squeeze out and slide down between us. The embrace was wet, messy and creamy. I can see why Anthony didn't put down carpet in the attic like Kelsey had wanted.

He kissed me passionately and fucked me hard, slamming against me and putting the brakes of the sex-rack to the test. It wobbled but didn't move. My pussy gripped tight around him and his cock felt huge. I was surprised at how easily I'd taken him, but there were many more things crazier about that night.

"Can you come inside me?" I asked him when our lips parted.

He nodded and pushed his forehead to mine. "Is that what you want?"

I nodded back. "I want it so bad."

"Tell me what you want," he said, and he upped his pace.

"I want your cum."

"Tell me where you want it!"

"I'm my pussy!"

"Yes!" he grunted, upping his pace.

"I want your fucking cum in my pussy," I told him.

"Yes!"

Each time I spoke Anthony called back more excitedly, upping his pace and fucking me frantically.

"I want your fucking cum in my tight pussy, Anthony!"

"Yes!"

He worked his hips hard. His cock slipped through my tight O and then he rose up on his tip-toes and pushed himself deep.

"Give me your cum!" I whined.

Finally he exhaled. I felt his cock throb and then I felt the burst of heat blast into me. It warmed me instantly and as one bout of thick, white cream entered me another exited through my nipples.

My tits leaked steadily as he began his stroke anew. He moved softly through me, shooting more of his cum into me until the texture of his cock turned slippery. It eased through me beautifully, rocking without friction and as stiff as ever.

"Oh, Anthony," I hushed. I wanted to embrace him so bad and hold him to me.

He bent his back and sucked on my tits as his cock continued to move through my tightness slowly. Finally he pulled out and I felt his cum dribble down my leg. It was all warm, just like the tit-milk from earlier that had made white tracks down the curves of my body.

He breathed heavily, sucking one last bout of milk into his mouth and swallowing it down. He leant against me, kissing at my shoulder and then my face.

He found my lips and we had one last kiss. It felt so passionate. I hung onto it as long as I could but Anthony moved away eventually.

He unfastened the straps that bound my tits. The pressure released and they dropped back against me. Then he unfastened the straps on my wrist. Instantly I reached out to touch him. My hands stroked down over his muscled chest and then teased at his spent cock.

"That was hot," I told him.

He bent to the floor and didn't say a word. He unfastened the shackles at my feet and when he stood up I fell forwards against him.

He took my weight and held me. We hugged tight and I nestled in his shoulder.

"That was hot, Anthony. I want to do that again."

"We'll see," he said, and his voice sounded tinged with regret.

"We have to do it again," I told him.

"We'll see, Jessica. Now come on. It's late."

He stepped back into his underwear and pulled them up. I stood naked in the middle of the room, my tits steadily dripping milk and my pussy dripping its cum.

"Put these back on," he said, and he handed me my panties. "Trap that cum inside."

I bit my lip at how naughty that sounded. I stepped into them and pulled them up to my pussy. I could feel his sticky cum spread against me.

He handed me my t-shirt. As I went to put it on he stopped me. He moved his face quickly to me again and sucked on my tits as though he was kissing them goodbye.

"You'll see them again," I told him with a wry smile. He tried not to smile back.

"Come on," he said, and he showed me to the ladder.

I descended, looking up at him as I did so. I could make out his terrific cock in his boxer-briefs and I reminded myself that it had just been inside me.

"I'm gonna clean up," he said, looking down through the hatch. "Go to bed, Jessica, okay? We'll talk in the morning."

I gave him a gentle wave and then walked down the hallway. As I lay in bed I could hear him moving above me. I wore a smile and a glow that burned bright until the next morning. I hardly slept but I didn't feel tired. I felt more awake than I ever had in my whole life. I couldn't wait until our next visit to the sex-rack.

THE END

His Secret Milking Rack 2 : Suckled Brats 13

Anthonycame down to breakfast later than usual. I gave him a smile as he arrived in the kitchen but it wasn't returned. He didn't give me anything at all in fact. He went straight to the counter and started fixing some cereal.

"Morning," I tried.

"Morning," he said back flatly.

He stood opposite at the breakfast bar and poured his milk. It was tough to picture him as the guy from the night before, but it didn't stop me from trying. I still had that imagine of him over me with his big cock on display.

"About last night ..." I began.

"I don't want to talk about it."

"Anthony! Come on, it's too important to ignore, isn't it?"

"Drop it, Jessica."

"We can't just drop it! It happened didn't it?"

"It did, but it shouldn't have."

He shoveled his cereal angrily as I looked at him with angst. I couldn't believe him!

"So just pretend it didn't happen?" I asked.

"What else can we do?" he said, tossing his spoon in the bowl. "I fucked you, Jessica. How can I come back from that?"

"Jeez, you don't have to *come back* from it. It's not that big a deal to fuck a girl half your age, is it? I wanted it too, Anthony. How do you think it makes me feel for you to gloss over it like this?"

He stopped for a moment. I don't think that thought had crossed his mind.

"Upset, I guess," he said finally.

"Right. So don't pretend it all away. What happened up there was special. I've never connected with anyone like that before."

He put both his hands on the counter and looked to the floor, shaking his head. "But we're not supposed to connect like that, Jessica, don't you see?"

"People connect all the time like that. It's twenty years difference."

"We can't do it again," he said.

"Why not!"

"It's wrong, Jessica."

"That didn't stop you last night."

"Well, I guess the moment took me."

"No!" I said defiantly. "No, you don't get to do that. You can't just do something like that and then disassociate yourself from it the next day and act like you're all innocent and conflicted."

"I'm not saying I'm innocent," he said, and his face now had a pleading look to it. "I'm just saying that what we did—what we did *together*—was wrong."

"But it wasn't wrong!"

"I milked your tits in the same rack that I used to milk my wife, Jess. You think that's normal?"

"I can just think of things that are much wronger, that's all."

"I'm all ears," he said, and he started eating his cereal again.

"You didn't fuck my ass," I said softly, judging his reaction.

He stopped chewing. "I didn't."

"So there's that."

"What kind of point are you making?"

"That if we *really* wanted to do something wrong you could have fucked my ass *and* milked me."

"I could, could I?"

"Now you'll never find out."

I took my dish to the basin and gave it a rinse. I could feel his eyes on me as I moved around him but I didn't say anymore.

"You'd have done that?"

"You'll never find out," I shrugged.

I was trying so hard not to smile. I left quickly so as not to start giggling in front of him. His face was an absolute picture. Anthony was just like the rest, of course. All a woman had to do was dangle her asshole in front of him and he was anyone's.

"Would you have done that, Jessica?" he asked as I left.

I said nothing. Instead I went straight up to my room and decided to head out for a few hours.

"Can I expect you home later?" he asked as I was leaving.

"I'll be back," I told him.

I gave him a look from the door. He was sat on the couch pouting. He looked hot, of course, but I wasn't going to admit that. I was still pretending to be mad at him. The best thing about being mad is the make-up sex.

I stayed out all day. I found anything I could to occupy myself. I spent time with my friend Hayley but it was so difficult not to divulge what had happened that I just had to leave and make excuses.

I caught a movie but I couldn't concentrate. The night before was playing on repeat in my mind the whole time as I sat in the darkness. I felt as though I could still feel his mouth wrapped around my nipples as he sucked the milk from my tits.

I found my hands wandering as I daydreamed. In the light of the cinema-screen it was easy to get lost. There was a loud noise from the screen and I startled. If being fucked by your older housemate was naughty then masturbating in the cinema was surely close to the top of the list too.

Afterwards I went to a drive-through for something to eat. Most of the day I clock-watched. I wanted to stay out just long enough for him to get worried. Eventually a text-message came through on my mobile. I couldn't help but smile when I saw it was from him. I didn't want to read it straight away—that would be too needy—so I made him wait just that little bit longer. I was starting to enjoy taunting him.

'Making something to eat if you'd like?' the message read.

'I've eaten,' I sent back.

I watched the little dots move as he penned a reply, but nothing came through for a while.

'You okay?' was what he eventually settled on.

'Yep. Be back later.'

I left it there, putting my cell back in my pocket. I knew just how to drive a guy wild and that was a feat that was even easier to accomplish on Anthony. I'd been pulling his strings the whole time I lived there. I wanted to teach him a lesson.

So for the rest of the evening I just kind of drove round aimlessly, killing as much time as I could before finally pulling up on our driveway at ten o'clock.

When I walked through the door Anthony was sat in the exact same spot. He moved in his seat as though he was going to get up but then thought better of it.

"Good day?" he asked simply.

"Uh-huh," I said and I walked straight upstairs.

I didn't come out of my room. Eventually he came upstairs too and I heard a soft knocking at my door.

"Is everything okay, Jessica?"

"You tell me."

"I don't want things to be like this between us. Can I come in."

"No," I told him.

"I want to talk to you."

"We talked."

Silence. After another few seconds I heard him walk off down the hall to his room.

I felt bad, especially because I was only half-upset with him, really. I could understand where he was coming from, but he'd put it so bluntly that it had upset me. I didn't just want to be a fling to him.

After enough time to think *I* started to feel like the bad guy. Eventually I messaged him.

'I'm not mad,' I told him. *'I'm just upset.'*

His reply came back quickly. *'I don't want to upset you,'* it said.

'Well you did.'

'How can I make it up to you?'

It was tough to tell how suggestive he was being over text. I decided to throw caution to the wind.

'You can meet me upstairs.'

Again I watched the dots bounce as he composed his message. I could feel the adrenaline and arousal coursing through me. It was electric.

'Jessica ...' was all the message said.

I didn't respond. Instead I took my chair down the hall and pulled at the loft-hatch again. He must have heard. There was no way he couldn't.

When I went upstairs the memories of last night came flooding back. The milking-rack sat across the room, looking like both an inconspicuous collection of metal and leather and the naughtiest object I'd ever seen in my life.

My cell vibrated in my pocket. *'Are you upstairs?'* the message said.

I ignored it of course. I walked over to the rack and touched the straps that had bound me the night before. I looked to the floor and imagined Anthony standing in front of me with his pants around his ankles and his hard cock waiting to be claimed.

My pussy was flooding with juices just at the thought. I shivered and then felt my whole body awaken to the sinful ideas that crawled through my mind. I'd promised him my asshole and I wanted desperately to deliver.

The yearning to touch myself was too much. I sat on the wooden floor, opening my legs and facing the hatch. I started to play, lifting my t-shirt and rubbing my fingers over the crotch of my panties.

The wetness broke through almost immediately. It was as though the room itself just *made* me aroused. So much had gone on in there that it felt like the memories hung in the air. I could just recall the attic at any moment and immediately become turned on.

I started to think that maybe I didn't even need Anthony. I gave my tits a squeeze but the milk didn't flow. I found it curious that Anthony seemed to know *just* how to get it flowing.

I let out a grunt of arousal and closed my eyes. I cast my head back to the ceiling-beams and pulled my panties aside to touch myself for real. The sensation of my skin making contact forced another grunt from my lungs.

When I opened my eyes and stared forward I could see my Anthony's face staring back. He was on the ladder and his head was poking up out of the loft-hatch.

"Coming to join me?" I asked.

"Jessica, we can't keep doing this."

"We don't have to *keep* doing it."

I continued to rub my pussy, watching Anthony and waiting for his resolve to crack.

"Go back to sleep," he said.

"Why don't *you* go back to sleep. I'm up here minding my own business."

He didn't move.

"Unless you came up here to fuck my ass, of course?"

His eyebrows raised. "So you did mean that?"

I gave him a slow nod. Truthfully I had no idea what it felt like to be fucked in the ass, but if there was a guy that I wanted to discover that with it was him.

He walked slowly up the ladder now and it felt like surrender. I watched as his body was revealed. I watched his bare shoulders emerge, then his fantastic pecs. I wondered if he'd be wearing underwear but I didn't have to wonder for long.

His Calvins emerged, bulging already with his delicious thickness. He had clearly already been thinking something naughty.

"I see you're ready," I said, nodding to his boxer-shorts.

"I see you're not," he said, nodding to my panties.

"I can take these off."

"It's not those that I'm talking about."

"Then what?"

He laughed. "You've never done anal before, have you?"

"No ..."

"You don't just stick it in," he said. "You have to get relaxed first."

"I'm relaxed," I said defiantly.

"*You* might be, but I bet your asshole isn't."

I moved one of my fingers down to it and pressed against it. He was right. It was shut tight and even the tip of my finger felt like a struggle.

"Take those off," he said.

He dropped to the floor and crawled forwards.

I hurried my panties down my legs and his face came between them.

"Relax," he said, sensing the tension in my face.

I took several deep breaths and my tits heaved against my t-shirt.

Anthony's hand came up to my chest and he squeezed. The milk immediately burst from my nipple and turned my t-shirt a darker gray. He had magic hands alright, but I was about to discover that he also had a magic tongue.

"That's it," he hushed.

I watched as his face moved close. I could feel his hot breath against my wetness. He took a few kisses at the inside of my thigh and then he placed his mouth over my pussy.

Naturally I burst with a cry of pleasure. My fingers ran through his hair and I held him on me, but Anthony wasn't *just* interested in my pussy.

At first I thought it was an accident. I started to giggle as his tongue flicked over my asshole. When it didn't move I realized that it was his intention all along.

Now I knew it wasn't an accident I could treat it for exactly what it was. I closed my eyes and focused on that strangely arousing sensation. His wet muscle flicked over mine, relaxing it just as he'd intended.

"That's good," I hushed, surprised.

He let out a short grunt and continued to work me open. His tongue became a point and he stabbed it forwards, forcing it a little ways inside my ass where he waggled it.

I squeezed at my tits and found the milk to flow out of them at my command too now. It was as though Anthony was the key and he had unlocked some valve inside me.

I hurried my t-shirt up and over my head. He looked up and started to rub at my tits, smoothing the milk over them and spreading it around my body.

I was back in my happy place again and so was Anthony. All his trepidations about the night before fell to the wayside as he taught me even more about myself.

"I guess we can't use the rack for this?" I giggled.

He paused and looked up. "Actually we can."

He got to his feet and held a hand out for me. I took it and he pulled me upwards. I arrived right beside him and put a hand on his chest.

Anthony put a small kiss on my lips and then I kissed him back deeper. I ran my hand over the bulge of his big cock, rubbing it back and forth.

"I want this in my ass," I told him. Truthfully I had no idea how I was going to take him.

"And you're going to get it," he said. He'd never sounded more serious in his life.

He bought the rack out from the wall and made some alterations. "Bend over it like this," he said, motioning.

I came to the top edge of the rack and bent forwards. My tits hung through the leather that had supported my back the day before.

"Put your hands out here," he said, and I reached them forwards so that each arm ran along the outer metal bars. My ass hung off the back, pointing outwards with the support of my legs beneath me.

"That's it," he said steadily, and then he pulled tight at the leather.

I felt the straps tighten on my wrist and then Anthony secured them. There was no escape now, not that I wanted it. I wanted to sink into sin and let him have his naughty way with me.

"That's much better," he said.

He dropped his boxer-shorts and stepped out of them. From my position it would be difficult to put my mouth around his cock, but it turns out that's not what he wanted anyway.

"That's some view," he said, standing behind me and looking down.

"I'm glad you enjoy it."

He let out a quick flash of a slap across my ass. It stung immediately and my tits fired out a jet of milk as the shock rang through my body.

The milk pattered on the floor and Anthony took a look. "Interesting," he said.

He gave me another smack and then moved his head quickly to witness the milk spurt out from my tits.

"*Good* girl," he said, as though I had a say in where my tit-milk went.

He rubbed at my ass steadily. I could feel the heat arrive in it from where he'd spanked me.

"Are you going to fuck my ass?" I pouted, looking back with faux worry.

"I am," he said.

I felt his cock at my pussy. He rubbed the tip up and down my snatch and then treated me to it, sinking it into my wet warmth.

I closed my eyes and exhaled, but Anthony didn't stay in me for long. Instead he pulled out and then smoothed the crown of his cock back and forth over my ass. I felt it turn slightly wet.

"That's it," he said steadily. "We'll use your cum as our lube."

"Fuck, that sounds naughty."

He sank into me again and I covered his length it yet more of my love. There was more than enough to give. He dipped his wick and then spread the resulting cum over and around my asshole again.

It felt way more malleable than when I'd first touched it. I felt something pressing at it and I let out a grunt as it burst through the tight knot.

I've done it, I thought. It felt so easy.

I looked back to see that Anthony hadn't yet put his cock inside me and the sensation that I could feel were two of his fingers.

"That was the first test," he smiled.

He pushed all the way to the knuckle and my tits leaked their milk gradually. It was as though their nectar was directly linked to various other parts of my body. If it wasn't so fucking hot I would be concerned. I hated the notion that I might be out and public, sneeze and suddenly find my t-shirt soaked with milk.

He started to slide his fingers back and forth through my knot and I moaned long and loud. Anthony breathed hard behind me, trying to control himself.

"That's it," he hushed. "Good girl, Jessica."

Finally he sprang his fingers from my knot. I thought I'd be feeling his cock soon enough but suddenly I was looking down through the leather straps at Anthony arriving beneath me. He moved his mouth up to my tits and sucked on them as they hung down through the bindings.

The milk flowed with ease, firing through my nipple and feeling incredible. The nipples turned stiff and he toyed with each, straining upwards and gulping down mouthfuls of my nectar.

My ass winked as I gasped my breaths, as though it was connected to my lung somehow. He sucked out another jet of my cream and then left me.

"You always know just what to do," I said, looking back at him adoringly.

Milk dripped from the corner of his mouth and he kept his lips tight. He moved his face to my ass and I closed my eyes to focus on his touch.

When it came I startled. I shook the bindings as I felt him push my milk up inside my ass. It was the naughtiest thing I'd ever known, and since yesterday I knew some pretty fucking naughty stuff.

"Anthony!" I cried delightedly.

The sensation was like nothing else, but I guessed it wouldn't be the last one of those I felt. I didn't know whether to hold the milk inside me or give in to the pressure and release it.

Soon Anthony was making my decision for me. His cock toyed with the tight knot of my ass and then he pushed forwards. I felt myself burst over him and then the milk ran down to the floor as his cock displaced it.

He pushed forwards and I let out a long, drawn-out groan. His cock eased gradually into my asshole and I felt the sin of anal sex for the first time.

"Good girl," he hushed, breathing hard and pushing deep.

My moans grew as he pushed deeper. Not only did I have to contend with the tightness of my muscle around him, but now I could feel the head of his cock stabbing curiously at the pit of my stomach.

He pulled back and more of my milk spattered out of my ass and hit the wooden floor. Shit, if these walls could talk they'd have some stories to tell. It had started with his wife and now Anthony had passed his curious sexual-peccadilloes onto me.

He started to up his pace, passing his cock back and through me gradually until the tightness was no longer an issue.

When the pain dissolved I could feel the lingering pleasure in the act. It took some finding, but the more he stuffed his cock into me the more merit I found in the gloriously dirty act.

He bent over me and placed his weight on mine. My legs shook and the rack took our weight. His hands came beneath and he pinched at my swollen tits, exorcising more milk from them that dappled all over the floor beneath me.

I stared down and tried to imagine how it would look like to see Anthony's beautiful cock in the naughtiest spot of all. How tight I must be gripping him—how full I felt.

"You're good at this," he said, whispering close to my ear. He kissed my shoulders and back, reaching around to squeeze at my tits the entire time.

His hands kneaded my breasts and compounded the pleasure. His cock moved forcefully through me like a brute, showing no sign of mercy.

My asshole gripped him tight, desperately trying to squeeze him free but being unable to compete with his thrusts.

He opened me up over and over, teasing his cock to the exit before slamming it home just as deep. Each thrust felt incredible and each one brought with it a spurt of glorious milk.

He pulled back off me and stood up now, taking charge of my body by placing his hands on my hips. He pulled at my body and moved the rack violently, clapping his hips forwards against me.

My asshole, it turned out, could take quite the punishment. It sprang open over and over, submitting to his actions.

My tits swung beneath me, letting out their steady stream of milk that once again showed no sign of abating.

"I want your cum," I whined, closing my eyes tight.

I pulled at the binding with my hand, struggling like how I thought I should.

"You're my fuck-toy now," he said, and I felt that same excited arousal as yesterday.

He was a completely different guy in the moment, and that was the guy that I wanted most of all right now.

He spanked me again, raining down a clap so loud that it rang through the house, followed quickly by the yelp that left my throat.

I rocked beneath him, fuck-drunk and helpless. His cock bounced in and out of me and his breaths rose. His groans and moans started to match mine and I knew he was close.

My pussy cried out to be satisfied and the fact that I couldn't was driving me wild. In its stead I focused on my asshole, hoping to find solace in the sensations I felt there.

Anthony's cock seemed stiffer than ever and it stabbed more fiercely at the pit of my stomach now. He built his thrusts and damn-near turned my asshole inside out as he ravaged me.

"I'm gonna fucking come," he announced now, and I was more than ready.

"Shoot it!" I whined. "Shoot it in my fucking ass, Anthony."

"Oh, Jessica."

He built to a flurry, gripping my hips hard and sinking his fingers into my skin. His thrusts hit me so hard that I could feel the ripples travel up through my body. I'd never been fucked so hard.

"Come for me!" I whined. "Come for me! Come for me!"

He clapped on, holding his breath and straining. Finally he exhaled and pushed forwards one last time. He went all the way deep and then throbbed. I felt his thick cum started to fill my ass. When he finally let out his groan I joined in.

"That's so hot," I told him.

Each pulse of his cock brought more cum with it. He rocked through me gradually and the texture changed. His cock turned slippery inside me and the hot cum made his passing easier. If only we'd had a lube like that from the start!

"Every drop, Anthony. Please. Every damn drop!"

He fucked me slow now, giving me long strokes and sending his cum all the way deep. Nevertheless some of it escaped and fell to the floor just like my milk before it.

Eventually he pulled back out of me, popping his cock free. My ass quickly closed tight as he left me, trapping his seed inside. I wouldn't have had it any other way.

When he was done he unfastened my bindings. For the moment I didn't get up. Instead I lay there, breathing heavy and letting the rack take my weight as my knees buckled and my legs shook.

"Was that what you wanted?" he asked.

I go to my feet wearily and turned to him with a giddy, fuck-drunk smile. "That was more than I wanted."

Milk streamed steadily from my nipple. Anthony stared at it and then moved his lips to catch it. He ran his tongue up my chest and wound it round the areola, then he opened his mouth wide and enveloped as much of my tits as he could.

He sucked and the milk rushed to my nipple and out into his mouth. I held him against me as he guzzled it down, rubbing the back of his head and watching him suckle me. It felt so loving and not in the least bit strange, although I imagine everyone else would think differently.

I let him have his fill of me and as he sucked he started to rub at my pussy. It didn't take long before I was right on the edge myself.

The act had been so lewd and naughty that I'd been on the brink of climax this whole time, but with nothing stimulating my pussy I found the orgasm hard to achieve.

Suddenly Anthony's hands were wandering all over me and with my ass full of his hot cum the next part was merely a formality.

I breathed deep, squeezing Anthony and holding my breath at intervals. Each time I'd exhale I'd rise up against the rack. I just didn't know what to do with myself.

"You're gonna make me come," I told him.

His finger cruised down alongside my clit, jerking the little node and using all his experience. My body tightened and shook and finally the climax burst out of me in a terrific, joyous wail.

"Yes!" I whined.

Anthony pulled his lips off my tits and came to my mouth. He started to kiss me, letting the milk fall into my mouth and around it.

My eyes rolled back and I swallowed down my sweet cream. I moaned to the heavens. He sure knew how to treat a lady.

"I love you," I told him. "I love you so much."

"I love you too, sweetie," he told me, kissing me all over as the climax continued to burst out of me.

I shook against him and he held me, keeping me safe like he always had. I could feel the warmth of him in my asshole still, and I felt him there for the whole rest of the night.

In my bed later the heat of him in my butt was a sinful reminder of the act. I went to sleep with a smile on my face that night, I can tell you. Maybe there'd be even more pleasure to extract from Anthony's secret milking rack …

THE END

Bound & Satisfied : Suckled Brats 14

My boyfriend Derren and I had been getting adventurous in our sex-life. I was nineteen and he was twenty-two, so he was almost always the instigator in anything new that we attempted. Couple that with my older housemates being out for most of the day and it was a recipe for some very interesting moments of sexual discovery.

I'd only been dating Derren for a few months and he was my first serious boyfriend. Well, it was as serious as I'd ever had so far, put it that way.

Jonah—my housemate—wasn't a fan, of course. He insisted Derren was just using me, but I was sure that was just a case of classic over-protective older guy.

"I wanna do it in their room today," Derren said, kissing me as he entered the house.

"Jonah and Helen's room?!"

Derren nodded.

"That's kind of off-limits, isn't it?"

"That's exactly why we should be trying it. We're pushing boundaries here, Alice."

"I didn't know fucking in your friend's bed was a boundary."

"Of course it is. If it's forbidden then it's a boundary."

"How far do these boundaries go?"

"Depends how many you want to conquer."

Derren kissed me again, only this time his tongue pushed through into my mouth. I kissed him back and breathed deep, feeling myself awaken to him. He was hot. As far as I was concerned he was really, *really* hot. He seemed to me like the coolest guy I'd ever met and I'd have done anything not to lose him. I guess young love is foolish ...

"And I want to tie you up," Derren said.

It was then that I noticed Derren was wearing a backpack. He took it off and produced several lengths of rope from it as I processed his words.

"Jeez!" I cried. "Are you planning a kidnapping?"

"It's just rope and handcuffs!"

"Is that a ski-mask?!" I teased, reaching inside.

Derren pulled a face. "This is serious, Alice."

"It is? Can't it be fun too?"

Derren didn't reply. Instead, he zipped-up his bag and looked to the stairs. "After you."

"Do you want something to eat or drink or ..."

"I just want you," Derren said.

To my nineteen-year-old ears the sentiment sounded romantic. Derren was here for sex and nothing else, but that didn't concern me. I was horny twenty-four-seven myself. Perhaps an older woman would have taken issue, but for now I was okay with being used like that.

"Come on," Derren said, and he moved towards the stairs.

He put out his hand and I took it, following him upwards. Derren lead me right to Jonah and Helen's room and we walked inside and looked to the bed.

"Good," he said. "They have something to tie you to."

The headboard of their bed was made with slats of vertical wood that could easily have a rope tied around them. Likewise the base had shorter slats that, with a bit of work, could also take a rope.

"This is kinda weird," I said, walking in to the room and looking out of the window. The driveway housed Derren's Honda Civic but was empty apart from that.

I looked back to the room. It was kind of surreal. I didn't spend much time in their bedroom and being in there with someone else just felt *odd*. I guess that was the exact reason that Derren was keen to find adventure here.

"So are we gonna have a safe-word?" I asked him.

"Do you think we need one?"

"Just in case," I told him.

"Harvard?"

"*Harvard?*"

"Yeah," he shrugged. "Unless you can think of something better."

I couldn't. I suppose it didn't really matter what the word was.

"Harvard it is," I told him.

"Now take your clothes off."

Derren turned to his bag and started unraveling the rope. I stood there a second, wondering if perhaps our moments together had lost their romanticism.

I pulled up my t-shirt and unclasped my bra, hoping that Derren might turn around and I could put on a show for him.

Instead, he busied himself in his bag as I undressed further. I stripped my yoga-pants from my legs and then downed my panties without ceremony. I stood naked at the foot of their bed.

Finally, Derren turned back to me and stalled a moment. "God, you look good."

I felt a warm glow and blushed.

"On the bed," he said.

I lay back on their big mattress, with their carefully-made bedsheets beneath me. Jonah and Helen never left their bed a mess, no matter what.

"Give me your hand," Derren said.

I let him have my right wrist and watched as he used the rope to tie it to the bed above me.

"Pull," he said, when he was finished.

I did. My hand barely moved. I relaxed it and the rope held its weight.

"Good," Derren said.

He got up to move to the other side of the bed and I could see his erection in his pants already. Derren was turned-on and I've gotta say, feeling that rope around me like that, I was too.

I held up my other hand and Derren took it, affixing it to the bedframe in just the same manner. He pulled tight and nodded, satisfied.

I wriggled my left hand and met the same restrictive movement as before.

"Pretty tight," I told him, my eyes sparkling.

Derren was smiling too. "Now your legs."

"Legs too?"

Derren nodded and started fixing the rope to the bottom of the bed. He ran the other end around my leg and made a couple of knots, then he took the other leg and did the same.

"Perfect," he said, looking down on me. "Now wriggle."

I pulled with every limb and felt my big tits shake on my chest as I did so. When I realized I could barely move at all I felt a rush of adrenaline surge through me.

"Prime for the taking," Derren said.

He opened his fly slowly and I watched as he pulled out his thick, hard cock. He pumped it slowly in his fist and then moved his jeans and boxer-shorts down his leg.

His cock bounced, jutting out from his body. It made me forget for a moment that I was tied up and I tried to move a hand towards him.

"I'll bring a blind-fold next time," he said.

I closed my eyes and mused. "I think I'd like that."

Derren took off his t-shirt and I marveled again at his muscled chest. He was well put together. Derren had been on the football team and the athletics team, running track mostly. He had thick, tree-trunk legs and a short, muscley frame. He was like pocket dynamite, and I could have described his love-making the same way: powerful but with a short fuse.

"Look at you," he said.

He got on the bed and knelt close. His hand stroked gently up the length of my smooth leg, then he turned it towards my inner thigh.

I sucked a breath and closed my eyes. My body was trembling already. Being tied-up like that really did give the occasion an added edge that normal sex just didn't have. I was at his mercy completely.

"There's another thing I wanted to try too," Derren said slowly, and he started to stroke my pussy gently with his finger.

I was soaked already. He captured some of my wetness on his finger and spread it back up over my folds, turning my sex all slippery and wet.

"What?" I hushed.

"These," Derren said, and he dropped his mouth to my nipples.

I let out a moan and felt his tongue explore me. The nipples stiffened and tightened.

"What about them?"

"I want to see if I can milk them," Derren said.

I furrowed my brow in confusion, but the expression didn't stay for long. Derren sucked hard and filled his mouth with as much of my breast as he could. I let out another moan and felt something surge towards the nipple.

"Milk me?"

He nodded, still sucking. His finger worked back and forth over my pussy. My clit stiffened and Derren found it, teasing in small circles around it.

He pulled back from my breast and knelt upright. I could see him focusing on the taste in his mouth. His face lit-up as though he'd found what he was looking for. He opened his mouth to say something, but the sound of a car-door stopped him from speaking.

At first, I wore a smile, but the second Derren started to panic I did too. He rushed off the bed and looked down on the driveway.

"Fuck!" he cried.

He dressed as quickly as he could.

"Who is it?!"

"He's gonna kill me."

"Jonah? Is that him?"

I tugged at the bindings as Derren got dressed.

"Oh, fuck!" Derren cried.

"Alice?" came Jonah's voice up the stairs.

He put a foot on the step and started to ascend.

"Untie me!" I hissed, looking to Derren.

He looked back at the door, then he looked to the window. He opened it wide and threw his bag out.

"No way!" I hushed. "No way!"

"He'll kill me, Alice!" Derren said, putting his leg up on the windowsill. Jonah was a big guy.

"It's ten feet!"

"I'll take my chances with the drop."

"But Derren, he—"

I stopped talking as Derren disappeared out the window. His hands gripped the edge and he lowered himself as far down as he could, then let go. By now Jonah was at the top of the stairs and approaching.

"Alice?" he called again.

I heard him check my room, then I heard Derren's car start outside.

Jonah must have heard it too. "That fucker," he cursed.

He walked quickly into the room, thinking it empty. He was all the way inside when he finally looked to the bed. I stared back at him sheepishly.

"Hi," I tried.

Jonah stared. I mean, he really stared. He looked first to my face and then down around my body all over. His eyes locked on my breast. I looked down at them too. A bead of white hung on one of the nipples.

"Jonah, I can explain!"

Shit, could I?

"Is that ... milk?" he said, pointing.

I looked down again. "I—I don't know."

I was more than taken aback at Jonah's ambivalence to my situation.

He put a knee up on the bed and reached over. His finger took the bead of milk off my nipple and he brought it to his mouth. He tasted it and then smiled.

"It's milk."

I didn't know what to say. I gave the ropes a tug with my hand.

"You think you can untie me?"

He looked to the open window. He walked to it and looked down to confirm that Derren had left. He shook his head and then looked back to me.

"And he left you like this, huh?"

I'd have given anything to close my legs and try to regain some of my modesty. Jonah turned back to the bed and stood at its base.

"Look at you ..." he said.

I started to blush. I was so fucking embarrassed at what I'd done—and in his bedroom too.

"All tied up and slutty."

I looked down in shame.

"Tempting me," he added.

That startled me. I looked up at him curiously. "You're tempted?"

"What man wouldn't be?" he asked, and he started to rub at my bare ankles and feet.

I breathed deep. Jonah's hands on me felt good. I guess this was one of those boundaries that Derren always spoke of conquering; cheating with an older guy.

"We don't have to tell Helen, do we?"

"We don't have to tell anyone," he said, and the nail of one of his fingers slid up along my calf.

He looked to my wet pussy and then over it at me.

"He got you quite worked up, huh?"

I bit my lip. Jonah's hand moved even higher up the bed and I felt the flow of wetness begin anew at my crotch.

"Did he milk you too?"

"No."

What was this whole 'milking' thing? Was it more common than I thought? Could every woman do it?

"Good," he said.

His hand moved up higher, racing to the top of my leg. My whole body turned tense, and the ropes pulled tight as they held me.

Jonah missed my pussy and instead move up to my torso. His fingers touched softly all over me. I got goose-pimples from how delicate he was being. I didn't know he was capable of being gentle like that, given his ordinarily heavy-handed nature.

"He should treat you like a princess," Jonah said, stroking underneath my breasts. "Not like this."

I swallowed. "How would you treat me?"

"However you wanted me to."

His finger was on my breast now moving just as softly as before. He circled my nipple and it sprang back to life, pushing out from my breast and vying for even more attention.

"Suck on me, Jonah," I whispered finally. I couldn't keep quiet any longer.

He moved quietly towards me. He stalled above my breast and then clamped it over the nipple just like Derren had done. I found my entire body spark to life as he suckled on me for the first time. This was *way* different to having your boyfriend do it, I can tell you.

He sucked a big mouthful of my tits and they responded with a huge jet of milk that startled me as it burst through the tight aperture.

"Oh, Jonah!" I cooed, looking down in disbelief.

His eyes stayed closed and he started to gulp, sucking more and more nectar from my chest. I didn't even know that I was capable of that, much less that I had *so much* to give.

"That feels so good, Jonah," I purred.

I pushed my head back into the plush pillow of his bed and yanked at my bindings. He switched breasts and I looked at the one he'd vacated. Milk flowed steadily out from the nipple like I'd sprung a leak. The creamy-white liquid made meandering channels as it flowed over the curves of my breast and down my body.

My other breast was quick to release its nectar too. It only took the slightest of licks and sucks from him before it too was dispensing warm milk straight into his mouth.

He feasted on me and I felt a bond like no other. I wanted desperately to cradle his head to my bosom but with my limbs bound my options were limited.

Finally he broke from my tits completely. He wiped at his mouth and then looked down over me.

"You taste so good," he hushed.

"Keep tasting ..."

Jonah gripped at his crotch. I looked at the thick slab of meat that sat beneath. He looked much bigger than Derren.

"Is that for me?" I asked.

"If you're hungry."

"I'm very, *very* hungry."

"I wouldn't be much of a gentleman if I didn't feed you," he said, opening his fly.

I watched him untuck his plaid shirt and unbuckle his belt. He looked like such a man, even compared to Derren. The way in which my boyfriend had fled made me question my notions of what it meant to be a man. Jonah left me in no doubt though.

"That's it," I whispered.

I looked to his crotch, waiting desperately for the reveal. He opened his jeans wide and then reached down into his boxer-shorts. He produced a thick length of flesh that easily dwarfed Derren's.

"Bring me that," I begged, wriggling.

He crawled forward with his cock held in his hand. When it was close enough to claim I pushed my head out and did just that. My lips rushed over the tip and Jonah pushed himself into me. I started to rock my head, opening my jaw wide so as not to bite.

"Good girl," he said, moving my hair aside to watch.

His cock passed through my lips over and over as I worked my neck. Eventually he started to move his hips, passing his thickness through me and fucking my mouth. I kept myself wide-open for him, feeling the rush of his veiny, swollen cock.

Whenever he left himself inside me, I'd circle the smooth crown with my tongue and relish the sound of his deep groans above me.

"That's good, Alice," he grunted. "So fucking good."

I could feel his eyes on me, but I didn't care. I wanted him to watch. I wanted him to stare as I took as much of his delicious cock as I could.

"Think you're ready for me?" he asked.

I had no idea what he meant but I gave a "Yes!" anyway.

He took himself from my mouth and moved away. He stood up from the bed and took his shirt off. I watched his big, hairy, barrel chest burst out and then marveled as he downed his pants. He stood naked and proud, his huge, wet cock hanging off his waist.

I waited for him to put himself between my legs but instead he lay the opposite way to me on the bed. His legs stretched up to the headboard and his face was somewhere around my hips. It didn't take me long to realize what was about to happen.

"Look at that," he hushed, and I could *feel* his voice against my wetness.

I looked to my right at his huge, veined cock. It sat there as stiff as ever, bouncing each time his blood pumped into it.

Jonah opened his mouth and moved it to my sex. I felt his tongue slide over me and then he enveloped the top of my pussy. He sucked at my clit and I felt the blood rush to it. It swelled in his mouth and his tongue jostled it.

"Jonah!" I burst.

I writhed and moaned as he feasted on me, running his tongue all about me and turning the rest of my pussy as wet as my tight O. Soon it was tough to tell my cum from his saliva.

"Yes, Jonah!" I cried, my lungs pumping.

I pulled tight at the ropes, shaking the bed as he continued in earnest. His tongue slithered around me and my breaths pumped out of me hard. They burst from my lungs, followed by heady moans.

"You're gonna make me come," I told him.

He rolled over on me and I felt his weight. He propped himself above me and his thick cock ran across my face. I kissed and tongued at it as best I could, but Jonah wasn't concerned with that for the moment.

Instead, he licked and sucked, driven on by the unmistakable pre-climax moans that lurched from me.

My body tightened and shook viciously. The pressure inside me built. My head turned light and I held my breath.

"Come for me," he hushed, speaking against my pussy.

It was the permission I'd been waiting for. The second he said it I started to climax, and as I did so my tits began to leak their nectar all over again.

Milk streamed from both breasts as I came. My pussy tightened and flexed against his busy, unceasing tongue. He felt the orgasm against his mouth but he didn't stop. He kept on tasting me until I used my knees to push him off. My pussy just felt so sensitive!

"Good girl," he told me.

I mouthed around his cock wildly, trying to get the tip into my mouth.

Jonah spun around and I thought he was going to give it to me, but instead he sandwiched it between my big tits and pushed my cleavage closed around him.

"Look at that," he hushed.

I stared down, watching his cock sprout from between my tits as he started to fuck them slowly. My body was still spasming intermittently and every time it did a burst of milk rushed out of my nipple and flowed between my tits. Soon they gripped him in a milky embrace, running the nectar along his length.

He fucked me and the milk sloshed in my cleavage, lubing up his cock. From the look on his face it must have felt incredible.

"Oh, Alice," he moaned, and his face looked more serene than I'd ever known it.

"I don't want you to come there," I told him.

His eyes opened. "Where do you want it."

"Inside me," I told him.

How's that for a fucking forbidden barrier, Derren?

"Good," Jonah said.

He took himself out from my cleavage and moved down the bed. He moved his legs inside mine and the two of us stared down at his cock as he began to wash it back and forth over my pussy.

Now milk, spit and cum made my pussy a glossy, wet mess. Jonah put the thick tip of his cock to my tight O and pushed forwards. I felt myself open over him. My mouth opened too.

"Jonah!" I burst, and he pushed forwards and gave me a quick rush of his inches.

I hissed a breath and moaned, feeling the brief pang of pain as he stretched me wide. Soon it was deep inside me, planted as far in me as it could go.

My pussy gripped him close. Jonah kissed my lips and put his forehead to mine.

"Take my fucking cum," he said.

"I want it," I nodded. "I want you to come inside me."

He started to fuck me, moving the whole bed and bouncing my tits as he did so. I tried to add what I could but the ropes made things difficult.

Jonah took it all in his stride though. He had the energy of both of us as he fucked me, pumping at the hips and giving me the whole length of his cock over and over.

It ran through me and I thought I was going to come all over again. My tits continued to leak, as though they were expecting a climax too.

Jonah dropped his mouth to them, managing to suck on my tits as he fucked me. They gave up their bounteous nectar all over again, squirting into his mouth. He swallowed down each mouthful as though it was fueling his body. He pumped fiercely, slamming down into me and smacking my clit with the bone above his cock.

"Come inside me!" I moaned. "Come inside me, Jonah!"

He pumped hard, and his brow furrowed. Sweat appeared from his hairline and his moans lost their control. He pumped hard and made joyous noises that I'd never heard him produce before.

"I want your fucking cum!" I wailed.

My tits bounced and milk sprayed everywhere, covering Jonah above me and the sheets below. He barely flinched as it burst against him. Instead, he continued to fuck me, plowing on until his inevitable release.

"Alice!" he cried, right on the precipice.

"Shoot it!" I told him. "Fucking shoot it!"

His cock swelled and throbbed. My pupils fattened and the excitement coursed through me. I felt him burst finally and I hummed contently as his warmth poured into me.

Jonah was growling. He thrashed above me, punching his cock in and out of me and giving me his rich seed.

"I want every drop!" I told him.

His eyes opened and locked on mine as he came inside me. It was one of the most incredible moments I'd ever witnessed. The debauchery of the occasion had cleared briefly and there was a moment of loving clarity.

He dropped a kiss on my lips and continued to fuck me, pumping his cum deep and pushing it even further. The texture of his cock inside me felt incredible.

"Good girl, Alice," Jonah said, kissing my lips again.

He pulled himself out of me and I watched his cock emerge. It was glossed in cum but it had never looked sexier.

"Give me that," I told him.

He moved above and let his cock rest across my face. I licked it and bounced it above me, tasting the saltiness of him. I was more than happy to clean it up.

As I mouthed and kissed along him Jonah squeezed my tits, releasing the last few spurts of nectar and rubbing them over me, as though he was intent on leaving me mess.

Finally, he steered his cock into my open mouth and let me suck along it until the only traces of his cum were left in my pussy and mouth.

"Perfect, Alice," he said.

He stepped away from the bed and looked down on me as though he was taking a mental snapshot.

"Gonna untie me now?" I asked, shaking my arm.

"See you later," he said, turning.

Just before he did I caught his smirk.

"Jonah, no!" I burst playfully.

He came back to me laughing. "I'm not gonna leave ya."

He unfastened the knots until I was completely free. The second I was I stood up and put my arms around him, kissing his chest.

"I want to be able to use my hands next time," I told him.

"Next time, huh?"

"Tell me you don't want that again."

Silence.

"I knew it," I said, kissing him.

"No more Derren, okay?"

"No more Derren," I agreed.

He pulled me closer and kissed the top of my head. I'd never felt more sure of anything in my life than my love for him in that moment. How foolish young love can be ...

THE END

He Suckled Me Before The Show : Suckled Brats 15

I could hear the audience still simmering outside after our electric warm-up act had performed. The crowd knew I was next and the excitement amongst them was humbling.

"Thirty minutes, Lana," my assistant Janine called.

I nodded. "I'll be ready. Leave us."

She gave a quick glance at my manager Samuel who sat beside me in our private enclave backstage. Sometimes I wondered if other people knew our secret and they just kept quiet.

You see, my manager and I had developed a ritual so strange that you might never fully understand it. It started a long time ago as I was coming up in the local scene back home. That seemed a lifetime ago now.

I used to play small bars with sometimes no more than twenty people watching. Whatever the numbers in attendance my nerves went crazy. I could scarcely contain myself.

Back then Samuel used to sit with me, consoling me and telling me I'd be great and that everything would be fine. He was like a father-figure to me. We'd met in one of the bars and I just found his presence so comforting. Before a performance I used to hold him against my breasts and just cradle him. I found something calming about mothering him like that, despite the distance in our ages. One thing led to another and soon Samuel was mouthing over my tits. I found the sensation amazing and we kept it up ever since.

The first few shows I cradled him as he feasted on my tits, but after a while my tits started to give something back. It was as though Samuel had induced them to lactate with the loving licks and kisses of his mouth. He wasn't shy in feasting on the nectar that he managed to release.

It was so intoxicating and relaxing that I forgot completely about the performance. It put me in an almost trance-like state, that led many people to suggest that I was medicating before a show.

I'd arrive on stage with drooping eyelids and a gleeful look, as though I was stoned or something. The reality was that Samuel had sucked my tits so good that I was floating on a cloud of euphoria.

By the time the concerts were in full-swing my nervousness was a distant memory. I was free to just go with it. I'd fall in love again with my own music and end up feeding off the energy of the crowd. It had genuinely helped my career. I'm not kidding!

Without him by my side I'd really struggle to get myself in that place. I'd be a trembling wreck and the performance would never get going. I was sure of it.

For that Wembley show I was wearing a long, white unbuttoned shirt with a black bra visible beneath that had been custom-made for minimal bouncing. My big breasts often got in the way of my earlier performances whenever things got too frantic on stage. I'd commissioned a designer to ensure that I could bounce away to my heart's content and not have two black eyes the next day!

Below that I wore a high-waisted pair of light blue jeans that hugged tight to my calves and cut off short to show off the designer high-heels on my feet.

"Is this the bra you were telling me about?" Samuel asked. His fingers stroked along the underside where the metal support-wire was hidden.

"It is," I told him, looking down.

I took a deep breath to relax. By now our ritual was unspoken. My manager knew just what I liked and I was happy to let him explore.

We sat on the chaise lounge that was now part of my rider. I looked down on my tits that Samuel's finger stroked and teased. By now my body was primed to react. My nipples turned stiff in my bra. The crowd roared my name outside.

"Relax," Samuel said softly. His words were like a purr in that deep Southern accent of his.

I let out a soft moan.

"Mr. Earl will take care of you."

A smile crept on my lips. I loved it when he called himself that.

He'd dressed up for the show and was looking even more dashing than usual. He wore blue jeans, a brown belt and plaid shirt, as well as his now-customary cowboy boots and hat. You can take the man out of Texas but you can't take Texas out of the man. Samuel's iconic style was getting a following all of its own.

"Relax," he said again, wooing me into that serene state that was my happy place.

He started to kiss at my cheek and then my neck. Despite our unusual relationship Mr. Earl kept a strange set of boundaries. He'd never kissed me on my lips or dared to touch me in other places. Likewise, I kept my hands to myself, despite a deep yearning to reach out and please him the same way he'd pleased me.

"Relax," he said between soft pecs.

I fell into the backrest and let him explore me. He kissed inside my white shirt at my collarbone and then down further over my milky skin. I loved the way his moustache bristled across my sensitive flesh.

I looked down and watched. He seemed so peaceful himself, despite the constant roar of the crowd beyond that flared up at intervals for reasons we were unaware of.

I watched him kiss at the top of my tits that bunched up out of my bra. They were the assets that my PR team had told me I needed to accentuate as much as possible. *Tits sell*, they'd told me. They certainly bought Mr. Earl's attention.

"Good girl, Lana," he hushed.

I pushed his cowboy hat back and it fell to the floor. My fingers teased their way in at his brow, pushing through his ashen locks.

He brought his hand up to my bra and pulled at the cups. His kisses teased lower but he couldn't quite make it to my nipple.

"Hold on," I told him. "Carys will kill me if you break my bra." She'd painstakingly made the thing.

He moved away and I pulled my shirt back off my shoulders. I tossed it over the nearby coffee-table and then popped the clasp at the back of my bra. My tits were immediately claimed by gravity.

"There," I hushed, smiling.

Samuel looked at my tits and shook his head with a soft laugh. "I'll never get tired of those."

"Good. I'll never get tired of you sucking them."

He drifted nearer and I felt back to the couch again. His hands carefully pulled the straps off my shoulder. I brought my arms out of them and he pulled the garment off my chest. My tits sat on my ribcage like gloriously ripe fruit.

The look in Mr. Earl's eye turned serious. He stared and his pupils fattened. He looked as though there was a bubbling lust inside him that couldn't be contained.

"Suck my tits, Mr. Earl," I hushed.

He moved forwards and pounced. I let out a joyous shriek and then delighted in the kisses that he adorned all over me. He moved from breast to breast at first, pricking each nipple with licks and sucks. His moustache teased over me and my scalp fizzed like static.

"That's it," I mewled. "Suck my tits, Mr. Earl. Please."

The world fell away. All that existed was he and I in that moment. I felt the rush of juices move to my pussy and to my chest. My breasts became pumped with fluid and primed for the milking that Samuel was about to deliver.

He started to squeeze and massage them, working towards the nipple in an effort to free the mounting milk through the tiny aperture.

My veins became more pronounced across my chest. They flared up and fed life into my breasts. They became ripe and ready—something which Samuel was more than attuned to. He increased his fervor and the two of us moaned happily as my tits finally gave up their nectar.

He mouthed over the nipples, sucking the fluid into his mouth. I fell into that happy place all over again. Thoughts of the impending concert fell by the wayside. The nervousness left me in an instant. It was as though Mr. Earl was exorcising me of an emotion that was somehow tied up in the milk of my tits.

The gap between my legs turned warm and I wanted desperately for Samuel to touch it and realize how worked-up I had become. Instead, he kept things within those awful boundaries of his. He cared only for my tits and the milk within them.

The nectar spiraled outwards. Samuel would squeeze hard and move his mouth away, making a show of the fine sprays of pure white that would shoot forward into his open mouth. Sometimes the milk would dapple on his moustache and look like decorative pearls. That was unbecoming of a cowboy, but Mr. Earl somehow managed to pull it off.

He wiped at his mouth and returned for seconds. I looked to the clock above. We still had twenty-five minutes-or-so before the start of the show. Shit, they weren't gonna start without me, were they?

"I want more, Mr. Earl," I told him.

"What more can you want, sugar?"

"I want more of you. You always treat me. I want to treat you."

"I don't deserve it," he laughed, and he put his mouth back over me.

"You—oooh—you do, Mr. Earl."

The milk sprouted through me and each time it did I felt a devilish tickle. The release was incredible. I wanted to give Mr. Earl a release just like it.

He swallowed down my nectar with aplomb. Despite doing it a hundred times it always felt brand new. Now though I wanted to take things up a notch.

"It turns you on, doesn't it?" I asked him.

He wiped his lips and pulled away. "It brings me a certain satisfaction, yeah."

"Show me," I sparkled.

Samuel pulled away and looked back to the door.

"No-one will bother us," I told him. "Show me what I've done to you."

"That wouldn't be proper, Lana."

"I don't want proper." I made a gesture at our surroundings. "*This* isn't proper."

"If anyone found out ..."

"And this is somehow better?"

"Lana, I—"

"Show me," I told him. "I want to see what this does to you."

He got up off the couch and stood before me. He squared himself and put his thumbs inside his front-pockets. I looked at the bulge at the front of his jeans.

I reached out and paused. "Can I ...?"

He nodded.

My hand squeezed and met the resistance of his thickness beyond. He felt so fucking stiff in his pants. I moved my hand along him and looked up at his face. His eyes were closed as though he was trying to take himself out of the moment.

"It feels so big."

Mr. Earl swallowed.

"Look at me," I told him.

His eyes opened and his head angled down. His brown eyes locked on mine and we stared into each other's soul. He took a deep breath.

"I want this," I told him, squeezing. "I want to treat you like you treat me."

"This is *your* moment, Lana," he said.

"It's *our* moment. I wouldn't be here without you, Samuel. I'd have fucked it up on some small stage years ago."

"You're stronger than that. You'd have made it."

"We don't know that. But I know this."

My hand moved across him. His cock stretched right into his pockets. I was desperate to see it for real. Before now I'd accepted Samuel's mouth without too strong a desire to search for more. Now though, before the biggest gig of my entire life, it felt as though I needed to thank him for all that he'd done. Mr. Earl wasn't too good at accepting the plaudits.

"Lana you've got a big show soon ..."

"And I think this will help to calm me," I said, focusing on the bulge.

I moved to his belt buckle. His hand came to mine and he held me.

"There's no going back from this, Lana."

I looked up at him. "We're already too far in."

I felt his grip relax. I fought his belt open and then popped the top of his jeans. I paused there and took a deep breath. I was only moments away from the big reveal. I could feel my heart beating fast and as it did so the milk pumped from my tits. I'd become so excited that they'd started to express all by themselves.

"Are you sure about this?" he checked.

"I'm sure."

I dragged at his pants and they dropped. His boxer-shorts dropped with them and I saw the chiseled cut of his muscles that seemed to point downwards to that forbidden object within.

I followed the groove of his muscles as it ran from under his shirt. It moved into his underwear. I dragged down their waist to reveal more of his fuck-gutters.

"Yes!" I purred, noticing that he'd shaved.

His hair was cut close with a tuft of manliness that sat above the shaft. Shit, there it was! The start of his cock. It looked thick, but that wasn't the half of it. The lower I dropped his boxer-shorts the more the barrel of flesh continued.

Eventually it sprang up out of his pants. I couldn't help but giggle and cover my mouth. Mr. Earl was big.

"I told you there was no going back," he said. I looked up and noticed he was smirking. He *knew* how big he was.

"Fuck, Mr. Earl! You're huge."

"I guess we were both blessed with something."

He wasn't talking about my voice.

"Now what do you want to do?" he asked.

I was speechless. "I—I want more," I told him.

His hand came to my face and then moved to my neck. I felt an excited chill as he gripped. The blood-flow ceased. My head tingled and Samuel moved his hips forwards.

His cock swung close to me. I reached out and took him, gripping the barrel of flesh and pulling him close.

I let out a strained grunt and opened my mouth. It ran over the smooth crown of his cock and plunged deep. I spluttered a breath over him just as Mr. Earl loosened his grip. The rush of blood and oxygen flooded back, driving me wild.

I ran him into me as far as I could before pulling back slowly. My lips stayed close around the barrel and I ran over the contours of his glorious cock. I had to open my mouth wide enough to make my jaw ache, just so that my teeth didn't graze him.

My tits dripped steadily the whole time. They seemed in tune with my arousal. The more excited I became the more my milk seeped through the tight aperture. The fluid was curving down under my breasts and running down my stomach.

"My outfit!" I hissed.

I wiped the milk before it made it to my high waistline.

"You could always take it off," Samuel offered.

I gave him another smirk. He took his cock and started to jerk it. He looked like such a fucking man with that huge weapon in his hands.

"I could, couldn't I?"

I looked at the clock again. I had bags of time. The crowd were still in high-spirits beyond, knowing that my show was imminent.

I popped the button on the waist and downed the zipper. I turned around and pushed my ass out towards him.

"Take them off," I told him.

Samuel didn't waste any time. His fingers slid down the small of my back and he gripped the waist, tugging them down over my big ass. My panties rolled down with them and my bare ass was revealed. Very quickly I was naked and vulnerable, and Mr. Earl was finally able to see what his milking-sessions did to me.

"You're soaked," he said in his southern drawl.

"That's what you do to me. It drives me fucking *wild* when you suck my tits."

"I'd better keep doing it then, hadn't I?"

He turned me over and pushed me back onto the couch. His lips came onto me again. He sucked, jerking his cock at the same time. This time my tits fired into him, releasing their cream in huge jets. Mr. Earl swallowed each one down, pumping his cock harder in response. It was as though we were feeding off each other's arousal.

He pushed both of my tits against each other and they each fired up their nectar. Samuel steered it towards his mouth and let some of it run against his shirt. He popped open his buttons and bared his chest, then he fired the milk again and let it scatter over him.

He brought his cock up towards my breast and squeezed again, taking the milk across his length. He steered it towards my mouth.

"Yes!" I growled, and I raced over him quickly. I tasted my own sweet nectar on his cock and felt my pussy explode again in a riot of juices.

"That's my girl," he said.

He set his cock into my cleavage and fucked it for a few thrusts. I pushed my tits together around him and looked down at his cock sprouting through my breasts. I tried to imagine it doing the same inside me.

"I want you to fuck me," I told him,

This time Samuel didn't give a warning. He wanted it too.

He took his cock out from my cleavage and then moved lower. He jostled my body into position and I let him move me.

He took off my shoes carefully and then dragged my jeans off my ankles, taking my panties with them. Finally, he pushed open my legs at the knee and looked at my soaked pussy. It glistened. Above it sat my flat stomach. Milk pooled in my navel as it streamed steadily from my plump tits.

"Fuck me," I told him.

Samuel moved me again and steered himself close. I took several deep breaths and felt an excited nervousness. I wasn't concerned about the concert. *This* was my real performance.

"Ready, sugar?" he asked.

I nodded.

He looked down and splayed the head of his cock back and forth. I let out a whimper, thinking that he was going to stick it in.

Instead, he spread the juices of my pussy back and forth along the folds of flesh, teasing me for just a moment longer.

"You're soaked," he hushed.

I looked down as he rubbed his cock over me, then I watched the tip disappear. I felt him at my soaked O.

"Yes!" I whined. "Yes!"

Samuel pressed forwards and I felt my body accept him. My pussy spread over him, engulfing his offering with an ease that surprised me. What surprised me too was the sudden burst of milk that erupted from me like a geyser.

It fired upwards, battering Mr. Earl's chest and falling down in a cascade. It pattered on the floor, rising over the sound of my moans that had faltered briefly.

"My God," he said, looking down.

His chest was covered and dripping in milk. The flow had subsided, but when Samuel pulled back and thrust forwards it fired out again.

"Oh, Lana!"

He fell against me and our wet bodies pressed together. His hips bounced against mine, sending his cock through me over and over. Every time he pushed forwards the milk flowed between us. The sinful moment seemed even naughtier with my milk sandwiched between our naked bodies like that.

"We've done it now, sugar," he hushed. He put his forehead to mine.

"I already wanna do it again."

"We haven't finished yet."

He upped his pace and pulled back. I let out a huge groan. It was the kind of groan that was sure to start a few rumors, but in that moment I didn't care. I just wanted Mr. Earl and everything he had to offer—and believe me: he was offering everything.

He plunged his cock all the way to the hilt, coating it in my juices. The whole front of my body was soaked and some of my milk had found its way down between my legs.

He fucked me hard, using my body to get off like I'd used his mouth all these years. I tried to stave off the climax, but I just couldn't. I almost felt embarrassed as I started to come after only a minute of having him in me.

"Mr. Earl!" I burst.

My whole body tightened. Samuel plowed into me, not stopping for one moment. I held off for as long as I could but the reliable thrusts of his thick cock were too much.

Eventually the climax burst inside me and my legs shook. My pussy squeezed around him, but Samuel didn't even seem to notice.

"That's my girl," he said instead, kissing my face as I moaned. "That's my girl."

I drifted away again, finding that place of serenity that was so often my home before a big show. All of my thoughts went. It was only the climax. The pleasure overtook my emotions and for a moment I was merely a body. My mind was elsewhere.

When it returned it was to the sound of Samuel's impassioned cries. His face wore an expression of elation that I'd never noticed in him before. It was pure ecstasy. This was Samuel how I'd never seen him. He was unshackled and primal, working towards that climax just as I had.

"Come," I told him. "I want you to come. Come inside me!"

"Oh, Lana."

"I want to go out there in front of all those people. I want to go out there with a pussy full of cum and stand before them."

"Oh, Lana!" he strained. There was a sudden urgency.

"I want my manager's cum inside me and I want to parade my body in front of all of those people. They won't even know."

"Lana!"

"Come!"

"Lana!"

"Come!"

"Oh, Lana!"

"Come in my fucking pussy, Mr. Earl!"

Finally, I felt his release. His thrusts slowed and all the tension left him. By coincidence the crowd outside let up a joyous roar as though I'd suddenly appear on stage.

"Lana," he hushed.

I looked up and saw that same serenity that I found. I felt his cock throb within me and the warmth poured inside. He rocked slowly and there was a new texture of stickiness within me now. His huge cock cruised through my slick core several more times. I looked up adoringly at him.

"You're my world, you know that?" I told him.

He dropped his forehead to mine.

"Kiss me," I told him.

He moved his lips to mine and we embraced. The moment felt more loving than anything. I breathed deep and basked in the kiss. I found his tongue and teased at it, feeling my breasts slowly release the last of their offering, just as Samuel was squeezing out the last drops of his.

He pulled back and his cock emerged. I looked down as if to prove it to myself. His cock wore an unmistakable sheen of hot cum.

"That's what I've always wanted," I confessed.

He stood up and looked back at the clock. "You don't have long before you—" Samuel began, but he stopped just as my mouth wandered over him again.

He pushed my hair aside and looked down on me as I cleansed his cock of our love. I dragged my lips off him, pinching them close. He still felt so hard in my mouth.

I leaned back and brought his cock to my chest. I pinched up towards his crown and one final, beautiful bead of cum appeared. My nipple wore a similar white dot of milk.

I touched the two together and circled his cock on me until the palette was mixed, then I brought his cock to me again and tasted cum and milk as one. It was incredible.

"The world is waiting for you," he said, lifting my chin. "Knock 'em dead."

I stood up and faced him. "I'm going out there with your cum inside me."

Mr. Earl shook his head. "You're naughtier than I ever knew, Lana."

"I can be naughtier," I teased. I'd leave it to his imagination as to how.

I put my panties on and the two of us dressed again. Thankfully there wasn't too much to my outfit. Samuel used a towel to wipe down the visible parts of me and then he stepped back and took another look at me.

"You like fine, fine, fine," he said.

I grinned wide. "Let's do this."

He walked me to the door and I burst out into the corridor. I ignored Janine's look as I emerged. I didn't need any distractions now. I strode down the corridor with my manager and lover in tow.

"Go give 'em hell," he told me, smiling.

I tapped at my mouth and winked. Samuel still had some milk in his moustache. He wiped at himself and I let out a giggle. I turned to the stage entrance and walked out. The crowd erupted, basking me in the warmth of fifty-thousand screaming voices.

Only Mr. Earl and I knew that *his* warmth was sunk deep within me. It wouldn't be the last time.

THE END

My Milk For Free : Suckled Brats 16

I guess you guys could call it free-use, but in our world we just call it 'normal.' If the moment takes us, we act on our impulses, and everyone here is absolutely fine with that. It's embedded in the culture of our society.

You might find it strange, but if I walk down the street and see a guy I want to fuck, it could only be a matter of seconds before I've got his hard cock deep in my wet pussy.

Likewise, I've been stopped on the way to work before by several guys who all took it upon themselves to give me the fucking of a lifetime. Everything here is fair game if you give off the right signals.

For my gangbang I wore a pair of crotchless pants. When I fucked that guy before he had the front of his pants open, which is another signal. They're little cues that we give each other. Everyone knows the code. You advertise what you want and wait for the right person to come along.

Whenever my tits got too full of milk, the signal was more than a little overt. I'd bunch them together, hanging them out the front of a custom-made t-shirt that you could buy in some of the clothing stores here. It pushed them up and out, making them look like udders that sat on my chest. I was never short of a guy or two that had found himself thirsty.

One thing that was still off-limits though, and something that our two worlds seem to share, is that doing any of this with someone considerably older than yourself is somewhat forbidden. Everyone has to draw the line somewhere.

But, because of this, a sub-culture had arisen. The risky nature of age-gap sex was a huge turn-on for all sections of society, and when all of our other boundaries had been smashed we set our sights on these new horizons.

I'd seen a few instances in the past. I remember when one of my friends from college had her father over to stay and he and another girl wound up fucking in the hallway. Got to be honest, it was hot to watch. None of us spoke a word of what we saw, and I secretly found myself incredibly jealous of what Kendra had done. Cassie's Dad was in his fifties!

Naturally thoughts of fucking an older guy were never far from my mind. I think the opposite is true too in that a fifty-year old would love to get his hands on a twenty-something. I'd found my college tutor, Mr. Williams, to be a particular tease.

"Nice ass," he'd say, staring at it before class began as it hung out the back of my pants.

"It's an anal day today," I'd chirp. They were rare.

It must sound so alien to any of you guys reading, but that was just the way our world worked.

Anyway, I digress. That day I wanted nothing more than to have a guy—or two—latched on to my chest and freeing me of my milk.

That might be another way in which our worlds differ. Over here some women are blessed with being able to lactate without any kind of real stimulus. Give me a willing mouth and I'm good to go, whereas in your world things aren't so simple.

That day I bounced happily from my apartment. My neighbor Alan was in the hallway. He was just about to enter his room when he turned back and looked to my door.

"Annabelle," he chirped, turning and looking straight to my big tits. "That kind of day, huh?"

"Sure is."

I noticed that his pants were open. I walked straight across and got to my knees at his feet. Mrs. Thompson, who lived in the apartment beside mine, walked up the stairs at the end of the hallway.

"Morning," she waved.

"Morning," I waved back.

"Morning," Alan said too, flopping out his cock.

"Lovely day for it," Mrs. Thompson said.

She was a sweet old lady and didn't dither. She'd seen things much crazier in her time. Before she was even through the door I'd steered my lips onto Alan's cock. I hummed, blinking up at him and feeling the blood rush into his dick.

"What are you up to today?" he asked.

I pulled my lips off his cock and jerked it as I answered. "I'm going to the park, I think. Try my luck down there."

"Plenty of people out and about already," he said, taking a breath. "It's a nice summer's day."

He stiffened up in my grip and I beat him faster.

"I'm thinking I might try and get two people on my tits," I mused. I put my mouth over his cock and popped my lips off him quickly. I'd sucked Alan many times in the past and I knew exactly how to get him off. You just had to start fast and not stop.

"Y—yes, I should think that would be an easy feat for you to accomplish."

He dropped one of his bags and stumbled back against his door. I moved forwards with him, beating my fist. My tits shook as my hand hammered over him.

"I can't wait," I snarled. "Two guys on my tits. What a way to start a weekend."

I popped my lips over him again. I felt him flare up and stiffen further in my hand. He was close.

"I had a nice lady treat me last night after dinner," Alan said. There was a tremble in his voice. "My date fingered herself as she watched."

I focused on his cock, watching a bead of cum appear on the tip. "That must have been nice."

"Very," Alan said.

The cum rushed up his dick and I put my mouth over the tip. I felt the lashings pour inside and my hand worked to pump them all out of him.

"I might be meeting her again later," he strained.

My mouth ran down his cock and I swallowed his cum. Alan always tasted nice. He was big on pineapple.

I pulled back off him and swallowed again, pinching towards the end of his cock. "Your date or the woman who sucked your cock?"

"My date."

One last bead of cum arrived on the tip of his cock. I moved over and sucked it off him and then stood up. "That'll be nice."

Alan picked up his shopping. "Have a nice day, Annabelle."

"You too, Al."

I bounced to my feet and walked to the stairs. My tits shook as I skipped down a couple of flights. I always preferred the stairs to the elevator. I remember once I got in the elevator with three guys and we went up and down the apartment complex for the next twenty-minutes as people got on and off around us. That was one cramped session, let me tell you.

Outside the sun was shining brilliantly. Alan was right. I felt its warmth against my exposed, milky tits. They'd already started to steadily drip. The veins in them were visible, hinting at the bounty to be had from within.

I tried not to make eye-contact with too many people. My goal was just to make it to the park, and I didn't want some tit-hungry fellas to jeopardize that.

The park was busier than usual. As I walked through I noticed people fucking on the grass. A woman at the entrance was taking a cum-shot on her face and from the way the spunk hung from her chin I was guessing it wasn't her first. She was glazed in it, but she seemed to be enjoying herself.

I breathed deep and drank it all in. I loved summers. The day was about to get better too. A woman approached, making a beeline for me from off the grass. She looked to be in her early twenties, the same as me.

"Morning," she said.

"Good morning."

She took off her sunglasses and it was apparent that she was staring right at my tits.

"I'm thirsty," she said, and her head moved to my chest immediately.

"I'm—ooh—I'm glad I can help," I struggled, taking deep breaths.

The milk rushed from my tits and into her mouth. She sucked hard, drinking in my nectar and moving her hand to my pussy as she did so. She rubbed against my warmth and feasted on my breast as I stood there in the busy park.

"Have as much as you like," I hushed, holding her head to me.

Several people watched as she sucked me. I took a brief look around and saw a familiar face. I raised a hand to wave, but no such greeting was returned.

My brow furrowed. Mr. Williams wasn't usually so stern-looking. He seemed entranced. He was walking right towards me. I wondered if I should alert my new friend.

"Mr.Wi—" I began.

"I'm thirsty," he said.

Fuck. This was it. This was the moment that I'd yearned for most of all. In a park full of people my older tutor was asking to suck my tits along with the mysterious stranger below.

The lady took her mouth off my nipple and wiped her lips. "It tastes lovely," she said. "Come and join—" She saw how old Mr. Williams was and did a double-take before looking up at me.

I shrugged. "We could show these people that it's not so much of a stigma."

Her eyes shifted left and right. "I think it's *hot*." She looked to him. "Come taste."

She stooped back to my breast and latched on all over again. I took several deep breaths, trying to calm myself. I could feel my pussy becoming damp, both from her rubbing hand and Mr. Williams's excitable expression before me.

"Please, Mr. Williams," I offered.

He moved in. I looked around sheepishly. People stared back in wonder, but none of them wore a look of disgust. It tended to be the very people in Mr. Williams's age bracket that found the notion the most disgusting.

"Good boy," I hushed, putting my hand on the back of his head.

I leaned back proudly as his mouth found my other nipple. His tongue tickled the stud to life and he started to massage my tits, working out a fine sprinkle of milk. He moved his mouth away and let it spray into him from afar.

"Ooh, let me try," the lady said.

She did the same and the three of us laughed, although mine was tinged with nervousness. It felt so wrong to have Mr. Williams on there, even in a world such as ours. He was thirty years my senior.

I looked around nervously, torn between how good it felt and how wrong it was. I wanted him to hurry up, but I wanted him to take it slow and treat me too.

"That's me," the lady said, pulling back and wiping her mouth. She gave me a kiss and I tasted my cream on her lips. "Look after him," she said.

It was just Mr. Williams now. I held him against me in the middle of the park's path. People walked past, some looking back and narrowing their eyes. Asses hung out of shorts and cocks got swallowed around me, but in spite of all of that I was the main attraction.

"What are you doing?" I hissed now, wondering what had gotten into him.

"I've wanted this," he said, swallowing. "I've wanted this for so long."

"It's dangerous here, Mr. Williams."

"That's why its such a turn-on," he said. "Come on. I know how wet you must be getting."

He put his hand between my legs where the lady's fingers had been only moments ago. He rubbed against me and I felt my juices flood to the fore. It was even more of a turn-on to have Mr. Williams do it. He was right. I loved how wrong it was.

He pushed both my tits together and popped his lips off the nipples of each, moving between the two. The milk fired forwards around his mouth messily, but Mr. Williams didn't have a care in the world. A fine spray of milk was nothing to worry about, especially considering the woman drenched in cum at the park entrance.

He pulled away completely and smiled at me. He nodded down for me to look. His fly was open. Fuck.

"I know you know what that means," he said.

"Mr. Williams," I groaned, looking around. Eyes stared back.

"If it's not you it'll be someone else."

"Someone nearer your age."

"Do this with me," he said. "Let's show them."

I didn't know what to do. As my mind fought to decide I noticed someone walking towards him. Her eyes were on his open fly. She'd spotted his offer and what's more, she looked to be in her fifties too.

Without a word I crouched to the floor in front of him and reached into his pants. He grunted as I tugged his hard cock over the waist.

I looked back to the approaching woman. "Sorry."

"Maybe next time," Mr. Williams said to her.

She frowned and walked away, unwilling to watch what was about to happen.

"Good girl, Annabelle," he said above.

"I can't believe I'm doing this."

He pushed forwards and I opened my mouth. I felt his mature cock slide inside and I surrendered to it immediately. The second it moved past my lips I was lost. I gushed a breath, breathing deep and forcing as much of him inside me as I could. People around us gasped.

"That's it," he said, holding my head.

People were really watching now. There was so much passion being injected into the act that it was tough to ignore. That was something else that was rare here. Mostly people just did their thing and left, but me and Mr. Williams were enjoying each other. A crowd began to form.

"Nice work," one guy called, and my eyes darted over. He was jerking his cock steadily on the inside of a small circle of people around us. He was enjoying the show.

I gave a thumbs-up.

Mr. Williams's eyes stayed fixed on me, looking down. He didn't seem to care that we were garnering an increasing amount of attention.

"Suck my cock, Annabelle," he groaned.

"Suck his cock, Annabelle," some of the crowd said, turned-on by the forbidden sight.

I relished being watched like that. I got off on the attention anyway, but this was something else. I could feel the crotch of my panties turning damp with arousal.

I rocked my head back and forth and kept my fist wrapped around him, creating a long, wet tube to slide him through.

Mr. Williams seemed to really appreciate that. He let his head fall back and roared at the heavens. The crowd around cheered and applauded.

"You two should fuck," one of the women said. She was on the floor with her legs split wide and her skirt pulled up. Her fingers toyed over her pussy.

"Yeah," several people agreed.

"You should fuck!" one guy yelled.

Mr. Williams pulled his cock out from his mouth and beckoned me to my feet.

"Yeah!" the crowd rejoiced.

Shit, now it was hard to back out. I felt like I was fucking for a cause now; as though we were pioneers smashing down barriers so adventurous people could follow us.

Mr. Williams helped me to my feet, and I blew a kiss at the crowd who laughed back.

"Fuck her," one guy said.

He pulled me towards him by the waist of my jeans. My tits jiggled as I bounced towards him. The nipples pressed against his shirt and the milk bled through.

"I want to fuck you, Annabelle," he said.

My eyes turned black with lust as my pupils fattened. I'd wanted him to say that for so long, and now here I was with a terrific choice to make.

"Take down your pants," the lady on the floor said. "Give him your pussy."

The crowd cheered and played around us. Strangers had started to connect around us, sucking on cocks or licking on pussy. It was as though we had become an inspiration or some kind of gathering point. More people flocked over and started doing things around us that moved the attention away. I didn't want that.

"Okay," I said loud. "Okay. Fuck me."

Mr. Williams tried to temper his excitement. I turned around and pointed my ass towards him, then I pushed my yoga pants down and took my panties with them.

"Fuck her ass," one guy cried.

Mr. Williams didn't want that, thankfully. He walked forwards with his cock in his hand and put it up under me. I could feel the wet, spit-drenched barrel against my folds.

"Fuck me," I begged, uncaring now.

He put one hand on my shoulder and used his other to steer his cock into me. I bent over double. My tits hung beneath me and leaked their nectar on the floor.

"Yes!" the lady on the floor cried. She was a pretty brunette and she was one hundred percent focused on the two of us.

I felt Mr. Williams's cock press against my O and then in one quick, sudden movement he sunk inside. My mouth hung open in shock and arousal. The lady on the floor bit her lip.

"She fucking loves it," she cried, working her pussy harder.

She was right. It was incredible. Mr. Williams's dick was big. I could feel that now.

My pussy gripped him tight and he started to rock back and forth. The crowd's attention had turned back to us. Mr. Williams was fucking me hard right off the bat and my tits were sprinkling their nectar downwards like some kind of spirograph on the park's pathway.

"Oh, Annabelle," he moaned.

He gave my bare ass a spank and then gripped my hips with both hands. His cock sprang in and out of me and each time he pushed forwards he jolted me.

The lady close by was moving towards me. I knew what she was aiming for immediately and I didn't stop her. Soon she was on my tits and licking them something fierce.

She carried on fingering herself too. Her hand flurried over her pussy and she moaned into my breasts. The vibration of her cries felt incredible, as did the ravenous nature with which she fed. It was as though the was starved, just like how Mr. Williams fucked me like he'd been starved of sex.

"Come on both of them," someone offered. "You should come on both of them."

Now that was an idea. It seemed the horny woman was a good addition to the cause.

For now though I was far too focused on the sensations that were creeping over me and taking control. I could barely function. I was a moaning mess of ecstasy, spurred onwards by Mr. Williams and his new assistant. The crowd cheered me on and my climax rumbled closer.

"Yes!" I whined, clenching my fist.

Mr. Williams shot his hand down and spanked me again. The slap felt fierce, and its heat arrived quick. It seemed to shock the orgasm out of me.

My pussy gripped tight around him and I gave an unmistakable grunt. The crowd cheered and the girl beneath me sucked with increased fervor as I started to come.

My pussy contracted on Mr. Williams, but he wasn't going anywhere. The look of angst on my face must have been incredible, because a couple of the onlooking crowd shot off their own loads. Some of it spilled forwards onto the grass while willing women caught others.

"Wooo!" one woman cried.

I tried to giggle but the climax was too strong. I bit my lip and let it flow through me. The milk spilled and its flow increased. The lady beneath me gasped off my tits and let the strong jet of milk blow over her.

Another member of the crowd saw the rushing torrent and moved forwards. It was another woman, keen to feel the heat and strength of my unrelenting cream. It was another person that had decided that perhaps age-gap sex wasn't so wrong after all.

Now two women bathed beneath me, rubbing my white milk all over their bodies as Mr. Williams started to fuck me again from behind.

Gradually my pussy opened and allowed him back through me. He didn't waste an ounce of time. He started to fuck me hard again, and all of the crowd seemed certain of what was to happen next.

The ladies beneath me latched on to my breasts now that the flow had ceased somewhat. The milk shot out of me in jets. I could feel it squeeze through the nipple and I could feel their tongues coaxing it out too.

Mr. Williams was working steadily behind me. My knees had bent from my efforts, but he was still going strong. He pounded quickly against me and I felt him turn tense. The orgasm built within him. I wanted it bad.

"Come on all of their faces," someone cried.

I looked to the voice and noticed that it was the lady from the park entrance. She was pushing cum towards her mouth. She gave me a wink.

"Yes!" I cried. "Come on our faces!"

Mr. Williams let out a grunt of approval and moved onwards. He pumped hard and then sprang out of me in a damn hurry. I spun on the spot and sat between the two women that had been on my tits beneath me.

They each swallowed their last mouthful of milk and then opened their mouths like hungry chicks. The three of us looked up at Mr. Williams. He stared down with a look of determination and ecstasy.

"Come! Come! Come!" the crowd chanted.

Mr. Williams wasn't gonna let them down. He smirked as though he knew it for sure.

"Come!" they blared.

He gave me a wink and then I watched the climax ripple through him. He tensed up through his body from his calves all the way to his shoulders, then he let out a terrific grunt and looked down as he pointed his cock towards us. I was first.

The cum shot out and I pinched my tits as it struck my face. It was all warm an incredible, but the force of the blast caused me to startle.

The crowd cheered and clapped, and Mr. Williams steered his ropes across the other participants. They giggled and pushed their tongues out far from their mouths to catch him across it.

He made a mess of all of us and I fought to keep my eyes open as the lashings of cum fell across my lashes. It was so heavy on my eyelids that they wanted to close, but I refused to let them. I stared up and smiled as Mr. Williams pumped out his spunk. It seemed from his volume that it had been several days since his release.

"Every drop," I told him.

The heat ran down over me and then one of our assistants rose on her knees and started to lick my face. I felt her tongue move the cum over me. She pushed it towards my mouth and we started to kiss. I could taste Mr. Williams's sweet stickiness between the embrace.

I passed the act on, looking to my right and doing the same to the cum-strewn face of my other cohort. My tongue wound over her and I held her face steady as Mr. Williams pinched the last of his cum from his cock.

The woman to my left had risen and she was sucking on Mr. Williams. I looked at her and then up at him. His eyes were still on me.

I rose on my knees and put my face close, making no bones about what it was that I wanted. Thankfully she surrendered his cock and steered it towards me. She seemed excited to share it.

"Good girl," she told me as she fed Mr. Williams into me. I felt fresh courage that these two strangers had joined me in the forbidden act.

Both of the girls moved downwards now to my chest. More of Mr. Williams's cum had been spilled there, as well as the steady drips that had fallen from my chin.

The two of them moved it around, coating my breasts in spit and cum until they were shiny and slippery. They pushed my nipples back into their mouths and sucked, rounding out the act just as it had begun.

The milk poured from me, losing none of its flow. I hummed along Mr. Williams's cock, keeping my lips pinched tight in a bid to cleanse him of his cum.

"Thank you, Mr. Williams," I hushed.

"Good girl, Annabelle," he said, and he stroked at my chin.

I gave him one last, long lick. I dragged my lips off him and let his cock fall. He was spent and with good reason.

A clap began around us, and it rose into a quick round-of-applause. Mr. Williams bowed and me and the two women got to our feet and did a tongue-in-cheek curtsy.

I raised my arms and put them around their shoulders, feeling a bond to my two sisters-in-sin. They took their cue and moved to my tits again, giving them one last lick and freeing another sprout of nectar.

"I'll have to get your numbers," I told each of them.

"Gladly," one giggled.

I looked back to Mr. Williams but he was nowhere to be seen. I searched amongst the crowd but he had disappeared, letting the three of us take the plaudits for our forbidden show in the park.

"Can I be next?" one older man had asked, stepping forwards.

One of my girls was straight to servicing him. She pulled his cock out and started to suck it, but I was too busy looking around for Mr. Williams to help. He was nowhere in sight.

I vowed to go and visit him later to discover what all that was about, but for now I decided to stroll the park. My sexual activities would no-doubt continue, but my best encounter of the day had already happened. Shit, it was my best encounter *ever*. How fucking naughty did that sound? Having my older college tutor fuck me and suck my milk in front of everyone like that.

Just imagine how that might have gone down in your world. Do you think you'd have enjoyed it? Shit, I hope so.

THE END

Coffee Liqueur : Suckled Brats 17

It was summertime and I was nineteen, meaning it would be my second working-vacation at Dante's bar in Tenerife.

I took the job when he'd offered it last year, mixing drinks for tourists and locals alike and enjoying the sea-air and endless ocean views. Dante's bar was one of the better ones on the strip, but recent events meant that he still had money-trouble. He'd been bailed out, but he was still very much trying to prove himself now that business was returning to the island.

I worked almost for free. He paid me very little, but I wanted for nothing and honestly, life on the island was too amazing to turn-down. I loved the relaxed pace of it all. It was in stark contrast to the city I grew up in in America.

"You see that table," Dante told me that evening, pointing. "Make sure you look after those guys."

I wiped down a few glasses and placed them back above the bar. "Who are they?"

"The big guy is Don Carlos," Dante said. "He helped me keep this place afloat."

"That's him?" I studied the large, suit-wearing, cigar-smoking guy that sat out on the veranda.

"He's big around here."

"He'd be big anywhere," I laughed.

"Just look after him, Mariana. Please."

"I'll keep an eye on their table."

"Two eyes," Dante asserted.

I nodded and he moved away, greeting a family of tourists who had wandered up to look at the menu.

The orders came in throughout the night and I fixed orders for the entire bar, making sure that Don Carlos and his group were never out of drinks of olives. He ate them like they were going out of fashion. I replaced the first few tiny bowls and then set a huge bowl down for him. He'd laughed but given me a polite nod.

"How's it going?" Dante asked, returning to the bar later in the night.

"Fine, I think. They're just drinking and talking—and taking the odd look down my top whenever I lean over the table."

"Don Carlos and his friends appreciate fine things," Dante said. That was one of the best compliments from him that I'd ever received.

Don Carlos looked up and gave me a signal, popping another olive in his mouth and biting around the stone.

"Go," Dante said.

I scurried across to the table, ignoring a guy who tried to stop me for drinks.

"Same again?" I asked.

"No," Don Carlos said. "I would like a coffee."

"How do you take it?"

"A Barraquito," he added. He made the signal to his three guests. "For everyone."

"Four Barraquitos, coming right up."

I turned away and walked to the bar. God, I hated making those. It was more about the presentation than the taste. Everything had to be perfect. Condensed milk first, with Tenerife's local liqueur on top, followed by a layer of espresso and then a further layer of frothed milk with a slice of lemon peel and a cinnamon dusting. Ridiculous, right? Well, the people of Tenerife take great pride in it, and Don Carlos was keen to see how deep my roots ran.

"What does he want?" Dante asked.

"Barraquitos. Four of them."

"At nearly midnight?!"

"You said to get him whatever he wanted!"

Dante lingered. "You want my help?"

"No way," I told him. "I can do this."

"Make it perfect, Mariana," he hushed.

"No pressure!"

"We have to show him we know what we're doing."

"I know!"

Dante rushed back to a table with their bill and left me on the bar. I prepped four saucers and the four small, tall glasses that held the drink.

The condensed milk and liqueur were easy. I liked to roll the alcohol off a spoon down the side of the glass to get that perfect line between the two liquids. The white with the yellow on top was a real statement.

Next came the coffee, which again came pretty easy with Dante's espresso machine. I poured that carefully down the side of the four glasses too, holding my breath and hoping that the lines split cleanly between layers.

"Careful, Mariana," Dante said as he returned to the bar to make some drinks for the few remaining customers.

"You don't think I'm being careful?"

He peered close and watched. I could hear his impatience in his steady breathing.

"Fetch the milk, would you?" I told him.

He turned around to the fridge and opened it. "Fuck!" he hissed.

I looked back. "What is it?"

"We're out."

"Out of milk?"

"The next delivery isn't until tomorrow."

"So go to the store?"

"They're closed!"

"Go to the bar next-door?"

"They hate us, Mariana. We took most of their customers when Don Carlos became my partner and not theirs."

I looked over to Don Carlos who stared. He seemed to sense something was amiss. When I looked back Dante was staring at me.

"What?"

He glanced down to my breasts. "You could ... do that thing that you do?"

I shook my head. "No. No way. Nuh-uh."

"Mariana, we need it!"

"I told myself I wouldn't do that again."

I started to turn red with embarrassment. A year ago I'd discovered what I guess you might call a skill. I was able to produce milk if I pinched and toyed with my tits in just the right way. Dante had found this out to both of our costs when he'd walked in on me showing this to a girl that I worked on the bar with last year.

"We're out of options," he said.

"Problem?" Don Carlos shouted, and the remaining guests turned around.

"Please," Dante whispered, before turning to Don Carlos and rushing over. "No problem at all," he said. "It'll just be a minute-or-two longer. Mariana wants it perfect for you."

"Then she's a smart girl," Don Carlos said.

I stood for a second in thought, but ultimately, I knew what I had to do. I wasn't going to let Dante down like that. Eventually I grabbed the metal jug beside the coffee-machine and walked into the kitchen. The chefs had thankfully cleared down and left already.

"Okay," I told myself. "Okay. Just this once."

I pulled up my t-shirt and took it off, then I unfastened my bra. My breasts bounced out and I moved my hands to claim them, taking their weight and pinching just how I had done in the past. My heart quickened and the electric sensation of each touch burst inside my body, moving its way to my pussy as though the two things were connected.

Just then the door behind me opened and I startled, spinning on the spot with my tits in hand.

"Mariana, we need—" Dante began, but he stopped in his tracks and stared.

"I'm doing it!" I told him.

He seemed mesmerized. It was that same look that he held when he'd first caught me, as though my tits were some kind of hypnotist's pocket-watch, swinging in front of his eyes.

"Dante!" I cried, snapping my fingers and letting go of one of my breasts.

He startled and looked to my face finally. "Don Carlos," he began.

"I know! It's coming!"

Dante backed out of the door and I returned to the jug. There was something flattering about having that effect on him if I'm honest. So often I was his employee and nothing more, but when he looked at me like that it made me feel desired.

I took to my tits again, massaging them and closing my eyes until I could feel the tingle. When my breasts turned to static like that I just knew the release wasn't far behind.

I took up the jug in one hand and squeezed at my nipples with the other, pinching the milk to the tight aperture and spraying it out into the jug. I let out a deep breath and let the flow ease out of me. It was so cathartic, but I didn't have time to enjoy it.

I squeezed rapidly, inducing the milk and firing it down into the jug. I'd switch hands when the flow decreased and fire a fresh, hot jet into the container until I had enough for four Barraquitos.

I hurried my t-shirt back on and stepped back out onto the bar, putting the jug of milk beneath the steamer spout on the coffee-machine.

It whirred to life and the milk frothed deliciously, turning all velvety and creamy. Dante had already cut the lemon-peel and slotted it on the glass.

Carefully I scooped out the frothed milk and then added a dusting of cinnamon to each. I set them all on a tray and walked out to the table.

"Thirsty work, all this talking," Don Carlos said, seeing me approach. His eyes went to my tits and I realized then that I hadn't replaced my bra. The milk was seeping against my white t-shirt.

"Here you are, sirs," I said, setting down the tray. Those with a good view stared down into my plunging cleavage, watching my tits more closely now that they were unleashed.

"Thank you, Mariana," Don Carlos said. I didn't realize he knew my name.

"Enjoy," I told him. There was some satisfaction to be had from knowing that he was about to drink my tit-milk.

Don Carlos looked at the drink. He took it up in his big hand and set it to his lips. He tilted the glass back and opened his mouth wide. In a second all my hard work had gone down his throat. He swallowed and ran his tongue around his gums.

"Now that," he began, and Dante's attention piqued close-by, "is incredible."

I beamed a smile. Dante looked relieved at the table behind as he cleared their glasses.

"Well done," Don Carlos said. "I haven't had one like that since my mother used to make them."

"It's my pleasure, sir," I told him.

"It's ours," Don Carlos said. He ran his eyes up and down my body. I put the tray up to my chest.

"Will there be anything else?" I asked.

"No," he said. "We'll be leaving soon."

I walked back to the bar and Dante followed with his tray. "Well done!" he whispered. "That's why you're my favorite."

I smiled warmly and met the twinkle in his eye with my own. It felt like we'd overcame something together. It felt incredible.

Several minutes later Don Carlos got up from his table. He didn't pay, of course. He never paid.

"Thank you, Dante," he said. "Tonight has been an absolute pleasure."

"The pleasure was ours, Don Carlos."

Dante stood to attention, nodding at each man as they passed him and left to walk along the sea-front.

When they were gone completely Dante turned to me and put both his hands on my shoulders. "You did amazing tonight, Mariana. I'm so proud of you."

My lips trembled. I felt myself start to well-up with tears, but instead a burst of milk shot from my nipple and spread across my t-shirt.

"I'm leaking," I laughed, trying to hold back the tears.

"Yes, you are," Dante said, standing back to admire my breasts as the nipple started to show through the wet, white fabric.

"I should change. Do you still have those t-shirts for the staff."

"I'll grab one."

I walked back into the empty kitchen and leaned against one of the brushed-metal tables. The t-shirt stuck to my tits as I lifted it off, but with some effort I managed to relieve myself of it. My tits sat on my chest all wet.

"Here you go," Dante said, walking in on me again.

"You always seem to catch me at the naughtiest moments," I smirked.

"I didn't think you'd take it off yet!"

I held out my hand for the t-shirt and Dante stared at my wet tits. I knew how good they looked. They were one of the things I liked the most about myself.

"Can you ..." he began. "Can you show me how you do that?"

"How I ... milk myself?"

He nodded. He was unable to meet my gaze for any stretch of time. His eyes kept wandering down to my milk-soaked tits.

"I just kind of pinch towards the nipple," I told him.

"Show me."

Dante held out a metal bowl. I put the t-shirt down beside me and moved forwards, putting my tits over the bowl.

He swallowed and looked at me. His nostrils flared and his pupils thickened. "Show me," he said.

I took my breast and he stared down, watching as I pinched off some milk into the bowl. It spattered and sprinkled, firing out from me under a great deal of pressure. It tended to do that when I was aroused.

"That sure is something," he said. "I can't quite believe it."

I did a few more and then a naughty idea struck me. I smirked before I even said it.

"Would you like to try?" I asked him.

His whole face opened up in shock. "Really?" he said. "I can?"

And here I was thinking he was going to politely decline. I started to laugh. I'd never known him more eager.

"Please do," I said, nodding downwards.

He moved his hand forwards steadily. When he touched my breasts the smirk left me. We were in unchartered territory now.

"Squeeze," I told him.

He did as commanded. I felt that electric rush hit me. My pussy dampened. A fine jet of milk sprayed out into the metal pan and he let out a breath of shocked laughter.

"I'm doing it," he said. "Fuck, I'm doing it!"

"Keep going," I told him. I closed my eyes and swallowed. "Keep going."

He pinched towards my nipple, squeezing my breast and releasing the pressure within. The milk sprang free, pattering against the metal until it started to pool.

I opened my eyes slowly and looked back at him. "Try it with your mouth," I dared.

His jaw tightened. "Can we do that?"

"I think we're already doing something we shouldn't," I shrugged.

He put the bowl down behind him and then came forwards, moving slowly. He was entranced. Shit, so was I. I couldn't wait to see his mouth on me.

"Suck them," I urged. "Suck my tits, Dante."

He rushed the last few inches, bringing his mouth to it quickly and enveloping the nipple. I felt him suck. My breast rushed into his mouth with Dante managing to suck it almost all the way to the back of his throat. I felt the pressure build. His tongue teased around the nipple and he suckled, forcing the milk from my breast and into his mouth.

When he tasted it he moved his head off me and looked up. "That's fucking incredible, Mariana. No wonder Don Carlos enjoyed his Barraquito."

"It tastes that good?"

"Here," he said.

He put his mouth to my tits again, sucking hard and filling himself up with my nectar. He moved off me and then brought his mouth to mine.

I pursed my lips and kept my eyes open as he put his mouth on mine. Our lips pressed together and my mouth opened. The milk rushed between, all sweet and delicious. Dante's tongue flicked against mine and we tasted it together.

I let my eyes close as his hand came around me. We kissed with the milk, swallowing it down slowly until it was only our two tongues fighting together.

As we kissed he kneaded my tits, letting the milk spray against his black shirt. Finally, he pulled back, swallowing and staring. It was as though he was waiting for me to protest.

"That was ... something," I hushed, biting my lip.

"Sorry," he said. "Sorry, Mariana, I got carried away. I should go clean up."

He turned and went for the door.

"No," I said, louder than I intended.

He turned and looked back.

"Stay here. Stay with me. Taste me some more."

He took a breath and shook his head, but I could see he was conflicted.

"Please," I urged. I looked down and noticed the thick barrel of cock that sat in his pants. The kiss had turned the both of us on.

"You're my employee," he said.

"And you're my boss. So, let's do something we shouldn't. Together."

I walked to him now and put a hand on his shoulder. I eased my lips upwards, hoping for another kiss. My hand moved across the front of his pants and I felt his thick cock beneath.

"I knew it," I smirked.

Dante started to grin too, despite his trepidations.

"Is that for me?" I asked.

"It shouldn't be."

"But it could be."

He said nothing.

I got to my knees in front of him and started to unfasten his belt. He looked back around him, running his hand through his hair and sighing. If he wanted to move, he would have.

"We can tell no-one, Mariana," he said.

"I would never tell."

I pulled open his pants. His white boxer-shorts beneath hugged tight to him. I could see the thick barrel more clearly now.

"That's what I want."

I tugged his pants down far enough and then went for his underwear. His cock slipped up over the waist of them and bounced in front of me. I startled at how big he was. I guess we both had a secret.

"Now *that* is a cock," I said, looking up.

Dante's worried look became a smile again. "Show me what you do with them."

Now it was my turn to suck on him, but I didn't want milk for a prize. I wanted his hot cum.

I put my hand around him and felt the strength of his arousal. His cock felt like it was made of oak. I ran my hand along it and then brought it to my mouth.

He let out a groan as all of that night's tension left him at once. I pushed my mouth down over him and flicked my tongue around the swollen head of his delicious cock. It was amazing to have him make those noises. I'd never given Dante this much pleasure in all my life.

"Oh, Mariana," he cried, holding my head against him.

He rocked his hips, pushing his cock into me as I held my head still. My hand worked back and forth, moving my spit over him until I had a chamber of wetness to jerk him in.

I hummed on him and breathed heavily. My tongue continued to toy around his sensitive tip and my pussy dampened in response, becoming as wet as my mouth. I could feel my juices against my panties.

Then, without warning, my tits started to leak too. It was as though I had reached peak arousal and the only way to manage the sensation was to let off my nectar steadily.

I pulled off his cock and looked down to assess the new state of my tits. The milk bled out from them and hugged my tits, rolling underneath and meeting my ribcage where it fell down towards my navel.

"They're milking themselves," I hushed.

"You're so beautiful," Dante said, staring down. It must have looked so surreal to have me holding his cock and staring back.

"And this cock is so fucking handsome," I said, running my tongue along it and keeping my eyes on him.

I put him back inside me and worked him some more, feeling his cock throb as the blood beat into him. My hands teased his balls and he moaned as though he couldn't stand it anymore. He grabbed my hand and pulled me up to my feet.

"Take off your pants," he told me, and he started to do remove his own.

He unbuttoned his shirt too and soon he was stood before me completely naked. I watched and then hurried to join him, unfastening my jeans as my tits shook on my chest.

He couldn't keep his hands off me. He put his mouth back on me and sucked at my breasts, filling himself with even more of my delicious milk.

I paused as he sucked and Dante took over, pushing my jeans down over my ass and taking my panties with them.

He moved off my breast and crouched, taking my pants and panties down and staring ahead at the strip of fur that sat above my pussy.

I watched as he studied me, curling my hair behind my ear and awaiting his approval. He said nothing as he took my jeans off my ankles, but then he pushed me back against the table. It screeched a little way across the floor.

Dante rushed forwards and put his face between my legs. I let out a wail of glee that was cut-off when he opened his mouth over me.

My legs parted as I tried to give him a good angle. Dante worked hard, lapping ravenously and teasing my clit with his tongue and mouth.

"That's good," I told him. "You're too good."

I hopped up onto the metal table and Dante stood up. He kissed me and I could taste me wetness on his tongue. He moved down off my face and kissed his way to my tits again where he sucked hard. I looked up at the bright lights of the kitchen and then felt his kisses go lower, following the trail of milk down my stomach.

I leaned back as he moved lower still, and I felt the cool of the metal table against my back. When I was all the way down Dante lifted and parted my legs, putting his face right over me and smoothing his tongue up along my sodden folds.

"Yes!" I whined. "Oh, Dante, yes!"

He ate messily, pulling at my flesh and smacking his lips on me. He spread my juices all around and worked his tongue as deep as it would go. The whole time the milk eased out of me, running down under my arms now and settling on the table beneath.

"Please," I moaned. "Please. I want you to fuck me. Please!"

The words came all on their own. I was naked an honest, telling him exactly what I wanted now in no uncertain terms.

"I want to feel that big cock inside me. Can you do that for me?"

Dante pulled his face from between my legs and wiped his mouth. "Come here."

He took my hand and pulled me up off the table. I fell close to him and put a hand on the hairy, bare chest in front of me. He moved as though we were going to kiss but then he spun me around and pushed my head forwards towards the table.

I let out a yelp of shock that soon became a moan of pleasure when I realized his intention. He gripped my hair tight and then used his other hand to guide his cock towards my wetness. When he felt it against him, he pressed forwards and pushed his cock into me.

I opened over him with a moan of: "Dante!" As I cried his name the milk burst out of me all by itself, spattering on the metal beneath me.

"Yes, Mariana," he growled. "Spray your milk for me."

I squeezed my tits and did as he dared. My milk fired from each nipple, cascading over the clean kitchen and making it one big mess all over again.

Dante started to fuck me, passing his big cock in and out of me and giving me the whole length at a steady, strong pace. He'd stab forwards and hit my ass, causing a grunt to lurch from my lungs each time.

He pulled me up closer to him and I felt his hairy chest against my back. His hands came under my arms and he squeezed at my tits, pinching the milk free and then rubbing it all over me.

"You're my dirty, naughty girl now, Mariana."

"I am, Dante. I'm your slut!"

"You're my slut. Taste this fucking milk, you slut."

Shit that was hot to hear him call me that. It was even hotter when he rubbed the milk all over my face and let me lick it off his hand.

"Fuck me!" I wailed. "Fucking fuck me!"

We both lost ourselves to our new roles. Dante became my master and I became his submissive slut, willing to please.

"Get on your knees and suck your cum off my cock," he told me, and like a good girl I did as he said.

I pulled off him and turned, marveling at how good his cock looked drenched in my cum. It would be an honor to cleanse him of it.

I sucked on him, rocking my head back and forth along him until there was scarcely any of my wetness left along his shaft.

"Give me your tits," he said. "Put them around my cock."

I bunched them together and brought them upwards. Dante set himself between them and I wrapped them around like a hot-dog bun. I started to bounce them in my hands, shooting milk against his waist and thighs as I jerked him in the milky embrace.

"I want your fucking cum," I told him. "I want your fucking cum, Dante."

"Keep doing that and you're gonna get it."

I bounced my tits over him and felt him go wild above. The creamy milk made an amazing lube. His cock ran through me, all veined and delicious. He was right on the edge.

I wanted to rub my pussy so bad. I could feel it dripping with wetness. My breathing started to match his and my heart raced. I wanted to touch myself but wanted Dante to get off first.

"Mariana," he strained, and his head rolled back to stare at the ceiling.

I worked my tits up and down, jerking him between them fast. My pussy quivered and dripped its juices. My tits leaked their milk and it ran down the both of us to the hard floor.

"I'm gonna come," he cried, and he looked down at the source of his joy.

"Do it!" I dared. "Fucking come."

Dante moved hastily, pulling his cock from my cleavage. The second he did I moved my hand to my pussy and teased my clit. It was so fucking swollen and charged. I worked my hand fast, strumming over my flesh and moaning loud.

"Mariana," he groaned.

"Fucking come for me," I grunted.

I felt my climax blossom inside me. My pussy flexed and all of my joy rushed to it.

"I want your cum!" I told him. "Come on my face!"

He let out a long groan and then I felt the first rush of heat. The second it struck me I flinched and felt my climax explode.

My mouth opened and I moaned long and loud. The next splash of cum struck me, lacing over me. I tasted it as it fell in my mouth and worked my hand faster as my climax flourished.

My pussy flexed and my thighs quivered. The milk ran freely from my tits, falling down my body. Dante moved and sent his next volley of cum across my chest. It mingled with the milky liquid, making a pearly cocktail of mess that slid down my body slowly.

"Oh, Mariana," he said. "You're so fucking beautiful."

I smiled warmly and then flinched again as he angled the next blast of cum towards my face. It struck me and I gritted my teeth, relishing the next hot blast.

It struck me again, hitting my forehead and rolling down. I must have looked a mess but when I blinked my eyes open carefully and looked up at Dante, I saw nothing but a look of admiration.

"That's my girl," he said.

"Your slut," I reminded him.

My fingers pushed slowly over my pussy and gradually the gravity of what we'd just done dawned on the both of us now that we were relieved of our lust.

I stood up carefully, looking at Dante bashfully as my face held his cum.

"Perfect," he hushed, pushing it aside to make space for his lips.

We kissed slowly, closing out the act. He put a hand on my shoulder and looked me up and down.

"Wow!" he cried. "We made a mess!"

I looked down and some of his cum stringed off my chin. "We sure did!"

Dante handed me my white t-shirt. "May as well use this," he said.

"I don't need to," I told him, and I pushed the cum towards my lips and into my mouth.

"You are something else, Mariana," he said.

He moved away for his clothes and I looked at his naked prowess. His spent cock hung magnificently. The tip was a pink hue with a bead of cum hanging off it. His hairy chest was dappled with milk from where we'd made a mess.

"Don Carlos seemed happy," I said.

"You seem to have a habit of making men happy," Dante said, turning back to me.

"I try my best," I told him, finishing off his cum. "I want to make you happy all over again."

THE END

Milk Trading : Suckled Brats 18

Mr. Shaw was quite a highflyer in the world of trading, and he kept it all very hush-hush. I was his P.A and part of a very small team. He'd disclosed it all to me one time when we went for a drink after work. I think he'd had a little too much to drink and he wound up telling me the whole sordid affair.

He'd started trading on the stock exchange, you know, all pretty normal stuff. He'd been successful and that had got him noticed, but not everyone that noticed him was straight-laced.

He'd agreed to be part of a new venture that promised a lucrative salary and boy had it delivered. Mr. Shaw had disclosed all of this from the bar he owned in the city. I was blown away when he explained things further.

You see, he trades milk and if that isn't crazy enough, he trades *breast* milk. All kinds. He trades in different nationalities, ethnicities, and ages. If a buyer wants Middle-Eastern, thirty-something breast milk, Mr. Shaw can get it. These buyers have *very* particular tastes and operate in wealthy, underground circles. Their milk is certified to an incredibly high standard to ensure it's exactly as advertised. There's a whole network of people around the globe working on this, but it's something you've probably never heard of. Shit, it'd be insane to think it existed at all. I certainly had my doubts.

Mr. Shaw had wound up retrieving his laptop and showing me the live markets to prove it all. There were ticker-symbols—they're the short letters that describe each stock—for every milk market imaginable, with live-prices and buyers. Some of them even had ratings as they were from a particular supplier.

They'd be delivered in refrigerated vans to millionaires all over the world. I guess a more main-stream example of something like this would be caviar; it's something for the rich to indulge in that's out of reach for most common folk. Well, breast-milk was exactly like that!

It'd taken me days for it to really sink in. Every now and then I'd forget and then I'd see him sat on his laptop and it'd all come crashing back. I wasn't even sure he'd remembered telling me if I'm honest, but I felt part of his dirty little secret. I was about to become an even bigger part.

We were nearing the end of our work vacation and one of the other women who worked for him had retired to bed early again. It was just Mr. Shaw and I around the pool, and I could see something was bothering him. He just wasn't himself.

"Everything okay," I ventured.

"Fine, fine," he said, pinching at the bridge of his nose.

"It's not fine, is it? Tell me what's wrong."

He gave a heavy sigh. "I don't know if I should be talking to you about this ..."

"It's already too late," I laughed. "I'm in the inner-circle now."

He gave another big breath. "Well, the price of white, twenty-something's milk is sky-rocketing right now and I just can't find the supply."

"The supply of milk? Can't you just give them any old milk?"

"The whole business is built on trust and standards. Doing something like that could crash the entire market. It has to be authentic."

"What's the price right now?"

Mr. Shaw looked to his phone. "It's at five-hundred dollars a milliliter at the minute."

My mouth hung agape. "Five-hundred a milliliter?"

He nodded.

"How much is in a milliliter?"

"There's around thirty of them to the fluid ounce."

"Why milliliters?"

"It's just easier internationally."

I did a few sums. "So, if I bought it as a shot in a bar it would cost me around twenty-thousand dollars?!"

Mr. Shaw looked up and thought. "Yeah, give or take."

"Holy shit!"

"There's a lot of money in this," he said.

"Why can't you get the milk? I thought it'd be easy?"

"Obviously there are margins. We can't pay suppliers that much, and it's *very* hard to approach a healthy white woman and ask her for her milk. They're far too guarded on the whole. I mean, you shot me quite the look of disgust when I told you."

"It wasn't disgust," I protested. "Just ... shock."

"Anyway, like I say, it's not easy approaching women and asking if they'd like to sell their breast milk, so the market isn't exactly saturated right now. Hence the price of milk."

"White, twenty-somethings ..." I began.

Mr. Shaw nodded and took a deep breath. "It's stressful, Hannah, I've gotta tell ya."

"How much do you pay for it?"

"We pay around one-hundred a milliliter at the minute but are thinking of offering more. It's just I don't want to eat into the margins. The distribution is costly, as is paying for people's silence. If this got out a whole host of wealthy individuals would be publicly embarrassed."

"I'll do it for two-hundred," I told him.

He stared across at me. "Two-hundred?"

I nodded.

"We can't do that," he said, dismissing the idea. "It wouldn't be right. I couldn't sell my own employee's milk like that. Could I ...?"

"You tell me?"

"Can you even produce?"

I shrugged. "How do I find out?"

"Some women have the ability. They just possess it, but most don't know until they try."

"So how do I do it?"

"There's kind of a skill to it."

"Show me."

"It's not gonna work on *me*," Mr. Shaw laughed.

I looked across the pool to the villa. It looked quiet inside. Vicky, a colleague much older than myself, had been gone for over an hour by now. There was little chance of her returning now.

"Show me," I told him again. "Show me on me."

He stared in silence. "Hannah, I ..."

"Just show me! It's two-hundred a milliliter, Mr. Shaw. Even if I only get a little bit out that'll be amazing!"

"We didn't agree on that price ..."

"Think of everything I could do with two-hundred dollars," I dreamed, ignoring him.

"If you want the money that badly I can give you more hours."

"I wanna earn it a different way."

"I can respect that."

"So, show me how I earn it."

He moved off his bar stool and came over to me. I put my shoulders back and opened my chest to him. One thing I had been blessed with was a great set of tits. They were probably my finest asset.

"What do I do?" I asked, looking down and then across at him.

"Well, we need to get that sweater out the way."

I didn't say a word, lifting my top up over my head. I think Mr. Shaw was expecting me to be wearing a bra, because when I saw his face again it was strewn with shock.

"You didn't know I had these?" I asked, cupping them and laughing.

"I didn't know you were just gonna take them out."

"How else are we gonna milk them?"

"Good point."

"My eyes are up here," I told him, laughing.

"But your tits are down there," he laughed. "They look like my ex-wife's when I first met her."

"I'll ... take that as a compliment?"

"You should. Her tits were incredible."

"Incredible?"

"Her milk was too."

"She could do it?"

"She could."

"Did you sell her milk?"

"From time to time, yes," he said.

"How long for?"

"It was just for fun, really ..."

"You milked her for fun?"

"Uh-huh."

"What kind of fun did you have?"

"All the fun of sex, but with some milking thrown in for good measure."

"Did you ... taste it?"

"Of course," he said. He seemed almost offended. "This was some of the finest milk on the market."

"How much was hers?"

"Well, supply was limited then so it wasn't quite five-hundred a pop."

"But mine will be," I beamed.

"If you can do it."

"What are we waiting for!"

"Are you sure about this?"

"Milk my damn tits, Mr. Shaw."

He started laughing. "You're the boss."

He moved his hands forwards and touched me. They felt warm against my breasts. They started to move around slowly, as though he was rubbing a crystal ball.

"How will I know if—"

"Shh," he said quickly.

I kept quiet as he touched me. It was as though he needed all his senses. After a moment or two I started to feel a simmer, as though my tits had fallen asleep. They were like static, fizzing on my chest.

"It feels ..."

"Tingly?" he guessed.

"Yeah!"

"That means you can do it."

I beamed wide. "So, let's do it."

"You really want it?"

I nodded. "Milk me."

He pinched and a bead of white appeared on my nipple.

"Is that two-hundred?"

"We should check the flavor," he said, and without a word he raced his tongue over my nipple. I think he forgot himself for a moment, because afterwards he looked up at me and the reality of what he'd just done dawned on him.

"Sorry," he said.

"Don't apologize. I wanted this. Does it taste good?"

He relaxed and smiled. "It tastes *amazing*."

"Better than your wife's?"

"Let's not compare."

"I'm better, aren't I?"

"I couldn't possibly comment."

"See if there's more," I said, nodding to my tits.

Mr. Shaw moved to them again and squeezed. I felt the rush of euphoria as my breasts burst. The milk spiraled out through the nipple and sprayed onto the poolside floor.

"Don't waste it!"

"Don't worry," Mr. Shaw said. "You'd be surprised how much there is."

"We should sell it!"

"We don't want to flood the market. The prices will go down."

"So, what do we do with the excess?"

Mr. Shaw smirked. "Thirsty?"

"Eww!"

"You don't wanna taste the richer side of life? Give it a try."

"I don't even know if I can reach my own nipple."

"Let's try that too," he said, and he lifted my breast.

I giggled but then moved my chin down to meet my chest. Mr. Shaw pushed my big tits upwards and I found the nipple. It was so weird to suck on my own breast, but not in the least bit unpleasant. I felt the same rush of excitement when my lips wound around them. Mr. Shaw squeezed and the milk shot into me. It startled me at first, then I felt its warm, creamy flavor.

"Oh, wow," I cooed, genuinely surprised.

"Good, right?"

"Amazing!"

"That's what they're paying for."

"I mean, I'm not sure if it's worth five-hundred a milliliter but it's damn good."

"Can I try it again?"

"Please," I said, offering him my breasts. "Knock yourself out."

This time he was much more sensual. His tongue wound around my tits and he sucked as much of them into his mouth as he could. I let out a shriek of excitement as he pulled me nearer towards him. The milk burst through the tiny aperture, filling his mouth until he needed to swallow.

I heard it all slide down his throat, but he wasn't done there. He took another suck and filled his mouth again, circling his tongue around the nipple until it turned stiff. I wasn't so sure that part was necessary, but I wasn't going to stop him. Mr. Shaw clearly had a magical mouth.

"Oh, Mr. Shaw," I purred, losing myself. I held him against me but he brought his face away and rubbed the milk from his lips.

"So good," he said again.

"Is that how you extract it?"

"We use a machine," he said. "I have one hidden away inside somewhere. It doesn't waste a drop."

"That doesn't sound as fun."

"Having fun, are we?" he smirked, looking to my tits. My nipple was stiff from his amazing cajoling.

"It's hard not to! It'd be like me milking your cock by sucking it."

"Good point," he said. He looked off at the night's sky as though he was imagining it.

"Are you having fun?" I asked.

"I get to spend time bonding with my assistant. What's not fun about that?"

"What about the rest?"

"I get to suck on some lovely tits too," he said. That was what I wanted to hear.

"Would Sir like some more?"

"Sir would be delighted."

He moved onto me again, pushing my tits into his face. This time he moved between each, sucking out the nectar and humming contently as he did so. It felt amazing to nourish him like that. It was like we were really bonding, you know? It's tough to explain, but I felt a deep need to care for and satisfy him.

"Fuck, you're something else, Han," he said, popping off my tits with a gasp and a heady sigh.

"Is this doing it for you?" I asked, looking down to his shorts. "My God, it is, isn't it?"

"A pair of tits in my mouth will *always* do it for me. You?"

"Are you kidding," I laughed. "It feels like I've wet myself."

"You're wet?"

I nodded and bit my lip. "I couldn't help it."

"I'm stiff," he hushed. "I couldn't help that either."

"Maybe ..." I began, and Mr. Shaw was hanging on my words. "We could help each other."

"I was just going to suggest the same thing."

"Come over here," I told him, grabbing his hand.

I led him over towards one of the loungers that sat close to the pool and I perched on the base. Mr. Shaw stood up at the end of it.

"Stay there," I told him.

I held his leg and stared up at his face. Mr. Shaw looked down, keeping his eyes on me. I knew what I was about to do was wrong, but it felt like we'd already done a whole bunch of wrong. I was just adding to what he'd started.

I dropped my head and looked forwards at his shorts. It was obvious where his package was. A long, thick bump sat in front of me.

"Is that *all* for me," I whispered. I reached out and touched it, confirming that he was as stiff as he'd said he was.

"It can be," he said, stroking my head gently. "If you want it."

"I want it," I hushed.

I straightened my back and moved my tits close to him. I brushed the nipples softly over the front of his shorts and Mr. Shaw watched. The nipples were still bolt-stiff and each time they touched the fabric of his shorts it felt incredible.

"You gonna take those down for me?" he asked.

"Can I?"

"Definitely."

I raced for the laces of his shorts like it was Christmas morning. I pulled them open and then dragged them down. His cock burst up and out of them quickly, followed by a sigh from Mr. Shaw as though he could finally relax.

I startled and flinched away, looking at the huge cock in the half-light. My boss's cock. It was big and beautiful and veined and perfect and I wanted it all to myself.

"Have I done this?" I asked.

"Well, I wasn't thinking about anything else," Mr. Shaw said, matter-of-factly.

"If I've done this then it should be all mine, right?"

"I don't see why not."

The pool filter trickled softly, and insects chirped. I reached forwards and swallowed nervously, wrapping my fist around his big cock and feeling its power in my midst.

"That's it," he said steadily. "Give it some milk."

I used my other hand to bring my breast up towards it, then I squeezed towards the nipple as though I was drenching a hot-dog in mayonnaise. It burst out of me, and Mr. Shaw groaned as it covered his cock. I worked it back over him with my fist, using my cream as a kind of lube.

"Perfect," he hushed. "So perfect."

"You like that?"

"Uh-huh."

Without thinking I raced my mouth over him, causing a greater moan to surge from his stomach. It bounced around the pool area, and I stalled, wondering if we should be making so much noise.

"Sorry," he hushed, but he guided my mouth back onto him.

He pushed forwards and moved through my lips. I tasted my milk again, only this time I had the magical taste of Mr. Shaw's cock to go along with it. It was the perfect vessel with which to drink my nectar off, but I doubt the elites did it like this. They probably used fancy champagne flutes or something, but I was more than happy slurping it off my boss's gorgeous dick.

"That's so good, Hannah," he groaned, smoothing my hair from my face.

I looked up at him and smiled, putting on a performance for him. My lips ran up off his cock and I licked along the shaft, bouncing the tip of it off my tongue and giggling.

"Give it some more milk," Mr. Shaw urged.

This time I brought both tits forward and squeezed them. The milk fired out waywardly, striking his stomach and cock. I struggled to aim it, but I don't think he gave a shit. He started to jerk his cock and find the streams with it, pumping hard and letting the milk douse him.

"Yes, Hannah," he cried, and he sounded so impassioned.

"You like my milk all over your big cock?"

"I love it!"

He jerked himself and I kept up the flow, firing my pricey bounty all over him. Mr. Shaw was right, I was surprised how much I had.

He pushed his shorts down off his ass and I helped to take his legs out of them. His huge, soaked cock swung in front of me. He stood before me naked, with all of his prowess on display. He was well-toned and athletic for a guy his age. He was a fucking catch alright.

He took a grip of his cock and brought it forwards again, feeding it to my mouth. His hand held the base firmly and the shaft swelled up in response. The thick veins pumped up his length and it felt deliciously swollen with arousal in my mouth.

I brought my tits around him now and Mr. Shaw let go. I stared to bounce on my knees and move my tits over him, jerking him in their soft embrace. I giggled and looked up with a wide smile.

"Like what you see?" I asked.

He nodded. "I love seeing myself sandwiched between those."

"Good," I moaned, looking down at the shiny, milk-glossed head as it emerged over and over from my big tits.

"But I want to please you too," he said. "You've been such a good girl that you deserve more."

"What did you have in mind?"

"How do you feel about this"—he pulled his cock out from my cleavage and held it again—"in your soaked pussy?"

I held my breath and closed my eyes, imagining just that. "Yes," I hushed. "Yes, I want that."

"So, take those off," he said, pointing to my little shorts. "Panties too."

I stood up. "I want you to do it for me."

I walked slowly to the covered bar, looking back over my shoulder and tempting him towards me. I approached one of the stools that sat in front of the marble bar-top and put my hands on it, arching my back and pushing my ass out towards him.

Mr. Shaw stood up steadily, tempering his movements. I wanted him to rush over and claim me, but he walked slow. His cock stuck out from his body all stiff as he moved towards me.

"I think I can do that," he said.

I bit my lip as he approached. I was so nervous but hid it well behind my giggles.

"Is this what you want?" he asked, curling his fingers down inside the waist of my shorts.

I nodded.

He slipped them down over my ass but left my panties where they were for the moment. The shorts fell to my ankles and I stepped out of them. Mr. Shaw's big hand came to my ass and he gripped firmly. I mewled back at him.

"Take off my panties," I whined. "Fuck me."

I was so desperate for him and he could sense it. I wanted his cock deep inside me and he knew it. Instead of taking off my panties he cupped a hand beneath and rubbed at my pussy.

"Mr. Shaw," I whined, pushing my head back.

My tits dripped their milk steadily. The arousal seemed to ease the nectar out of me drip by drip until it was a steady stream that curled under my tits and ran down my stomach.

"You feel so fucking wet," he said. "I can feel it through your panties."

I was soaked, and not just with milk. I was so ready to be fucked. I wanted to show him how turned on he'd made me by swallowing him up in my slick folds.

"Fuck me," I begged.

"You want Mr. Shaw's big cock?"

"Give me that big cock, Mr. Shaw," I told him.

He moved my panties down now and I felt them come off my sticky crotch. They fell to the floor too, but before they were even at my ankles I could feel his big thickness arrive from below.

He rubbed himself up and down until he found the wettest part of my pussy, then he guided his cock upwards and I felt myself widen over him.

"Mr. Shaw!" I hushed, tensing and closing my eyes.

I fought against crying out in satisfied pleasure. Instead, I let out a long, low grunt as I felt his cock push all the way up inside me. I was finding out just how big he really was.

The deeper he drove the faster the milk flowed from me. Mr. Shaw put his hands to my rib-cage and felt the flow.

"You're really leaking now," he whispered, leaning over and kissing my ear.

I felt the chill of the kiss tingle down my spine and mingle with the pleasure in my pussy. I got goose-pimples all over as he gave me every inch of himself and then breathed close to my ear.

"You earned this," he told me. "And you'll earn a whole lot more."

I shuddered gleefully at the giddy thought of having him fuck me again and again as he took my milk. It sounded like the perfect partnership to me.

"Now let Mr. Shaw have his fun," he hushed.

"Fuck me," I told him. "Fuck me. I want your cum, boss."

I surprised myself at how eager I sounded.

"You do, do you?"

I nodded. "All over my tits."

"I think I can do that," he said wryly.

He took a grip of my tits and squeezed as he thrust in deep. His hips hit my ass and I let out a croak. He kept a steady rhythm to begin with, surging his cock home and showing me just how big he was.

I closed my eyes and groaned. The milk poured from me, unceasing. I never even knew I had any at all, never mind a bounty to rival a damn dairy-farm.

Mr. Shaw pinched at my nipples and then started to focus on himself, gripping my ass and looking down as his cock rushed inside me over and over.

"You gonna give me that cum?" I asked, looking back.

He nodded. "You're gonna get it, Han."

He sounded so certain. It made me shudder with ecstasy. I closed my eyes and smiled, but the force of his thrusts turned that into a look of pleasured anguish soon enough.

I looked down at my bouncing tits and the puddle of milk on the floor beneath them. He must have milked me of tens-of-thousands of dollars already, but I didn't care. This act was priceless to me in that moment. It was a confirmation of a deep, deep love.

"I want it," I moaned, grabbing my own tits and pinching them.

The milk fired forwards across the bar top. Mr. Shaw gripped my hips harder and pumped faster. He became animated behind me, working towards the grand finale.

"Come!" I told him. "Come! Come all over my *fucking* tits."

"Ohh, fuck!" he groaned, long and loud.

"Yes! Yes! Yes!"

I could feel the excitement. I could feel the impending release. I'd never wanted anything so badly.

"Come!" I told him.

"Oh, Hannah!"

"Come!

"Hannah!"

"Come on my fucking tits!"

Mr. Shaw pulled out fast and I dropped to my knees, turning towards him. I reached up and took his cock from him, jerking it for him as he stood over me.

"Oh, Hannah!"

His eyes closed and his body tensed. I pumped fast, rubbing the juices of my pussy back and forth along him. My tits dripped, hanging before him and waiting to be smothered by his love.

"Yes!" he burst, and he looked down at the source of his pleasure.

I kept jerking, holding my tits up on my forearm and presenting them. Suddenly a rush of cum shot up his cock and I felt it against my hand. The barrel throbbed and a volley of hot spunk burst out, crashing across my tits.

"Oh, yes!" I smiled as he exhaled. "Yes! That's it! Cover my tits!"

I pumped fast and watched the cum pour out of him. There was so much! Each rope pounced from his cock and lathered my tits, latticing them in thick lines of hot, white cum.

He took his cock from me and I started to rub the cum into my tits, pushing it up and over and massaging my nipples. It mingled with the milk and turned all pearly and white.

"Fuck, that's hot," he gasped. He'd put all of himself into his climax. He was breathing heavy and pinching the last of the cum from the tip of his cock.

"Good boy," I told him, looking up right into his eyes.

He stared down at the vision of sin beneath him. I ran my hands over my tits and rubbed in his cum as he jerked himself slowly.

"How much does this trade for?" I asked, nodding down.

"My cum?"

"Your cum and my milk," I giggled. "Do people drink that?"

"Try it."

I took my fingers across my tits and then showed him as I put them in my mouth and sucked along them. It tasted beautiful, like salted caramel. I took another load on my fingers and ate it up.

"I'd buy it," I told him wryly.

"We'll have to cook up another batch soon," he said.

"Agreed."

"So, you think you wanna let me sell that for you?" he asked.

I nodded. "Two-hundred?"

Mr. Shaw nodded and put out his hand.

I looked to mine. It was still covered in milk and cum. I pulled a face at him.

"I don't care about that," he said. "Deal?"

I reached out and took his hand. We shook firmly.

"Deal."

"I think this is the start of a beautiful relationship," he smiled.

THE END

More Milk Minister : Suckled Brats 19

Caroline Peters pushed through the door of number ten Downing Street with a rabble of unanswered questions trailing in her wake. The press outside was ravenous. They smelt blood.

She fell back against the door and let out a deep breath, but she couldn't be still for long. Her close aide Henry stood beside her; he had ever since she'd taken the job. She'd received plenty of criticism for that move too, despite his credentials.

"Breathe," he said. It seems odd to employ someone to tell you to do that, but Caroline often found herself forgetting, even after twenty-two years of doing it.

"They want me to fail, Henry," she said.

"They do, and that's why you mustn't. Prove them wrong. All of the bastards."

Just then the next onslaught came as Caroline's Press-Secretary arrived in front of her with a clipboard clutched to her suit-jacket.

"The Telegraph are asking for a statement regarding the recent expenses scandal. As are The Observer. The Mail would like to know if you plan on hiring any more personal friends to office and the Daily Star haven't stopped calling with regards to rumors surrounding you are your aide." She glanced at Henry

"Rumors?" he asked.

The Secretary flashed Caroline a quick look.

"Tell the Telegraph and the Observer we are actively investigating, tell the Observer that Henry is a very well qualified aide and don't tell the Daily Star anything. We don't want that gathering any traction."

"I'm afraid it already is," the Press Secretary said. She pulled a page from her clipboard and turned it around to show Caroline.

The Prime Minister studied it. It was a page from Reddit with users speculating wildly on the nature of Caroline and Henry's relationship. Some of it was very close to the truth.

"He's my aide!" Caroline cried. "What kind of relationship are they talking about?!"

"Well, with him being so close to you ..."

"He's my *aide*. That's what aides do!"

"I'm flattered, truly," Henry said, placing his hand on his chest.

"Ugh," Caroline grunted, clenching her fists. She could feel her stress-levels rising. "I need to be alone for a few minutes."

She looked to her Press Secretary and waited for the overt hint to register.

"Oh!" she said suddenly. "Yes. Of course."

She retreated with her clipboard just as someone else approached.

The Prime Minister held up her hand. "Stop," she said simply.

She and Henry walked ahead to her office. Inside she bolted the door and fell against it. Henry stood opposite her.

"It's been quite the day, huh."

"It has, Henry" she said, feigning a child-like voice.

"Aww, we'll get through it," he said. He stepped forward and embraced her, holding her head to his broad chest. Having been in politics for most of his life Henry Barlow knew all too well how vicious an arena it could be.

"Can we do it again?" Caroline asked.

Henry's hand stopped rubbing her back. He looked to the locked door.

"The rumors are circulating, Caroline."

"Then it's already too late."

"Your secretary can make them go away."

"I don't want to stop. It feels too good."

Henry sighed. "I'll get the blinds."

He slid towards the window, keen to keep himself from view. He twisted the cord and the blinds closed, then he moved along the wall to deal with the other windows.

In the mean-time Caroline was looking at herself in the mirror. She was fixing her shirt and opening a few buttons, revealing the deep cleavage that she kept hidden from public view. It didn't do well to have a leader who put too much skin on show in England. The older generation just wouldn't stand for it, and it was them whose votes had won her the election.

"Sit in my chair," Caroline said, offering Henry the resplendent seat of office.

Henry ran his hand along its back. He'd had his own desires of office but had put them to one side in support of Caroline. People will do strange things when they're in love. And lust.

Henry sat in the chair and leaned back into its cool, leather embrace. It felt stiff and yet comforting all at once, being more of a symbol than a practical seat. Nevertheless, he enjoyed it. He knew what was to follow.

"I feel full today," Caroline said, touching her breasts gently. It was the result of a terminated pregnancy following a fling with one of her underlings. She told herself she'd have made the choice regardless of her leadership charge.

"I'm sure I can help relieve some tension," Henry said. He set his hand on the arm of the chair and stared forward with command. It made Caroline blush.

"You always know how to take care of me."

"Come here."

Caroline walked slowly across the floor, stepping out of her high heels on the way. The wooden floor beneath felt cool. The rug beneath her desk felt soft as she stepped over it. She perched on the arm of the chair and Henry started to rub her lower back.

"Open your shirt," he said softly.

Caroline bit her lip. She leaned forwards and turned on the desk-lamp that sat before them. An orange light filled the immediate area.

"That's better," Henry said, looking up from her breasts and into her eyes.

Caroline popped open several buttons until her black bra was visible beneath her dark blue shirt.

"They're all for you, Henry," she whispered.

Henry moved his face forwards and buried them in her cleavage, kissing her soft skin and breathing deep. Caroline sighed too. Her aide's stubble bristled over her skin and his breath felt warm. Her nipples pricked as the adrenaline pumped through her. No-one had ever used their time in office like this, she was sure of it. What a thrill!

Henry started to unfasten the rest of her buttons and then he pulled the bottom of her shirt out from the waist of her pencil skirt. He pushed it wide open and ran his hand up over her bare stomach. His hands squeezed at her tits. Caroline felt one of her legs prickle like static as all her stresses gave way. The scandals, affairs and rumors disappeared briefly and all that was left was the sensations she felt at the capable hands of her older aide.

He squeezed each breast in turn, breathing deep against them and feeling his cock turn hard in his pants. He sat in that chair and felt absolute power. He felt as though he could do anything. Caroline wanted him to.

"Yes, Henry," she urged, throwing her head back and shaking out her blonde hair. She took great strides to make herself appear less attractive in front of the public.

Henry kissed at the top of her tits, flirting his lips around the frilly material above each bra cup. Caroline felt the wetness arrive at her pussy as Henry teased her. He'd never gone that far, of course, but she'd always hoped he might. Until that day the most he'd ever done was take the milk from her tits with his mouth. That was enough for Caroline.

"I want to drink you in," Henry said, looking up at her for approval.

"Suck my tits, Henry, please. I want your lips around me. Taste me."

Henry pulled down one cup and quickly raced his lips over the pink, stiff nipple that appeared. His tongue tickled around it. He teased the tip of it into the tiny recess of the stud and Caroline felt a wave of euphoria cascade through her body, exploding at her pussy.

"Yes, Henry," she grunted, holding his head against her and running her fingers through his thick, black hair.

He opened his mouth over her and licked messily, pushing as much of her breast into his mouth as he could. His jaw rocked and he started to suckle, flicking his tongue over the nipple and stimulating a response from his boss.

Caroline closed her eyes and hummed contently, feeling the milk begin to spurt through the tight aperture. It blasted outwards in a spray, but Henry caught each drop. He rolled his tongue over the ambrosia in his mouth, tasting its creamy sweetness.

He swallowed it down and felt a relief that was almost as great as Caroline's. His hand rubbed at his cock slowly. He didn't want her to see just how much he was enjoying himself.

"Let me feed you," Caroline moaned.

She pulled back her shirt quickly and then took off her bra. Her big tits hung down right in front of Henry's face. They swung like a hypnotic pocket-watch and Henry felt their allure all over again. He didn't have to bridge the divide though; Caroline would do that for him.

He sat back in his chair as she crawled up onto it, straddling his lap. He had to imagine that she was oblivious to the stiffened cock that sat in his pants. It yearned for her attention, but he was fearful of ever getting it. It was a step too far, even for them.

"Squeeze it into my mouth," Henry said, opening wide.

Caroline did and a spurt sprinkled across his face. Henry caught some of it on his tongue and let the rest fall down his cheek. He seemed caught in a moment of bliss at having it all over him like that.

"Mind your shirt," Caroline said, catching the errant drops on her fingers. She moved them to Henry's mouth and pushed them inside. His tongue rolled around her fingers and cleansed the milk from them.

"Let's take this off," Caroline said, tugging at the lapel of Henry's suit-jacket.

He leaned his back off the chair and Caroline helped him out of it. She placed it on the desk behind them and then ran her hands down over his powerful chest. As she sat down on his lap she could feel the stiffness in his pants, but it didn't immediately register.

Henry knew, of course. His back was straight, and his fists gripped tightly at the arm of the chair. He didn't want Caroline to notice how excited this was making him. It was as though the admission would be a blow to his control.

Caroline felt the stiffness against her ass finally. "Is that ...?" she began.

Henry blushed and swallowed hard, flustered. "I couldn't help it."

"I had no idea I had that effect on you," Caroline said, and she rose up on her knees and fed her breasts into his mouth again. She'd thought the act more maternal than sexual, although she couldn't deny it's many effects.

He opened wide over the nipples and gripped each one, pressing his fingers deep and pushing out towards the nipple. A jet of fine milk sprayed out from each, and he did his best to catch it. Some of it speckled the leather of the chair behind him.

"Your shirt," Caroline said, pulling at his tie. "Let's take this off too."

He was reticent, but he didn't stop her when she started to unfasten his tie.

"This is dangerous," he said, but offered nothing else.

"Isn't it!" Caroline rejoiced. It wasn't the reaction Henry wanted, but he found it thrilling all the same.

There came a sudden knock at the door that startled the pair of them. Caroline felt her adrenaline peak.

"Not now," she called.

Her and her aide held their breath as they held each other. They stared at the door, wondering just how locked it really was.

No other sound came. Gradually the pair relaxed and finally Caroline turned to face Henry again.

"Your shirt," she said, unfastening a button. "Come on. Quickly."

Henry unfastened his buttons and Caroline pushed the shirt open, swooning as she rubbed her hands over Henry's hairy, toned chest. Henry took good care of himself. He knew that mental strength and physical strength often went hand-in-hand.

"That's it," Caroline hushed. Her pupils were fat with lust. She felt like a horny teenager on her first sexual adventure.

Henry leaned away from the large back of the leather chair and took off his shirt. Caroline grabbed it and placed it behind her onto the steadily growing selection of clothes that adorned her desk.

"That's better," she said, and she celebrated the act by spraying a fine jet of milk out of her tits at Henry.

He hurried his face forwards hungrily, opening his mouth over the sprinkle of white and latching right on to Caroline's nipple. He sucked her breast into his mouth and swallowed down the bounty that he received. It seemed endless.

Caroline massaged her breast with her hand while Henry soothed the other with his mouth. A moment later he switched, treating her other nipple to the flicks of his tongue and the vacuum-like clasp of his lips.

She held him against her and looked down as he fed on her tits. There was something impossibly good about the act. It felt amazing to nurture someone and have so much control, control that she found herself lacking in recent times. Her excitement began to outrun her inhibitions.

"I want more," she hushed.

"More?" Henry asked, looking up and licking his lips.

"More," Caroline said, and she reached beneath and placed her hand on Henry's hard cock.

"I—I don't know about that, Caroline."

"Allow me to change your mind," she said, slipping down off the chair and crouching beneath the desk.

Henry looked down on the excited face of the Prime Minister as she sank to her knees, desperate to please him. He felt great conflict, but he was ultimately only human. He didn't stop her when she fumbled at his belt, but he didn't help her either. He told himself that would be too much.

Eventually Caroline opened his pants. She teased her nails down inside and ran them over the fabric of his boxer-shorts until she found his unmistakable stiffness.

"That's what I want," she said, looking up dreamily. "I've earned it, haven't I, Henry?"

Henry pursed his lips and held her gaze. He nodded.

Caroline's smile grew wide, and Henry couldn't help but smile too. It was rare to bring her so much pleasure these days.

She tugged at the waist of his boxer-shorts and giggled as they started to move down. Henry took his ass up off the chair and Caroline's next frantic tug showed great progress. Henry's boxer-shorts descended until the black, thick hair became visible. It was a sure-fire sign that Caroline was close, and her pussy knew it. She felt her wetness bleed into her panties as she gave another tug.

This time his pants moved down over his cock, stretching it downwards. She could see the thick hilt, but it didn't give too much away yet, save for Henry's terrific girth. This was a real *man's* cock.

Caroline reached inside and took him in her hands. Henry felt the cool of her soft skin against him. He swallowed hard and tried to keep his composure as he stared down and watched Caroline free him completely.

Her whole face lit up when she saw the true majesty of what she was holding. Henry was big. He was the kind of older man who just *had* a big cock and there was nothing more to it than that. He didn't show it off, or talk about it, or hint in any way at its size. He just had it.

"Holy shit," Caroline said. She took it in two hands and caressed it, looking up at Henry and expecting him to share her disbelief.

"I'm glad I could impress," Henry said.

"You've done more than that. It's so big and beautiful."

Henry felt flattered, but he didn't feel it for long. Caroline pounced on him unannounced and forced the head of his cock deep into her mouth. She opened wide and Henry felt the dangerous but exciting brush of her teeth and the flex of her tongue on the underside of his cock.

"Caroline!" he cried, but he had nothing to follow it up with.

She pushed down until Henry touched the top of her throat. Her hands massaged his big balls and then wandered up to jerk the base of his cock. She pulled her lips back and released him, looking at his cock in a new light now that it was drenched in her spit.

"It feels so good," she said. She watched with wide, sparkling blue eyes as Henry's cock moved under her command. She ran her fist along the barrel, marveling at how much of him was left unclaimed.

Caroline started to use two hands, but still the crown of Henry's cock remained uncovered when she gripped both along the barrel of his dick.

"It's beautiful," she said again. She gave the head a kiss as both of her hands jerked him.

Henry's knuckles whitened as he gripped the armrest. He pushed his hips upwards and moved more of his cock into Caroline's mouth. He was part of the act now.

Caroline opened her mouth wide and let Henry rock gently through her lips as he made love to her mouth. By now the juices of her pussy had bled clean-through her panties. She could feel the stickiness on the inside of her leg.

"I want this," Caroline urged.

Henry could guess at what that meant, since he thought she was already *having* it.

Caroline looked back to the door and then to the clock on the wall. She stood up in front of Henry and went to the zipper at the side of her pencil-skirt.

"Caroline ..." he warned, but he lacked all conviction. He wanted his cock buried inside her more than anything, he just couldn't admit it.

Caroline took no notice of him, letting her pencil skirt fall to the floor to reveal her stockings and suspenders. She unfastened them slowly and then teased at the waist of her panties. Henry was smitten.

"You're something else, you know that?"

"I could say the same," Caroline said, looking again to his delicious, stiff cock.

He took a hold of it and started to play. It was intoxicating. Caroline had never seen him anywhere close to anything like this before. A small pair of shorts during a game of squash was about the nearest she'd come to seeing him naked—not that she'd wanted to beyond simple intrigue. If she'd known what he was packing she'd have come sniffing for it long before now.

Caroline turned away from him now and showed him her bare back that curved out at her hips. She rocked them as she pulled her panties down. Henry watched as his naked cock and the Prime Minister's bare ass shared his line-of-sight. He couldn't quite believe it.

Caroline wriggled out of her underwear and felt the crotch stick to her wetness. She pulled it down and let her panties drop, then she looked back over her shoulder with a smirk.

"Ever fucked a Prime Minister before?" she said.

"Never."

She turned and shower Henry the full majesty of her nudity. His eyes wandered all over her. He looked down at the kempt strip of fur that sat above her pussy. He could see the light from the lamp catch her wetness as she opened her legs and straddled him on the big chair.

"Give me what I want, Henry," she hushed.

She leaned in and kissed his lips. Henry took hold of his cock and found her wetness, washing it back and forth over the lips of her pussy.

"Yes," she whispered, nodding.

She straightened up and put her tits in his face, dropping her pussy at the same time. Her mouth opened in a moan as Henry felt the warmth of her embrace around him.

"Yes!" he grunted, putting his arms around her and squeezing her ass.

Caroline pushed her tits against her aide's face, and he moved his mouth to find her nipples. She dropped down further and took his big cock inside her. When Henry started to suck on her tits she came almost immediately.

"Of fuck!" she strained, reaching out to grab the top of the chair's backrest. She squeezed hard and thought about pulling off him. She was so sensitive and had waited so long. She hadn't expected to reach her climax so quickly, but Henry had primed her without even realizing it.

"Yes, Caroline," he urged, spotting the signs.

With his permission she let go. The orgasm tore through her and the moan that escaped was loud enough to hear out in the halls. It wouldn't do anything to quell the rumors, but Caroline didn't care about anything in that moment apart from the feeling—that glorious feeling.

The euphoria shivered through her. Her jaw was tight. She grunted out the release, contracting and squeezing her mature aide's big cock that sat inside her.

She rose and dropped slowly, jerking him in her pulsing pussy and determined to give him the same release that he'd given her.

"Oh, Henry, I love you," she growled, leaning over him and kissing the top of his head.

Henry stayed busy at her tits, squeezing and sucking. The milk poured into him, its flow increasing now that Caroline had surrendered.

He swallowed it down and felt the loving nourishment gloss his throat. Caroline's pussy hugged his cock close, massaging his full length like no pair of hands ever could.

She could feel her stomach bulge whenever she dropped down on him as her body made way for the powerful intruder.

She leant over and worked her ass, rocking it up and down. If anyone were to burst through the door now, they'd get a pretty good look at some Prime Ministerial asshole as her cheeks clapped open and closed.

Henry's attention wavered away from Caroline's tits for the first time. Now he was focused on himself and the sensation that her rhythmic writhing had coaxed out of him.

He could feel the tingling below the waist. His balls moved all on their own, priming themselves for release. He found the tightness unbearable. He hadn't had a pussy so young in a long time.

"Give me your cum," Caroline whispered.

Henry started to tremble. That didn't usually happen. Usually, his release was quick and fierce, but Caroline's love was giving him something more than normal.

It felt as though his whole body was about to explore. The trembles built and he gripped the chair to try to control them. His whole body was tense. All he needed was permission.

"Come," Caroline urged. "Come inside me. I want it. I need it. Give me your come."

With each of her urges she heard Henry grunt back. His responses became more rushed and urgent.

"You want to give it me, don't you?"

"Yes!" he managed.

"So, give it me. Give me that *fucking* cum!"

The injection of sass was all Henry needed. When he heard the Prime Minister demand his cumshot like that it left him with little choice.

Suddenly he took her up in his arms and started to thrust up into her. Caroline sat steady, trapped in his embrace. He bounced up off the chair desperately, then he lifted her up and laid her back on the desk behind her.

"Fuck me!" Caroline dared.

Henry used the table as leverage, slamming into Caroline and watching her tits spin beneath him. He looked down and watched as his cock disappeared over and over. It was an image that would never leave him.

"Shoot it," Caroline said.

"Oh, fuck."

Henry lost control. His thrusts lunged forwards and lost their rhythm. He knew he was going to come. He felt the surge of spunk at the base of his cock and the euphoric sensation that came with it.

"Yes!" he grunted, looking down at the source of his pleasure.

Caroline waited. Her face opened in a smile and then a giggle as Henry let out another grunt that signified his release. She felt him pulse and felt the heat arrive. His cum fired deep and Henry started to rock again slowly, pushing it inside her and feeling the texture of their love-making change.

Caroline's pussy became slippery with cum as Henry continued to come. His release was bounteous. People in politics didn't come often, so when they did it was *huge*.

"You're still going," Caroline whispered, looking down her body as Henry's hips rocked.

The cum flowed out of her pussy and onto the desk. It felt like a sleight on the whole of the United Kingdom, but Caroline couldn't have cared. She'd wanted only one thing in that moment and had got it.

Finally, Henry pulled out of her, looking down at his spent cock. The realization came flooding to him, but he dealt with it as he always did. His face was calm. He looked down on her.

"That was beautiful," he said simply.

Caroline sat up on the desk and angled her chin up. Henry dropped his lips to hers and they kissed. She could taste the remnants of her sweet cream on his tongue.

"Good girl," Henry said. "You're a good girl."

He held her against him, and she sank into the embrace.

Eventually she moved away from him. As the hug ended the reality of everything came back suddenly. She was the Prime

Minister once more, and not a vulnerable younger woman looking for love.

She regained her hard exterior as Henry moved away from her. He pulled up his pants and grabbed his shirt.

"Back to your duty," he said.

"Unfortunately."

Caroline found her panties and slid them up her legs, trapping Henry's seed against her. She'd walk round with it inside her for the rest of the day. She was on BBC News later.

"Try not to stress too much," he said. "It's all just a bit of fun, isn't it?"

Caroline smiled warmly, then another knock sounded at the door.

"It's the Daily Star," her secretary said.

"If it's about the rumors tell them to get fucked," Caroline shouted, putting her tits away.

Henry started to laugh. "Now you're getting it."

THE END

The Boss's Raffle Ticket : Suckled Brats 20

"You should see this girl," Henry said, leaning in to speak close to his boss's ear. "She can do it all."

Mr. Cooper took a sip from his bourbon and ice and looked up to the stage. The company had put on an amazing event so far, full of the debauched activities of which Mr. Cooper was accustomed. He left the organizing to everyone else so he could really enjoy the show. He kept his wife in the dark, of course.

"Tell me more," Mr. Cooper said, standing proud in his fitted Italian suit. Some of his employees milled around him, hoping to be next in line for some small talk.

"Her tits," Henry said, drawing a shape with his hand. "You wouldn't believe what they can do."

"Tell me, man," Mr. Cooper said, losing his patience.

"She can shoot milk right from her nipples. I've never seen anything like it. Tastes incredible too. I had twenty minutes with her the other day. Even used my bonus to pay for it."

Mr. Cooper took a bigger swig. "Good use of a bonus."

"It was endless. I wanted so much more but I couldn't afford it. But I can afford these." Henry held a clutch of raffle tickets. "It's being drawn in the next few minutes. Can you believe she's in the room right over there?" Henry nodded to the large, wooden double doors.

"She is?" Mr. Cooper said.

"Yeah? Didn't you organize this whole thing?"

"I organized the organizing." Mr. Cooper was far too busy to plan a party. He paid someone to do that, and he paid them well. John had never let him down yet.

"Fuck, I hope I win. Those tits, boss. That milk ..."

Henry clutched his tickets tighter and stared towards the stage. "Is it starting soon?"

"Uh-huh. As soon as the tickets sell out."

Mr. Cooper moved away, pushing past some of his employees in the direction of the stage.

"Good luck!" Henry called after.

He approached the front and spoke to the guy selling the tickets. He was from accounts.

"How much for the rest?"

"Boss?"

"The rest of the tickets. How much for what's left?"

The man from accounts looked down at a sheet of paper and did some quick math. "Five thousand dollars."

Mr. Cooper reached inside his breast-pocket and produced a clipped collection of hundred-dollar-bills.

"Here," he said, and he placed down five thousand like it was nothing.

The faces of the men in line dropped a little, but they couldn't help but admire the sheer audacity and bravado of their boss.

"The raffle draw will begin imminently!" the compere shouted from the stage.

Mr. Cooper walked back into the audience and stood beside Henry, clutching a much larger stack of tickets.

"Best of luck, boss," Henry said.

"You too, Henry." Mr. Cooper didn't mean it. He suspected Henry didn't either, the way he'd spoken about the mystery-woman.

A drum-roll started and the eyes turned to the stage.

"And the winner of a full hour with our lady Gisele ... is ..."

He stopped the whirring sphere of balls and put his hand inside. "Nine, nine, seven!"

He showed the ball to the audience. There were only a thousand tickets. Most of them knew who'd won already.

Mr. Cooper looked down at his clutch of nine-nines. The rest of the audience waited for him to realize.

"I—I've won," he said, showing a rare smile.

"Fix!" one of the audience-members shouted as a joke.

The men laughed and then an applause rang out. Mr. Cooper went to the stage to collect his prize, nodding at his well-wishers.

"Congratulations, sir," the man on stage said, and he handed Mr. Cooper a key. "Now go unlock your prize."

Mr. Cooper turned to his employees.

"I hope you appreciate that this was all fair game," he said, raising a glass. "I wouldn't have entered at all if Henry hadn't told me the kind of prize I'd be missing out on."

There were jeers around the room as the men drank. Twitter would have a field day if they ever found out what still happened in these rowdy boys' clubs.

"Now if you'll excuse me, I'm in mind of something different to drink."

He raised his bourbon and then sank it as the room applauded louder, laughing and shaking their heads. It was comforting to know the boss was just as degenerate as all of them.

He walked through the crowd to even more cheers and approached the double doors.

"Go get her, boss!" the men cried.

***

In the next room Gisele waited. She could hear the rabble intensify beyond the doors. She swallowed with nervous excitement. She liked to put on a show for her clients. She got just as much satisfaction from it as they did, although she could never confess that. For now, she was getting paid to do something she loved. Whoever came through the door would be just another customer.

At least that was the idea, but Gisele had got ahead of herself.

She listened to the door unlock. It opened and the noise poured in. So too did a tall, suited, older guy with an athletic build. Gisele let out a sigh of relief. The guy looked handsome from the back. He wasn't fat at least.

But then he turned around and everything changed. She stared across into the eyes of the man opposite. His face dropped too.

"Tori?" he said.

"Mr. Cooper?!"

He closed the door and locked it quickly, then he turned back to her. His adrenaline started to bubble.

"You ... *you're* Gisele?"

Suddenly her tiny dress, stockings and burlesque-style corset weren't enough. She felt decidedly on show, which had been the intention of course, but she wasn't expecting her friend's father to walk in. She hadn't ever imagined he might win the prize.

"*This* is what you do?" Mr. Cooper asked, aghast.

"It's a job like any other, isn't it?"

Mr. Cooper laughed. "No it isn't. It absolutely isn't."

"Well, it pays the bills, okay?"

"If you wanted a job that pays the bills you could have asked, Tori. Instead of doing ... *this*."

"And you could have offered. You were perfectly okay with *this* when you walked into the room smirking like the cat that got the cream, Mr. Cooper."

"Meg didn't say anything." That was his daughter. "I didn't know. I thought you worked at that shoe store out of town."

"I quit."

"To dance and feed guys your breast milk?"

"I like to dance, yeah, and I'm good at it, okay. Now go give that key to someone more deserving, because I'm here to do my job. What the hell are you here for?"

Mr. Cooper twisted the key in his hand and looked back to the room behind him where the party continued. He wasn't about to let one of those reprobates in here with Tori.

"We've got an hour, haven't we?" he asked.

Tori sat heavily on the red leather Chesterfield sofa. "Unfortunately."

Mr. Cooper put his hands in his pockets and kicked around on the ancient parquet flooring. They'd rented an old country house for the event. They didn't want any prying eyes.

"So, is it true?" he asked eventually. "About your, umm ..." He nodded to Tori's chest.

"What? My tits?"

She leaned back and looked down at them. The corset had bunched them up into a thick, inviting cleavage.

"Yeah. Can you do what the guys said you could?"

Tori nodded. "Yup."

"That's ... interesting."

"The most interesting thing about me, I guess."

"Don't say that," Mr. Cooper said, and he started to walk towards her slowly. "I know you've got much more to offer than that."

"But what if I want to do this? You ever consider that?"

"Why would you want to do this?"

"Because I enjoy it? The same reason you entered the raffle, right? Because you thought there was something enjoyable about it too."

Mr. Cooper was lost for words on both counts. He couldn't fathom how anyone could enjoy it, and he couldn't bring himself to deny that he might enjoy it too.

He sat beside her. "What do you enjoy about it?"

"I don't know. I guess I like the excitement it brings people. I like the look in their eyes. I like holding them to my breasts and caring for them. Maybe it's because I never felt cared for."

"You were cared for," Mr. Cooper said. "Tom did a good job, didn't he?"

"He was never home!"

"He was working, Tori."

"Exactly."

"Working to give you a better life. Not to give you this."

"He could have worked half as hard and given me his time instead. I don't care about the money."

"Well, you've got my time now."

"An hour? An hour in which you're supposed to be sucking on my tits?"

Mr. Cooper swallowed. He wasn't used to feeling uncomfortable.

Tori leaned back against the sofa and sighed.

"We can all be better," he confessed.

"Damn right we can."

He put a hand on her thigh to reassure her. Tori could feel him through her fishnets.

"What can I do? Show me what I can do?" Mr. Cooper asked.

"You can do what you came into this room to do."

Mr. Cooper's face turned serious. "You don't mean that."

Tori shrugged. "You're only here for one thing. So am I. Have at it. Let's stop pretending."

"Tori, you're forgetting yourself."

"No, I'm not. No, I'm not. I know exactly who I am. This is me, Mr. Cooper. You can either like it or leave."

Mr. Cooper pulled at his collar and then unfastened his top button. He wasn't used to being talked to this honestly. The room suddenly felt very hot.

"I'm glad it was you," Tori said. "Out of everyone, I'm glad it was you."

"Why?"

"Because you're the only one I really wanted."

"Wanted? In what way? You want me to ..."

"You always looked like you had so much love to give whenever I came round your house."

"You can find that anywhere, Tori."

"I want to find it here. Help me feel loved."

"How am I supposed to do that?" Mr. Cooper asked, exasperated.

"Do what you came in here to do," Tori reiterated. "Treat me like I want to be treated. Respect me."

"Putting your tits in my mouth is a sign of respect?"

"Yes," Tori nodded. "I chose this for myself. You chose to enter the raffle. Here we both are. Do what you came here to do."

Mr. Cooper let out a laugh and looked to the door. He was glad too. Glad that it hadn't been one of the rabble outside that had walked in on Tori and done untold things. A nineteen-year-old shouldn't have to put up with those guys.

"What if it wasn't me?" he asked. "Would you have ...?"

Tori nodded. "You're still not getting it. I didn't fall on hard times, Mr. Cooper. I want to do this right now. Maybe it isn't forever, but it's for right now."

It was hard for Mr. Cooper to come to terms with.

"You look like you need some help," Tori said. "So, let me help you."

She put her hands inside the bust of her corset and pulled down. Her big tits popped out from her top, bunched up and inviting.

Mr. Cooper gasped, but didn't turn his eyes away. He looked at her breasts and then up at her. She rose her eyebrows and nodded.

"Go on," she said. "I want you to."

"Tori, I'm not sure if I—"

"Go on," she insisted. "Let me help you some more."

She reached a hand behind Mr. Cooper's head and brought him forwards. He didn't put up a fight. Instead, he fell right onto her tits and opened his mouth.

Tori let out a breath and sighed. "That wasn't so hard, was it?" she whispered.

She held him against her and watched him feast. Seeing a guy who was usually so dominant and controlling do something as submissive as this was a real turn on to her, as was its forbidden nature.

"Oh, Tori," he groaned, circling his tongue around the nipple. It stiffened up gloriously.

"I've got two, remember," she said, guiding him onto her other breast.

Within she could feel the tingle as the pressure mounted. She didn't quite know how she was able to produce her milk, but it was happening, nonetheless.

Mr. Cooper felt the sweet burst as the first fine spray shot into his mouth. He pulled back, startled and looked up at Tori.

"I told you," she said.

He looked to her nipple. A bead of pure white hung off it. He licked his lips and ran his tongue around the inside of his mouth.

"Come and get some more," Tori insisted.

Mr. Cooper clasped his lips back over her nipples and she let her head fall back. She moaned softly, feeling her pussy dampen. Ordinarily she didn't go any further than this with the clients, but this was no ordinary client.

Mr. Cooper circled the nipple with his tongue and sucked hard, breathing in as much of her tits as he could. The milk started to flow faster and he began to drink it down. He could feel his cock growing in his suit-pants. It was running out of space in his boxer-shorts. He shuffled on the seat.

Tori noticed. She looked to his pants and saw a distinct trouser-tent growing at his crotch.

"Is that for me?" she asked.

Mr. Cooper pulled off, alarmedr. He realized where she was looking.

"That's, uh, an accident," Mr. Cooper said. "Coincidence."

"Shame," Tori said. "I'd have liked it if it were all for me."

Mr. Cooper bit his lip and mused. "What if it was? What would you do?"

"I'd treat you to something that not every guy gets in here."

"What?"

"My pussy," Tori said simply. "I'd treat you to my soaking wet, shaven pussy."

Mr. Cooper wiped at his mouth. His cock twitched in his pants.

"Okay," he said. "Okay, maybe it is because of you."

Tori smirked. "That's what I like to hear."

"I didn't expect it either."

"I think there's a lot you didn't expect today, huh?"

"You can say that again."

Mr. Cooper looked to her tits and squeezed them. The milk scattered out and sprayed his face.

Tori laughed. "You look cute."

Mr. Cooper wasn't used to being called cute. Being a fifty-something businessman was far from cute. Most of his employees feared him. Tori did not.

"You look good enough to ruin," he said, smirking.

"You gonna keep that thing all to yourself?" Tori asked, nodding to his pants.

"I didn't think you did that?"

"I can make exceptions," Tori said. "Besides; getting ahead of yourself aren't you? I just want to see it."

"You just want to see it, huh?"

"I wanna see what you're hiding."

"Nothing to hide," he said, leaning back.

"So, show me."

He stood up and took off his suit-jacket, laying it over the arm of the chair. Tori's eyes dazzled as she watched Mr. Cooper's hands go to his belt buckle. He unfastened it. She loved that noise of clanking metal.

"Pull out that hard dick," she hushed, staring right at it.

Mr. Cooper watched Tori watch him. She leaned forwards on the edge of her seat. Her big tits hung down, dripping their milk.

"Show me," she hushed.

He pulled his pants open wide and dropped his boxer-shorts with them. His cock fell out from under his shirt, all stiff and weathered. It was an older-looking cock than Tori was used to, but she found it mesmerizing.

"Yes," she whispered.

Mr. Cooper gripped it, holding the base.

"Jerk it," Tori said, watching.

He started to move his fist over it slowly. Tori looked up into his eyes.

"Naughty," she smiled.

Tori moved her hands to her crotch as she watched him, pulling up her tiny skirt and showing him what she had on underneath it.

Her panties were a lacy lingerie set and either side of the material Mr. Cooper could make out the shaven skin of her pussy. It looked smooth and inviting. He wanted to move the crotch aside.

"You going to play with me?" he asked.

Tori rubbed down herself, jostling her clit and awakening her pussy. It started to drool.

"I'm gonna do whatever you need me to," Tori said, and she moved the crotch of her panties aside to show him what he was missing.

Mr. Cooper gasped and jerked harder, staring at the glistening slit. Tori fingered at the sticky O, moving her cum up and down along her petals and studying Mr. Coopers face closely. She grinned as she watched him enjoy her.

"That's what I want," Mr. Cooper asserted. "I want your milk and your pussy."

"And I want your cock," Tori groaned.

She thought about pushing her fingers inside but instead she moved forwards off the sofa and crawled on her knees towards Mr. Cooper.

As she arrived, he relinquished control of his cock, letting it hang free and unclaimed. Tori studied it, licking her lips.

"That for me?" she asked.

Mr. Cooper nodded. "Take it."

She gripped her hand around it and felt the strength of Mr. Cooper's arousal. Her hand glided over it, moving the skin over the stiff muscle beneath. He closed his eyes and let out a deep, satisfied breath.

"Those men outside don't deserve you," Mr. Cooper hushed.

"I'm all yours."

She opened her mouth and moved towards him, but didn't yet make contact. She lingered around him, teasing him a little by putting her mouth close to his cock. Mr. Cooper grew impatient above. He was used to getting what he wanted.

A smile broke on her lips, but Mr. Cooper didn't see the funny side. He gripped her hair and pushed forwards, filling her mouth with his hard dick.

Tori was shocked but opened her mouth anyway and pushed her lips over Mr. Cooper's big, weathered cock. She felt his arousal fill her. She could feel his heartbeat as it pumped the blood up his length. She listened to him groan above her.

"Good girl," he said, bunching her hair and moving it aside.

He watched his cock disappear inside her mouth. It was quite the sight. They'd been through so much together but never anything like this. He'd never even *dreamed* of anything like this and yet here they both were. Little did Mr. Cooper know, but Tori *had* dreamed of this. She'd told no-one, but the fantasy had always been there, hidden deep. What woman didn't want to fuck her best friend's father?

Mr. Cooper held her head and kept it still, thrusting his hips slowly and making love to Tori's mouth. Her tits dripped steadily, pattering on the parquet flooring.

"Let's not waste that," Mr. Cooper said.

He walked a few paces to the rug in the middle of the room. He took off his shoes and then his suit-pants and underwear, then he started to unfasten his shirt.

Tori rubbed her pussy and watched. She started to squeeze her breast and Mr. Cooper watched the white milk run down over her nipple.

Mr. Cooper kept quite the physique, despite his age. He'd always said that it was important he stayed fit and healthy. He had an image to convey as the boss at work. People needed to look up to him.

"Come here," Mr. Cooper said, and he got to the floor and lay on his back.

Tori crawled over towards him, smiling. Her tits hung from her chest, drawing little patterns of milk on the floor as they swayed.

"Over me," Mr. Cooper hushed.

She hung her tits above his face and Mr. Cooper quickly reached his mouth up to them. He suckled on the teat and urged the nectar out of her once more. His mouth filled with the creamy ambrosia, and he swallowed it down gladly.

"There you go," Tori said, stroking his soft hair aside as she cared for him.

Mr. Cooper's big cock sat on his stomach and from here Tori could reach it. She took him in her hand and started to jerk, listening to him hum contently against her ripe tits.

"You like when I do that?" she asked. "You like it when I jerk your cock, Mr. Cooper?"

"Mmmm," was all he could muster, not wanting to break free.

He swallowed the nectar down gladly, remembering that Henry had told him how good it tasted. How right he was.

He feasted and gulped her down, taking her nourishment with aplomb. He switched breasts and squeezed just the same all over again, giving himself another tongue-lashing as Tori moaned above him.

She jerked his cock, staring at it and watching her hand move over it. The whole thing was surreal, but it was a moment that Tori didn't want to be absent from.

"I want that big cock," she cooed.

She crawled down over Mr. Cooper and soon her breasts were replaced with her frilly mini-skirt. Her face was over his cock, and she started to suck him all over again.

Mr. Cooper could only stare at the crotch of Tori's panties for so long without wondering what was underneath

"Take those off," he said eventually.

Tori pulled them down quickly and shook them down her leg. When she settled again with her knees apart over Mr. Cooper's face he got a good look up at what she truly had to offer. It sat above him glistening like a glazed donut.

"Put it on me," he urged.

Tori sank her pussy onto his face and felt his mouth envelop her. He mouthed and sucked, messily tasting her snatch and coaxing out her clit.

"Yes!" Tori burst. "Yes!"

For the moment she couldn't concentrate on the blowjob. Mr. Cooper's lips and tongue were just too good. They sucked and pulled at her flesh greedily and Tori found herself at the edge of climax instantly. Few men ever seemed to care about her orgasm.

"Oh, Mr. Cooper," she whimpered, her jaw tight.

She pushed it out and groaned, closing her eyes tight and hanging her head. Mr. Cooper felt her blonde hair drape over his wet cock, tickling it. He tensed and his cock bounced.

"Mr. Cooper!" Tori strained.

Her pussy burst on his mouth and Mr. Cooper felt the contractions. He pushed his tongue into her tightening core, probing deep and tasting her creamy sweetness. Tori seemed to be full of amazing tastes.

"That's my girl," he said, gripping her ass tight as he continued to taste her.

Tori smudged his face with her sex, rocking back against him and feeling his stubbled chin against her clit.

"I want more!" she begged.

She turned around on top of him and quickly put his cock beneath her mini-skirt. Mr. Cooper looked down over his toned abs, spying the hilt of his cock. The rest of him was disappearing up under her skirt. Soon he felt the warmth of her sticky O.

"You want it?" she asked, staring down on him as she hovered over his dick.

Mr. Cooper nodded.

"Come get it," Tori smirked.

He took a grip of her hips and pushed upwards. Tori tried to tease a little longer by moving up away from him, but Mr. Cooper gripped her hips harder and thrust upwards.

"Yes!" she burst, feeling him spread her muscle open.

Mr. Cooper found the inviting warmth of her pussy and knew instantly that he was going to come. If the sensation alone wasn't enough, then the dripping big tits that hung in his face were.

"Suck my fucking tits, Mr. Cooper!" Tori cheered.

It sounded as though there was a cheer in the adjacent room too but neither of them noticed.

Mr. Cooper sucked hard but was losing his focus. The pleasure mounted around his cock and he concentrated on the wet, firm grip of Tori's pussy around him

"Come inside me, Mr. Cooper!" she demanded, and again the noise in the room beyond flared up.

Tori started to bounce, leaving Mr. Cooper with no choice at all. As much as he wanted to carry on fucking her there was nothing he could do to stop himself from bolting. Tori bounced, jerking his cock within her and smiling down knowingly.

"Come," she told him. "Come. I know you want to."

Her tits shook on her chest, dripping down milk all over him. He felt the wash of euphoria rush over him. Here it came.

"Tori!" he strained, and his hands gripped her hips.

She slowed. She watched the pleasure etch itself on his face and bit her lip, gasping when she felt his cock throb within.

"Shoot it!" she told him, and she felt the heat arrive.

Mr. Cooper's eyes opened, and he looked down at the source of his pleasure. He let his head fall back to the rug and Tori stroked his face, guiding him through.

"Come inside me, that's it. Fill me up. Fill up my pussy."

She rocked slow, easing down and feeling her pussy turn sticky and silky as it flooded.

"Every bit of cum," she told him. "I want it all."

She kept Mr. Cooper inside her until his groans had subsided, along with the pulsing throb of his cock. Mr. Cooper opened his eyes slowly and stared up, his demons exorcised.

"That was something," Tori said, and she sat down all the way on him. Mr. Cooper's cock pushed the cum deep.

"You can tell no-one, do you understand?" he said

She smiled and briefly entertained the idea of toying with him.

"No-one," he reiterated.

"I understand, Mr. Cooperf."

She pushed off his stomach and eased up off his cock with a groan.

Mr. Cooper closed his eyes and felt her pussy unsheathe him one last time. He looked down at his cum-glossed dick and then watched as Tori pushed her hair behind her ear and went for it one last time.

She plunged his cock inside her and cleansed him of the cum, sensually lapping it off him until his cock was clean. It was as though she was readying him to return to his underlings.

"This won't be the last time," she smirked, and she tossed Mr. Cooper his clothes.

Mr. Cooper dressed in silence, but it wasn't awkward. Tori admired him as he once again became the big, bad boss that his employees feared. She knew another side to him now.

"Not a word," he cautioned, raising a finger.

He went to the door and unlocked it, slipping back out into the room. Ninety or so men looked in his direction in silence.

Mr. Cooper's face was stern. It was mere seconds away from belying his panicked guilt. Thankfully he was saved.

"Nice work, boss!" one man cheered, and then the men erupted in frat-boy revelry.

Mr. Cooper wore a look of relief that he tried to transform into confident pride.

They charged their glasses and drank, then turned their eyes to the stage for the next prize. Mr. Cooper looked back at the locked door, thinking of Tori behind it.

On the other side of the door Tori wore a permanent smile, sitting on the couch with her hands on her knees. She looked at the mess of milk on the floor and her mind thought back to the crazy, debauched act. She hoped to soon have more than that to reminisce on. She hoped to snare him again and have him on her tits, just as they both wanted.

THE END

Drinking My Nectar : Suckled Brats 21

You know what guys can be like with hobbies. They soon become obsessions. After Mr. Blakes wife split he'd gone through the ringer of activities. Now, inexplicably, he was a beekeeper.

I guess it's kind of become a noble pursuit. Seems every time I turn on the news, I'm hearing about how bees are necessary for the future of the human race.

If I'm honest I kind of find them fascinating, and as a hobby it was one of Mr. Blake's better ones. Building ships in bottles seemed utterly pointless to me, but this new venture seemed to have purpose. Honestly, anything to keep his mind off his ex was good I guess. I don't think he'd been laid since she left, despite me encouraging him to get out there and meet people.

I dropped in to see him for a coffee, but naturally he didn't answer the door. By now I knew what that meant, so I walked around the outside of his house and peered in over the back gate.

I could see him in his full regalia, moving slats of wood out of his hives and harvesting a batch of honey.

"Hey, Mr. Blake," I called, waving.

He spotted me and waved back. He looked like an astronaut in his getup.

"I'll let myself in," I told him, and I hooked my hand over the top of the gate and slid the bolt across.

I never wanted to get too close when he was around the hive. I think the smoke he let off relaxed the bees, but Mr. Blake regularly got stung through his protective outfit. I wasn't taking my chances. I hung back.

"What brings you to this neck of the woods?" he asked.

I took a seat on the bench he kept that overlooked his flower bed. "Can't a girl come visit?"

"She can," he said. "But she rarely does."

"It's a two-way street, Mr. Blake. Everything works both ways."

"Can I get you a drink?" he asked.

"I'm good. I'm happy watching."

"Watching?"

"You and your bees."

"Oh, they're restless today."

"Anything to do with you having your hands on their honey?"

He laughed his big belly laugh. "A little, I'm sure."

"How often do you harvest?"

"Two or three times a year."

"Oh, so today is really special, huh?"

He smiled through his net. "*Very* special."

I'd tasted his honey before I'd moved away and it had been incredible. It was so unlike the store-bought stuff. You could tell it was all authentic, if you know what I mean. Just one man doing his thing.

"I can't wait to taste it again," I told him.

"Won't be the same this year," he said.

"Why's that?"

He nodded to the patch of flowers in front of me. "Different pollen."

I sat forward and looked at the different colored petals. "That matters?"

"Oh, yeah. Can make a world of difference. I got these plants in from New Zealand for this year's batch."

"Which plants?"

Mr. Blake moved away from the hive and pointed close to the middle of the big patch. "The white ones there with the deep-purple center."

I leaned over and looked. They were kind of mesmerizing and looked like nothing else in the whole bed.

Bees buzzed across the top of the grass, visiting each flower in turn and loading up their butts to return to the hives that Mr. Blake tended to, keen to replace the honey that he was taking.

"What do you do with the wax?" I asked, still staring at the flowers.

"Candles, maybe," he said. "Been reading some people use it as sex wax."

"*Sex* wax?"

"Yeah."

"Mr. Blake, there's no such thing."

"Sure, there is! You pour it on your lover when it's hot."

"Pour it on your lover? That's just *wax*!"

"Sex wax," Mr. Blake reiterated.

I shook my head and started to laugh, but suddenly I caught an image of him playing with his sex wax.

"You used it like that yet?" I asked.

"Need someone to use it with," he said.

"You still haven't been out on a date?"

"I've been busy, El."

"With bees?"

"With all kinds of stuff."

"You need to be getting busy with a woman, that's what you need," I told him.

"Maybe that flower will help," Mr. Blake said, nodding again at the patch.

"The white one?"

"Yeah. It's supposed to have *powers*. If you believe in all that stuff, anyway."

Well, I *did* believe in all that stuff. I stared at the flower again and felt it's strange pull. No wonder the bees were drawn to it to.

"What powers?" I asked.

"It's an aphrodisiac, for one. And then there's some other stuff that I don't even wanna say."

"What?"

"I'm not saying."

"Spoil sport," I teased. "Lemme take a sniff."

"No, El," he said, taking a step forwards as I moved.

"It's just a flower, Mr. Blake."

He seemed unusually tense. "Just one sniff, okay? I don't know how potent this stuff is."

"It's a flower, Mr. Blake. No-one ever died from sniffing a flower."

He took his pruning scissors and walked over to the flower. He snipped the stalk and then handed it to me

"Careful," he said.

He walked back and set the beehives back to how they belonged as I held the flower in my hand and studied it.

I felt woozy just holding it, but I didn't want to let on. There was nothing worse than Mr. Blake being right.

He carefully removed his outfit and then walked around the flower bed towards me.

"Ellen!" he called, and it was then I realized I hadn't been hearing a thing. I was too rapt on the flower's deep, purple inner-petal. "I knew I shouldn't have let you have that thing."

"No," I called as he came close, and I took the flower and gave it a deep sniff. Its pollen rushed inside me. My pupil's bloomed into big dark pools as I looked to him.

"Ellen!" he said, snatching it. "That's a powerful thing."

"I thought you didn't believe in all that stuff?" I asked dreamily.

"I don't."

"So, smell it," I giggled, stroking a finger down over his shirt.

He looked at my hand as it touched him, keeping his expression stern for now. God, he looked good when he was angry. *Why did he have to be twice my age? Why couldn't he just be some hot guy?*

He put the flower to his nose and took a defiant sniff, then I watched his eyes blacken and deepen just like mine. He dropped the flower and stared right into me. It felt like he was taking a glimpse into my soul.

"Mr. Blake, you're staring," I said, bashfully.

"I'm just appreciating the finer form," he said.

"I feel funny," I told him, and my hands moved to my tits where a new sensation was beginning.

"I wish I could touch those like that."

"Mr. Blake!" I swooned playfully.

"What's wrong with them?" he asked. "They look fine to me."

I looked down to my breasts that sat bound in a bra and beneath a tight t-shirt. They felt kind of funny to touch. Suddenly they were incredibly sensitive. The nipples perked up beneath my bra.

Mr. Blake took a hold of his crotch now.

"Quit making fun," I cried. "Something feels weird."

"No, I feel it too," he said, gripping himself.

"What's it feel like?"

He moved his hand away and I replaced it with mine quickly. I mean, I didn't even think. I just thrust my hand right onto his crotch and felt his hard cock beneath.

"Feel it?" he asked.

"I do. It's hard."

"Out of nowhere," he said.

"Try these," I told him, and I pushed my breasts out toward him.

Mr. Blake, like me, wasted no time at all. He reached out with two hands and gripped a breast in each one. He squeezed and I felt a terrific rush of euphoria that eased a moan out of me.

"What was that?" he asked.

"I ... I kinda like it."

Jeez, what must we have looked like? Mr. Blake's neighbors weren't exactly close to the house—they all had huge back yards—but from the right vantage you'd be able to sneak a glance at an older guy and a younger woman, touching each other in the most intimate of places, fully clothed.

"I'm liking what you're doing too," he said, looking down. I hadn't realized but I'd been gently squeezing along his cock.

"Mr. Blake, that flower ..."

"That flower was everything we needed to express our love."

He stepped into me and put his lips on mine. I didn't even flinch. I just started kissing him all deep and passionate like it was the most normal thing in the world. His chest pressed against mine and I felt another burst of euphoria. This time it came with a new sensation: wetness.

I looked down at my t-shirt to see that the gray was starting to turn darker. My brow furrowed and I looked to Mr. Blake.

"The side-effects are true," he said, gasping.

"What side-effects?"

"The one I didn't want to tell you about."

"And that's"—I reached my hand down the front of my top and worked my way towards my nipple—"milk?"

"I don't believe it," he said, and he gripped my wrist, studying my finger.

"My tits are leaking, Mr. Blake," I giggled.

He opened his mouth over my finger and sucked along it, savoring the taste. Shit, it was so hot to be in his mouth like that.

"It's as sweet as the honey," he said, his eyes widening.

"Really?"

He nodded. "Taste it."

I reached down into my top again and swished my finger across my wet nipple. I pulled it out and studied the bead of white. He watched closely as I wound my tongue around it and lapped it up.

"Fuck," I burst. "That *is* good."

"More," he said, and I could agree with that.

He took the bottom of my t-shirt and started to lift it. I giggled, looking back over my shoulder at the thankfully empty windows of his neighbors.

Mr. Blake pulled the garment up and started to kiss my exposed stomach. I held him against me as he pushed the t-shirt up over my tits. He stood up and stared into my big cleavage, then he moved his face forwards and started to kiss my breasts.

"Mr. Blake," I hushed, closing my eyes.

He pulled the shirt up over my head and went back to business at my breasts. His fingers pushed into my waist and then moved up towards the clasp of my bra.

"I want you so bad," he said.

I knew exactly what he meant. My tits weren't the only thing that was leaking. I put a hand back on his stiff cock and rubbed along it. He felt *huge*.

He popped the clasp of my bra easily and pulled me close to him again. His lips fell on mine and our tongues entwined. Meanwhile he pushed the bra strap off my shoulders, so that only his body was holding it on me.

Finally, he pulled back. My eyes stayed closed as the bra fell from me and Mr. Blake got a good look at my firm, wet tits.

I opened my eyes to see him staring. His hands came in again and he pushed them together. They responded by firing out a spray from each nipple that Mr. Blake smiled gleefully at.

"So much milk," he hushed.

He moved his face close to the spray and let it pepper him. He opened his mouth over one of my nipples and started to suck straight from the source. I could feel the milk rush through my nipple and the sensation made my insides shiver. I burst with excitement and looked down on him as he fed from me.

"Suck the milk from my tits, Mr. Blake," I whined.

His face looked so serene and peaceful as he fed from me, but every now and then it would flare up with lust and he'd suck and bite at my nipple.

The whole time it burst with milk, sending out jets of nectar that Mr. Blake happily swallowed down. His garden was suddenly our own private sanctuary of sin—a kind of Eden but with a different forbidden fruit.

He moved his mouth to my other nipple and drank down its offering. I was suddenly *full* of milk, but Mr. Blake was on hand to relieve me. I hoped to relieve him too.

"I don't want you to do *all* the sucking," I told him.

He looked up over my tits and into my eyes, spotting my suggestive smile.

"Stand here," I told him.

I took his shoulders and guided him round so that he stood in front of the bench. I opened his belt buckle, smirking at him. He knew what was to come.

I slipped the leather through its metal clasp, my tits shaking the whole time. They dripped steadily, bouncing and bobbing while I snatched at the opening of his jeans.

When I'd popped open every button of his fly, I pulled his pants wide. I looked down and teased the front of his boxer-shorts forwards. I could see down into them. Inside his big cock lay in wait, yearning to be free.

"I hope that's all for me," I told him.

"I want you to have as much of it as you can stomach."

I pulled suddenly, sending his pants and underwear down in unison. His huge cock sprang out, but before either of us had time to take it in I pushed him back hard.

He put his hand out behind and fell into the bench. His cock swayed and then settled upright. I fell with him quickly, embracing his hard dick and thrusting it right into my mouth.

Mr. Blake hissed a breath in shock and then quickly relaxed. My warm mouth covered him in spit and sank down along his cock, pushing it right to the top of my throat.

I felt him move my hair aside but for now my eyes were closed. I was scared to confront the act, but I guess I had to look at what I was doing sooner or later.

"Fuck, Ellen," he said. "This is so wrong, and I love it."

I pulled up slowly off him, then looked right up into his eyes with my cock in his hand. He smiled and shook his head in disbelief. I tried not to blush.

I looked down at the bright, plump head of his cock and sank down on him again. I gave a slow pump along him with my lips and then came off the tip again, kissing down the underside of his cock and looking beyond it at his gaze.

"You are something else," he whispered.

I giggled as I started to tongue his balls. Mr. Blake tossed back his head and let out a satisfied groan. It was so hot to hear how much he was enjoying me.

I sucked at one of his balls and then slid my tongue back up his cock, feeding him into me all over again.

My tits just did not stop leaking the whole time. I could feel the nectar dribbling down over my stomach and messing the top of my jeans. Some of it ran in down to my panties.

Mr. Blake held my head on him as I covered his cock in spit, but then I had the idea to cover his cock in something else entirely.

I sat up and started to guide my tits towards him, and he became even more excited.

"Yes, babe," he said. "Put those milky tits around me."

I trapped him amidst the cleavage, closing my tits around him with my hand. I started to bounce slowly, dragging his hard cock through the soft flesh.

My nipples sprayed out their cream, coating his cock and making a mess of his crotch. The white pearls of liquid hung on his pubic hair.

With my other hand I started to rub at my hot crotch, getting more and more excited the entire time. I could feel the wetness of my pussy bleed against my panties. Fuck, I had to get him inside me.

"Oh, baby, that's it," he said, looking down.

His face was contorting wildly, but I didn't want his cum yet. I wanted to get it where it belonged. I wanted to commit fully to this sinful act.

"You gonna hold on for me?" I asked, looking up.

He came down off his cloud, breathing heavily. "Yes," he said. "I can do that."

I gave his cock a kiss and then stood up in front of him. I unfastened the front of my jeans. Mr. Blake pulled everything off both ankles and tossed it aside, then he pulled his shirt off and showed me the rippled muscles beneath. He sat naked on the wooden bench as I undressed before him.

"That's it," he said. "That's what I want."

He started to jerk his cock as I undressed. It was so fucking hot and naughty. I mean, I just couldn't believe what we were doing, but I had no intention to stop. The thought just didn't occur. I wanted to put on a show for him and have him enjoy me.

"Is this what you want?" I asked, pointing down at my pussy as my jeans sat open.

He nodded, jerking his wet cock.

I turned away from him and pushed them down over my ass, taking my panties with them. I could hear him grunt as he jerked his dick, fighting to be patient.

"I'm gonna sit on that *big ... fucking ... cock.*"

"Yes, you are, babe."

I got out of my jeans and stood astride, flexing my ass and rising on tiptoes. I felt a kiss of wind brush over my wet nipples. My whole body flooded with goosebumps. I could feel my body bubbling with excitement. I just *knew* that I was going to be satisfied.

Finally, I turned to face him. He slowed the movement of his hand, and I watched his eyes draw all over me, looking from my kempt pussy up to my dripping tits and back down.

"Come and fucking sit on me, Ellen," he said, holding his cock up right.

I walked with purpose and confidence, striding forwards. I put a knee on the bench and straddled him. His cock sat below my pussy, dangerously close. My tits hung against his face.

"Give it me," I told him, and I started to drop slowly.

He kept himself where he was, fighting the urge to thrust up and claim me. Instead, he allowed me to drop slowly and find his cock with my tight, soaking O.

I felt it slot on him and slide down slowly. His thickness eased inside me, opening me up with a satisfying stretch. I threw back my hair and put my tits against his face as he moaned.

I could feel his passion in vibrations against my breasts as he let out a groan of pleasure, then he raced his lips back over my nipples and took a good mouthful of milk.

Shit, the sensations were too much. I burst with desire and felt my whole body become charged with excitement. His mouth fed on me, drawing the milk through my nipple as I continued to drop down on his long, thick cock.

The more and more of him that I fed into me the strong the sense of excitement became. I sucked in huge breaths and gasped them out in stuttering moans. My whole body went tight. I hadn't expected to come so easily.

I sank all the way and when Mr. Blake's big cock hit as deep as it could go, I gasped my eyes open and stared of into the distance.

I held his head against me and started to come, wriggling on his thick cock. Mr. Blake sucked on my tits the whole time, squeezing my ass and pushing his face against me. He feasted on my breast, forcing as much of my flesh into his mouth as he could.

My pussy gripped and flexed around him, coating him in my creamy wetness. I was a mess. My vision swirled with fantastic colors and the whole world seemed to open up to me. Everything was more vibrant. The birds sang and the bees seemed to buzz louder than before.

Mr. Blake swallowed down his mouthful of milk. "Yes, baby."

It felt like a beautiful partnership. I was feeding him my nourishing tit milk whilst he was feeding me his huge cock. I yearned for more. I started to bounce slowly, coming out the other side of my climax.

I started to bounce on him now, my tits knocking against his moaning face. Whenever he felt thirsty, he clasped over the nipple and took a few jets of my warm milk in his mouth, but otherwise he just sat back and enjoyed me. It had been a long time since he'd had a twenty-year-old woman bouncing on his cock.

He stretched his hands across the back of the bench and gave me full control of his cock. I wasn't going to neglect the privilege. I held him against me and twerked my ass down, swallowing up his cock over and over and turning it all white with my cum.

As I increased my pace Mr. Blake's hands moved around me. He started to breathe deeper and moan louder. His grip became sterner, burying his fingers into the flesh of my ass as he took big fistfuls of me.

"Make me come," he told me.

"Just like this," I told him. "I'm gonna make you come just like this."

I worked over him, popping my pussy on and off him. His cock got swallowed up again and again, becoming stiffer and plumper as I continued. It was just a formality now.

"Oh, Ellen, you're gonna make me come," he told me.

"I want it, Mr. Blake. I want it!"

"Oh, Ellen!"

"Give me that fucking cum. I deserve it. Give it me!"

I started to thrash on him, bouncing faster than I ever had. My tits dripped against his bare chest. Mr. Blake's brow furrowed in pained pleasure.

"Ellen!"

"Come. Come in my fucking pussy. Give me that thick, hot load."

"Ellen!"

That last strain was unmistakable. Finally, he pushed his ass up off the bench and sank his cock deep. He wanted to give me his all.

I held him against my tits and cooed with delight as he let off. Mr. Blake strained out each rope, signaling them with grunts that started loud and faded off.

I felt the heat within me. The texture inside changed too. I became all sticky and full, and then gravity took over. His cum started to roll out back over his cock.

I lifted slowly off him and looked down at the mess, then I sank my pussy back on him gladly and felt him fill me up again.

"Every drop," I whispered, kissing his face.

Mr. Blake was spent. His eyelids hung heavy. He smiled blissfully.

"You just came inside me," I told him, kissing his face.

"And I'd do it all over again."

He raced back over my tits and gave one final, loving suck. The nectar rushed into his mouth, and I could hear him swallow it down.

"Mr. Blake!" I burst, shaking my tits on him.

I got up off him slowly, easing his cock out of me. I looked down on it. It was covered in all of our juices. My cum had mixed with his and the whole thing looked like a stick of marble.

I can't let that go to waste," I told him, crouching before him again.

His eyes lit up and he concentrated again while I mouthed him. I tasted our sweet, salty cum. It was like caramel on my tongue. I sucked up all I could and then popped my lips off the crown.

He looked like Mr. Blake, but in no way that I'd ever known. It was so jarring to see him all naked and aroused before me like that, but it didn't feel wrong. It felt like we'd explored a facet of our love for each other that most people don't, and it was all thanks to that tiny, white plant.

"That's some flower," I said.

Mr. Blak looked over me at the bloom behind. "It blossoms for several months," he hinted.

"Several months, huh?"

He nodded.

"Then I think I'll be stopping by more often."

THE END

Draining My Milk : Suckled Brats 22

Since moving out Mason was always on hand to fix any problems in my new apartment. He worked for the building, but my apartment alone felt like a full-time job for him. Well, I'm not complaining. Some of the issues I just *can't* fix, and Mason's got a wealth of experience behind him.

That day he found himself studying the kitchen basin with me a few feet behind him.

"You say it's leaking?" he asked.

"Yeah."

"Like, *dripping*?"

"No, it's leaking underneath."

He opened the counter beneath the basin and looked inside. "Ahh," he said.

He crouched and I leaned over behind him. You could see a small puddle of water that was collecting inside.

"You said the faucet is loose too?" he asked.

"Uh-huh."

"Jeez, is anything right with this basin?"

"Water comes out of the faucet at least," I shrugged.

It was then that I felt the tingle. It was something that had been happening more and more recently, and I have no idea why. To my knowledge, women's breasts don't just start leaking milk for no reason.

"So, you've got a leaky drain and a loose faucet?" he said.

"It seems so." The tingle grew.

"Can you just run the tap slowly for me?"

I went up above and twisted the top of the faucet. The whole thing rotated a few degrees but then a steady stream of water came out.

"Okay, stop," he said. "I can see where it's leaking."

He fidgeted around beneath for a few minutes.

"Can you pass me the wrench?" he asked.

I fished in his tool bag and handed it to him. I could feel a strange wetness all of a sudden. I looked down and noticed my t-shirt becoming darker at my nipples. *Fuck, not now.*

"I'm just gonna go and—" I began.

"Stay here," he said. "I need you for this part."

Fuck.

"Can you just hold the faucet for me to stop me from twisting it from below?"

I reached forward and took a firm grip. I felt him twisting from below and fought against him.

He strained. "There. Can you turn the flow off?"

I looked to the faucet. "It isn't on."

"It's still leaking," he said.

I looked down at the basin's drain to see a whisp of white disappearing down it. I followed the trail to my nipples and saw my t-shirt steadily dripping white milk.

"Is it off?" he asked again.

"Uh-huh," I said.

"Some of it got my face. It's sweet. Weird. Lemme just tighten this."

He strained again beneath, and I watched him wriggle. I looked back at the door and thought about making a move.

"There," he said, and he emerged from beneath. "All fixed."

His eyes caught mine and he looked immediately to my t-shirt. I folded my arms across my breasts.

"Did it splash you?" he asked. "We got a wet t-shirt contest going on?"

"Mason!"

He stood up and it was then that I saw my milk on his face. It rolled down his cheek slowly. He wiped his hand at it and then looked at his finger.

"Huh," he said. "It's ... white."

"Could just be some gunk from the drain."

He sniffed it. "It's never usually that color."

"Could be anything," I shrugged, keeping my arms firmly across my chest.

To my horror he poked his tongue out from his mouth and tentatively tasted the whiteness on his finger.

"I thought so!" he announced. "It's milk!"

He looked to the drain and the residue of white that was still present. "Huh," he mused.

I started to turn red. I didn't know how long it would be before he put all the pieces together. I could feel the milk against my bare forearms as the cogs of his mind whirred.

"Milk," he said suddenly, looking to me. He saw me blushing and then looked down at my arms. "Milk!"

I looked down too and noticed that I was no longer doing a good job of hiding it. It had bled right through my t-shirt and its whiteness was more than apparent.

"You're *leaking*," he cried, stepping forwards.

"It's nothing," I said, twisting away.

"It's not nothing, Sophie, it's *something*. What's causing that?"

I sighed. "I don't know. It keeps happening."

Mason wore a look of concern and intrigue. "You keep leaking milk?"

"It started a few weeks back. Just one night and *bam*. Milk."

"Just like that?"

I shrugged and moved my arms away. The two of us looked down at my breasts. They were sodden, and the t-shirt left nothing to the imagination. It pulled close to each breast, hugging the nipple. The milk continued to stream out of them.

"Damn," he said. I'd never had a guy study my breasts so closely before.

"Okay, Mason, jeez."

"It's just ... I've never seen anything like it," he said in awe.

"Sorry for not being as pleased about it as you are."

"I'm not pleased, Sophie, just ... *fascinated*."

He didn't let up from looking. He continued to stare, and his arm reached out as though he was going to go a step further.

I waited, cautious. It felt dangerous, but I wanted it. I wanted him to reach out and claim me. I wanted to see where this would lead.

His eyes were black with desire. "It just came out of nowhere, huh?"

"Uh-huh," I told him, studying his face. He was captivated by my body in a way no-one had ever been before. It made me feel special, despite the circumstances.

"It just doesn't stop, does it?" he said.

"It will in an hour or so."

"An hour of this," he said. "Shit. You could open your own café."

"Mason!"

He laughed. "Sorry, Soph. Just messing around."

"You ever seen anything like it?"

"No on two counts."

"On two counts?"

"Firstly, I've never seen a pair of tits do that before. Secondly, I've never seen a pair of tits look so fucking incredible, Soph." He looked me in my eyes. "Where have you been hiding those?"

I was blushing for a whole new reason now. He wasn't shy about giving me compliments in the past, but they were never so sexual. My leaking breasts seemed to be having an effect on him, and they were affecting me too.

Whenever they leaked, I felt an impossible arousal that I could only sate with an orgasm. It was as though my body flicked a switch suddenly and decided not only that my breasts were going to leak milk, but that I was going to be incredibly excited by their doing so.

"They're just tits, Mason," I shrugged.

"They're very special tits," he said, and he held my shoulders and stared.

I bit my lip, wondering whether to move this to the next level or even *how* to move it to the next level. It isn't every day that your older handyman develops a deep attraction to your breasts.

"Do you want to see?" I whispered, saying the words so quietly that I could deny I said them if I didn't get the reaction I wanted.

"Now? Here?"

I nodded.

"Please," he said. He took a step back. "Show me."

I took a deep breath and felt the wet t-shirt hug around my tits. I gripped the bottom of my shirt and pulled it up over my head, feeling my tits drop out from beneath and hearing Mason swoon soon after.

"Fuck, Sophie. They look incredible." He stepped forwards and put out a hand. "Can I?"

I nodded, dropping the shirt. I looked at his hand as it touched me. It felt warm against my breast. He stroked his thumb over the nipple as it steadily eased out droplets of white.

"It's just *leaking*," he said.

The nipple stiffened beneath his touch, and I closed my eyes. I let out a soft whimper.

"Fuck," Mason said, then he squeezed.

I startled as I felt the rush of fluid leave me. I opened my eyes to see a spatter of wetness on his shirt now.

He looked down slowly in shock and then started to laugh. "They shoot milk, Soph!"

"Try them both."

He took a breast in each hand and pushed them together. "Here goes."

He squeezed up to the nipple of each and they both fired out a fine spray of milk that peppered his t-shirt some more.

I laughed and Mason did too. We were getting carried away. He squeezed again, only this time he moved his mouth to meet the milk's source.

I opened my mouth to gasp but a moan replaced the sound. Mason's mouth clasped over my nipple and he started to suck.

My hand held his head against me in an instant, as though it was instinctive. I cradled him to me and felt him begin to suckle, working the milk out of me and swallowing it down audibly.

"Fuck, Mason, that feels so good."

I ran my hands over his back, trying to convey my appreciation in my touches. I rubbed down around his t-shirt, over his broad shoulders and around to his chest. None of the touches seemed to return the sensations that he was giving me.

"Mason," I whispered distantly. I was practically *floating*.

He switched breasts and gave the other the same treatment. Finally, he popped his lips from the node and looked up at me, licking his lips.

I looked to his mouth. This was the moment when things could get crazier ... if we wanted.

He moved his mouth to mine but left the final few inches of contact up to me. I wasn't going to stop here. I was too far gone. Besides, Mason's lips had barely satisfied. I wanted more. Much more.

I bridged the gap and put my lips to his. We started to kiss, and I tasted the sweet nectar on his tongue as it swashed against my own.

My hand moved down to the waist of his jeans, and I hooked a finger inside. He stepped closer and my breasts pressed against him.

They leaked into his t-shirt as the kiss blossomed. His hands wandered down my bare back and to my ass, squeezing it tight before moving back up. He pulled away after a few more seconds. I looked down at his top and saw the two dark circles where my milk had bled through.

"Guess I better take mine off too," he said.

"Guess you better had."

He made no show of it. He lifted his t-shirt over his head quickly. He was confident for good reason. The muscles below looked effortlessly sculpted. I had no idea he kept himself in such good shape. The yearning to run my hands over him was too big to ignore.

I put a hand on his chest. I could feel his heart beating fast beneath it. He pulled me close again and we kissed. Now the milk fired against his chest and with nowhere to absorb it trickled down his body, breaching the waistline of his jeans.

He pulled back suddenly and looked down. I followed the white trail into his pants.

"That felt funny," he laughed.

"You can take those off too," I shrugged.

He smirked. "You'd like that, wouldn't you?"

"I'd enjoy it," I told him. "But not as much as you."

I raised an eyebrow suggestively and Mason got the hint. He didn't waste any time. He popped the button of his jeans and opened it wide.

"Like to do the rest?" he said.

Fuck yes.

I crouched to the floor in front of him and put both hands up to grab the waist of his underwear. My tits shook and dripped. I yanked at the waist and pulled both garments down at once. His jeans fell below his knees and so too did his boxershorts.

I startled and angled my head backwards as his big cock sprang up from his pants. He was halfway stiff already, and from his hand atop my head I was guessing he wanted some help with the other half.

I didn't even stop to think. You don't hang a cock like that in front of your face and then turn it down at the last second. I did what any woman would—but what few women had. I opened my mouth over his cock and started to get him hard.

It was so fucking surreal, but then so was everything else. He'd already sucked the milk from my nipples—this felt pretty tame in comparison.

I felt the blood pump into him as he grew in my mouth. His hand stroked down over my cheek and he groaned.

"That's it, Sophie."

I pulled my lips back and stared at his cock at full mast. The veins surged up along the length, igniting the head that shone now with my spit.

I gripped him in my fist and jerked him slow, watching the skin move over the muscle. I kissed the tip, tonguing gently at the little slit on the end and giggling up at him.

"Let's test out this basin," he said. "See if my handiwork is up-to-task."

He helped me to my feet and then moved me around so that I stood at the counter over the basin. His hands came around to the button of my jeans and he popped it open, putting his head on my shoulder and kissing at my neck.

"Are you going to fuck me?" I whispered.

"Yes."

That simple *yes* sparked something deep inside me. I felt my wetness break inside, and my pussy flooded with juices. It knew I was going to need them.

He pulled my jeans down roughly and took my panties with them. His hand came down to my stomach and pushed down, finding the little patch of kempt fur above my pussy.

His fingers moved through that and to my clit. It was already breaching the hood, swollen and ready. He tickled it as he kissed the lobe of my ear. A shiver of excitement went through my spine, exploding down near my stomach and pussy. My petals felt as though they were fluttering with excitement.

"Fuck me, Mason," I gasped. There's something I thought I'd never say in my life.

He came up close, gripping his cock. He dropped his knees and put it under me. I could feel the thickness against my wet pussy lips. I moaned as he ran his cock along them, not yet venturing inside.

"Fuck me!" I whined, desperate.

I pushed my ass back as he sought me out. I felt his hard cock at my O.

"Yes!" I gasped.

He pressed his cock into me, and I let out a moan. As he filled me up my breasts burst, sending a jet of milk out into the basin. It swirled down the drain, with more joining it as Mason started to hit a steady stride.

"Good girl," he told me, gripping my ass. "There's a good girl."

My tits bounced as his hips hit my ass over and over. His big cock pushed deep, striking a spot far inside me. It felt like no-one had ever been that deep in me before. Shit, with only two notches on my bedpost I suppose that's not much of an achievement.

I turned my head back and Mason started to kiss me again as he fucked me. His hard cock moved steadily with a pace I began to depend on. Every time it hit deep, I moaned along with him. Our breaths started to race, and my tits continued to flow. They seemed to have a ceaseless supply.

"That's it, Sophie," he said, pressing his head to me.

He reached under my arms and gripped my tits. He seemed excited by their leaking. He pinched them and the spatter pounded against the metal basin below.

"That's it, Mason," I gasped. "That's it!"

The stimulants were too much. Mason's hands on my tits and his cock in my pussy were one thing, but the rushing tickle of milk as it spurted through my nipple was something I couldn't ignore.

"Mason!" I strained, tightening my shoulders.

He took me in a close hug and fucked harder, sensing my release was close. He seemed to know my body better than I did, but perhaps that came from experience. Mason was in his late forties and had surely had his fill in the past.

The orgasm exploded inside me, and so too did my tits. In the past I noted a brief increase in their flow, but nothing like this. Mason pinched and the milk flew wildly, like a hose with no-one holding it. Some of the nectar found the basin but more of it found the walls.

Neither of us gave a shit in that moment. Mason was too concerned with jackhammering my pussy and I was too concerned with trying not to leave earth entirely.

I felt my pussy grip him as it contracted. He pressed on against the squeezing, battling back with squeezes of his own that caused even more cream to spurt from my chest.

He rubbed the milk back against me, turning everything real messy. My pussy leaked its cum and gave our lovemaking a whole new texture. It was as creamy as the milk on my tits.

"Fuck, Mason, that was huge," I told him, gasping.

"I don't wanna waste any more of that milk."

He pulled out of me, and I felt a string of my cum leave with him. It fell against my leg as he twisted me.

I stumbled as my jeans locked around my ankles, but Mason held me steady. I breathed hard and deep in front of him, my tits rising with my shoulders.

He looked down and bunched them in his hands, pressing them together and moving his face to the cleavage. His tongue wandered all over it, lapping up the nectar before visiting the source.

He swallowed down more of my ambrosia. I nursed him against me, stroking his hair and trying to give him the tenderness that he seemed to crave.

As he feasted his hand found my pussy and he started to rub his fingers along it, ramping things up towards the next wave of sinful taboo.

"I want to look you in the eyes while I fuck you," he said.

I bit my lip and nodded. "I want that too."

He put his hand to my throat and used his other to hold his cock and seek out my groove. I leaned back against the basin and tried to give him the access he needed.

He pinched at my neck, and I felt my head turn light. He pushed forwards at the hips and his cock eased through my tight O again. He went deep.

"Yes!" I strained.

His fingers pinched either side of my neck, giving me a sense of danger and excitement the likes of which I'd never known. But you've never known danger until you take you're a stranger's cumshot deep inside you. *That's* real danger.

He pressed on, fucking me and keeping his grip on my throat tight. My tits bounced on my chest and the milk fired off wildly. So much for not wasting another drop.

"I'm gonna come inside you," he insisted, staring into my eyes as they reddened.

I knew I could handle him. I don't know how, but I just knew it. Besides, it felt so good that I didn't want it to stop. If this is what choking was like, then choke me all fucking day. I felt my pussy start to swell as my head turned light.

"Take this hard cock, Sophie."

He loosened his grip and I felt the rush of oxygen return. The blackness faded and gave way to an intense burst of color. Everything suddenly seemed more *real. Fuck. My own handyman is fucking me.*

"You want this hot cum?" he asked. "You want my cum?"

"Fucking come in me," I snarled, finding something inside myself that I didn't know I had.

Mason nodded. "That's what you want, huh?"

"Give it to me. I want it. I need it. Come inside me."

We both looked down. Through the cleavage of my big, wet tits I could see his cock slamming in and out of me. He was soaked in my cum, but my pussy was about to receive a whole new load.

"Come inside me, Mason," I whined. "Please."

He put his hand to my throat again and squeezed my tits with the other. The milk fired out and my airway tightened.

The flow of oxygen lessened, and the sensations became heightened. Everything doubled. I could feel each ridge and vein of his as his cock passed through me. I could feel how ready he was to explode.

"Come!" I snarled.

Mason found a higher gear and fucked me so hard that the entire basin started to shake. A squeaking noise began as the counter took the strain, but neither of us gave a shit. I just wanted his cum and it looked like he was dead set on giving it me.

"Oh, Sophie!"

"Yes!"

"Oh, Sophie!"

"Yes, Mason! Yes, Mason! Come! Come!"

"Sophie!"

Fuck, I'll never forget the way he said my name. It told me for definite he was going to come. It sounded so desperate, but sure of itself all at once.

I braced myself. Mason let go of my neck and the euphoria hit me just as his cum did. It was warm inside me. The expression on his face was incredible. He looked so serene.

"Come, Mason," I dared, running my hands over his milk-soaked chest.

He squeezed at my tits and pumped slow, firing off his ropes with each grunt. His body shook out the climax, as though it was being given to me with great effort.

He pushed all the way deep, sending his seed so far inside me that it felt like it made pregnancy a damn certainty. Shit, at least I already had the milk ready.

"That's good," I told him, caressing his face. "That's what I wanted."

He smiled and pulled back slowly. My mouth opened as my pussy gasped off him one final time. I could feel the heat of his cum spill down the inside of my leg.

Suddenly I heard a pop of wood and then I dropped about an inch. I froze in front of him, naked and with my jeans and panties around my ankles. I daren't move.

Mason started to laugh. He guided me off the countertop gently and I turned to look at it. It looked like it had come off the wall almost entirely.

"Now I have a reason to come back," he said.

I looked back at him and laughed.

"We'll fix it," he said.

My tits dripped steadily. "Can you fix me?"

Mason looked to my breasts. He hooked some of the milk off with his finger and tasted it again.

"I don't think you're broke," he said. "Just ... different."

I smiled warmly. "Thank you," I told him.

"For breaking your basin?"

"For fixing me."

"I was hoping you'd keep leaking," he laughed. "I'd like to fix you a few more times."

"You're more than welcome to drop by in future and assess your handiwork."

"It looks like I've got another job on my hands here," he nodded.

"How ever will I repay you," I teased, affecting a distressed damsel's accent.

"I can think of a few ways."

"I want to hear them *all*."

THE END

My Dripping Milk Gave Me Away : Suckled Brats 23

The farmhouse I live in is always so damned busy that it's tough to catch a break. Between Mr. and Mrs. Jenkins, their three daughters and their two dogs, there's really no let up. There are constant distractions everywhere, so to get away from it all I started to head out to the barn at night.

It started with books. I'd head out the front door and across the yard to the barn where the horses were kept. I'd climb up onto the mezzanine where Mr. Jenkins kept the hay and I'd just fall into it and open my book. I could spend hours up there.

There was something comforting about the gentle sounds of the horses beneath too. I could really lose myself out there.

I'd been doing it for months and everyone just left me to it. However, the reasons for my nightly trips changed dramatically in that time.

It started innocently. I'd gone over there to read like always, only this particular chapter was very risqué. I hadn't seen it coming. I found myself flustered beyond measure and being out there all alone meant that there was only one thing for it. The eventual orgasm was enormous.

Since then, I'd kept up the habit. Now, at nineteen, I still made my way over to the barn every night. Mr. Jenkins and his family knew it was my private space, even if they didn't know what I got up to out there.

The types of books I read started to change too. I'd sneak them out of the library in my bag, making sure to take out something more innocent to cover my tracks.

A few months ago, I'd read this naughty book about a guy who likes to suck the milk from his wife's tits. Since then, I'd been massaging mine every time I masturbated in the hope that I might be able to produce some milk of my own. So far, I hadn't succeeded.

It was a fairly cool night, which were the ones I liked best. I could really snuggle into my blanket and sink into the hay. It also meant I didn't get too sweaty when I started to play. The last thing I'd want to do is return to the house all flustered. I mean, it would just be obvious, wouldn't it?

I strode across the yard that night, feeling hornier than usual. Sometimes the moment just got to me. The more I thought about how naughty I was going to be, the bigger the urge to climax became. I'd end up teasing myself all day and then finally let it all out up there on the mezzanine of the barn. It felt like I could be as loud as a wanted. Shit, if anyone heard anything I'd blame it on the horses!

I pushed open the barn door and put on the small light. It had a soft, orange glow and was perfect to read under.

I raced up the ladder and into my safe space. I wrapped the blanket around me and started to read, but before long my imagination got the better of me.

I wriggled out of my bra and then pulled up my t-shirt. My big tits sat ready on my chest. I was sure that today would be the day that I'd finally have my milky breakthrough.

I wore a skirt to make things easier. Mr. Jenkins just thought it was a fashion choice, but it was really for ease. He had raised his eyebrows when he first saw me in one, but knew better than to comment. I was a live-in worker at the farm, and as long as I did my jobs Mr. Jenkins didn't care too much about everything else.

My panties soon came down and my legs opened. I started to fantasize that I'd been supplanted into the book that I was reading, and that suddenly the manly pirate that the story centered around was now infatuated with me. I imagined him ravaging me below the deck, sucking at my tits and getting nice and hard just for me.

I started to whimper. The moans carried away on the night's breeze. My whole body tightened, but I didn't want to come yet. I wanted to ride the precipice for a while longer and dine out on that feeling.

My fingers paused and I took deep breaths to try to calm myself. I felt a tingle at my breasts and then a rush. It was like they were calling out to me to be squeezed.

I brushed a finger over the nipple and felt something wet. In an instant I bounced from my fantasy and looked down at my chest. I held my breast up to the faint light and spotted the unmistakable white that sat on the nipple.

"Milk!" I gasped, overjoyed. "It's milk!"

I'd done it. Finally, I'd done it.

I bit my lip excitedly and tried to relax back into the fantasy. My excitement was *huge*—I mean, you just have no idea how long I'd been trying for this. I thought it was impossible, but against the odds I'd managed to make myself lactate with only a few weekss of training.

I started to pinch my nipples and the milk began to flow freely. It scattered out and I gasped in shock, rubbing my pussy hard. The sensation of milk springing through the tight aperture on my chest was incredible. It was like a tickling rush of excitement.

My eyes rolled back, and euphoria consumed me. I just couldn't believe it. I started to come, trembling against the hay. I could hear the pitter-patter of milk as it trickled down onto the floor below.

"Yes!" I gasped, spreading the flowing cum back up against my pussy.

My chest was covered in milk, and I started to rub it back against my body. I guess I hadn't really considered my return journey to the house. I was just so elated to have finally been able to lactate that all my sensibilities went out of the window. And it was during that moment that I received an even bigger shock.

"Gina?" I heard Mr. Jenkins call from across the yard outside.

I stopped, jumping from the moment as though I'd been slapped in the face.

"I left my damned wallet in the saddle," Mr. Jenkins said, his voice getting nearer.

I couldn't speak. All I had to do was just give him a 'yeah' and the whole thing could have just been over, but instead, I was silent.

He came into the barn below. I looked through the crack in the floor and saw him looking around.

"Gina?" he called curiously.

I tried to pretend I wasn't there. I could hear my heart pounding in my chest and feared that Mr. Jenkins may be able to too.

"What the heck?" he muttered.

I had no idea what he'd seen, but he sounded shocked. I tried to move silently and look at what had startled him. He was down on his knees, touching the ground.

I heard a patter on the floor. The adrenaline burst around my body as I followed the milky trail upwards and noticed that my breasts were still leaking.

I gasped and covered my mouth.

"Gina?" Mr. Jenkins said, hearing me. "You up there?"

Speak, Gina.

But I couldn't. I put a hand over my mouth and prayed that a giant hand would come from the sky and pluck me from the situation.

"Milk?" I heard Mr. Jenkins say suddenly, and then I heard him on the ladder beside me.

The panic was huge. I was so exposed with no hope of dressing in time. My legs were open, and my t-shirt was pulled up over my exposed tits.

I looked to the top of the ladder as Mr. Jenkins's hand arrived. He strained to push himself up. It was only then that I found my words.

"Don't!" was all I could say. *Nice work, Gina.*

"Huh?" he asked, and then his face came into view.

I froze. We both did. I sat across from him, naked and vulnerable. Mr. Jenkins stared. I could see the shock in his eyes as they glinted in the orange glow of the lamp.

"I ... I ..." I began, but I had nothing to follow it up with. I mean, what do you say? *'Sorry, I was just milking my tits and having an enormous orgasm?'* I had no words.

"Gina ..." Mr. Jenkins said, and he seemed just as speechless. "Your tits ... you're ... leaking."

I looked down nervously. The milk was streaming steadily from my nipples and running down around my naked midriff. It ran through the gaps in the wooden flooring and dripped down below.

"I ... I'm sorry," I said finally.

"Sorry? You don't have to be sorry. I'm sorry I interrupted," he said.

His eyes tried to look everywhere else apart from at me. It sounds weird, but I *wanted* him to see me. I wanted him to notice how turned on I was.

He swallowed. "I'll leave you to it, I guess."

"You ... don't have to."

The silence between us felt huge. I let the words linger. Mr. Jenkins's big shoulders rose and dropped steadily as he breathed, contemplating the offer.

"What would happen if I stayed?" he asked.

I looked down at my tits and then across at him. I found a modicum of confidence now that he had shown some interest.

I narrowed my eyes and pretended I was one of the characters in my naughty books. "You'd wind up with a mouthful of milk. At the *very least.*"

Mr. Jenkins looked back at his house. "Anyone ever come out here?"

"They know not to."

He ran a hand down over his mouth. I could see him thinking. While he did his gaze traveled up along my legs and to the glistening slit that sat between them.

I moved my hand towards it, stroking my fingers close. His eyes locked on the target and he waited for me to do more.

"You could be my first," I told him.

Mr. Jenkins hoisted himself up the rest of the way and stood tall over me. Now I looked up at him from my blanketed spot amongst the hay. He was a big, bear of a man—the kind of guy you felt safe around, purely because there was no-one else big enough to fuck with him. Mr. Jenkins could look after himself, but right then, I wanted him to look after me.

"Squeeze those tits for me," he said. "Show me what you've been doing up here."

I put the book aside and looked up at him. He started to unclasp his belt. I froze again and stared at the bulge in his pants.

"Squeeze your tits for me, Gina," he reiterated.

He paused and waited for me. I pushed both tits together and felt the spurt of milk through each nipple. As the cream blasted forwards, I let out a sigh of relief. The milk pattered at his feet and disappeared down through the floor.

"That's my girl," he said, and he whipped his belt out through its loops.

I bit my lip and pinched my nipple. The milk sprayed out from me, landing on my stomach, skirt and legs.

"Rub your pussy," he told me.

I moved my hand down and pushed the milk into my groove. It mingled with my cum and I spread the mixture up along my little petals. The adrenaline was giving me an added boost of confidence.

"That's my girl," he said, and he opened the button of his jeans.

"Are you gonna show me," I asked, sitting forward on my knees.

"Be patient."

I sat on my heels and placed my hands on my naked hips. My big tits hung down, pushed together on my chest. Mr. Jenkins moved a hand into his pants, and I held my breath.

"You want this, don't you?"

I nodded.

"I'm gonna let you take it out for me."

He put his hands by his side.

I looked up at him and then down at the bulge in his pants. It was only feet away and it was mine if I wanted it. Fuck ... I *did* want it.

"Go on," he urged.

I sat up on my knees and put both hands on his jeans. I looked up into his face, studying it for any change in mood. He stared down and waited.

I slipped down the zipper and then wriggled his jeans. I started to giggle when I couldn't take them down, but Mr. Jenkins didn't offer any help.

"If you want it, you've gotta earn it," he said.

I scrunched my nose and really pulled, dragging his pants down and taking his underwear with them. When they started to move, I was able to pull the down faster. My face opened with relief as his pants dropped, but the expression soon changed to shock and then joy.

His cock bounced up out of his boxer-shorts and then sat there stiff. It jutted out from his body amazingly. My mouth opened in shock, and I sat back on my heels, admiring what was in front of me.

"It's so big," I cooed.

"Think you can fit it in your mouth?"

I stared at him to make sure he was being serious. "I'd like to try."

He nodded for me to continue. I rubbed my thighs impatiently and then sat up and went for it. I took him in my grasp and felt the strength of his arousal.

"Wow," I gasped.

My hand started to pump along him—which was something I'd read about—and my mouth started to salivate.

I could feel more moisture arrive at my pussy too as my body awakened to what was occurring. Suddenly I didn't have to use my imagination anymore. Suddenly it was all right there in front of me, and it looked glorious.

You can have a cock described to you a thousand times, but nothing quite prepares you for staring down the barrel of one.

I moved my face towards it, opening my mouth in the hope of swallowing up his bulbous crown. I was just about able to without having him hit my teeth.

"Good," he said, and his big hand gently smoothed my hair aside. "That's good, Gina."

I pushed more of him into me and started to rock my head over him. My lips closed tight around his cock, and I jerked him in my mouth.

"That's it," he said. "Squeeze my balls."

Shit, I'd never read about that before. I cupped his sack and started to squeeze gently. He responded with a moan. I must have been doing good.

"And jerk it too," he said.

Damn, there was a lot to remember. After a moment of practice, I was able to suck over the head of his cock while jerking him with one hand and using his balls like a stress-reliever in the other.

He was making noises that I'd never heard from him before. He was usually that stoic, silent strength type-of-man, you know? The kind of guy who daren't smile because it would be a sign of weakness.

Well, now he was letting me in and showing me another side of him, and it felt like a privilege to witness.

I started to gain confidence the more Mr. Jenkins started to relax. I was giving him pleasure and in turn that was giving *me* pleasure. But I didn't truly know the heights of pleasure. Yet.

Eventually he pulled himself out of my mouth. I looked up at him, wondering if I'd done something wrong. He beat his cock close to my face and stroked my cheek with his thumb.

"Lie back in there," he said, and he nodded at the seat of hay that I'd made behind me.

I fell back into the blanket. Mr. Jenkins got on his knees and pushed my legs open. I bit my finger and looked at his face as he spied my pussy again.

His face fell onto it, and I gasped. I didn't have him down as a pussy-eater. He mouthed over my petals quickly and started to lick along me. I lost myself instantly. I'd never known anything like it.

"Yes!" I whispered, clenching my hands in fists.

I didn't know what to do. It was one thing to give yourself pleasure, but another thing entirely for someone else to do it. This was the first time that I'd felt someone else on me, and it was a moment I'd never forget.

He ate me messily. I wasn't sure if guys were supposed to do it like that, but he was spitting and licking and pulling with his lips and everything. I felt my pussy get plump and swollen as the arousal rushed to it. I was gaping for him, and he hadn't even tried to fuck me yet.

The O of my pussy opened and the cum leaked out from it. Mr. Jenkins whipped it up with his tongue and spread it back against me, then he came off my pussy completely and wiped at his chin.

"You're ready," he said, but then he spied my tits.

I hadn't even noticed, but they'd been streaming out milk this entire time. My engines were revved, and that seemed to mean a near constant flow of milk.

"Look at you," he hushed, and he took my tits in his big bear hands and squeezed.

I moaned and fine jets of ambrosia sprayed forwards. They scattered against his plaid shirt. He opened the buttons quickly and took it off. Beneath lay his muscled chest, looking like it had been carved from wood and then dipped in hair.

The only thing he wore now were his pants and underwear, but they were both bunched around his ankles above his heavy work boots.

He fell on me and started to suck the milk right from my tits. I felt his weight and sank deeper into the hay and deeper into sin. I looked down and moved his hair aside, cradling him to my tits as he fed from me. I felt as though I'd turned provider suddenly, but I was happy to. My maternal instincts were in overdrive, and they were mixing in a dangerous cocktail with my arousal.

"That's it," I gasped. "Feed on me."

He mouthed over my nipple and stimulated it over and over, firing huge jets of milk into his mouth. He gulped them down steadily and started to breathe deeper. It was as though he was charging his body and using my nectar as the energy source.

"That's good," I told him.

At this point I wasn't even sure we were going to fuck. I was happy to cradle him against me and let him have his fill, but the way he was breathing was telling me he wasn't yet done. Finally, he popped off my node and wiped his mouth.

He looked down at my pussy and rubbed his fingers on it, then he pushed two inside. My mouth opened in a silent moan, and I gripped his wrist.

"There you go," he said. "That's it. Let me open you up."

I tried not to scream. His fingers were so much bigger than what I was used to, but if I had any hope of taking his cock then I'd have to get used to them pretty quick.

"Good girl," he said.

I felt proud that I'd managed not to shout out. My tits cried their milk and my breaths returned, quick and hard.

"Fuck, Mr. Jenkins, that was a lot."

"And you took it, sugar," he said. "You took it well."

He pulsed his fingers back along my core, giving me a teaser of what it was like to be fucked for real.

I wriggled back into the hay and started to mewl. My hands ran all over my body. I just didn't know what to do. I started to squeeze my tits again, feeling the warm milk cascade over me.

Mr. Jenkins's fingers felt much nicer now as my muscle relaxed around him. I could feel him probing deep, but there was only so far he could go.

"You're ready," he told me.

"Fuck me!" I cried.

Mr. Jenkins was on me quick, nudging my knee open with his. He took a hold of his cock and put it to my pussy, then he pushed forwards into me.

I started to moan. He put his hand over my mouth and then pushed inside my pussy, pressing his chest against my wet tits.

His weight felt amazing against me. I moaned into his hand and looked into his eyes. He kissed at my cheek and steadily moved his hand off me now that the initial shock of his size was over.

I took several deep breaths as he moved deeper. I'd never had anything that big inside me before. It felt like our two bodies had become one. It was beautiful.

"Yes!" I growled, and my tits spat out their milk in defiance.

His chest took the brunt and the milk sat between us, running over our bodies as he started to pump against me.

His big cock squirmed into me, and I wriggled down on it. I felt impaled by it, such was its size. Mr. Jenkins took a grip of my neck and started to fuck me harder.

"That's what it's like, sugar," he said over and over, and my eyes rolled back as I enjoyed him.

I felt my head prickle as he starved me of oxygen, but Mr. Jenkins seemed attuned to it, as though it wasn't his first time squeezing someone's neck. I wasn't scared. I surrendered myself to him, trusting him to keep me safe.

He loosed his grip on my neck and everything came flooding back ten-fold—including the sensation of his girth moving through me.

"Mr. Jenkins!" I whined. "I want your cum." I nodded, pleading with him. "Please. Please. Give me it."

"It wouldn't be proper if I didn't," he told me.

I bit my lip excitedly, but then a lunge from his hips made my brow furrow in pained ecstasy.

He swept me up in his arms and hugged me close as he found another gear. His hips hit against me, and his cock surged deep over and over. I gripped him tight and he used me to jerk his cock.

"That's it, Gina," he said, and I could hear him losing himself bit-by-bit.

"Fuck me, Mr. Jenkins!" I begged. "Fuck me!"

I was impatient for his release now that it was so close. Before I was happy to ride the edge of climax, but now I wanted its full force, and soon.

"I need your cum," I told him, stroking his face. "Please come inside me."

He pulled back and looked down over my naked body. My tits bounced as he fucked me, spurting their milk upwards.

I looked down and saw his impossibly big cock disappearing into me again and again. His breaths rose. His cock stiffened and seemed to inflate further.

"Gina!" he cried, and he paused and tilted his head to the light.

I'll remember that moment as long as I live. It was a snapshot of Mr. Jenkins moments before release. His face looked so serene. He was unlike himself. It was as though this rare beast had gifted me a glimpse of his true nature.

I stared wide-eyed and then watched as he grunted out the first rope.

I felt him throb within me, then my insides started to turn hot. Mr. Jenkins grunted, announcing each lashing. I took every one and each time I did my tits seemed to fire out a jet of milk, as though all of these things were somehow linked within me.

"Oh, Gina! Oh, Gina, yes!"

He stroked my face and rocked his hips, pushing his seed all the way deep with his big, burly cock.

I took it innocently, staring up in wonder as he filled me. I had no thought to the danger of it. My only thought was how beautiful it was to be deflowered by such a big, powerful man.

"Good girl," he said, seeming spent.

He pulled back out of me. I took one last look at his cock. It was shrink-wrapped in a film of both of our cum. He pulled up his jeans and put himself back inside, standing in front of me and breathing heavy.

I lay back on the hay, disheveled. I looked up at him and blew a jet of air up my face that moved my hair.

Mr. Jenkins chuckled but then turned serious. "This is just between us, okay?"

I nodded. "I'm not telling anyone."

He ran his eyes over me one last time and shook his head in disbelief. "I'm gonna come out here again tomorrow, okay?"

I smirked. "I'll make sure I'm ready for you."

"Make sure you do," he said, putting his shirt back on. "I'll go fetch you out a towel."

I looked down, noticing how covered I was with milk. It had run down onto the waist of my skirt, turning it damp. It sat around my midriff, a ring of milk.

I kept my legs open as he dismounted the ladder, and I saw him take one last look between my legs. I fingered gently, trying to feel his cum.

"I'm coming back for that tomorrow," he said.

I pushed a finger inside and searched out his seed, but it was so deep.

"Please do," I told him.

I stayed quiet as he left the barn. When he was halfway across the yard, I punched a fist in the air in celebration and rolled in the hay beneath me, giggling.

"I can't believe it!" I cried, and I felt like a character in my very own book, discovering herself for the first time.

THE END

Lacto-Tolerant : Suckled Brats 24

Mr. Fogle was a veritable Willy Wonka when it came to a dining experience. He'd been experimenting with various menus for years now and he'd finally created his magnum opus.

He'd sent the invites out to his newsletter of loyal fans and followers. Mr. Fogle had accrued many over the years who wanted an evening to remember, not just fine food. That was where I came in.

Since becoming pregnant several years ago to an absent father, Mr. Fogle had cared for me like no-one else. He'd found the idea of my breast milk so intoxicating that he'd started to incorporate it into his meals.

At first, I found the notion ridiculous, and it had taken a long time for him to convince me. To begin with I just gave him a sample of my milk, but when I'd tasted one of the first dishes he'd made I was beyond impressed. It was *so* good, and I couldn't believe one of the main ingredients had been sourced directly from me. Since then, I'd given him all the milk he needed.

I believed in Mr. Fogle, and my trust was paying off. I commanded quite the salary now that I was so integral to his fantastical new restaurant.

Tonight was opening night and nerves were high. Mr. Fogle had asked something special of me. It was to be the talking-point of the evening, and the moment when his masterplan was revealed. You see, this wasn't just a place that people came to eat ...

"You're gonna be great, Debbie darling, I just know it," Mr. Fogle said, holding my biceps and giving me a kiss.

I stood before him in my French-Maid's outfit. A white bib covered my chest, and my black skirt barely covered my panties. The top of my suspenders were visible underneath.

In the kitchen beyond Mr. Fogle's team of expert—and discreet—chefs made their concoctions.

"The first party has arrived," informed one of his staff.

"Excellent," he said, beaming a smile. Mr. Fogle didn't get nervous—of if he did, he rarely let it show on his face.

He moved into the dining room to greet them, bursting through the door with immediate smiles and frivolities.

"Welcome to *Lacto*," he cheered, and he embraced the couple at the door who looked to be in their early twenties. It looked as though it wasn't Mr. Fogle's first time meeting them.

"How are you both?" Mr. Fogle asked. "Did you buy that house in Greenwich in the end?"

"We decided against it," the husband said, "but we're both very well."

"And *very* excited," the lady added. She looked through and spotted me waiting awkwardly. "Is that her?" she said, pointing.

"It might be," Mr. Fogle said, and he rushed to the door to close it. He gave me a quick wink before he hid me away. I was part of the big reveal later, and Mr. Fogle didn't want to spoil things.

I heard laughter and cheers come from the room outside as it filled with more people.

Behind me chefs milled around in the kitchen and wait-staff walked between the two rooms. I stayed to one side, nervously playing with my phone as members of Mr. Fogle's staff hurried by.

I watched the dishes be transported through the room—dishes with my breast milk filling them. Since lactating had begun, I'd managed to keep it going with constant stimulus, sometimes with mr. Fogle's help. We'd gotten *more* than close over the years. Closer than most people would be comfortable with, but he assured me we were safe here tonight among his handpicked company.

Around an hour passed before he returned. He came through the door with that same infectious smile as always, dressed immaculately in his suit.

"You're going to be great," he said. "Are you ready?"

I hopped off the table where I was sat and presented myself. "How do I look?"

"Ravishing," he said, "which is just as well."

He came close and put an arm around me, squeezing my ass. I blushed and turned my chin in to my chest, looking up bashfully at him.

"Is it going to be okay?"

"It's going to be *great*," he said. "Everyone out there is so nice, Debbie dearest. You're going to do wonderfully."

I took a breath. "You think so?"

"I know so, but be prepared for anything, okay?"

"*Anything?*"

Mr. Fogle winked, then he motioned to a nearby waiter. "The trolley." He looked back to me. "Just relax. No-one's going to hurt you and you're going to enjoy yourself very much. I'm going to be there the whole time."

I smiled at him. He had a way of calming my nerves.

"Now on the trolley," he said, and he nodded behind me.

I looked back to the long stretch of metal. It looked almost like a gurney. Mr. Fogle covered it in a black sheet and then patted it. "Like we practiced," he said.

I hopped on and lay back.

"With me," Mr. Fogle said to the waiter, and he pushed me towards the door that led out to the restaurant.

Mr. Fogle flung open the doors and spoke loudly; "Ladies and Gentlemen. The main course!"

He presented the trolley, and it was pushed into the room. I stared up at the ceiling as the applause and cheers began. There must have been four couples in there and they were all on their feet.

I saw their faces beaming down as I was rolled beneath them and set between two tables that separated each group of four. The trolley was a snug fit, completing the length of table.

"She's beautiful," one of the women swooned, looking down on me with sparkling eyes.

"You taste lovely," her husband said. It was the strangest of compliments, but I guess it was high praise in the restaurant world. Several others around the table agreed.

"It's delightfully velvety," one of the women said.

"Thank you," I said. It was so surreal to be lying down amongst them like that, but it was something I'd have to get used to if this was going to become a regular thing.

"And now," Mr. Fogle said, approaching the table, "the moment you've all been waiting for."

One of the older ladies did a series of excited claps with her hands.

Mr. Fogle reached down to my bib and looked me in the eye. He gave a wink and I melted just a little bit more for him.

"Voila!" he said, and he pulled back the fabric to reveal my exposed, bounteous tits. "The source of all our joy."

"Wow," hushed the crowd.

I looked around at each of them. They seemed mesmerized.

"And who would like to try first?" Mr. Fogle asked, looking about them.

I bit my lip and waited.

"Perhaps I should show you how it's done?" he said when no-one offered. "I'll get you started, Debbie dearest."

Mr. Fogle moved over me and put his hands to my breasts. I waited for that same massaging squeeze that he ordinarily gave me, but it didn't come.

I looked to him. He was frozen and staring at my tits. He took a deep breath. Just as I realized what he was about to do he began doing it.

He dropped his face to my chest and latched his mouth right over my nipple. I tensed up and my eyes spread wide in shock, but when he started to suckle the sensation began to lull me. My eyes floated around the ceiling, and I let out a soft moan. I could feel my nectar rushing into his mouth.

"My, oh, my," a gentleman in the group said. "That's something."

I could hear the pleasure in his words. Mr. Fogle gulped me down audibly and then came up for air, wiping his mouth and smiling wide at the crowd.

"Beautiful," he said.

A woman raised her hand. "Can I be next?"

"Please," he said, and he offered me to her with a hand.

I bit my lip and gripped the edge of the trolley tightly as the lady to my right brushed her blonde hair back and moved in over me. Her husband stepped behind her and took her hair. She placed her lips over me, and the amazing sensation returned. I moaned softly as I felt a woman's lips for the first time. She sucked and tickled.

"Really play with her," Mr. Fogle encouraged.

Her tongue flicked over my engorged stud, and I started to feel the excitement in my pussy now too.

"That's it," Mr. Fogle said. He could tell just from my expression that I was feeding his guest.

The milk rushed out through my nipple over and over.

"She has two, remember," my boss said. "Would anyone else like to try?"

A man raised his hand. He had black hair and a dashing, square jaw. Mr. Fogle nodded for him to continue, and his wife bit her lip excitedly as she watched him move in on me.

He arrived at my other breast, and I felt the new experience of two people on me at once. Their tongues delighted me and the milk burst forth.

"It's incredible," the lady said, pulling back. "Try it, honey."

She offered my breast to her husband, and he stooped to feed on me. I moved my hands and cradled both men to my chest.

"That's it," Mr. Fogle said, his eyes sparkling with joy. His plan was coming to fruition. "Let's all get a little more relaxed, shall we?"

He took off his suit-jacket and so too did some of the other guys. He the proceeded to remove his bowtie and unfasten his top button.

"Let's all get a little more casual," he said, and he put a hand on the waist of the lady whose husband was busy on my tits.

She looked back to him, then I watched as Mr. Fogle kissed her. I felt a pang of jealousy and with it a burst of milk so fierce that it sent my two suitors rushing back from my tits.

Milk burst up from each nipple like a geyser and fell back down against me, pattering my dress and white sheets.

"An explosion of milk," Mr. Fogle wowed.

"I'd like to try it," another lady said, and she was joined at my breast by another woman.

"Have at it, Mrs. Nunez," Mr. Fogle said to the Latino-looking woman.

They ate from me sensually and I tried to relax as Mr. Fogle had instructed. I watched as he continued to kiss the younger lady in the room, but then something took my mind from him completely. I could feel a hand at the inside of my thigh. I looked down to see the lady on my breast moving her hand towards my crotch.

I closed my eyes and opened my legs wider. I wanted her to feel how wet I'd become. I wanted her to make Mr. Fogle jealous, just like he was making me jealous. The second her fingers touched me I let out an over-the-top moan.

"Yes!" I burst, and I checked through my lashes to make sure Mr. Fogle was looking.

"Good girl," he said, moving close. He crouched and put his face to mine, whispering near my ear. "Good girl. Do whatever you need to."

"She's fingering me," I whispered.

"Good," he said, and he looked down at his guest's hand.

"Well done, Mrs. Chamberlain."

She gave him a narrow-eyed look of lust but kept her lips around my nipples, sucking hard. The milk burst from me in its ceaseless flow and her fingers became more adventurous.

She pushed at my mound and then hooked her finger inside the crotch of my panties, running it back and forth slowly over my shaven folds.

"Let's take them off," a man said who'd been watching.

"Good idea, honey," Mrs. Chamberlain said.

Mr. Chamberlain reached under my frilly black dress and grabbed the waist of my panties. I lifted my ass off the table and let the older man drag them down.

"Good initiative, sir," Mr. Fogle said, nodding at him.

"I'd like to show some initiative too," a man said who was yet to do anything.

"And what's that, Mr. Graham?"

Without a word Mr. Graham unzipped his pants and produced a big, black cock, stroking his hand up and down its length slowly.

"Delightful," Mr. Fogle said, and he looked to me. "Do you like it, Debbie?"

"I love it," I whispered.

Mr. Graham walked closer and put his ebony length close to my lips. I stared down the barrel and then looked up at him.

"Be my guest," he nodded.

"If she won't, I will," Mrs. Chamberlain said, her mouth dripping with milk.

She moved her fingers over my pussy and sought out my wetness. When she found it, she pushed her fingers up into me and I let out a moan.

"She's soaked for it," she said. "Go on. Suck it."

Mr. Graham stepped into my moan, filling my mouth with his hard, black cock. I moved down on him and hummed. I was being pleasured from nearly every angle, and Mr. Graham was now a recipient of the pleasure too. I tried to use his monolith as a vessel to transfer my horniness through.

Steadily he started to work into my mouth.

"I can't leave you on your own, Mr. Graham," Mr. Fogle said. "Although I'm afraid I can't quite compete."

I pulled off Mr. Graham's cock and tried to get a look as my boss downed his pants too. He stepped right out of them and then took off his shirt, standing only in his socks and polished black shoes.

"About time, Mr. Fogle," a lady said.

I looked back to see that she was rubbing at the bulge on her husband's pants. He was stood with his hands behind his back, watching the show.

"We can't leave Mr. Graham here on display alone, can we Mrs. Hanlon?"

"We cannot," Mrs. Hanlon said, then she turned to her husband and crouched at his feet.

She took him out of his pants quickly and then put her mouth right over his cock. I couldn't quite believe it.

Mr. Graham jerked his black length close to my face, but I wanted Mr. Fogle's. I stared at him. I'd never been more in anticipation of something so much in my life.

Mr. Fogle downed his boxer-shorts and his huge, hard cock came springing out, sitting proud on his waist underneath a kempt rectangle of hair.

"You're not far off at all, Mr. Fogle," Mr. Graham said.

I was so smitten that I hadn't realized where Mr. Chamberlain had gotten himself. He was pushing up my skirt and moving his face to meet his wife's fingers that were still buried deep in my snatch.

She fucked me with them and then moved them out, presenting them to her husband who sucked my juices off her fingers.

"She tastes great all over," he swooned, then he planted his mouth right onto my pussy.

My head came up off the table as I groaned. Another fierce jet of milk burst through my nipples, causing Mrs. Nunez to gasp off me. Her mouth dripped with milk, and she looked at me with a shocked look of lust.

"You're *incredible*," she said, and then she put herself back on my breast.

Mr. Fogle walked over with his hard cock on display and put it close enough for me to reach.

"Go on," he insisted. "There's a good girl."

I reached up with my head and opened my mouth over him, sucking his cock while the rest of his guests tended either to me or to each other.

Mr. Chamberlain tongued at my folds and sought out my clit beneath its fleshy hood. He nibbled at it and I shivered. The milk burst through me each time he delighted me like that.

"Enjoy the feast," Mr. Fogle said, presenting the scene. It was like one of Caligula's orgies.

Mrs. Graham got up onto the table that had thankfully been cleared for the main course. She split her knees wide and pulled her dress back, then she moved her panties aside and showed her pussy to the room.

"Look at that," Mr. Fogle said, stroking my face but looking at Mrs. Graham.

She fingered along her folds and closed her eyes. Her husband beat his cock faster close to my face.

"She's a goddess, isn't she?" he asked Mr. Fogle.

"And no mistake."

I hummed on my boss's cock for attention.

"And not the only one," he said, looking down on me.

He moved his hips and started to fuck my mouth as the revelers relaxed around us. They started to entertain themselves, but my breasts were never left unmanned. As I sucked at Mr. Fogle's cock several different people dropped in to sample my milk. Some of them would finger me, others would move down off my nipples and tongue at my pussy. One even made a go at my ass, but the logistics didn't quite work out.

The whole time I lay on the trolley, sucking whatever was put it on front of me. Mr. Fogle moved around the room and I kept my eye on him. I hadn't yet seen him fuck someone. Mr. and Mrs. Graham had been fucking for the past ten minutes, their black bodies sweaty and glistening in the light from above. It was so hot to watch.

"Come on, Mr. Fogle," Mr. Nunez said, standing behind him. The two of them were naked and each sported a hard cock. "I think it's time you showed us what we all want to see."

"And what's that?" he asked.

"Fuck her," Mr. Nunez said, nodding at me.

"Yes!" jeered the crowd.

"Fuck this fine beauty," Mrs. Chamberlain said, her legs wrapped around her mature husband. "It would be an honor to see something so incredible."

All the couples turned to the action as Mr. Nunez pushed my boss forwards.

Mr. Graham pulled his cock out from his wife. Her white cum was strewn along his length. He came to the foot of the trolley and pulled me down it with ease. I let out a shriek of delighted pleasure and some of the crowd laughed.

"She can't wait," Mrs. Chamberlain said, looking down on me fondly. She was right.

"Look at her," Mr. Nunez said, staring up between my open legs. "So tight."

Mrs. Nunez put her hand round Mr. Fogle's cock and tugged him forwards. "Come fuck her," she said, her green eyes dazzling.

She put his crown to my soaked pussy. I lifted my legs and spread them. Mr. Nunez held one while his wife held the other.

"That's it," Mr. Graham said. His wife came behind him and started to jerk his cock.

Mr. Fogle moved into me, and I felt my pussy stretch over him. The crowd gasped relishing the act. It was rare to see an older woman fuck someone over twenty years his junior.

"Good girl," Mrs. Chamberlain said, her head rocking as her husband continued to fuck her.

Mr. Hanlon was too busy eating his wife's pussy to notice, but she was staring at the act from one end of the table and moaning in ecstasy as she did so.

"Take it all," she said. "All of that fucking big cock."

Her husband stood up and wiped his mouth, then he put himself inside her and turned her face to his. He started to kiss her.

Mr. Fogle looked down and watched himself disappear inside of me. As he pushed inside the flow of milk at my tits increased. It started with a stream that ran down onto the soaked, black cloth, but soon the strength of my flow was such that it sprouted from each nipple like fountain water.

"Oh, look," Mrs. Chamberlain said, and she fell back on the table and attempted to drink from me while her husband fucked her.

She sucked the milk into her mouth and drank it down, then she let it wash over her beautiful, mature face. Her enjoyment of my milk was making me turned-on, and Mr. Fogle's big cock inside me was certainly adding to the excitement.

He pushed into me and then started to fuck me, building his pace.

"Good," Mrs. Nunez said.

Mr. Fogle moved his hand to her pussy and started to tease her. Her hold on my leg wavered.

Mr. Nunez mounted the table and moved over me. I took his cock in my mouth and started to suck and lick him. Sometimes he'd slip out from me, and I'd tongue at his balls as he held them over my face. The whole thing was wild.

Mr. Fogle continued to fuck me, sending that beautiful cock of his in and out of me over and over until I had no choice but to come.

When my eyes opened and my head lurched up from the table to moan, I noticed that Mrs. Nunez was now crouched behind my boss, presumably tonguing at his ass.

I shivered and trembled. Mrs. Chamberlain came up and held my face.

"Good girl," she told me, kissing me over and over. I could taste the sweetness of my milk on her tongue.

I felt something on my other breast and looked to it to see Mr. Nunez pumping the cum from his cock.

This made my orgasm flare up even more. Milk burst out from my tits wildly and scattered about me.

"Congratulations, Mr. Nunez," Mr. Fogle said, taking a moment to applaud. "We have our first arrival."

"And soon our second," Mrs. Graham said.

I looked to her as Mr. Nunez's cum lashed my tits. She was pumping her husband's cock hard and pointing it right at her face. I watched as his thick, white cum hit her skin, contrasting its blackness. It looked incredible. I could see each and every lashing. She moaned as it hit her and then started to rub it over her face.

Mrs. Hanlon was quick to get involved suddenly. She came over to Mrs. Graham and started to lick the cum from her.

"Now it's time for mine," he said, looking down on me.

Mr. Chamberlain was tonguing between his wife's legs. I knew how good he was at that. She lay her head back on the table and started to moan right next to me as he made her come.

Her noises were getting me excited. I could feel the blood rushing to my pussy. I started to breathe deep, and my head turned light. I couldn't help but smile.

My nipples tingled and shot out their milk. It mingled with Mr. Nunez's cum on my right breast, turning all pearly and smoky.

"Come inside her," Mrs. Nunez said, her words muffled by my boss's wet ass.

He thrust in and out of me and I felt his cock stiffen further and then swell. The look on his face was like nothing I'd ever seen before. The room was a cauldron of lust.

"Come inside me!" I burst, feeling my own climax explode at my pussy.

I started to wriggle and writhe on the table, joining Mrs. Chamberlain in ecstasy.

Mr. Fogle pumped hard, cheered on now by the crowd.

"Come," they said.

His moans rose and he lost himself. It was the culmination of months of hard work, and I was to be the joyful recipient of it.

His hot cum burst inside me, announced with a groan. His cock throbbed and the muscle along it pulsed.

"That's it," Mrs. Hanlon said, taking a break from eating cum to watch Mr. Fogle's delivery of more.

His seed felt warm and welcome inside me. My pussy squeezed him as I continued to climax.

"Good girl," Mr. Fogle said, straining.

Each rope fired into me and inspired more climaxes around the room.

Mr. Hanlon staggered to Mrs. Graham's face and let himself off all over it. She took it gladly, coming herself as she rubbed her beautiful pussy. Her cheeks were awash with spunk, but Mrs. Hanlon made short work of it. She sucked it all up like a hoover and then started to kiss the black goddess with it in her mouth, passing it between their mouths.

"Yes," I grunted finally, and Mr. Fogle slowly pulled back his cock.

Mrs. Nunez looked down for a good view, watching as my boss's pearly evidence became apparent.

"There it is," she said, biting her lip. She looked up at me. "He came inside you."

Mr. Chamberlain grunted and started to come all over his wife's stomach. She hummed contently with her eyes closed. She was utterly spent. I knew how she felt.

There was one final gift to be had. When Mr. Fogle moved back far enough Mrs. Nunez took his place. She thumbed at my swollen clit, causing me to jolt and shoot bursts of milk up from my tits.

"There's no end to it," Mrs. Hanlon said, impressed by my ceaseless flow.

Mrs. Nunez crouched and put her mouth right over my pussy, working her shoulder vigorously to finger her own pussy as she ate Mr. Fogle's cum from me.

"There's a good slut," Mr. Fogle said, putting his hand on her head.

She tongue-fucked me until she got off, shivering uncontrollably at the foot of the trolley. Degradation seemed to be her kink.

Her husband got down and took a fistful of her hair, then he pushed her face back onto my cum-drenched pussy.

She tongued and tasted me, and I lay back and enjoyed it all, feeling like a princess. I couldn't believe I was getting paid for this. I couldn't believe Mrs. Nunez was *paying* for this!

Finally, she took her mouth off me and fell back on the floor, breathing deep. She was satisfied. We all were.

"And that," Mr. Fogle said, "concluded the first feast at *Lacto*."

There was a rapturous round of applause, although some people were more spent than others.

"I do hope you've enjoyed your meal," Mr. Fogle said.

"Oh, yes," members of the party said.

"I'll be coming back for seconds," Mrs. Chamberlain said.

"Thirds here," Mrs. Hanlon said, having already eaten two cumshots from Mrs. Graham's face.

"It was a pleasure," Mr. Graham said.

"Oh, the pleasure was all mine," Mr. Fogle said, "as Mrs. Nunez here has just tasted."

She smiled wearily and waved a hand. The orgasm had tired her out.

I sat upright and looked around the room now, viewing the sin from a fresh angle. "It was such a delight to feed you all," I said.

"It was beautiful," Mr. Graham said, holding my hand sincerely and looking into my eye. "Just magical."

"Like nothing I've known on this earth in all my fifty years," Mr. Chamberlain said.

I put a hand to my heart humbly but felt Mr. Nunez's cum and my milk instead. "I can't wait to see you all again."

"It won't be for a few months," Mr. Fogle said. "I'm afraid we're fully booked."

I opened my eyes, shocked.

"Yes, we have a whole new group in tomorrow," he continued.

I bit my lip in anticipation. I felt so close to this current party that I couldn't imagine being with another.

"Enjoy them," Mrs. Graham said, with only the smallest amount of cum on her face now. She sounded so genuine.

"She will," Mr. Fogle insisted, putting a hand on my knee.

I fell back against the trolley wearily. I was fuck-drunk and tired, but excited for more. I couldn't tell if it was nerves that I could feel in my stomach or Mr. Fogle's warm seed.

What I can tell you though, is how delighted I was to be part of *Lacto* and all the adventures that came with it.

THE END

Join The Mailing List[1]

Get <u>7 FREE EROTICA STORIES</u> and <u>WEEKLY DEALS</u> when you join my Mailing List[2] - http://eepurl.com/b0ma0X

---

1. http://eepurl.com/b0ma0X

2. http://eepurl.com/b0ma0X

More Titles From Taboo Inc.[1]

Brat's Cream Mega Bundle 24-Pack : Books 1 - 24[2]

[3]

The 'Brat's Cream Mega-Bundle 24 Pack' includes books 1 to 24 of the naughty breast-feeding series that sees alpha males milk their brat hucows in sinful fashion.

This collection will leave you dripping, just like the udders of these bountiful beauties.

Brat's Cream Lactation Bundle : Books 1 - 12[4]

---

1. https://itunes.apple.com/us/author/tori-westwood/id596852358?mt=11

2. https://itunes.apple.com/us/book/id1437586714

3. https://itunes.apple.com/us/book/id1437586714

4. https://itunes.apple.com/us/book/id1341482412

5

The 'Brat's Cream 12 Pack Lactation Bundle' includes books 1 to 12 of the naughty breast-feeding series that sees alpha males milk their brat hucows in sinful fashion.

This collection will leave you dripping, just like the udders of these bountiful beauties.

Stories include : *'Milk Masseur,' 'He Sucked My Chest,' 'His morning Milk,' 'A Need to Nurse,' 'Bursting With Milk,' Milked For a Bet,' 'Wet Nursing Him,' 'My Swollen Chest Needs Milking,' 'Suckled By Him From His Hospital Bed, 'He Catches Me Milking Myself,' 'Emptying in His Mouth'* & *'His Sucking Secret.'*

Brat's Cream Lactation Bundle : Books 13 - 24[6]

The 'Brat's Cream Lactation Bundle' includes books 13 to 24 of the naughty breast-feeding series that sees alpha males milk their brat hucows in sinful fashion.

This collection will leave you dripping, just like the udders of these bountiful beauties.

Stories include : *'Tied Up & Milked, 'My Leaking Big Chest,' 'My Magical Milky Chest,' 'My BDSM Milking,' 'Milked By Two Men,' 'A Squirt of Milk in His Mouth,' 'His Milking Subject,' 'She Catches Him Milking Me,' 'Milk Swap,' 'The Rough Lactation,' 'Milk My Big Chest, Mister'* & *'Milked By My British Boss.'*

Lactation Erotica - Brat's Milk : Books 1 - 12[8]

9

The *'Brat's Milk Series'* bundle includes 12 sinful stories of lactation erotica from the *'Brat's Milk'* Series, featuring big chested brats getting emptied by dominant alpha males. Read on as these feisty teens get drained by the very men closest to them, culminating in hot sex that'll leave you dripping with desire.

Includes : *'Doctor's Hucow,' 'Farmers Milk Maid,' 'Hitchhiker's Thirst,' 'Doctor Milked My Breast,' 'Caught And Milked,' 'Milk Instructor,' 'Bound and Milked,' 'Saving Him With My Milk,' 'Boss's Office Milk,' 'Brat's Milky Cocktail,' 'He Drinks My Milkshake,'* and *'My Forbidden Milking.'*

---

9. https://itunes.apple.com/us/book/id1221016113

About the Author

Millie King writes naughty lactation erotica that'll leave you dripping, along with the main character!

Dominant men drain younger women of their nectar, guzzling down their ambrosia while getting harder and harder by the second until they have to get emptied themselves!

License Notes

Fuck, I'll never forget the way he said my name. It told me for definite he was going to come. It sounded so desperate, but sure of itself all at once.

I braced myself. Mason let go of my neck and the euphoria hit me just as his cum did. It was warm inside me. The expression on his face was incredible. He looked so serene.

"Come, Mason," I dared, running my hands over his milk-soaked chest.

He squeezed at my tits and pumped slow, firing off his ropes with each grunt. His body shook out the climax, as though it was being given to me with great effort.

He pushed all the way deep, sending his seed so far inside me that it felt like it made pregnancy a damn certainty. Shit, at least I already had the milk ready.

"That's good," I told him, caressing his face. "That's what I wanted."

He smiled and pulled back slowly. My mouth opened as my pussy gasped off him one final time. I could feel the heat of his cum spill down the inside of my leg.

Suddenly I heard a pop of wood and then I dropped about an inch. I froze in front of him, naked and with my jeans and panties around my ankles. I daren't move.

Mason started to laugh. He guided me off the countertop gently and I turned to look at it. It looked like it had come off the wall almost entirely.

"Now I have a reason to come back," he said.

I looked back at him and laughed.

"We'll fix it," he said.

My tits dripped steadily. "Can you fix me?"

Mason looked to my breasts. He hooked some of the milk off with his finger and tasted it again.

"I don't think you're broke," he said. "Just ... different."

choking was like, then choke me all fucking day. I felt my pussy start
to swell as my head turned light.

"Take this hard cock, Sophie."

He loosened his grip and I felt the rush of oxygen return. The
blackness faded and gave way to an intense burst of color. Everything
suddenly seemed more *real*. *Fuck. My own handyman is fucking me.*

"You want this hot cum?" he asked. "You want my cum?"

"Fucking come in me," I snarled, finding something inside myself
that I didn't know I had.

Mason nodded. "That's what you want, huh?"

"Give it to me. I want it. I need it. Come inside me."

We both looked down. Through the cleavage of my big, wet tits
I could see his cock slamming in and out of me. He was soaked in my
cum, but my pussy was about to receive a whole new load.

"Come inside me, Mason," I whined. "Please."

He put his hand to my throat again and squeezed my tits with
the other. The milk fired out and my airway tightened.

The flow of oxygen lessened, and the sensations became
heightened. Everything doubled. I could feel each ridge and vein of
his as his cock passed through me. I could feel how ready he was to
explode.

"Come!" I snarled.

Mason found a higher gear and fucked me so hard that the entire
basin started to shake. A squeaking noise began as the counter took
the strain, but neither of us gave a shit. I just wanted his cum and it
looked like he was dead set on giving it me.

"Oh, Sophie!"

"Yes!"

"Oh, Sophie!"

"Yes, Mason! Yes, Mason! Come! Come!"

"Sophie!"